The Antique Dealer of Algiers

Cover photo: Old illustration of the fig tree Algiers bazaar. Created by Allon and Prior, published on Il Mediterraneo Illustrato, Spirito Battelli ed., Florence, Italy, 1841

Edited by Linda Anne Beavan

ISBN: 978-618-85229-0-9

Thessaloniki, Greece

ikaragogos@gmail.com

Ioannis N. Karagogos

The Antique Dealer of Algiers

to Nikolas, Maria, George, Menas and Michael

Facts, events, dates and actions of historical persons are all true.
Motives, intentions, dialogues and secret deals are all product of pure imagination.
Edward Aguillon never existed.

PART ONE

I waited outside the church for ten minutes but the baron didn't appear. I had arrived on time to find no one was there and I'd have recognised a waiting baron, I'm sure.

A priest came out of the church and I figured something was wrong. He was an Orthodox priest with a beard and black robes.

"Excuse me, Father, this is Sant'-Antonio Taumaturgo, isn't it?"

"No. This is San Spiridione, an Orthodox church. Serbian Orthodox."

"Oh, my goodness! Do you know where…?"

"Right over there." He smiled and pointed in the direction of the Grand Canal.

"Thank you, Father."

"God be with you, my son," I heard him say as I hastily made off.

When I got to the church of Sant'-Antonio, again, no one was there. I looked around and saw a man walking in the opposite direction about fifty meters away. I was sure it was the baron.

"Si…" Luckily, no one heard me. Was it right to call a baron *Sir*? I should be more careful. I'd slipped up once already.

"Baron Victor von Kalchberg!" I shouted, running towards him.

He turned and looked at me sternly, having every right to do so. I caught up with him and began to apologise, explaining and apologising again.

He was disapproving at first but then he smiled.

"It could happen to anyone," he said. "How about that coffee now?"

He needs my product!

The baron was the president of the *österreichische* branch of Lloyd bank in Trieste and I had almost blown it with a simple mistake. Later, I wished I had. I wished I hadn't caught up with him at all but how could I have known at the time?

The city was busy already but that was no surprise. It was the fourth largest city in the Austro-Hungarian Empire.

We settled comfortably to continue our conversation at the nearby *Stella Polare*, a splendid café on the banks of the Grand Canal near the church of San Spiridione. It was probably the largest café I had ever been in. At the same time, we were able to admire the many beautiful women who passed us by.

Our discussion began with our mutual friend, Flavio Cavanna, a lawyer from Genoa, and continued with ancient history and the poetry of Dante. Unbeknown to us at the time, our meeting would be the reason the name of the street was changed at a later date to the *Via Dante Alighieri*. Von Kalchberg informed me at some point that a good friend of his, who was also interested in my merchandise, would be joining us.

"Leopold is the son of a very good friend of mine. He started his collection recently and I would like to help him out. I am interested, too, of course, but my collection is already quite extensive. His father is my best client, you know, and I always take care of my clients," said the banker.

Shortly afterwards, a tall, athletic-looking man approached our table. The president of Lloyd bank introduced us and Leopold ordered a coffee. Like Cavanna, he was a lawyer and made no secret of his enthusiasm for antiquities. It wasn't very clever of him but I assumed he was so rich, he didn't have to worry about being clever. Rich, handsome, educated, he had it all.

We were the same age and almost the same height, but unlike me, he was born into a wealthy, noble family that owned land in Moravia and Hungary. Rich was not the most accurate word to describe him and though I had no idea at the time, one of Austria-Hungary's richest men was standing in front of me.

He was very pleasant and had a good sense of humour. He ordered cakes and sweets, having been indecisive at first as to what should accompany our coffee. Each of us took the opportunity to share our knowledge of history, which inspired me to raise the price I would attach to the historic treasure that lay aboard my ship.

It was going to be a beautiful day, it seemed.

We leisurely entered the port of Syracuse. We were there to deliver a cargo of beer and load a new shipment of lemons for Marseille. However, a surprise awaited us at the port. We were surrounded by around twenty armed men as if we were criminals.

The Mafia types wouldn't even let us unload. They grabbed and blindfolded us and bundled us onto a carriage. We were taken someplace and thrown into different rooms, or cells to be more precise, and our blindfolds removed. We must have been close to a village because I could hear people talking, chickens and roosters crowing and the sound of passing sheep.

Two months ago, I was drinking coffee in the Stella Polare in Trieste and now this?

I understood from what they were saying that they'd expected us the following day and were forced to hold us somewhere until their boss could 'look us over'. This was bad news. Very bad news.

The next morning, I was blindfolded and taken somewhere nearby. When I could see again, I found myself with the rest of the crew in a large room with huge windows. The summer sun shone through them and reflected on the white shirts of four angry men sitting at a table in front of us. One of them was around fifty, the others were older. Armed men stood against the walls around the room. I recalled some of the faces from the day before, others were new. Nice Italian guys, with guns.

Next to the table stood a familiar young man, happy-looking, with beautiful hair. He was well-built and his left leg was posed slightly forward. He looked at us and smiled arrogantly despite being completely naked. Did he have no shame?

It was only then that I understood the irony of his smile. He was the reason for our downfall.

My name is Edward Aguillon and I was born on January 1st, 1863, on the very same Thursday as another important Frenchman called Charles Pierre de Frédy, otherwise known as Pierre de Coubertin, father of the modern Olympic Games. I'm sure you've heard of him, though you've certainly never heard of me and I am also a 'father' of the twentieth century. It's true, as you'll soon find out.

I was born in the city of Algiers, the son of a French farmer. My grandfather died in the battle of Ligny, in pursuit of Blücher's Prussians. The battle took place shortly before the Battle of Waterloo. My father was destined to become an orphan of a heroic French *cuirassier*. It was a poor and miserable life and he followed in the footsteps of other poor Frenchmen when we conquered Algeria by acquiring a decent plot of land and managed to make a good enough living to support his wife and two sons. Soon afterwards, two more sons were born. I was the fourth.

The French considered themselves superior to the locals, forgetting the misery they had suffered in France. Was anyone actually *local* in Algeria, except for the Berbers, of course, but let's not get into that now.

As far as I was concerned, Algeria was just another version of France. I had nothing else to compare it to. I would happily run through the fields and play on our small farm, making traps for the chickens and hounding the hares. Walking by the sea was also enjoyable. I knew that Paris, Marseille, Biarritz, Austerlitz and Jena were just across the Mediterranean Sea and mixed them all up in a beautiful way. Beautiful places with lots of cheese and plenty of wine for the adults to drink in celebration of Napoleon Bonaparte's victories.

My older brother Nikola and I acted out the Napoleonic wars. I always wanted to play Napoleon and he was kind enough to let me. He played the part of Nikolas Davout or Joachim Murat. The battle of Austerlitz was my favourite, while he preferred the battle of Jena where we defeated the Prussians. I later discovered that Davout was the protagonist of that battle. We played the Battle of Waterloo, too, but with a somewhat different ending.

I loved walking up and down the city side streets with my family, admiring the white houses of Algiers and visiting Mr Elazar Amsallem, my father's best friend. He was an Algerian Jew and we exchanged visits once or twice a month. It seemed he knew everything from the beginning of mankind. He had a passion for history and would describe major events or minor historic details as if he'd been there at the time. Whenever we kept company, it felt like an important event was about to take place.

He had a pottery shop that also sold other stuff in the Bazaar of the Fig Tree in Algiers and regularly invited his friends for drinks and sweets. The shop wasn't very big but was always full of customers whom he greeted with a smile and always found time to talk to.

It was always clean with everything in place and it smelt beautiful. It was my favourite place to go when we visited the city. Above his desk was a large painting of a young man. I noticed fairly soon that the painting was different every time I visited and eventually realised that this was neither random nor by accident.

Sometimes, the young man in the painting was wearing a big straw hat and a white waistcoat, sometimes a woollen cap and a heavy tunic. Sometimes, there were grapes on his head and sometimes apples. Sometimes, a boat on the sea was visible behind him, sometimes a house buried beneath heavy snow or an almond tree in full bloom.

"What are you looking at, young Edward?" he asked, kneeling down and looking directly into my eyes.

I pointed to the painting. "He's different," I said.

"Ha! So you noticed. Well done! Henri, your son will grow up to be a great man. He is very clever. He pays attention."

"Why do you say that?" asked my father.

"It's the painting. Don't you see?"

"What about it?"

"Have you never noticed before, Henri?"

"Noticed what?"

"The young man is different, father. Can't you see? Last time he had yellow leaves on his head."

"But it is not the same young man as last time, dear Edward. Can you guess why?"

"Why…? Er…because you sold the painting?"

"No, it is not for sale. The last time you saw it, it was October. Now it's November."

"And the young man is wearing different clothes?"

"No, it's a different man. Last month, it was October. This young man is called November. July has blond hair. May has green eyes. April has a big nose and February is somewhat shorter."

"Are they real?"

"Of course they are, young man. You recognise their names, don't you?"

The names of the months danced around inside my head, singing Algerian folk songs in a never-ending festival.

"So, Elazar, you change the painting every month?"

"Yes, on the morning of the first day of every month. It's the first thing I do," said Mr Elazar.

"I admire your patience and consistency, my friend. I never noticed, to be honest."

"This is how I test my friends' alertness, Henri," said Elazar, smiling.

"Thank goodness I have a clever son like Edward! Come here, my boy!" he said, and threw me into the air. I loved it when he did that. "Clever Edward!"

I was very proud. I fell into my father's strong arms...The arms of a son who had lost his courageous father before he even got to know him. The hands of a hard-working man, proud of his children. Proud of me. My beloved father.

The good times came to an end far too soon, however. It was 1870 and I was almost eight years old when my older brother, René, left to fight the Prussians in the Franco-Prussian war, never to return home. He was killed in the battle of Sedan on September 1st. It was in that same battle that Napoleon III, a nephew of Napoleon, was captured. I will never forget how my mother cried for days and nights. There was much heartache in our home and all over France. My father was particularly distraught and it took a month for him to pull himself together. Those damned Prussians caused so much sorrow!

The architect of this disaster was Otto von Bismarck, the Iron Chancellor. It was all his fault. He was born in Schönhausen, west of Berlin in the Prussian province of Saxony on April 1st, 1815. Napoleon was preparing to face the Seventh Coalition having escaped from Elba. 1815 was undeniably a bad year for France.

Bonaparte should have burned Berlin to the ground while he had the chance. The Prussians killed my grandfather and my brother, and if it wasn't for them, Napoleon would have scored another victory at Waterloo.

The Prussians had won the Franco-Prussian War. Four years earlier on Friday 27th July 1866, in North America, and for the first time in human history, the recently constructed trans-Atlantic telegraph cable, established in Newfoundland, delivered its first signal.

European news, July 27. Highly important intelligence. 'A treaty of peace has been signed between Austria and Prussia.'

On that very same day, a newcomer entered the scene - The German Empire.

That's correct. In 1866, they won the Austro-Prussian war, also known as the Seven Weeks War, also known as the German Civil War, also known as the Unification War, also known as the War of 1866.

It should be remembered as the 'The War The End Of Which Became Known In America On The Same Day' and there are reasons this war of such short duration had so many names. Think of a small-time criminal trying to escape arrest. This was Bismarck. Incidentally, he was born on April Fool's Day. The shrewd Prussian named the war precisely to suit his needs.

Now, please pay attention!

Before the Franco-Prussian war broke out, Bismarck met Napoleon III in the beautiful town of Biarritz. He sampled quality French wine with a variety of cheeses and admired the Atlantic Ocean and the beauties of France. He was guaranteed French neutrality in the event of an *Austro-Prussian War.* Actually, it was a war against Austria, Bavaria, Saxony, Hanover and certain minor German states.

Napoleon III had no reason to worry. Bismarck would never have called it a *Unification War,* which would result in another large kingdom on France's border right in the heart of Europe.

Austria didn't see it coming either. Maybe because the Prussians were Germans after all, and hadn't learned their lesson when the powerful Kingdom of Piedmont was created. This led to another successful unification and the creation of the Kingdom of Italy in 1861. The new Kingdom of Italy was now allied with Prussia, which meant that the Austrians would be fighting against both with no major allies of their own. They should have approached Napoleon III first.

In conversation with Franz Joseph, King of Austria, Bismarck would have persuaded him that the League of the Three Emperors should probably refer to the war as the *German Civil War.*

When speaking to the Bavarian King Ludwig II, he would have called it the *Unification War,* because as previously mentioned, the Bavarians were allied with the Austrians against the Prussians in that particular war. Make sense of that, if you will!

Otto probably called it the *Seven Weeks War* when talking to his field marshal, Helmut von Moltke, and the *War of 1866* was probably the term used by the bellicose officers of the Prussian army.

Voltaire was right, however: *'Where some states have an army, the Prussian army has a state.'*

Napoleon III undoubtedly regretted it when, five years after the cheese and wine tasting, he was captured in Sedan. The Austrians probably regretted the Austro-

Prussian War, too. In 1864, two years before they fought with the Prussians, the Austrians had aided the Prussians in the German-Danish war, also known as the Second Schleswig War.

The Austrians allied with the Prussians against the Kingdom of Denmark because they did not want Christian of Glücksburg as their new king after the death of Frederik VII. The war ended on October 30th, 1864, with the Treaty of Vienna. The 1860s turned out to be quite a decade for the Prussians!

Meanwhile, between 1861 and 1865 on the other side of the Atlantic, the American Civil war was taking place, but in Europe, we couldn't have cared less.

Mr Elazar was a great help to my father at this difficult time for our family.

"You have four sons, Henri! Three young Frenchmen who will make you proud and one brave warrior watching from above who needs you to make him proud. René deserves it, Henri!"

Though younger by a few years, he stood by my father like a wise brother and helped him go about his business. They took long walks together and gradually, my father regained his more recognizable, stable-minded look. He was the father I knew again.

One afternoon, Mr Elazar paid us a visit. He was holding a strange object. He and my father sat in the garden and my mother took them two glasses. My brothers had gone out so I watched them as they talked. Today was a special day for him and he had brought us a gift.

"Do you know something, Henri? When my grandparents were driven out of Spain, they could never have known that one day, their grandchildren would become citizens of the country that gave the world a magnificent gift. A miracle the world had never seen before."

"Napoleon Bonaparte!" I shouted. I couldn't help but intervene.

"How old are you, young Edward?" he asked with a smile.

"Eight, Mr Elazar."

"Madame Aguillon, would you bring us another glass, please?" he said to my mother and turned to me again.

"Today, young man, you will have the privilege of tasting a superior and unique drink. But don't tell your brothers. And believe me, Edward, if Napoleon were alive today, he would agree with me." He held up a strange-looking bottle.

The neck of the bottle was very long and the lower half contained the liquid.

"See this unusual bottle? You hold it by the neck so as not to hide its sacred label leaving it visible for all to admire. Look! D.O.M. Do you know what that means?"

"Tell us, Uncle Elazar."

"Deo Optimo Maximo."

"What does that mean?"

"It means 'To God, Most Good, Most Great'. The monks of the Order of Saint Benedict used it as a dedication for their works."

"Is it holy?"

"No, young Edward, but the recipe is very old. A Mr Alexandre Le Grand discovered it in the family library in a 16th-century *'grimoire',* which belonged to the Benedictine abbey of Fécamp."

"Where is Fécamp?"

"It's in the north of France. It's a beautiful town on the coast of Normandy."

"What happened next?"

"The *'grimoire'* belonged to his grandfather, Elie Couillard, a *'procurer fiscal '*, who acquired it during the French Revolution. This wholesome elixir of twenty-seven herbs and spices was created at the Abbey of Fécamp during the Renaissance. Dom Bernardo Vincelli, a Venetian Benedictine monk, was its creator. According to legend, the liqueur initially gained its reputation during a visit to Fécamp by King Francis I.

"*'Foy de gentilhomme! Oncques n'en goustai de meilleur!'* he was said to have exclaimed. It means *'On my honour! I have never tasted anything better!'* "

"King Francis said that?"

"Yes, and King Francis was not just a king. He was also *'le Père et Restaurateur des Lettres'*, the *'Father and Restorer of Letters'*. It was he who initiated the French Renaissance by attracting Italian artists such as Leonardo Da Vinci to work for him."

"What an amazing king!"

"He was also known as *'le Roi-Chevalier'*, the *'Knight-King'* as he fought against his great rival, the Holy Roman Emperor Charles IV, who was also King of Spain."

"A Knight-King?"

"That's correct. Alexandre Le Grand recreated the medicinal formula, marrying myrrh with juniper, and saffron with lemon rind and used this uniquely shaped bottle with its distinguishing label.

"De Opio Maximo!" I repeated enthusiastically.

"No, Edward! Deo Optimo Maximo."

He opened the magic bottle and poured us a glass of the liqueur. Mine, just half-full, but a fine, yet unfamiliar aroma infused my brain when I held it to my nose.

That night, I tasted the Benedictine liqueur for the first time in my life and I will never forget it. My father was equally impressed and Uncle Elazar, with his amazing gift for story-telling, told us many tales about Benedictine monks, kings and knights and elixirs sealed in mysterious bottles.

I was fascinated.

Somewhere on the coast of Normandy, in the north of my great and glorious country, in Fécamp, is a place dedicated to the production of a Renaissance-period elixir for the modern world. Deo Optimo Maximo. Wow!

It was a very important day for Uncle Elazar and it was equally important that he had chosen to share his happiness with my family. On October 24th, he had been informed that he, and around 35,000 other Algerian Jews, had acquired French citizenship by means of the décret Crémieux.

The law was named after Adolphe Crémieux, a French lawyer of Jewish descent, who was Minister of Justice and founder of the *'Alliance Israélite Universelle'* a decade earlier.

I stayed up late listening to Mr Elazar's stories but no matter how many times I begged, I was not allowed a second glass of the elixir.

"It is obvious that a unified German Empire will greatly disturb the balance of power. The aftermath of Waterloo, you understand, and the Congress of Vienna, have brought enormous change to the continent."

"The Austro-Prussian war, you mean?" said my father.

"The 'Seven Weeks War', Henri, was the first phase of the war and was Bismarck's goal from the outset. Once he'd achieved the unification of all the German states under the Prussian umbrella, a new Europe was born."

"Italy was born ten years ago."

"But that is not the same, Henri. Don't you see?"

"To be honest, I don't."

"Ok, my friend, let me explain, starting with the underlying truth of the matter. We have the great powers of Europe: England, France and Russia…"

"You're forgetting the Austrians."

"No. According to Voltaire, the Holy Roman Empire was not Holy, not Roman and not an Empire. And for good reason, he claimed. Now if Napoleon had put an end to the Holy Roman Empire, what remained did not belong to the great powers of Europe. Piedmonte was complete in 1861, the Prussians with their seven-week war in 1866, and the Slavs were on their way to take the eastern territories."

"They could have annexed the Slavs, though."

"Maybe, but I don't think so. Anyway, let's stick to the simple facts. A newcomer wants to join the club and will do anything to achieve it. In 1815…"

"A dreadful year…"

"…the Prussian King Wilhelm played a major role in the Battle of Ligny as Commander of a battalion."

"He was probably the one my father hunted down in Ligny. Damned Prussians!"

"He arranged for his son and heir to marry Queen Victoria's daughter, the Princess Victoria. The Prussians agreed that the wedding of Frederick and young Victoria should take place at the Chapel Royal of St. James Palace in London because Queen Victoria insisted her eldest daughter should marry in her own country. The couple had a son. Young Wilhelm II is four years older than Edward.

"Returning to King Wilhelm, his sister, Princess Charlotte of Prussia, married Nicholas I of Russia and became Queen Alexandra Feodorovna. The marriage took place in Russia two years after the Battle of

Waterloo. She died some ten years ago, in 1860, I think. The Prussians acted wisely by extending their relationship with Russia, and I am pretty sure Bismarck had something to do with it. King Alexander's mother was a Prussian princess and we must not forget that Catherine the Great was a Prussian princess, too. Do you understand now?"

"But you say that France is alone."

"Well, it depends."

"On what?"

"On France's effort to find allies."

"In whom? The Austrians? You said they don't count."

"Well, the Prussians made the effort, so the French must make an effort, too. Where diplomacy is concerned, nothing is finite."

"Look here, Elazar, the Prussians didn't exactly surrender the Battle of Ligny, you know! Blücher lay trapped under his dead horse for several hours. I am sure my father rode over the damn Prussian, and if it weren't for the devotion of his aide-de-camp, Count Nostitz, his life would not have been saved. He threw a greatcoat over the commander to obscure Blücher's rank and identity from our cavalry. We repeatedly rode over him. My father was killed by a Prussian, who lay down and pretended to be dead! It was father's friend, André Bizier, who killed the swine!

"Blücher was unable to resume his duties for some hours and Gneisenau took command, withdrew the defeated army and rallied it. Gneisenau did not trust Wellington. Can anyone trust the English? But he obeyed Blücher's last orders and led the army's retreat in the direction of Wavre, rather than Liege, and secured the possibility of uniting the Prussian army with Wellington's. Blücher bathed his wounds in a liniment of rhubarb and garlic, fortified himself with a generous dose of schnapps, and was revitalised enough to take command of his troops again.

"Field Marshal Gneisenau feared that the British had reneged on their earlier agreement and favoured a withdrawal, but Blücher convinced him to send two corps to join Wellington at Waterloo. It proved fatal. He led his army on an incredibly muddy march and they arrived on the battlefield of Waterloo in the late afternoon of Sunday, 18th June, by which time Wellington had all but lost the battle. Any later, and Blücher would have found that Wellington had taken flight.

"And I'm pretty sure Wellington would have been faster than Blücher."

"So what are you trying to say, Elazar? That France should make friends with English pigs or Queen Feodorovna's son, Alexander of Russia, because of Blücher's damned overcoat?"

"But Henri, if it hadn't rained heavily in the days before the Battle of Waterloo, Blücher might have been lucky enough to find Wellington hidden under his overcoat, too. All I'm saying…and I'm proud of what I say…is that from now on, *WE* need to find allies anywhere we can, regardless of the outcome of this damned war because, at this rate, all royal weddings will take place in Berlin.

"Actually, the only king to outsmart the Prussians was Christian IX of Denmark.
In March 1863, his daughter Alexandra married Edward, Prince of Wales, the son of Queen Victoria and heir to the throne of England. Three years later in 1866, his other daughter, Dagmar, married Prince Alexander of Russia. Thus, both daughters will become Queens of England and Russia in the near future.

"Christian IX of Denmark did a fine job with his offspring. Not only did he have the greatest storyteller in the world - Hans Christian Andersen – to tell them fairytales but he was also able to secure extremely favourable marriages for both his daughters. Oh, and I forgot to mention, his son, George I, became King of Greece in 1863."

"Do you think we should become allies with Greece to punish the Prussians, Elazar?" asked my father, laughing. They poured themselves another glass of the Benedictine liqueur.

"The English would be a better option, I think."

"Yes, the English will always be there to control things. Only the other day you told me that one in three people on this planet falls under the rule of Queen Victoria."

"Almost. And the rest will be ruled by one of her grandchildren."

"But the English are married to the Prussians."

"There will be other opportunities, Henri. The *'Belle Alliance'* won't last forever. The sooner the Prussians become like Napoleon, the sooner the alliance will be broken. This newcomer, who wants to join the club will do anything to earn his place in it, you know. Prussian princesses marry in Russia, unlike English princesses who marry in England. Our newcomer will build contacts at any cost, just like his strength, and by the time he has gathered enough strength, his contacts will be irrelevant. From then on, marriages will take place in Berlin alone."

"But Uncle Elazar, the Prussians are busy fighting all the time and have no time for marriages. So the Danish outsmarted them. If they continue fighting, no more marriages will take place." I said, trying to add something important to the conversation.

Mr Elazar smiled and looked at me.

"You are absolutely right, young Edward. You are a very clever boy, and do you know something else? This Benedictine liqueur is the same age as you."

"But Uncle Elazar, you said it was ancient."

"Yes, but it was originally produced in these wonderful bottles in 1863. I'll reveal more secrets some other time. Now before I leave, I have something just for you. Something that was also born in the same year as you."

He reached into his bag and took out a white book.

"Books are not like liqueurs; they don't need presentation. They speak for themselves," he said and handed me the book.

"*'Five Weeks in a Balloon'*. What's it about, Uncle Elazar?"

"Read it and tell me. It's this young writer's first work. He has a vivid imagination, they say. Tell me his name, Edward."

"Jules Verne."

When the wretched Franco-Prussian War ended three months later on January 26th, 1871, everything was lost. On May 10th that year, the Treaty of Frankfurt took place and gave Germany most of Alsace and parts of Lorraine. It became known as the imperial territory of Alsace-Lorraine. The word *revanchism* evolved from this treaty and it doesn't take the imagination of Jules Verne to understand what it means. It was derived from the word 'revenge'.

Damned Prussians!

I lost my mother two years later. And quite suddenly. It's the greatest loss a boy can suffer. It changed everything. I was a lost soul. I couldn't bear the reality of it. I couldn't bear Algiers.

I began to spend a lot of time in Mr Elazar's shop, helping out and picking up his mail from the post office. He sent and received letters from all over the world. All those postmarks, all those names, all those picture-postage stamps were an unexpected gift to me. Unknown people from far-away places with no pain in their lives. How lucky they were!

I was there on the first of every month when he took down the painting and hung a new 'Month' in its place. There was only one frame with a special wire attached to the back to hold the picture in place. He followed the same careful procedure every time, removing the special screws, releasing the painting, putting the new one in place and tightening the wire again.

"Come with me, Edward," he said one day and led me to his home over the shop. "Look, this is the library." He opened the door to a large room.

"Wow! So many books!" There were books everywhere. Thousands of them.

"They are all yours to read whenever you like. Take one book at a time and return it when you are ready to read another."

"Thank you, Mr Elazar."

"Just one thing. You see these two coffers?"

"They look very old."

"Yes, they are. Never open them, ok?"

"Ok," I said. I would never have opened them anyway.

Why would I open the coffers with so many books at my disposal? But why did he tell me not to open them in the first place?

There was a famous school for girls in Algiers. It happened to be the first Franco-Arab school for Muslim girls offering a European-style education. The girls learned French, Arabic, arithmetic, geography, sewing and embroidery. It was called the Luce Ben Aben School and was founded in 1845 by Mrs Eugénie Luce.

Mrs Luce was a French schoolteacher who left her husband, abandoned her family and immigrated to Algeria in the early 1830s. By the 1840s, she had become a major participant in debates on educational policies, insisting that women were a critical dimension of the French effort to bring about fusion between races. Her funding, however, was discontinued by the authorities in 1861, at which point she abandoned the teaching of spelling, grammar and sewing and focused solely on embroidery.

Embroidery is the craft of decorating fabric or other materials using a needle to apply thread or yarn. This same needle was used by Yasmine to secure my heart on a sunny Tuesday, the fifth day of October in 1881.

My brother Nikola and I were walking past her school when a group of Muslim girls came out having finished their lessons. I picked her out amongst her friends. She was somehow different. Our eyes met at some point and that was it. I had never felt that way before. My heart beat like mad and I thought my head would explode. My brother told me later that my face had flushed bright red.

In the days that followed, I found myself walking along the same road at the same time, searching for those eyes of hers. Sometimes I was lucky, sometimes not. I got to know her name and that she had three brothers and one sister.

Nikola helped a lot. He would walk a short distance behind me and her friends would walk a short distance in front so Yasmine and I could walk together for a while. I thought it was our secret but somehow, more people knew.

One day, I was in Mr Elazar's shop. It was almost one in the afternoon and there were just the two of us.

"Edward, some things are simply not meant to be. You will both get hurt."

"What do you mean, Mr Elazar?"

"I know what I'm talking about, Edward, I assure you. Come now, let's have a glass of liqueur."

He carefully took out a bottle of Benedictine and poured two glasses.

"Look at the bottle, Edward. It's specially constructed so that when you grab hold of it, your hand does not cover the label."

"You've told me that already, Mr Elazar."

He continued as if he hadn't heard me. "The label is so precious it makes you feel privileged. The embossed stamp, the D.O.M., the colour. King Francis, the monks, the Renaissance..."

"Yes, it's unique."

"No, Edward. There is a more accurate word to describe it."

"And that is?"

"Nonsense," replied Mr Elazar in a voice quite unlike his own.

"Nonsense?"

"Obvious, absolute and complete nonsense, my boy!"

"What's come over you, Mr Elazar?"

"King Francis never visited Fécamp and Dom Bernardo Vincelli probably never existed but you still believe anything they tell you. Mr Le Grand simply connected an alcoholic drink with rich, well-kept secrets of the Renaissance period. Who are you to decide whether good old King Francis said what he was supposed to have said? Your ability to taste this liquid is considered a privilege. It was simply an opportunity to give it royal approval... *'Appointed by His Majesty King Francis'*, because after the Revolution, there were no more kings.

"Mr Le Grand not only invented an excellent liqueur, Edward, but applied a unique sales technique that had never been used before. It's as much 'nonsense' as you can possibly imagine.

"And one more thing. King Francis was also known as *'François du Grand Nez'*, or Francis Big Nose," he said, pointing to his nose with a smile.

A sailor came into the shop and asked for a water bottle. Mr Elazar paused for a moment to serve his customer. He carefully took one of the bottles from the shelf.

"This particular water bottle is very special," he said as if it were exactly what the sailor was looking for. "When he was young, my father, Aaron Amsallem, travelled across the desert south of Morocco for five days and would never have made it if his water had not been stored in this type of bottle. The great Berber caravan of Oman navigates the Sahara using only this type of bottle, you know.

"Look how it's sealed with special tape so it doesn't leak, no matter where you put it. It holds one and a half litres of fresh water. Here, see how light it is."

The sailor took hold of the bottle.

"Maybe it isn't suitable after all. Would you like a more ordinary one? How about those in the basket?" he continued.

"How much does it cost, Mr?"

"Seven francs… take it if it's something special you're after."

The sailor gave Mr Elazar ten francs and left with the bottle. The shopkeeper turned to me.

"Now, back to our conversation. I understand you are in love but it is not meant to be. It's ok to talk to her a little, but don't touch her. If you carry on, you will die like Romeo and Juliet and do you know why, Edward? You only want her because you cannot have her."

"That's not true."

"Believe me, if you spent more time with her, you would agree. She is like a special water bottle you cannot have. You were fooled by those stupid stories about Mr Le Grand and his liqueur and mine about this water bottle. The only difference is you don't have seven francs. Those seven francs do not exist, Edward. Not in this world.

"There are many beautiful women in this world, Edward, believe you me. Women more suitable for you, Edward. Women that can make you happy."

"You are wrong Mr Elazar. Phileas Fogg was English and Aouda an Indian. He rescued her and took her to England. Maybe I'll take Yasmine to America, one day," I replied, swallowing the liqueur in one gulp. "Thank you for the drink. See you again."

I was slowly going mad and my family noticed, except for my father, who was busy at the time due to a microscopic, yellow, sap-sucking insect from North America. Let me explain.

At the time, France was establishing itself as a world leader in winemaking, as far as quality and quantity were concerned. In 1875, total wine production was 84.5 million hectolitres. Things couldn't have been better for France as it continued to expand its everlasting empire of wine exports. However, several English botanists managed to destroy this effort. Yes, the English once again, but without Blücher's help this time.

They had collected specimens of an American vine, unaware that native grape varieties were at least partially resistant to this American bug. By contrast, the European wine grape was very susceptible to it and *phylloxera,* the scientific name for the bug, spread rapidly across the continent. Some estimates claim that between two-thirds and nine-tenths of all European vineyards were destroyed. In France alone, total wine production fell to almost a quarter of its previous capacity.

My father recognised it as a great opportunity, maybe after talking it over with his friend Elazar. Until then, we had a small vineyard to produce wine for family needs. Like all other French people in Algeria, we cultivated mostly fruits and vegetables.

One day, while we were having dinner, my father informed us that from now on, winemaking would be our main business.

"We will produce the best French wine in Algeria," said my father quite calmly, and continued eating like everyone else.

Henri Augillon was the first farmer in Algeria to change course a year before the French government initiative for Algerian farmers to produce wine to combat the epidemic spreading across French vineyards.

Algerian agricultural workers began to expand their vineyards up and down the country. Large quantities of wine flowed from Algeria to France and to other countries around the world. Algeria developed a reputation for the production of high quality and an extensive range of wine.

My father worked very hard to adapt to the new situation as his wine business grew. I had no idea that once he realised my situation, it would be the end of the world as I knew it. He had heard my two brothers joking about my secret love for the girl at the Ben Aben School. He demanded an explanation and the damage was done. He spoke to me for hours, explaining why I should forget about talking to the girl again. During our conversation, he was calm and understanding, at least I thought he was. As the days went by, my feelings didn't change and I decided it was time to demonstrate them.

One day, I went to the Luce Ben Aben School earlier than usual so I could see her before she came out with her friends. Just before the end of lessons, I went into the school to look for her and asked her if she would like to walk out with me. Everyone's eyes were upon me, but I didn't care. We walked and talked together, and it was on that day that I kissed Yasmine for the first time. I was the happiest man on earth.

The following day at dinner, my father informed us that the newly built SS Alesia had embarked on her maiden voyage. She had departed from Livorno in Italy bound for New York via Tarragona in Spain, Bône, Algeria and Malaga.

"She will arrive in Algiers in two days' time. Edward! You'll be on board when she leaves. You'll be working in the kitchen," said my father calmly, and carried on eating unlike everyone else.

And so it was. Two days later, I was saying farewell to my father and brothers at the port. I didn't even see Yasmine before I left. However, just before I boarded the damned ship, two of Yasmine's friends came walking by. As they approached, one of them hurriedly stuffed something into my hand.

"From Yasmine," she said.

Whatever it was, I quickly hid it in my pocket and looked around for her. She was nowhere to be seen. I boarded the ship and was introduced to a rather anxious sailor, who showed me my bed and the locker I would use to keep my belongings in. He urged me to hurry up to the kitchen, but thankfully, he was very understanding when I politely asked if I could take one last look at Algiers before the SS Alesia set sail.

I admired my beautiful city from the deck but my eyes were not fixed on the white houses with balconies. I was looking for Yasmine but couldn't find her anywhere. I put my hand in my pocket and I took out her farewell gift. It was a piece of white fabric beautifully embroidered with red and gold thread. Yasmine had stitched her name in red in the centre.

Would I ever see her again?

I burst into tears as I searched for her. The sound of clanking chains signified the anchor was being raised.

"Damned ship! Damned SS Alesia! I wish it would burn down right here in Algiers. Goodbye Yasmine, my love."

The SS Alesia was an ocean liner built for the Fabre Line, the Compagnie Francaise de Navigation, established a year earlier in 1881. An ocean liner is a passenger ship primarily used for transportation across oceans. Liners may also carry cargo or mail. The Alesia had twelve first-class and a thousand third-class passenger cabins. It was built by Thomas Royden and Sons, shipbuilders of Liverpool, and her port of registry was Marseille.

France and England are doing good business it seems.

I wasn't old enough at the time to realise that business has nothing to do with countries, friendship and allies. For me, it was just another sign that the French were making allies to take back Alsace and Lorraine and burn Berlin to the ground.

My first insight of this awkward friendship with our eternal enemy was Jules Verne's *Around the World in Eighty Days.* When I read the book, I was disappointed at first that Phileas Fogg was an Englishman. Why on earth would a French writer do such a terrible thing and promote an Englishman as the first person capable of such a great achievement.

Travelling around the world in eighty days was like a modern-day Herculean chore. Such an achievement should have been performed by a Frenchman, not an Englishman. We have been at war with the English for centuries, for heaven's sake!

To be able to live with it, I decided it was part of a bigger plan. Wise Frenchmen, like Mr Elazar, decided that it was necessary to approach the English. It was not by accident that Phileas Fogg managed to succeed with the help of a brave Frenchman, Jean Passepartout. And although Phileas was the protagonist, the smartest and bravest move in the whole novel was made by the brave Passepartout.

He took the place of Aouda's deceased husband on the funeral pyre, pretended to rise from the dead, scared the hell out of the Hindu priests, and saved Aouda just before they burned her alongside her dead husband. Practically speaking, both men travelled around the world in eighty days, didn't they?

So the underlying message to the English was: 'I, the Frenchman will help you. I will save the girl and I will give her to you. Now help me get Lorraine back.'

Jules Verne was a genius.

The SS Alesia was not the best place for a man of my age, especially when working in the kitchen. The only advantages were that I learned how to cook and got to see America. New York was magical and the Fabre Line was the only transatlantic route to southern New England. Thus, I was able to visit Rhode Island and Boston.

Although there was something fascinating about this new world that promised a life of opportunities, I was never really excited by the idea of living in America. I'm glad I wasn't in the same position as all those people immigrating to the new world. I felt really sorry for them.

Of course, I had no idea at the time that, thirty years later, their children would return to Europe to fight in the Great War. My war.

I was far more excited by the larger Mediterranean ports. Alexandria of Egypt, Beirut, Naples, Palermo, Piraeus, Constantinople, Monaco and Marseille, which was our home port.

Docking at a port, however, was a welcome short break from the tedious work in the kitchen aboard the Alesia. It may sound foolish, but when our steam engine broke down in the middle of the ocean in December 1883, I almost welcomed the break from the monotony. I had only been at sea for a year and had absolutely no idea of the danger that lay ahead. Luckily, on December 4th - it was a Tuesday I think - we were spotted by the SS Anglia near the coast of Mauritania, in northwest Africa

The next incident, however, was the one that would force me to bid farewell to the oceans forever. In September 1887, on the crossing from Marseille to New York, a young man came into the kitchen and asked for some food and water for his uncle, who was ill with diarrhoea was vomiting. He could not speak French, so gestured what he wanted to say. He was a seventeen-year-old Greek called Alexander. His surname, which sounded like Schenas, was very difficult to pronounce, so I called him Alexá the Great. I informed the doctor myself because I wanted to help the young boy who seemed scared. The doctor feared even more when he examined Alexander's uncle. Diarrhoea and vomiting were the classic symptoms of cholera. In those days, it happened all the time. Whenever you drank water in cities or aboard ships, you were risking your life because, at the time, there was no way to guarantee its purity.

... when our steam engine broke down in the middle of the ocean in December 1883, I almost welcomed the break from the monotony

Indeed, there was an outbreak of cholera on the ship. Eight people died and the ship was placed in quarantine on arrival at New York. By October 10th, twenty-five passengers had died. Alexander's uncle was among them. From a small window inside the ship, I could see the flame of the Statue of Liberty. In reality, I was imprisoned. Ironically, it had been unveiled a year earlier on October 28th, 1886. A gift from the people of France. Our gift. As ridiculous as it sounds, once the statue was in place, the whole continent became somehow more attractive.

Two more passengers died and miraculously, the ship came out of quarantine on October 26th. Two days before the beautiful lady celebrated her first birthday, I was free to walk the streets of New York. That Wednesday when I stepped ashore, I knew it would be my last visit to the New World. I wasn't destined to be the master chef on this or any other ship. How wrong could I be?

Before returning to the Alesia, I posted a letter to Mr Elazar, proudly sticking an American stamp on the envelope. It was the last letter, or so I thought.

I tried to help Alexander, who was devastated by his uncle's death by introducing him to a group of Greeks but to my great surprise, they were unwilling to help.

They had troubles of their own I suppose…

With no other solution at hand, I felt obliged to do him a favour when he asked me to help him get back to Greece. I had already made my decision to quit the Alesia so it wasn't much of a risk. I knew the ship well and there were places I could hide an extra passenger. As for his food, that was no problem for someone working in the kitchen. We returned to Europe without any surprises.

By the time we reached Marseille, I could speak some Greek and he some French. I told him I would be staying in Marseille and could no longer look out for him. His destination was the port of Salonika, which was under Ottoman rule at the time.

He was very happy when we docked in Marseille and said he could walk the rest of the way. He gave me his address telling me how obliged he felt and said he would do anything for me if I ever made contact. I had made a good friend and little did I know that one day, I would take him up on it, though in a rather bloody way.

As far as my future was concerned, I had no idea what to do next so I checked in to a cheap hotel in the beautiful city of Marseille to relax for a few days. It was the *Quatre Chats* hotel. I landed my next job there, though rather awkwardly.

One morning, as I was finishing my breakfast in the hotel restaurant, I heard loud voices coming from the reception. I made my way there out of curiosity and found two men shouting at each other. It was obvious from their voices they were of Italian origin. One of them was huge, completely bald and was squeezing a black beret in the face of the other, somewhat shorter Italian. The shorter yet brave Italian, was articulating with his hands to the rhythm of his beautiful, melodic Italian voice.

I wasn't afraid, despite how scary the big guy looked. He must have been in his fifties and you could tell by his black beret and blue jersey that he was a seafarer. A whiff of salt and gradually increasing tension filled the air and the Italian bad language drew other residents of the *Quatre Chats* to the lobby.

The situation escalated when the shorter Italian swiftly drew a knife from his pocket and scowled.

The residents of the *Quatre Chats* held their breath with fear. So did I.

The larger Italian swore angrily as he stepped back, giving the knife-bearer a victorious advantage.

Or so he thought!

The decisive seaman, agile for his size, surprised his opponent by grabbing the blade of the knife using his beret as a glove and turned it away.

In a blink of an eye, their roles had changed.

"Capitano! No! Per Favore!"

"Baco!"

Capitano pointed the blade at Baco and spat in his face before turning his back on him and proudly making his way out of the *Quatre Chats*. Baco, however, was furious that Capitano had spat at him. He grabbed a chair and ran after him intending to smash it over his head.

"Capitano!" I shouted, standing in Baco's way. I grabbed his raised arms in an attempt to prevent his devious attack. It was a spontaneous reaction to defend the huge Capitano against the vicious Baco but there was no risk involved.

I was quite big myself and strong enough to immobilise Baco, but it was Capitano's reaction that brought fear to his eyes and sent him running in the direction of the other *Chats*, stumbling before he finally made it to the door.

"Grazie!"

"De rien, Capitano!"

"Antonio Caporaso."

"Edward Aguillon."

And this is how my new job as cook aboard a small Italian merchant ship came about. Capitano Antonio Caporaso was the owner and captain of the *Bella Messina*, a two-masted schooner.

He was from Messina, as the name of his vessel implies. The third son of a Sicilian farmer whose livelihood depended on…lemons.

In the middle of the eighteenth century, the Scottish doctor James Lind discovered that vitamin C could help combat scurvy. This disease was a huge problem for the British Navy, who eventually adopted Dr Lind's recommendations to increase sailors' intake of vitamin C. By the late 1700s, captains had started giving lemon juice to their crews. Naturally, this drastically increased the demand for citrus fruits. Sicily was blessed with great quantities of this yellow fruit, which until then had mainly been used for decoration. Sicilian growers reaped the benefits of the massive increase in demand.

In 1837, seven hundred and forty barrels of lemons were exported from the island. By 1850, that figure had jumped to more than 20.000, and the day I started working for Capitano, 2.5 million cases a year were being exported to New York alone.

Poverty was widespread in Sicily at the time and the lemon boom provided an incentive to steal citrus trees. It was a huge problem for Antonio's family as thieves were very tempted and no one was there to safeguard the trees. It was then that the Mafia stepped in, protecting the growers at every stage of the supply chain. From the groves to transportation and storage at the port.

Young Antonio enjoyed the protection the Mafia provided for his family. One day, however, he got into a fight with the son of the local Mafia leader. So as not to worry his family, he left home to work for his uncle, transporting lemons and other goods to Mediterranean ports. When his uncle died, he took over the business and became the Capitano.

The navigator, the businessman, the administrator, the disciplinarian. Capitano's word was law.

"Listen to me, Frenchman. My first responsibility is the ship. This vessel has to be in perfect condition so everyone aboard is safe. The second is the crew. Every soul aboard the Bella Messina is worthy. Everyone! The third is the cargo. The reason this vessel carries these souls is to deliver the cargo in perfect condition and on time. Understood?"

"Yes, Capitano."

"Now, which of these responsibilities can you deliver on?

"What?"

"Pay attention Frenchman! Ship, crew or cargo! What are you here for?"

"To cook." I trembled, waiting for an answer, expecting him to disapprove. He remained silent. "The crew… I will cook for the crew… take care of the crew," I answered in multiple ways, hoping to get it right.

"Wrong answer, Frenchman."

"So what is the ri…"

"All of them! Your role is included in each of my responsibilities. Your work is indispensable for everyone and everything aboard this vessel. Life at sea is hard and this is no ocean cruiser, you know!

"I need to be sure that when the sailors sit down to eat they are happy to be here, even if I yelled at them five minutes ago. Understand now?

"How can I possibly deliver on time and how will I take command of this ship if you don't do your job properly?"

"I understand, Capitano."

It seemed ideal. Short trips and many port stops and it was usually quite a few days before Capitano found new cargo to transport and close his deals. It was a good life for the crew and a good life meant one thing only. Women.

But first, let me tell you about the crew.

The most dominant figure was definitely Moroccan. His name was Mehdi, but everyone called him Moroccan. He was even taller than Capitano, and when not at work he would play with a small knife that seemed to disappear between his huge fingers. He was very strong with enormous hands that made ropes look like single threads. He didn't say much but consumed an unbelievable amount of food. As the ship's cook, I was safe because I knew he relied on me.

Most of the time, he stayed on board the ship. Even when we docked he would only go ashore for a short time, mainly at night and only to certain places. There was a reason for that.

The ports of the Mediterranean Sea are a hive of activity where people communicate and information is exchanged like no other place in the world. Sailors, dock workers, fishermen move about, watching and talking. Moroccan could easily be found if he wasn't careful and for some unknown reason, he didn't want to be found.

Then there was Emilio Di Batista. An Italian from Napoli, around my age, maybe two or three years older. A nice guy and boy, could he talk! He was the equivalent of three of Moroccan's type. He had been working aboard the Bella Messina for six years and knew most of the ports quite well. He was an outright liar who exaggerated most of the time, but he was the perfect company for exploring the Mediterranean ports and their whorehouses.

He was good at picking fights and a very good seaman. Our similar age and my appetite for listening to stories would contribute to us becoming good friends, though he hated books more than he hated being silent.

There was another Italian from Palermo called Massimo Gianneli, who was a bit like the second-mate or boatswain, or both in one. He was around forty and the only one with a family back home. He had a daughter and a son and was planning to move to America with his family soon. He seemed to have the right answers when asked any questions.

Finally, there were two brothers from Africa, the so-called Tana brothers, Berhane and Tafari. Berhane was twenty-one and Tafari nineteen. They were also new aboard the Bella Messina but not new to sea life. You could tell by watching them dive from the highest point of the mast. They were full of energy and enthusiasm to learn and do all it takes to sail a two-masted schooner, no matter which way the wind was blowing.

Like Moroccan, they were always playing with their knives and he would show them new tricks, being the master himself. As brothers, they looked very alike and if you were in any doubt, you could always tell them apart by the large medallions they wore, even when diving from what seemed like the sky.

As I was the only *Frenchman* on board the ship, this was destined to become my name for the next five years. My main job was to cook, but like everyone else, I would help out wherever I could when help was needed. During those wonderful years, I visited all the ports of the Mediterranean, all the islands, the Portuguese ports, the Spanish and French Atlantic coasts, the Netherlands, the British islands and of course, the north coast of my beautiful country, Normandy.

Let me tell you about them, one at a time. There's no rush.

Our first voyage was from Marseille to Malta, transporting mainly soap and fabric. From Malta, we travelled to Siracusa where we loaded up with oranges. It was there that I saw the Mafia guards making sure the cargo was properly loaded onto the ship for the first time. From there, we sailed to Venice where we delivered the oranges, once more under the supervision of the Mafia. We stayed in Venice longer than usual because Capitano had some important business meetings there.

I noticed that Capitano was in a particularly good mood. He had fully shaved his head, was dressed like a real gentleman and looked very impressive. He stood up straight with his shoulders back and set off for his important meetings with important Venetian people.

I would have given anything to be a fly on the wall and listen to the important things they said! I was very curious and envious of his 'business'.

I set off to buy my important food supplics with Gianneli, who also took the time to show me around in this unique city. A much different walk to the one with Di Batista.

Piazza San Marco is the principal public square of Venice and is generally known as La Piazza. Napoleon called it the 'drawing room of Europe' and had the famous Horses of Saint Mark forcibly removed from the basilica and carried off to Paris, where they were used in the design of the Arc de Triomphe. After Waterloo, the

Austrian Emperor ordered the return of the horses to Venice.

Gianneli and I wandered around and headed west, where he showed me an impressive building with many statues on its facade. There were also maps and ships made of marble on its exterior.

"You see those statues, Frenchman?"

"Very impressive!"

"They're the Barbaros. A great Venetian family. The maps indicate the places where Antonio Barbaro served. His statue is in the centre. He is surrounded by representations of Honour, Virtue, Fame and Wisdom. He was the chief benefactor, you see. The other statues are of his brothers."

"Is this a family museum?"

Gianneli laughed.

"No, a church."

"A church?"

"Santa Maria Zobenigo.

"Santa Maria?"

"Surprised?"

"But where is Santa Maria? There are no Christian figures."

"Money, money, money, my friend."

"Money…" I murmured.

"It's not the wind that moves the Bella Messina, Frenchman… it's money. Damned money."

In Venice, we loaded an assortment of boxes with all the luxuries in the world. Perfumes, women's things, dresses, hats, spades, taking extra special care and when it was all aboard, we set sail for Smyrna on the west coast of Asia Minor.

On our journey across the Aegean Sea, something strange happened. The ship came to a halt close to an island the name of which I did not know. It was a scheduled stop and it seemed everyone knew about it, except me. Capitano looked at the seabed and sometimes raised his cleanly-shaved head to examine the coastline, searching for a sign I assumed. He instructed the others to anchor the vessel in a specific location in the middle of nowhere.

Filled with curiosity, I asked what they were doing but only got smiles for answers. They were anxiously executing their orders.

"Stop!"

He'd found what he was looking for, it seemed. He put his knife between his teeth, dived into the sea and was gone for quite some time. I began to worry, but judging by the calmness of the crew, I was the only one concerned. Suddenly, he reappeared.

"Moroccan!" he shouted.

Moroccan was playing with his knife and was not surprised. He knew what to expect and he too put his knife between his teeth and dived into the sea after Capitano. The two brothers followed in exactly the same way. Was this a 'bite the knife and dive' competition? As soon as they dived overboard, absolute silence reigned in the blue surroundings of the Bella Messina.

"What are they doing? What's going on?"

"Patience, Frenchman, patience," said Gianneli.

I turned to the other Italian. "Emilio! What's happening?"

Di Batista couldn't stay silent so he sang a beautiful Italian song in an effort to prolong my ignorance and increase my anxiety.

All of a sudden, I saw a head, then another, then another. Four heads gradually appeared on the surface of the water. It looked as if they were holding a fifth person who couldn't swim. As they approached, we dropped them a rope and carefully pulled the 'non-swimmer' on board.

Voila!

It was an ancient Greek urn. I couldn't believe it! It had probably been waiting for centuries for Capitano to come along.

It was crafted centuries ago for the needs of another world. A world that was now lost forever. Maybe it was from a sunken city or a sunken ship. Who had made this beautiful thing? Who had used it? What was the story behind it? What secrets did it hold? Why were we taking it?

The urn was full of algae, mud, mortar and seashells and was covered in sand. Some flecks of paint were visible, however.

Everyone was excited about our finding and not for the love of history, for sure. Once it was safely on board, Capitano ordered the crew to release the boat into the water. This time, the four divers went closer to the shore. Moroccan rowed slowly, while Capitano and the Tana brothers carefully searched the seabed.

"Stop," shouted Berhane and dived into the water. His brother and Moroccan followed. I couldn't see clearly but it was obvious they were bringing things to the surface before diving down again. Capitano carefully placed their findings in the boat. After an hour or so, they were back on board the ship, as happy as fishermen who had caught their best catch ever.

"Donna Julia, here I come," shouted Capitano in glorious tune as he admired the massive urn drying on the deck.

In Smyrna, we unloaded the luxury items and took on a consignment of raisins straight away. Once the last box was on board, we cast off. There was no hanging about.

"Frenchman, come here."

"Yes, Capitano."

"You see that small island over there? It's called Delos."

"Ah, I know that island. It's where Apollo and Artemis were born. Their mother…"

"Yes, yes… but look and listen to what I'm saying, goddamit! A Frenchman was in charge of excavations there until 1880."

"That's great!"

"I think so, too. His name was Theophile Homolle. And there are more French people there now."

"Great!"

"I think so, too. Now go and get shaved and put on some nice clothes. Then, you and Moroccan will take the boat and go ashore. Make it look like you own the place, ok?"

"Well…"

"If anyone talks to you, start speaking quickly in French about Apollo and all that nonsense, ok?

"But…"

"There's a lot of stuff there. If you get into trouble, Moroccan will cover for you. Then take the boat and return but take whatever you can."

"Capitano, I…"

"Shave!"

We reached Delos at midday. The sun was burning hot and we were sweating like pigs. Moroccan was better off because he always wore light clothing but I was dressed formally and my clothes were unsuitable for such high temperatures. I hoped, however, that my appearance, posture and native French would do the job.

When we went ashore on the island of Delos, I was a different man. I surprised even myself. When two men near the small harbour started walking in our direction, I smiled and greeted them. "Bonjour! Bonjour! Ignorez-moi! Continuez à travailler. Continuez à travailler!"

Would that do?

Probably.

I could tell they were Greek because they hardly understood and when they heard me speak French, they stood up straight. I continued towards the centre of the sacred island; the island that had never needed walls or guards because Apollo was protecting it, even from those who didn't know him, like the Persians.

Even when the collective funds of the Delian League were kept there, no guards were needed. It's true. No one dared. No one would dare anger the god Apollo.

In 478 B.C., after the Greek victory in the Battle of Plateaus at the end of the Second Persian Invasion of Greece, the Delian League was founded to continue fighting the Persians. It was an association of Greek city-states under Athenian leadership.

In 454 B.C. however, Pericles thought it was wrong to bother Apollo with economic matters or thought he might not do a good job of protecting the monies. The Athens city walls would do a much better job, so he took the money there.

You would be wrong to think that Apollo didn't mind. Look what happened to Athens and Pericles. The great plague of 430 killed him and his family and an estimated 75.000-100.000 people died. And this took place during a war with Sparta, the so-called *Peloponnesian War.*

n 1887, I was like a modern small-time version of Pericles trying to remove something from this sacred island. It was less important than the Delian League collective fund, and would not worry Apollo, Homolle or whoever was in charge of the place now.

I walked around the island with an air of self-confidence and Moroccan at my side. I approached a group of three workers to evaluate their work on a lion-like statue.

"Trés bien! Trés bien!" I said and ordered Moroccan to help them. He was taken by surprise but could do nothing about it.

Once they'd got used to Moroccan helping out and my loud, fluent French, I decided to make a move.

With the little Greek I had learned from Alexandros on the Alesia, I gave clear instructions to one of the workers to take two small statutes and put them next to the boat. Later, I did the same with an urn and a deer. I walked about, refusing to stay in one place and talk.

Please note. Moroccan and I did not move anything. The workers on the excavation site did the moving. Do you understand?

Obviously, for a reason.

Once we'd gathered enough items, I ordered Moroccan to follow me. I did not say anything to the workers. We made our way to the boat, loaded the stuff on board and Moroccan hastily rowed away.

"Can't you go any faster, my friend?" I asked as arrogantly as I had spoken to the workers.

"You French are one of a kind," he said and we both began to laugh.

Maybe Pericles laughed too when he took the money to Athens. But Apollo didn't forget. Twenty-four years later, the god of light sent Nemesis.

Between taking the ancient Greek treasures on board and our arrival in Venice, the situation had become clear. I could see why Capitano was happy to have me among his crew and it wasn't for my French cooking skills. He wanted me for my French language, French accent and my imposing posture.

Once our consignment of raisins was taken care of, Capitano took me to the marketplace to buy new clothes. It was an opportunity to admire the streets of this unique city once again and proudly send letters to my father and Mr Elazar.

Capitano paid for my outfit with his own money. He had chosen clothes that would make me look intellectual. I was intellectual already, of course, with all the books I had read, I just didn't know it. What you are and what you make yourself out to be are two different things, however. He also bought a hat for his clean-shaven head. The marketplace in Venice was full of beautiful things, beautiful buildings and beautiful women.

"Frenchman, if we play our cards right, we'll make a small fortune out of this junk. Don Gianmarco Basilio is a very rich man. He collects this stuff like a maniac but he is no fool. He might be desperate to get his hands on it but he won't be willing to pay much."

"Ok, so this is where I come in?"

"Yes. Until now, I've been quite naive. I took Di Batista with me to sell the junk. He could see we wanted the money and had no other option; that we wanted to leave with the money instead of taking the stuff back.

This time, we'll go together and you'll say you want to keep it for a rich Frenchman. A Monsieur *De la Crois* or something, use whatever name you like. Just don't go into detail. Speak as little as possible and don't smile. I want Don Basilio to fear he's losing us as suppliers."

"I have another idea, Capitano. Why don't we tell him to come to the ship if he's interested? Show him we are willing to leave with the treasure."

"Bad idea", said Capitano flatly, though I did not know why.

Three years later, it would have been obvious but that was then not now. In the meantime, I'd find out what a bad idea it was in the worst possible way.

When we got there, I couldn't believe how luxurious Basilio's home was. Or palazzo, should I say? I was more anxious about meeting his wife - Donna Julia Basilio - however. Emilio had described her as a unique beauty. He also mentioned that she noticed him, as all women do, of course.

The treasure was unloaded from the carriage and carefully transported to the Basilio's palace. As usual, the items were covered over.

"Don Basilio, it's been almost a year. How are you? You're looking well. Allow me to introduce you to my associate, Monsieur Edward Aguillon!"

"A Frenchman? It's been almost ninety years since we saw one in Venice."

"There was one here on May 12th, I think, in 1797. That was ninety-one years ago," said Edward proudly.

"And, like you, he was also good at mathematics and wanted to become a professor so he traded at least, but ended up as emperor. Life can be tricky, especially when you experience history in the making," Edward continued.

"Napoleon was actually making history, Don Basilio. Let's remember that, shall we?"

"I couldn't agree more. In any case, history is the reason you are here, Monsieur Aguillon."

Napoleon had conquered Venice on May 12th, 1797 during the War of the First Coalition. I heard Mr Amsallem emphasise that date many times because of the importance of it for his people. Napoleon was seen as something of a liberator by the city's Jewish population. He removed the gates of the Ghetto and ended the restrictions on where and when Jews could live and move about the city.

Venice became Austrian territory when Napoleon signed the Treaty of Cambo Formio on October 12th, 1797. After many exchanges during the Napoleonic wars and later revolutions, finally, in 1866, Venice, along with the rest of the Veneto, became part of the newly created Kingdom of Italy.

The sixties, remember? It was after the Third Italian War of Independence. Exactly the same time the damned Prussians won their multi-named war against the Austrians. The Austrians had to fight on two fronts. Napoleon III was half-asleep and failed to see what was coming. He would be next, as I have already explained but I just can't help mentioning it again when I think of Alsace and Lorraine.

After my first exchange with Don Basilio, I could see how happy Capitano was about the way I made conversation with his client. He probably noticed how happy I was, too, when Donna Julia Basilio entered the scene.

Emilio Di Batista was a liar. She was even more beautiful than he'd described. She was probably one of the women Mr Amsallem was talking about, when he wanted me to forget about er… oh yes, Yasmine.

Yasmine? That seemed a long time ago.

We were offered a glass of *Fernet*, which is a type of *amaro,* originating in Milan.

"Fratelli Branca have been producing it since 1845. It's one of the best known Italian *bitters.* It was originally marketed as a cure for cholera, stomachaches, nervous disorders and other such things. Can you imagine that?"

I didn't mention the cholera episode aboard the SS Alesia less than a year before. It was easy enough to avoid and I also didn't mention the Benedictine liqueur.

That was not so easy. I noticed, however, that Don Basilio was aware of the history of his favourite Italian liqueur sold in an unremarkable bottle.

"Things are happening in Europe, you know. The German Emperor, Wilhelm I, died on March 9th. The new king is his son, Frederick III. The lucky man has Queen Victoria as his mother-in-law."

"I don't consider it lucky, Don Basilio," said Capitano smiling.

"Well, if your mother-in-law reigns over practically all the men on the planet, you can bet she won't have time to bother you, right?"

Everyone laughed, except Donna Julia, of course. Don Basilio continued.

"Frederick will be a great king. He is much more sophisticated than any other ruler in Europe, at the moment. The German Empire is running like a well-tuned clock; Bismarck made sure of that, and with Frederick as king, the German Empire will thrive."

And as if that wasn't enough about this new Prussian king, Don Basilio continued in his admiring tone.

"His mother Augusta insisted that her son receive a classical education, so he was thoroughly tutored in both military traditions and the liberal arts. His private tutor was Ernst Curtius, a famous archaeologist."

Indeed, the new Prussian king broke with family tradition at the age of eighteen and entered the University of Bonn where he studied history, law and governance and public policy. Not the typical Prussian militaristic approach. All these were instrumental in his embracing of liberal beliefs.

"You seem to know a lot about him, Don Basilio."

"He was here in Venice during the winter, but I did not see him. I met him in the past because we share the same interest in archaeology, you see. Didn't I tell you? He has been appointed Protector of Public Museums in Berlin. It was largely due to him that a great number of artistic collections were acquired and housed in Berlin's new museum, you know. Probably the greatest of all the Hohenzollerns. He smokes a lot, by the way."

In 1880, clad in the uniform of a Prussian field marshal, Frederick, and his English wife Victoria, attended a service at a synagogue in Berlin to demonstrate his opposition to the anti-Semitic ideas of Heinrich von Treitschke and the court chaplain, Adolf Stoecker. Frederick gave a speech denouncing the anti-Semitic movement in Germany as 'a shameful plot of our time'.

Don Basilio continued. "Within Junker circles, of course, Frederick is widely criticised for his actions in support of the Jews."

"Junkers?"

"The young lords, derived from 'Jung' and 'Herr', young man."

Understandably for a young Frenchman like myself, it was impossible to resist, especially in front of such a beautiful woman. I was very angry hearing about this new Prussian King and at some stage, I exploded.

"I am very surprised how easily the Prussians, or the Germans if you like, have accomplished so much in the field of science, while at the same time, they thrive on conceiving and believing their own lies. Oversimplified, ridiculous versions of history and humanity!"

I told them stories of the Prussians, Napoleon, Waterloo, my grandfather, my brother and of course, Alsace and Lorraine. I spoke in French and although Capitano did not clearly understand what I was saying, he soon realised that the atmosphere was becoming strained.

"Don Basilio, I think the small treasures we have brought you are deserving of a generous offer. Otherwise, they will end up in the hands of a Frenchman like him," said Capitano quite sternly.

Basilios laughed out loud and I was rather ashamed. I suddenly remembered the reason we were there and Capitano telling me to say as little as possible. Capitano gave me a look I would never forget.

"No problem Caporaso, I enjoy hearing the French language. Edward is mostly right. I should add though, that while still a prince, King Frederick was opposed to military action in all those wars with Denmark, Austria and France. However, once the war had begun, he supported the Prussian army wholeheartedly and took positions of command. He was praised for his leadership on the battlefield. He is certainly not a coward. I have read that even French journalists praise his abilities and character."

Indeed, following his victory, Frederick spoke to two Paris journalists. 'I do not like war gentlemen. If I should reign, I would never make it.' 'The Crown Prince has left countless traits of kindness and humanity in the land that he fought against,' remarked one French journalist. Regarding his behaviour and accomplishments, The Times wrote a tribute to Frederick in July 1871, stating 'the Prince has won as much honour for his gentleness as for his prowess in the war'.

"I do apologise, Don Basilio. As you said earlier, we are here because of history and history not only involves wars but more importantly, art and science, the beauty of civilisation. Unique masterpieces created more than 2,500 years ago in the vicinity of the Mediterranean."

You should have seen the look on Donna Julia's face! Life is full of little surprises. I didn't dare believe she could be mine.

I do not have those seven francs, as Mr Elazar said. Or do I?

"Monsieur Aguillon, they say that a French architect is planning to build a unique tower in Paris. A tower that will be the tallest in the world and different to any other tower built to date. Gianmarco and I are planning to visit it when it's completed."

I had no idea about that but it was easy to glance over it. I had been bored to death by another tall, French tower some months earlier in the port of New York.

"I am curious to see the result too, but I would strongly recommend a visit to New York to see the Statue of Liberty. It is one of the wonders of the modern world, like the Colossus of Rhodes in ancient times." I turned to the captain. "Mr Caporaso, do you think we could transport it aboard your ship when we find it?"

We enjoyed a delicious meal and then moved on to view the merchandise. As expected, Don Basilio was not very enthusiastic about our findings but was very good at hiding his feelings. On the other hand, we stood as equals this time and were prepared to leave with our treasure if necessary.

The urn was pretty impressive due to its size and painted sections were visible under the stoned sand.

Capitano insisted we clean it on board the ship but I informed him that would be dangerous. We could have damaged it and what's more, the mystery that lay beneath would have guaranteed us a bigger profit. I also insisted on keeping the other findings for another time. Capitano also brought along two small items that were probably a pair of ancient earrings. He thought he could raise the price if Donna Julia was charmed by them.

"Monsieur Aguillon, it is certainly not the statue of Winged Victory of Samothrace. I was there when they revealed it in Louvre four years ago…

"And I am more interested in visiting Paris to see it again than seeing a new Tower of Babel. For your amphora, Capitano, I will give you this much," he said, showing Capitano the money like a fisherman showing bait to a fish, and excluding me from the negotiations at the same time.

Capitano was disappointed when he saw the amount and he mistakenly let it show. It was time for the French cook to stir the soup.

"Don Basilio, thank you for the wonderful meal and your generous offer but we cannot agree. Maybe we will have something for you in the future."

"I am not giving you any more money, Monsieur Aguillon, you can take it with you."

I smiled and approached Capitano to consult with him, whispering but emphasising certain words. "….Monsieur Le Grand….", "… Palais Benedictine…" Then, we prepared to leave. But the bait was too good not to catch a fish.

"One minute, Caporaso. Do you honestly intend to give this treasure to that Frenchman who thinks he is Alexander the Great? Le Grand! Does he think he can open another Louvre in Normandy? And that French Benedictine liqueur is nothing special!"

"I find it quite unique, Don Basilio."

"You are French, too."

"And I would very much like to see this treasure at the gates of the Palais de Benedictine. But to tell you the truth, there's something else I am curious about."

"Really?" asked Don Basilio ironically. "And what is that?"

"The mystery that is hidden beneath. The beauty the ancient Greeks conveyed to us. The story it tells.

"Maybe it's Hercules killing the Lion of Nemea or Jason's Argonauts taking the Golden Fleece. Maybe it's Zeus in all his glory on Mount Olympus. Maybe it's Theseus and the Minotaur. Even Odysseus? Who knows? I must admit, Don Basilio, I am dying of curiosity."

I had never seen Capitano so happy. On the way back to the ship he laughed like a child. He couldn't believe how much money we'd earned from the sale of a single urn. Don Gianmarco Basilio gave us ten times more than his original offer and Capitano did not give the earrings to Donna Julia. Luckily, I managed to patch things up after my foolish monologue.

Damned Prussians!

"I have to admit, Frenchman. I never liked your cooking but today I am grateful that I met you in Marseille. There were times when I wanted to punch you in the face. I couldn't understand what you were saying but it sounded as if we were going to be thrown out of the house."

"Capitano, I lost my older brother in the Battle of Sedan in 1871, in the Franco-Prussian War. Whenever I remember him, my heart bleeds. I cannot help it."

"I'm sorry for your loss, son. It must be hard. It is hard, but you know, brothers, sons and fathers are killed in all wars. Even the glorious Napoleonic Wars. Even in

Alexander the Great's glorious campaign. War means pain, son. The ultimate pain."

"Yes."

"Thank goodness the new king hates war. Fortunately, he fought bravely as a prince because he will have nothing to prove to the German… what are they called?"

"Junkers."

"That's right. In Sicily, I used to pick fights just for the sake of it. To prove myself. It was stupid. But anyway, today is a big day, dear Frenchman, and we are going to celebrate. Oh, and who is this Le Grand by the way? How did you know?

"He is one of our prospective customers, Capitano. One of the best, I guess."

"It was quite a success, son."

When we got back to the ship, Capitano couldn't stop talking about what had happened and the money we'd earned.

At this point, there is something I need to explain.

The Bella Messina is a ship that transports goods and the crew make a fair living from it. Not the best though, and not equivalent to the amount of hard work involved and being continually on the move. The ancient treasures were an extra. Capitano could have kept the proceeds for himself but that would have led to more competition. Sooner or later, the crew would have gone their own way and shared his secret. He stood to lose everything, so Capitano made a deal with us.

"Of all the money we earn from the ancient Greek treasure, half goes to me because the ship is mine, as are the risk and expenses. The other half is yours to share equally between you. You say nothing, I say nothing. I think that's fair enough!"

Capitano was a clever man. He could easily have done a deal with me and we could have shared the biggest part of the profit but he would have lost my trust and I could have exposed him to the others at any time. It would give me power over him.

As you probably realise, I was given the credit for this unexpected, large income for all of us. The others showed their gratitude any way they could. Gianneli was the most grateful of all.

"Frenchman, three more deals like that and next year, I'll be in America with my family. Thank you, my friend."

Unfortunately, the happiness was short-lived because I soon forgot Capitano's wise words about war and pain. I wish I had given it more thought at the time. I really do.

"Mr Edward Aguillon! Aguillon! Aguillon!" shouted the heaver looking up at Bella Messina from the dock.

That night, there was a private party. Beautiful women, plenty of wine, lots of food I didn't have to cook and cabaret music. We sang, we danced and we drank more wine.

We had great company, too. Venetian women who wanted our money and money in our pockets earned with women in mind. Except for Gianneli, of course.

Rather surprised, I went ashore to talk to the heaver but he simply gave me a piece of paper and left.

Get on the white boat was the message written on it. I only told Capitano, who smiled and told me to have fun. He knew what it meant.

Soon, a white boat approached the Bella Messina.

I did as I was told and got on the *special* boat. Donna Julia was waiting on board. Her extravagant dress exposed her bust and without a word, she embraced me and kissed me.

The boat took us to a beautiful house where on a bed as big as the SS Alesia, we celebrated throughout the night.

Nothing was beyond my reach, it seemed. I had those seven francs, after all.

I was very proud of myself when I returned to the ship but all was lost when I discovered Capitano and Di Batista knew what I had been up to. They, too, had those seven francs.

Donna Julia was the last of the Barbaro family. A successor to one of the most powerful Venetian families for centuries. The family's wealth came from the salt trade. Records show that the family moved from Pula to Trieste in 706 and then to Venice in 868. At the time, the family name was Magadesi. In 1121, a naval commander called Marco changed his surname from Magadesi to Barbaro.

The family was recognised as one of the leading families of the Republic of Venice but its fortunes diminished after Napoleon's defeat of Venice when they were forced to convert most of the Palazzo Barbaro into apartments. In 1851, all that remained of the once-powerful Barbaro family was a couple of elderly, poverty-stricken brothers who lived in the garret of the Palazzo Barbaro.

John Ruskin, a leading English art critic, wrote that the poverty that descended on the last remaining members of the Barbaro family was justice for the family having rebuilt the Church of Santa Maria Zobenigo as a monument to…themselves. Had they never heard the story of the tax collector and the Pharisee? The Pharisee indeed praised himself before God but they built a shrine to themselves as well!

It seems bizarre that in the sixteenth century, there was division between the Venetian families who opposed and favoured the influence of The Holy See, a law that barred church officials from holding political appointments in Venice at the same time. These people, who as Ruskin pointed out, were 'a manifestation of insolent atheism', had a say on matters of the Church. And it was these same people who forbade the Jews to go wherever they liked.

An atheist called Napoleon saw to these matters. "I want no more Inquisition, no more Senate, I shall be an Attila to the state of Venice," he said.

Hubris brings Nemesis. And now their offspring, the last Barbaro alive, and undoubtedly beautiful, gives herself to any sailor she meets at her Palazzo Barbaro apartment. What could be more desperate? Poor Don Basilio Gianmarco! But you have your collection and the Winged Victory of Samothrace to admire.

She's a goddess, at least, and can't cheat on you!

After the sale in Venice, everyone's attitude changed for the better. I was the 'golden' Frenchman, invaluable to them now. Even Moroccan with his wild appeal and permanent silence was more willing to show his gratitude. As for the Tana brothers, I was not only a cook but a hero, though I could neither play with knives nor dive like a dolphin. As time went on, I got to know them better and discovered how they joined the crew of the Bella Messina.

They belonged to the Amhara ethnic group that occupied parts of the northwestern highlands of

Ethiopia. They learned to swim in Lake Tana, the source of the Abay River, better known as the Blue Nile. It is the river that joins the White Nile in Khartum, where they merge to become the famous River Nile which empties into the Mediterranean Sea, having blessed the areas on its way with its precious waters.

They grew up in the small village of Bahir Dar beside the lake, where the Blue Nile begins its intricate journey, heading first south-east and later flows to the north-west, as it had done for thousands of years.

They came from a large family and had many brothers and sisters, who helped their father fish the Labeobarbus *barbs*, Nile *tilapia* and sharptooth catfish until they left two years ago.

"Why did you leave?"

"We wanted to see where our river ends," was their answer.

Indeed, Capitano found them in Egypt. They travelled on foot to the port of Djibouti in the Horn of Africa and there, they managed to sneak aboard a British merchant ship and escaped to Egypt.

"The Suez Canal was constructed by Ferdinand de Lesseps, you know. He was a Frenchman."

"Don't worry, you're a better cook than him," said Berhane, poking fun at me.

There, they worked as heavers in the port of Alexandria. He saw them diving and swimming like fish after loading tons of boxes earlier in the day. Capitano realised at once he could make great sailors out of these two young men. And he was right.

No one ever admitted it but I got the impression that the fight in *Quatre Chats* was to do with Capitano's decision to take non-Sicilian crew on board. It didn't happen very often. In fact, in the few ports I'd visited so far, I think we were the only multi-national schooner. It was just a hypothesis, however.

In November that same year, the Bella Messina docked in the port of Genoa. Capitano negotiated deals for cargo to transport and I was given the task of seeking out possible clients for our ancient findings. Dressed like a gentleman, I roamed the city of Genova. I stopped at the beautiful *La Superba* tavern to eat and find out about collectors in the city.

As luck would have it, Luigi, the owner, was not just friendly but extremely talkative. He told me Genoa had been nicknamed *la Superba,* - the proud one - due to its glorious past. It was from him that I learned about the powerful lawyer, Flavio Cavanna, trusted by the rich merchants of Genoa and who had connections throughout Europe. His mother was from Saxony.

"He is said to have connections with the royal families of England and Germany; the most important ones. I prefer Franz Josef of Austria but you have to admit, nowadays, Victoria and Wilhelm are the most powerful monarchs in the world."

"Maybe you are not that well-informed, my friend," I said, taking advantage of the opportunity to provide this wonderful man with some extra information.

"Who me? Why do you say that?"

"Haven't you heard the news? King Wilhelm died in March. His son Frederick is the new king, and from what I've heard, he's doing very well in his new role."

At first, Luigi gave me a strange look, then he smiled and finally laughed the Italian way, slapping his knees. He laughed so much that I couldn't understand what he was saying but eventually, it became clear.

"When you say he's doing well in his new role, what do you mean exactly?" he asked, burying me in the hole I had just dug for myself.

"His new role as King of Prussia and Emperor of Germany, I guess," I replied reluctantly as he finally stopped laughing. Ironically, he repeated my exact words.

"Maybe you are not that well-informed, my friend," he said. "King Frederick died on June 15th after ninety-nine days on the German throne."

"What?"

"From cancer of the throat, I heard. His son is the new king, Wilhelm II. He's about your age, not even thirty."

"Unbelievable! King for ninety-nine days! It was only in the spring that I learned of his reign and in the very same year, I learn of his death."

"Kings die, too, you know."

"This year, two Prussian kings have died. It is rather unusual."

"The king is dead, long live the king! 1888 is the year of three eights and three kings," said Luigi and went off to speak to his other customers.

At the time, it was nothing more than a strange development but years later, I realised it was a fatal development. As far as my business was concerned, that is.

King Frederick died peacefully of cancer, which had developed due to his smoking habit which had come from America, just like *phylloxera*. Maybe the forthcoming war, my war, was the silent revenge of the Native Americans because it was European greed that slaughtered the Indian population. Maybe.

Not exactly relevant but a year earlier, on the other side of the Atlantic, the first Triceratops was discovered. It was mistaken for a gigantic species of extinct bison. The Triceratops was officially named and described by American palaeontologist O.C. Marsh in 1889. That makes 1888 also the year of three horns. Strange, don't you think?

I found Cavanna - the lawyer, and it turned out that he was also interested in archaeology. We sold him a small statue of a woman for an unbelievable price. Once again, the crew could hardly believe it.

I was good at my job. Very good.

The time passed quickly. We'd created a network of good customers throughout the Mediterranean, who paid enormous sums of money for the items we fished out of the Aegean Sea or stole from excavation sites. Delos, Ephesus, Troy. Things were going so well that even Gianneli considered changing his plans about going to America. The Aegean Sea was the real El Dorado.

This situation created a special bond between us. We all knew that we needed each other to continue at the same pace. There were two crucial factors. Finding the sites where archaeological treasures were buried and expanding our clientele. I focused mainly on the second task, while Capitano concentrated on the first.

He would make conversation with other captains anywhere he could to find out about any rumours, theories or stories.

We had already discovered two more locations. One in Artemisio, which was on the way to the port of Volos and one on the coast of Naxos. In Volos, we usually loaded fabric made in Tyrnavos, the largest city in Thessaly.

Naturally, there were difficulties.

Once, while we were heading to Constantinople, we thought we'd check out Xerxes' ships that had sunk during his Greek campaign. The exact spot was claimed to be near Mount Athos. We were told that the sea was deep and dangerous but we were far too confident.

The seabed disappeared just twenty meters from the steep, rocky shore and waves appeared out of nowhere. I had never been so scared in my whole life. When we reached Constantinople, I looked for a whip to punish the sea, as Xerxes had done.

I understand him now.

In any case, the fairytale life we were living had to come to an end, like all fairytales. And it ended on a minor detail we had failed to pay attention to. As our voyage continued, we became more confident and less careful. And when I say we, I mean I.

Remember what Capitano said when I suggested we bring Don Basilio to the ship?

"Bad idea."

"Capitano Antonio Caporaso..." and after a silence, "…we grew up together. I always considered you a friend, despite our differences." The silence continued. "My father helped your uncle to buy his ship."

Conte Antonio Cucinotta paused again, stood up and walked around the room. "We protected your earnings, we protected your business, your family…" He walked over to the damned Kouros statue and put his hand on his head.

"…and you? You are ignorant enough to deny us an introduction to your new friends."

The men with the guns laughed but the elders at the table didn't bat an eyelid.

As I said, things were looking bad.

I figured that Capitano had run into trouble with this man in his youth. The trouble that banished him to the sea. I felt guilty. It was due to my mistake that Capitano and my friends were now in big trouble, too.

I always considered the Austro-Hungarian Empire, the heir to the Holy Roman Empire, a great market for our products. But we had had no customers there, and while drinking coffee with actual Viennese aristocrats at the *Stella Polare* in Trieste, I got carried away.

Capitano had other business to deal with that day so I went alone. We agreed I would meet with the banker simply to investigate and arrange another meeting to show the merchandise and close the deal.

When Leopold politely asked to see it, however, I accepted, thinking that Capitano would be pleased to see business progressing and the expansion of our clientele. Both men came to the ship, saw the merchandise and Leopold enthusiastically made us a very generous offer. I told him we'd get back to him the following day after I had spoken to Capitano. They greeted us politely and left.

Later that day, Capitano returned to the ship and I told him the good news about the promising market we were about to conquer.

"How did you move the marble? Did Moroccan help you?"

"No, the baron and his friend came here."

"Here? Aboard the Bella Messina?"

"Yes," I said calmly.

I thought my Italian was good but that was the first time I'd heard such words spill from Capitano's mouth. He was furious and thrashed about the ship. All of a sudden, he stopped and stared in the direction of the port. He was looking for something or someone.

All was quiet. No one was there. People were minding their own business, fishermen, workers, kids playing. There was no one else. This was Trieste in Austro-Hungaria. Whom or what was he afraid of?

"Capitano…" I said. "Scusate me, non capisco."

He calmly sat on the stool, put his huge hands on his knees, shook his clean shaven head and stared on the floor. Total silence reigned aboard the Messina. A short while later he stood up and went to his cabin.

"Bad idea," he said. "Very bad idea!"

The following day, we rejected Leopold's offer, even when he doubled it. We never mentioned it again and moved on to the next port. And the next. And the next.

You might remember what I mentioned earlier about the ports.

You might also remember what I said about the Mafia watching every step of the supply chain.

Now put those two together and see what happened. As for me, it wasn't until I came before those angry Italians that I really understood what was going on.

Adesso capisco.

The Bella Messina had belonged to Capitano's uncle and when he died, Capitano inherited the business. The Messina was bought with Mafia money; a loan good old Uncle Giovanni had fully repaid. However, things are not that simple where the Mafia is concerned. Admittedly, the entire business would not have survived without the Mafia. But they weren't the bad guys, not yet.

Capitano reported to them on all the deals and transportations he undertook, even if there were no lemons involved. Sometimes he was asked to pay a percentage, somctimes not.

But the Mafia's eyes were everywhere. The dockworkers would mention any strange moves, anything unusual, out of normal routine, even the minor things. Like a famous banker and a rich aristocrat paying a visit to the Bella Messina on a normal morning in the port of Trieste.

Information travels fast. Ports are like information networks and the Mafia had no difficulty discovering the reason for the visit of such notorious men.

"If someone has to be killed, kill me, Antonio, but let the others go. They have done nothing wrong," said Capitano flatly when the men with the guns stopped laughing.

I knew nothing about Conte Cucinotta. If I did, I'd have died of fright. Sometimes in life, it is better not to know too much, to be ignorant of the situation around you but behave as if you know everything. When you want to speak to a girl who is out of your league, for example. On some occasions.

This proved to be one of those situations.

It couldn't have got any worse, so I reckoned it was impossible for Conte Antonio to know the history and size of our "antique" business.

"Conte Cucinotta, may I have your permission to speak, please?" I stepped forward and he nodded after checking with the elders - Dons, Contes or whatever they were.

"My name is Edward Aguillon. I am French and I come from Algiers. I have been the cook aboard the Messina since January of 1888. All my life, I have dived to catch fish. In the last four years, I have cooked fresh fish for my fellow shipmates. On one voyage, I dived into the Cretan Sea and caught an octopus. It was lying on the statue before you. I begged Capitano to take it onboard. He didn't want to. He said it was junk.

It was me who found the banker in Trieste and brought him and his lawyer friend to the ship. Capitano wasn't even there. When I told Capitano about the banker's offer, he said that I could not sell it without permission because it was more money than he thought it was worth. Even when the Austrian doubled the price, he refused to sell anything. That's why this statue is here today."

As I told my story, I tried to figure out how much they actually knew. The bastards were as idle as the Kouros with the infinite smile on his face. Suddenly, one of the older men leaned forward and put his elbows on the table. I took it as a sign to continue. He wanted to hear more, so obviously, he knew nothing.

"Conte Cucinotta, you can be sure that if by fishing I was making money, Capitano would ask for your permission."

Conte Cucinotta played another card. "What about Antonio Cavanna, the Genoan lawyer, Frenchman?"

It was a tough question, but if he knew the scale of the business we were doing with Cavanna, we were as good as dead. I instantly realised that the bastard who saw Baron Von Kalchberg aboard the ship in Trieste had spoken to him, and Von Kalchberg might have said that he knew about the Messina from Cavanna, the Genoan lawyer. Once I'd figured that out, the rest was easy.

"Cavanna was the first person I tried to sell this statue to but when I discovered he had Prussian roots... Well, my grandfather was killed in the Battle of Ligny by a Prussian, my brother was killed in the battle of Sedan by a Prussian... those damned Prussians!" I bowed my head and could barely hold back the tears.

I earned the sympathy of some of the men and it was obvious they didn't know everything. I could easily make them doubt. But Conte Antonio Cucinotta was very clever and was determined to hang the crew of the Bella Messina, or Antonio Caporaso, at least.

Men like him need to send a signal, a reminder if you like. If they haven't killed anyone for a while, it might show weakness. Who knows how a Mafia mind works?

"But the banker is Baron von Kalchberg. He's a Prussian too, Edward, isn't he?" he continued.

"Yes, but I didn't plan to sell him anything. I used him to get to Mr Leopold Berchtold. He is Austrian."

"They are Germans too, you know."

"Yes, but they were also outsmarted by the Prussians. They helped them beat the Danish and then the Prussians beat their former allies in just seven weeks. Bismarck called it the Unification War. The Austrians didn't behave like Germans and I don't think they'll ever forget it, Conte Cucinotta. I can't forget it either."

"Wilhelm, Germany's new king, dismissed Bismarck a year ago. I hope that makes you feel better." He paused. "Now, what else did you find in the sea, Edward?"

"A vase and a pair of earrings," I hastily replied. I didn't give a damn about Bismarck at that particular moment.

"Are they onboard the ship or did you sell them somewhere else?"

"There's this beautiful woman in Venice, Conte Cucinotta, and I used them to meet her, to be with her. There was no other way I could have done so."

"Donna Julia!" said Conte Antonio Cucinotta. One of the older men nodded his head. He had probably met her too.

The glorious Barbaro family!

I was in big trouble and figured that now was the time to get us all out of danger, once and for all.

"Before taking the job as cook on the Messina, Conte Cucinotta, I worked on the SS Alesia, shipping immigrants to America. I often talked to them and heard their stories and I discovered they were going there to do exactly what we are doing in Europe. A Greek immigrant told me he was going to Florida because the climate is good for growing lemons. I guess he's not the only one. I'm sure many others followed his example and more will do so in the future. Soon, that will cause big problems for lemon exports."

The three old men leaned forward and put their elbows on the table. Now I've got you, dear Sicilians!

"If we dug up all the statues in the Aegean Sea, Conte, there would probably be enough to fill ten rooms the size of this one. There are probably about another six men as crazy as the baron who would pay good money for them but it is not a business you can count on for the future.

"On the other hand, the Greek who is about to harvest his first crop of lemons will undoubtedly need someone to protect his business and expand it. And who are the best people to do that? None other than people like you, who have made a successful job of it for so many Sicilian families.

"And there are probably other products besides lemons that could benefit from the service you provide, Conte Cucinotta."

Conte Cucinotta's eyes lit up and he smiled deviously. Stern and silent, the three elders struggled to hide their enthusiasm. I couldn't see my friends' faces as they were standing next to me but I bet they were relieved, especially Capitano.

On July 15th 1891, the Mafia extended its business worldwide. It was a Wednesday.

As it happened, I was right. Sicily faced serious competition in the marketing of citrus fruits, particularly from Florida, which meant a great loss of profit. Due to decreasing profitability in the citrus industry in the 1890s, many Sicilians, including members of the Mafia, migrated to America. They simply followed my advice.

I had saved my life and my friends' lives too and was very proud of that. You probably think I should feel guilty because of the crimes the Mafia committed all over the world in the decades that followed.

But the Mafia did good things too and were not associated with organised crime as they were in the years that followed. Other crimes made the Mafia look like a humanitarian organisation, as you will soon find out.

What's more, the global expansion of the Mafia saved the world, civilisation, and humankind itself. And that is no lie. Unimaginable maybe, but this easily overseen historical fact is there for all to discover. Maybe you already realise but just never joined the dots. Read on, and I am sure you'll agree with me.

"How did you do it, Frenchman?"

"What?"

"How did you came up with all those lies?"

"How did you know what they knew?"

"I don't know. I assumed they couldn't possibly know everything."

"You seemed very confident."

"Well, what can I say? I could tell by the gestures and faces they were making. It was obvious they knew nothing."

"How did you do it? We were there too, you know."

"What did you see?"

"I really don't know and I don't remember now, anyway. I sensed it somehow, while I was talking, I sensed it."

"You sensed it?"

"I really can't say…I can't describe it. Sorry!"

"Don't be sorry. You saved our lives."

"We all owe you big-time."

"We certainly do, Frenchman. I was sure I would never see my kids again."

"You owe me nothing. We are a team, we are partners…friends. We're a family."

"We are our own private Mafia, right?"

"Weren't you scared, Frenchman?"

"I was at first. But as soon as I got talking, I forgot my fear. The words just spilt out of my mouth. I was trying to find out what they wanted to hear."

"How do you know about such things?"

"Well, I just…I don't know. When I was a kid, I used to spend a lot of time at my father's friend's shop. I watched people as they came and went. Then on the Alesia, I watched the immigrants."

"So you watched the immigrants, did you? If you'd known what kind of man Cucinotta was, Frenchman, what an enormous…, you'd have kept your mouth shut," said Capitano, who had been silent until then. He looked at the port of Palermo from the stern of the Messina as night began to fall.

"I was convinced he was going to kill us all," said Capitano. "Me for sure, I don't know about you. I would have been dead now. You saved my life, Frenchman." He paused for a moment, took a breath and then continued.

"His brother was the most decent man in the whole of Sicily. Angelo Cucinotta was his name. A gentleman. He was fair, logical, kind…a great man. He knew how to handle situations. He was a natural leader. He was a man I truly admired. He was four or five years older. He would have ruled all of Sicily by now."

"What happened, to him?" I asked.

"One morning, he was found dead. Someone killed him with a knife. The killer was never found but it is a common secret that it was his fucking brother. That bastard Antonio killed his brother. His own brother. His mother's son."

"Good god! His own brother!"

"I bet if you'd known that, you'd have had second thoughts about talking to him, right Frenchman?"

"That's for sure!" Thank God I knew nothing about him. I'd have kept quiet if I'd known."

"There's one more thing I'd like to know, Frenchman. What you said about the lemons in Florida. Something to do with a Greek immigrant. Was that true?"

"Well, one Greek I got to know very well came back, for sure. He is probably in Greece right now. I even have his address. Florida is definitely a good place to grow lemons but I never met anyone who talked about lemons on the ship. I suppose immigrants imagine another kind of future in America."

"You're some man, Frenchman! You gave them another perspective and it was a real success. Who wants to collect statues when the whole world is open for business, eh?"

"So now they will let us mind our own business, right Capitano? The Aegean Sea is still there with all that treasure waiting for us, as it has been for centuries."

"There's something else I need to tell you," said Capitano. He looked serious and sad. "It's not just lemons we're taking on board in Palermo. Cucinotta asked me to pick up our new crew member. He also asked me to keep him hidden onboard for the next couple of years."

"Like you keep me hidden, Capitano?" asked Moroccan.

"Yes."

That was it. We all knew what it meant. Conte Antonio Cucinotta wasn't letting us get away with anything. He was doing someone a favour by hiding the boy on board and at the same time, he had a man watching our every move. Brilliant!

The kid we took on board in Palermo was a horrible, nasty person. Guido Moffa was a sailor who had killed his superior while working on an ocean liner. He had killed a boatswain with a knife after an argument about something minor and it was obvious he didn't feel guilty about it in the slightest. Arrogant and foolish, he behaved like the boss from the moment he came on board, making our lives miserable, especially Capitano's. It was very hard being the captain of your ship and having to put up with a young idiot handed power by Conte Cucinotta.

I often thought Capitano would throw him overboard. But Antonio Caporaso was kind and generous enough not to do such a thing. He was just patient. So patient, that the situation became very odd indeed.

We shipped consignments of lemons to various ports and at some stage, Capitano got a good deal on a shipment of soap from Marseille to London. We would be leaving the embrace of the Mediterranean Sea for the first time. We were to travel north but it made no difference to us that we were no longer in the vicinity of the Aegean Sea. The statues, the excavations, the 'ancient junk' were safe where they were. That chapter was closed.

Massimo Gianneli wasn't on board when we set sail for London. He was the first to quit the Messina. He had saved enough money to take his family to America and start a new life in the land of opportunity.

"Give my regards to the beautiful French Lady, Massimo."

"Who?"

"The statue of Liberty."

"I hope the French are successful with Alsace."

"And Lorraine?"

"And Lorraine… and Lorraine!"

"Have a nice life, Massimo Gianneli, and all the best to you and your family!"

"Have nice a nice life, Frenchman!"

We had a great time in London while Capitano cut new deals and met beautiful English women. Moffa went crazy and Di Batista decided to marry a girl from Ipswich and stay in England forever. Berhane and Tafari were unstoppable. Girls would come to the ship asking for them.

It was paradise. Every port is a sailor's paradise. And I must admit, English girls really know how to kiss, though I never thought about marrying one…or two. Even Moroccan was more relaxed but still went about carefully and only at night.

In London, Capitano loaded a shipment of bottles and fine quality paper for transport to Normandy, to Fécamp in particular. That's correct. The place where the Benedictine liqueur is produced. I was very excited. I would buy dozens of bottles to send to Mr Elazar, or so I thought, but things turned out differently.

We arrived in Fécamp on January 11th, 1892. The first thing I did was visit Palais Benedictine. My main concern was to take in every small detail so I could describe it to Mr Elazar. Capitano came with me because he'd always wanted to see the place that was used five years earlier as bait for Don Basilio. Seeing Mr Le Grand's treasures, we calculated how much money he would generously pay us for our findings.

The following day something terrible happened.

From the ship, dark smoke could be seen rising into the sky. Moroccan and I rushed to the source of the smoke. The Tana brothers, always faster, were already there.

The Palais Benedictine had gone up in flames. People were trying to extinguish the fire with buckets of water, but it was obvious it would do no good. The fire brigade had not yet arrived. They were probably still loading their carriages or preparing the horses.

On the spur of the moment, I shouted out to a man in front of me in my mother tongue.

"Listen! My friends and I are going to try and rescue some of the antiques inside before it's too late!"

I turned around to find that Moroccan, Berhane and Tafari had already disappeared inside the Palais. The man had big eyes and a small, pointed beard. He shrugged his shoulders in desperation.

We had risked our lives but I honestly don't know why. Maybe it was out of respect for unique treasure, including the ones we hadn't sold. Respect for our segment of the market.

Berhane and Tafari, who always over excelled by stretching themselves to the limit didn't hesitate to enter the darkest, smoke-filled places. In a state of panic, I realised that I had briefly lost sight of Tafari, though not of Berhane, who caught my eye every now and again.

Where is Tafari?

I recalled the last time I saw him going down a corridor. *I should have stopped him, but I didn't.*

I ran down the corridor shouting but there was no response. My vision was completely obscured and it was difficult to breathe. Then, I stumbled on a shield and fell.

"Tafari!"

He was unconscious but breathing, thank God! I lifted him onto my shoulder and used the shield to make our way out.

Once we were out of the building, Tafari's breathing slowly began to improve as he returned to the land of the living. I didn't go back inside the Palais and would never enter a burning building again.

In two hours, we managed to rescue about thirty pieces of Mr Le Grand's collection, placing the items carefully in a safe location just outside the Palais. Then, we could do nothing more than watch the fire reduce the glorious building to ashes. The Palais was completely destroyed. Berhane and Tafari returned to the ship for some fresh air and to escape the smoke. Moroccan and I stayed close to the treasure we'd rescued. It was crucial to leave it with someone reliable. I sat on an antique, throne-like chair and Morrocan on a statue of Cerberus, the three-headed dog that guarded the kingdom of the dead. It had done a good job today. Capitano soon arrived and stared at the scene of the disaster.

Some women brought us drinking water. The men, who had tried to extinguish the fire were still there, their faces blackened from the smoke. Some lay down, some just sat there watching the powerful flames. Disastrous yet spectacular.

The fellow I had spoken to when I arrived on the scene was there too. Though tired, he did not look as desperate as when I first saw him. At some stage, he approached us and looked over the items we had saved. He was followed by a shorter man wearing fine clothes. We got up from our unusual seats.

"I thank you from the bottom of my heart for your enormous effort. These items are invaluable to me. You risked your lives to save my collection. I don't know where you came from but I'm extremely glad you came. My name is Alexandre Le Grand and I'm the owner of this place."

"It's an honour to meet you, Mr Le Grand. My name is Edward Aguillon, I'm from Algiers."

"I'm Mehdi from Morocco."

"Antonio Caporaso. The proud *Capitano* of these brave men. My ship, the Bella Messina docked here yesterday. I am very sorry for your loss, Mr Le Grand. We visited the Palais yesterday and we were quite amazed."

"The important thing is that no one was hurt. I was very proud of this palace and I can assure you I will rebuild it even bigger and more glorious than before. I don't know how long you will be in Fécamp, but it would be a pleasure to extend my hospitality to you one day. My father was a sea captain and Xenios Zeus is my favourite Greek god."

That night, I sat alone on the prow eating raisins from Smyrna using Yasmine's gift as a plate.

Berhane came and sat next to me.

"What is this, Frenchman?" he asked, looking at the handkerchief.

"It is a gift from my first love, my friend. Yasmine."

When he heard her name, Berhane went quiet and looked out to sea. He broke his silence five minutes later.

"You saved my brother's life today, Frenchman. I should have protected him but failed to do so. If it wasn't for you, Tafari would be dead and I would be dead, too. I could never live with myself if he died."

"We all acted pretty naively today, going into a burning building like that, my friend. It just happened to be me that found him."

"You searched for him, I know, Frenchman," he said and then went quiet again for a few more minutes. "Do you know why we left our homeland, Frenchman?" he asked.

"To see where the Nile ends," I said. I noticed the whites of his eyes were red.

"I was a fisherman, you know. All of my family were fishermen. One afternoon, we returned early and I went directly to her…She was with another man."

Berhane began to cry as he continued his story.

"I always carry a knife, as you know. All fishermen do. She pushed her way in front of him to stop me from…her eyes closed as she put her arms around me."

He was silent again before saying her name. *"Yemsirach!"*

This was Berhane's dramatic tale.

Blind with jealousy, he accidentally killed the woman he loved. He had to leave his family and go into hiding. His younger brother followed him on his journey. But at least they were better off than Moroccan because there weren't many Ethiopians in the Mediterranean Sea.

"This is for you," he said and took off his medallion. He put it over my head.

"I can't accept it. It's…"

"Yours."

"Thank you, Berhane but you wear it all the time. It must be important…"

"It is important."

On closer inspection, I noticed two small shells facing each other in the shape of a small box. It was tightly sealed.

"What is this?"

"It's absolute power."

"What?"

"Zewditu Notzo is a root that has total control over life and death."

"How come?"

"If even the smallest amount enters the body, that body will stop breathing."

"A poison?"

"Not just any poison. The body will carry on functioning as if nothing has happened but when the eyes go to sleep, they will never open again."

"Berhane, I am very sorry for saving your brother. I won't do it again, I promise. Please take it back, Berhane. I love my life and remember, I am the cook."

"Frenchman, the Zewditu is sealed in the medallion for all eternity. You have the power, now."

"But why don't you keep the power, and I just…"

"I am giving it to you out of gratitude, as a seal of our friendship and you can do whatever you like with it."

We stared out over the dark sea for a long time that night.

By the time I fell asleep, I had already become used to keeping death sealed in my medallion.

The next day, we put on the elegant outfits we had bought in London and waited for Mr Le Grand's carriage to pick us up. Berhane and Tafari didn't want to come at first, preferring to stay aboard the Bella Messina, but Capitano insisted.

Le Grand's well-dressed follower had come in the morning to inform us of the time. Moroccan looked very impressive in his English suit and obviously, Moffa had to come with us. The little bastard didn't even ask if he had been invited. He simply took it for granted. Once again, Capitano held on to his nerves.

We had the most wonderful, eclectic meal I had ever eaten. Mr Le Grand not only sold superb treasures but also lived among them. I was amazed at how calm he was considering how disastrous the previous day had been. He had invited us to dinner, which was very admirable but strange at the same time.

Moffa was like a parasite. He had no manners and showed no consideration.

"You mentioned ancient Greece yesterday, Mr Le Grand, and there is something I have to tell you."

"Really?"

"In 356 B.C., in ancient Ephesus in Asia Minor, the glorious temple of Artemis, one of the seven wonders of the ancient world, burnt to the ground. That same day, on the other side of the Aegean Sea, Alexander the Great was born. He was the man who conquered Asia and the whole of the ancient world."

Mr Le Grand looked at me cautiously. He seemed to admire me and what I had said. He was almost pleased, maybe because I had compared his Palais to the Temple of Artemis or because a man named Alexandre Le Grand would have a special bond with Alexander the Great, or both. Or maybe it was because he was the master of nonsense telling stories such as this.

"Good point, Edward," he said. "Good point."

Little did we know, that in 1892 on the other side of the English Channel, a baby was born. That baby would grow up to become an Air Chief Marshal. His name was Sir Trafford Leigh-Mallory, the Air Commander of the Allied Invasion of Normandy. On July 6th 1944, so-called *D-Day,* the American army would break Hitler's Atlantic Wall and invade Europe freeing it from Nazi tyranny.

Just as Alexander the Great died in Babylon, never to return in Greece, Sir Trafford Leigh-Mallory died in November 1944 en route to Ceylon to take up the post of Air Commander-in-Chief of South East Asia. His aircraft crashed in the French Alps and Leigh-Mallory, his wife and eight others were killed.

Some may argue that the real master of the Normandy Invasion was not born that year, since General Eisenhower or President Franklin Delano Roosevelt were in command. If Notre Dame had burned to the ground in the space of my – very long – lifetime, the birthplace of a future invader of France, whether it were Great Britain or America, might have concerned me. But it didn't, so it was pointless worrying about it.

When the meal was over, Mr Le Grand turned to Capitano.

"Mr Caporaso, you must be very proud of your crew. With your permission, I would like to make you an offer of a job."

To our great surprise, he made each of us an open proposition, except for Guido, of course. Capitano was surprised but took great pleasure in the fact that Mr

Le Grand had immediately disconnected Moffa from the rest of us. It took him just five seconds to reply.

"Mr Le Grand, even if I wanted to, I could not stop you from doing so. It will take many men to compensate for the absence of these brave sailors but I would hate to prevent what is best for anyone."

"I cannot abandon Capitano and the Messina, Mr Le Grand, but thank you anyway," said Moroccan. The Tana brothers followed suit.

They turned and looked at me as a new chapter in my life was about to begin.

PART TWO

It was six o'clock in the evening and I was admiring the wonderful view of Paris from the restaurant inside the Eiffel Tower. It was amazing to be inside the tallest building in the whole world. Donna Julia Basilio was the first to tell me about plans for the tower and I'm sure she would never have imagined it this tall.

Ironically, many intellectuals, writers, painters, sculptors and architects protested against its construction. Even Alexandre Dumas was among those who strongly objected and signed the *Artists against the Eiffel Tower* petition. It was sent to the Minister of Works and Commissioner for the Exposition, Adolphe Alphand, and published by *Le Temps*. Eventually, building went ahead, however, and it was used as the entrance to the 1889 World's Fair. France was celebrating the one-hundredth anniversary of the French Revolution.

It is said that writer Guy de Maupassant dined there every day. When asked why, he said it was the only place in Paris he could eat without looking at the Eiffel Tower. I had never seen Paris without it, so I can't say. I knew I would miss it, for it was scheduled to be destroyed.

But for now, here I was at the 1900 World's Fair enjoying the unique view of Paris. I am sure Guy de Maupassant enjoyed the view too, though it must have been hard for him to admit he'd objected to its construction. After waiting for a quarter of an hour, the stranger arrived.

Visiting a fair - any fair - is like being on a business trip without travelling. You meet people from all over the world, your clients, partners and even your prospects. As a result, you eat, drink, talk and if you are smart, you listen.

I had been standing proudly in the middle of the exhibition grounds admiring a German crane that could lift twenty-five tons. Twenty-five tons! Damned Prussians! The stranger stood next to me and introduced himself. Well, he didn't exactly introduce himself, as I was still unaware of his name but we had a brief conversation and he kindly invited me to dinner. He was well-dressed and obviously very rich. One thing I didn't know was his nationality. His strange accent told me he was neither French nor English and probably not German.

"Now, Mr Aguillon, tell me if you please, what do you think of the Dreyfus Affair?" asked the stranger after his fifth sip of wine and a quick chat about the tallest tower in the world.

"Yes, of course," I replied. "It's very important, I think, that one distinguishes the case from the man himself. Alfred Dreyfus as a person is one thing and the Dreyfus Affair another. The importance of the matter, its impact on French society and especially now, after certain things have come to light, should not confuse those who seek the truth - the actual facts, I mean – and neither should it stir patriotic sentiment or emotions of betrayal.

Tell me, what do you think of Alfred Dreyfus as a person?"

The mysterious man stared at me persistently but did not answer my question. There was an awkward silence and the atmosphere was somewhat strained. I drank some wine and in an attempt to escape the uncomfortable situation, I changed the subject.

"It is very sad, you know, that this place won't exist in nine years from now. In 1909, the Eiffel tower will be gone. It was intended that way from the beginning. A tower built in two years and easy to deconstruct only to be demolished after twenty. Maybe the Prussians will have built a bigger crane by then and we could even have lunch inside it!"

I laughed and expected the stranger to appreciate my sense of humour. Unimpressed, he stared at me in silence and a few seconds later, flatly repeated his question.

"Mr Aguillon, please tell me, what do you think of the Dreyfus Affair?"

Who is this man? What does he know? What does he want from me?

"I want you to be close to the customer, Edward. Customers, money, whar."

"Excuse me, Mr Le Grand?"

"*Whar* is an ancient Greek word. It means 'this is the reason', 'this is why'. It comes at the end of the sentence. It saves time, whar."

"Ah! Oh, ok."

I had reached the age of twenty-nine. I was tall and handsome with an impressive moustache and looked like a real gentleman. By good fortune, Mr Le Grand had seen me throw myself into the flames to save his collection and had come to appreciate the knowledge of a man born in the same year as the Benedictine liqueur. He found in me the ideal ambassador of Benedictine culture and I became a proud salesman of the world's finest liqueur.

The truth is, the liqueur sold itself. Mr Le Grand was a genius at advertising and had already laid the ground for sales of Benedictine to thrive. He persuaded several renowned artists to create posters and placards to be located around France and abroad. Artists such as Alphonse Mucha, the Czech painter, illustrator and graphic artist, Georges Goursat, the famous caricaturist, also known as Sem, and Lopes Silva.

A decade after its launch, when I was ten years old, the Benedictine liqueur was selling 150.000 bottles a year. Its commercial success was so overwhelming that in 1876, Mr Le Grand founded Benedictine S.A., a company dedicated solely to the production of liqueurs. In 1882, the year it entered the Bourse, France's securities market, the enterprise opened a new distillery to boost its production from 350.000 bottles annually to almost a million.

By applying corporate sponsorship, cooperating with artists and acquiring medieval collections for the Palais Benedictine, the liqueur gained legendary status.

My role was mainly to impress the clients, close the deals and ensure they were kept. My life as a Benedictine ambassador, as Mr Le Grand called me, was fantastic. In a Europe that was enjoying long-lasting peace and the new technological evolutions of electricity and steam, a generation of rich, super-rich, elite, who were willing to spend an enormous amount of money on 'the good life' sprung up. I had the privilege to associate with this elite. Though not an equal, I was a special guest, who kept the liqueur flowing in the prestigious salons of Europe using my wealth of knowledge of world affairs. The railway lines were expanding rapidly and I could reach the major European capitals in a day or two. In the past, it would have taken weeks or months.

Mr Le Grand gave me freedom of movement and I was able to choose the areas to focus on. As long as numbers increased, I was a free entrepreneur. And indeed, the numbers increased. Mr Le Grand, on the other hand, concentrated on rebuilding the Palais larger and more glamorous than before.

I attended events, parties and gatherings and made friends with the aristocracy. I was a member of eight patriotic organisations in Paris, Bordeaux, Marseille and Nice.

Alsace and Lorraine were at the core of them all. I attended any related gathering, supporting student organisations and university institutions that kept the flame of revanchism alive.

My favourite event was Le Bazar de la Charité. It was an annual charity event orchestrated by the French Catholic aristocracy in Paris since 1885 when it was first organised by Henry Blount, the son of banker Sir Edward Blount, an English financier of railway enterprises in France.

When the damned Franco-Prussian War ended, Blount dined with Otto von Bismarck at Versailles after the fall of the city and left for London at the end of March 1871. He was convinced that the British should have come to France's rescue. He spoke his mind to William Ewart Gladstone, the prime minister. Blount was also a commander of the Légion d'Honneur.

The Bazar was held in a variety of locations by a consortium of charitable organisations that shared renting fees to reduce costs and group potential buyers. For me, it was a wonderful place to associate with the elite of Paris and meet beautiful, upper-class women.

The most notorious was Duchess Sophie Charlotte. She was a magnificent person, having rejected many kings and princes before marrying Prince Ferdinand, Duke of Alençon. Her sister was Empress Elisabeth of Austria, king Franz Joseph's, wife also known as Sissi.

The Klomser Hotel in Herrengasse was located in the heart of the city in the very heart of Europe

In January of 1867, she became engaged to her cousin, King Ludwig II of Bavaria, the man who had fought against the Prussians in the 'Multi-Named War' the previous summer. The engagement was agreed upon on January 22nd, 1867. Three days later, Sophie met the official photographer's son, Edgar Hanfstaengl. Numerous photo sessions with the royal bride regularly brought Edgar to the beautiful Possenhofen Castle. They developed a bond and fell in love. After several postponements, the wedding was called off by Ludwig in October. Another proposed husband was Archduke Ludwig Viktor of Austria, brother of King Franz Joseph, the husband of her sister Sissi. The last potential suitor was Duke Philipp of Württember. The first two were homosexuals and she eventually married the latter's cousin, Prince Ferdinand, Duke of Alençon.

She knew how I felt about the Prussians and would often joke with me.

"If I had married Ludwig, the Bavarians would never have fought against France, my dear Edward, and if I had married the other Ludwig, the Austrians would have helped France. You were unfortunate, though."

What more can I say about the damned photographer, Edgar Hanfstaengl? Or about the invention of photography, or even about the invention of cinematography? You'll soon find out.

As to be expected, I seized any opportunity to declare our mutual hate for the Prussians with my French customers. Especially now that Bismarck had been dismissed by Wilhelm II in 1890, as Conte Cucinotta had kindly informed me. Wilhelm gained my appreciation for the move but the information I gleaned about Queen Victoria's grandson was not ideal.

I thought Bismarck, the Iron Chancellor, the man who initiated the wars of the sixties, occupied Alsace-Lorraine and then literally isolated France using diplomatic manoeuvres, had got what he deserved. However, I now knew that the new king dismissed him because Bismarck had wanted a peaceful foreign policy. The king wanted more. Can you believe it? More! If the grandson of the man my grandfather had hunted down in Ligny wanted more, what more could I ask possibly ask for?

I never missed an opportunity to blame the Prussians, when I was with Frenchmen, of course. Once, while in the beautiful Belgian city of Louvain, I was talking to one of our dealers, Jean Perdu, whose views I was well aware of. He originated from Paris and I happened to share my thoughts about the Prussians with him, trying not to appear too fanatic, to begin with at least.

On my visits to Berlin, Munich and other cities of the German Kingdom, I tried to understand their people. Their technological progress was clearly a result of their brilliant minds but how could the same people naively believe in the ridiculous historical theories of the Austrian Jakob Philipp Fallmerayer, that 'all Greeks simply died', or Heinrich von Treitschke's view that 'the Jews are our misfortune', or Adolf Stoecker's 'race is, without a doubt, an important element in the Jewish Question'?

Take note: there were anti-Semites in France, too. Especially after December 1894, when the scoundrel Captain Alfred Dreyfus - a French Jew - was caught communicating French military secrets to the Germans. If it weren't for Mr Elazar, I'd have been convinced of a hostile Jewish conspiracy. The traitor was imprisoned in

Devil's Island on French Guiana. I knew Mr Perdu well, however, and that he was of Greek and Jewish origin. He laughed aloud when I expressed my thoughts; I can still hear him.

"Don't you understand, Edward? It is for the same reason. This is how they explain the world around them. They understand how electricity works and simply take it for granted that humans work like machines. A machine either works or is broken. A race is either good or bad. One day, God pressed a button and all the Greeks from Antiochia to Constantinople and Magna Grecia died. It's as simple as that.

"My mother was Jewish, my mother's father was Greek and I was born in Paris," he continued. That makes me a dead, bad Frenchman, right?

"This, however, is their main strength or hope, even. Because once they realise that humans function differently to machines, once they get this single piece of information correct, that's it. No one can fool them. Let me tell you, Edward, Frederick III was the only man that could and would have done so. Prussia's final hope. Wilhelm is different altogether."

"He is very anti-Semitic, I hear."

"They say he even called his father a weak, cowardly man, controlled by the Jews because of his support for the Jewish community. Can you believe it?

"Thousands of Jews believed in Jesus Christ, in Jerusalem, in Salonika, in Korinthos. It says so in the Bible. The Apostle Paul first taught in the synagogues, didn't he? Those Jews became Christians and their children spoke the language of the place they were born. Greek mostly. Their grandchildren spoke Italian maybe, then French. Now, nineteen centuries later, we have 'Völkish' stupidity, which talks about race. I do business with Jews. Some are good businessmen, some are bad. As far as the good ones are concerned, they know how to do deals and keep them."

"But every successful businessman does that."

"Exactly, Edward."

I know what you are thinking. We, the French, realise that all human beings are different but the Prussians don't.

I repeat. We, the French, realise that all human beings are different but the Prussians don't. Is that true?

Now, I understand how naive we were by doing exactly what we were accusing the Prussians of doing. We were anti-Prussian, denying the Prussians differences between themselves as people and accusing them of doing what we were doing ourselves. We'd been blinded by Alsace-Lorraine, I suppose. Now I understand that, but I failed to recognise the irony of it at the time.

The most important event at that time of my life, however, was not destined to happen in the salons of a large capital, but in a post office of a city that always seemed to get me into trouble.

Trieste, to be precise, where I found myself again in July of 1895. I was expanding my network in the city. I went to the post office to post an order to my company, and while I was there, a young girl came in to post a letter. She was a tall, Italian beauty. Dark hair, beautiful eyes, wonderful body. She was one of the most beautiful women I had ever seen. Again.

"Mademoiselle!"

"Si?"

"Italiana?"

"Si."

"Is this the way to the Piazza Grande?"

"Si."

"Adiamo adesso?" I said, giving her my hand.

"Si!" she said and our hands touched for a brief, magic moment.

Her name was Virginia Agujari and her father, Tito, was a painter. We went for a coffee at the *Caffè degli Specchi* in the Piazza Grande. I chose this place for a special reason.

The walls of the café were lined with engraved mirrors. Each mirror recounted a historical event that occurred in nineteenth-century Europe. The light from the candles and oil lamps reflected in the mirrors illuminating the café with shimmering light. This allowed me to stay with my lady friend until after sunset. Nicolò Privolo, the man who opened the café in 1839, intended it to be that way. Patrons would sit for longer because of the better lighting.

"Edward Aguillon, is that you?"

"Baron von Kalchberg! What a surprise," I said thinking how my connections to the Empire's elite would impress Virginia. It's also marvellous when an important person sees you with a beautiful woman you can proudly introduce them to.

"How are you, young man? What are you doing in Trieste?" he said, looking at Virginia, amazed by her beauty."

"I work for Benedictine Liqueurs now.

"Please allow me to introduce you to Mademoiselle Virginia Agujari. Virginia, Baron Victor von Kalchberg, President of the Österreichische Lloyd Bank."

"Virginia Agujari? Are you from Trieste, Mademoiselle?

"Si."

"Magnificent! It was nice to see you, Edward, though I wouldn't want to disturb you two. Call in on me at the bank, maybe we can do business this time.

Benedictine is a good company to do business with. Have a good evening, my friends!"

"Good evening, Baron von Kalchberg."

Regardless of the lighting or how important or trustworthy the baron was, Virginia had to leave early every time I took her there because of her father.

The third time we met, I went to her home to ask her father to marry her. To marry Gina.

He refused in the worst possible way saying that his daughter was only fifteen years of age and that I should leave and never see or even think about her again.

That was impossible, however. Needless to say, sales of Benedictine spiked in the area. I needed to buy time and stay in the region. But to no avail. For the next six months, I stayed in the cities of Venice or Vienna, to be close to Trieste but so as not to spend too much time there. I was in love and a man in love is entitled to do such things.

Just before the end of the year, on December 2nd, 1895, I received the worst news for a man in love. Her father had agreed for his sixteen-year-old daughter to marry Johann Edler von Reininghaus. Damned Prussians!

And so it was. On January 21st, 1896, my Gina married the son of Johann Peter von Reininghaus, founder of the famous brewery in Graz. Correct. Beer conquered liqueur. How on earth did that come about? He was the owner and I was just an ambassador, you might say. But was it better to be the Ambassador of the Austro-Hungarian Empire than the King of *Serbia*, shall we say?

As a matter of fact, some years earlier, King Milan of Serbia had offered Serbia to the Austro-Hungarian Empire, preferring the enjoyable lifestyle of the Austro-Hungarian elite to the problems of a small kingdom. It was said that Franz Joseph refused to avoid offending Russia. The same King Milan was also said to have had an affair with an American-born British socialite named Jennie Spencer, later to become Lady Randolph Churchill.

Anyway, I'd lost her and left with my pride intact to sell my liqueur in London, where I would kiss English women and forget about Gina. But I couldn't forget her and there was nothing I could do about it. She was no longer Gina Agujari but Virginia von Reininghaus and she lived in Graz with her husband. Their first son was born that very same year.

The damned Prussians had annoyed me again but the equally damned year of 1896 wasn't over yet. Remember the story of Captain Dreyfus? Was he or wasn't he a scoundrel? Evidence came to light, primarily through an investigation instigated by Georges Picquart, head of counter-espionage, which identified the real culprit as a French Army major named Ferdinand Walsin Esterhazy.

When high-ranking military officials suppressed the new evidence, a military court unanimously acquitted Esterhazy after a trial lasting all of two days. The Army laid additional charges against Dreyfus based on forged documents.

The problem was that the French were divided like never before into Dreyfusards and anti-Dreyfusards. The former were pro-republican and anticlerical, and the latter, mostly Catholic and pro-army. But it was not that simple. There was no way of telling who believed what. The boundaries were not clear by any means and for an innocent salesman, who simply wanted to agree with his customers, it was a dangerous trap.

"I feel very sorry for Dreyfus. To be sentenced to Devil's Island while innocent is difficult to accept," I said, trying to start a conversation with a customer I thought might be a Dreyfusard.

"Don't be so naive, Edward. The Prussians are only helping to save the rat from trouble. Don't you see? I can't believe it! Your grandfather knew how devious the Prussians are, Edward. Dreyfus is a German traitor. He should be hanged."

That was the first and last time I voiced my opinion on the subject. From then on, I did what any decent salesman does. First, ask and then agree with the customer.

Amidst the Dreyfusian confusion came Pierre de Coubertin, who made me more envious than ever. Until then, I had considered aristocrats to be lucky scoundrels. However, this aristocrat, born on the same day as me, founded the International Olympic Committee in 1894 at the age of thirty-one, and two years later organised the first Olympic Games, which took place in Athens. He will always be known as the father of the modern Olympic Games. This man's vision and political skills led to the revival of an event practised in ancient Greece. Coubertin idealised the Olympic Games as the ultimate ancient athletic competition. I admired that. I was envious of his achievement and wanted to do something even greater. And as you will see, I did. My time was yet to come.

After the Bazar de la Charité in May, I left for Athens to promote the Benedictine liqueur during the Olympic Games, spending the summer of 1896 in the land where democracy was born. Mr Le Grand had made an excellent job of linking his liqueur to the Renaissance period and would be even happier to associate it with ancient times. Diagoras of Rhodes, perhaps the greatest winner of all, drank a liqueur similar to Benedictine, or the Spartans added it to their black soup. Or maybe Aristotle drank it. Who wouldn't want to drink what Aristotle had drunk?

Aristotle once commented on the drinking habits of the poor. Those who could not afford a vineyard drank something made of barley. The notorious beer. Aristotle said the difference between beer and wine was that when you drink too much wine you fall face up but when you drink too much beer, you fall face down.

'Drink Benedictine liqueur and stand tall with an enlightened mind,' I proposed. Mr Le Grand liked it at first but eventually rejected the slogan.

"Aristotle whar," he said.

Before leaving for Greece, I wrote a letter to my old Greek friend Alexander from the SS Alesia. He was the Greek I met when cholera broke out on board the ship. I asked him if he could come to Athens and meet me and gave him the address of my hotel.

I couldn't have regretted it more.

When I saw him, I hardly recognised him. He had changed so much.

While we were having dinner at a restaurant, he talked about his revolutionary ideas, about changing the world and how anarchy was a man's last hope. (We'll come to anarchy later.) It was very difficult to disagree with him, so I kept nodding my head. That was probably all he wanted. After the meal, I explained my very busy schedule and that it would be difficult to meet him again.

I asked if he needed money and he couldn't resist borrowing some. I gave him a fair amount and told him he wouldn't need to return it since we were old friends. Only then did I recognise the innocent boy I had met almost ten years before. A boy now lost forever.

So there I was, trying to promote my liqueur in the newly-founded Kingdom of Greece. Newly- founded but twice the age of the German Kingdom with a king I could associate with in many ways. Remember Mr Elazar telling my father the story about Prussian diplomacy at weddings?

George I was elected King of the Hellenes at the age of seventeen on March 30th, 1863 - the year that I was born - by the Greek National Assembly, which had deposed the Bavarian King Otto. Bavarians were not Prussians. In fact, they fought against them in the multi-named war but gradually, I was beginning to see all Prussians as Germans and all Germans as Prussians. It seemed the natural thing to do.

Most importantly, however, was that George was a Danish prince, born in Copenhagen and seemed destined for a career in the Royal Danish Navy. There, he was called Prince William. His nomination for King of Greece was both suggested and supported by the Great Powers: The United Kingdom of Great Britain and Ireland, the Second French Empire and the Russian Empire. Germans didn't exist in those days and the Prussians were planning to fight Denmark. It was the sixties, after all.

Ironically, George ascended the royal throne before his father, Christian IX, who became King of Denmark on November 15th the same year. The following year he would fight against the Prussians and the Austrians. I have already mentioned the German-Danish war. I shouldn't repeat myself, despite my love of cursing the Prussians for those wars.

I was certain that King George hated the Prussians. He was eighteen years old when his father lost a war to them. If only we could drink a glass of Benedictine and curse the damned Prussians together!

It did not come about, however, because I met a very sensual Greek widow, who had a beautiful country house in Kifissia on the outskirts of Athens, where I spent most of my time breaking one record after another, due to the extremely good climate, I might say.

As for King George, our paths did not cross.

The following year, in April of 1897, I read about the Greek-Turkish war in the newspaper. I was certain the Turks would invade the countryside of Kifissia and was concerned about my widow.

When May came, I attended, as always, the Bazar de la Charité. That year, the Bazar took place from the third until the sixth of May and was held at 17, Rue Jean-Goujon in a large wooden warehouse.

Fascinated, I went inside to admire the decor. The warehouse had been transformed into a medieval street using painted wood, cardboard, fabric, papier-mâché and any other flammable material you could imagine.

On the afternoon of the second day, as I was speaking to a beautiful young Parisian lady, I suddenly heard loud voices. Before I knew it, flames spread everywhere and women ran around shouting. Damned cinematograph!

That year, one of the key attractions of the Bazar was a cinematograph installation, which functioned with ether lamps. All that wood, cardboard and paper was not a good idea.

The projectionist's equipment caught fire and the fire spread instantly. Unlike Fécamp, where I naively dashed into the flames, I instantly dashed out, thinking only of saving myself. The memory of the smoke was enough to make me run for my life without another thought. I fled through the courtyard and managed to escape through the kitchen window of the adjacent Hôtel du Palais.

Unfortunately, a woman in front of me couldn't fit through the window due to her voluminous dress so I lifted and shoved her out to in order to escape. I saved her to save myself. The hotel cook, Mr Gauméry, helped me out. God bless him and his manager, Madame Roche-Sautier!

I was the same man who, five years earlier, had thrown himself into a fire to save the collection at the Palais Benedictine. The same man who now fled desperately and without a care in the world for the people around him. I failed to understand how this had come about. Had something changed in me, was it the fear of a similar experience in the past, or it was because I just did what everyone else did? This would later be called the psychology of the masses.

To make matters worse, I discovered that Duchess Sophie Charlotte insisted on staying behind until all girls, visitors and nuns working alongside her had been rescued. A Dominican nun who had managed to escape from the inferno explained that she saw the Duchess get down on her knees and pray.

One hundred and twenty-six people - mostly female aristocrats - died and over two hundred others sustained injuries. The poor Duchess! She was fifty years old. Even her personal maid was unable to recognise her body as it had been severely disfigured by the fire. Only her dentist, Mr Lavanport, after two hours of examining bodies, was able to identify her by her gold fillings. It was the first time that a person had been identified by forensic dentistry.

The disaster made international news. It even surpassed the news of the Greek-Turkish war.

A few days ago, I was wondering what would happen to my Greek widow if the Turks invaded Kifissia and here we are in the centre of Paris, enjoying the peace and political stability, having to mourn for so many people, so many women who were trying to do good. Is this technological evolution really worth it?

An anonymous benefactor donated an amount equivalent to the sum raised the previous year for the charitable purposes for which the Bazar had been organised. It was the last time.

As for the lady I rescued, so to speak, she found me later and thanked me for saving her life. She was Italian and her name was Maria something…Delli. Though still shocked by the disaster, she wanted to thank me and invited me to dinner with her husband. I politely declined at first, saying I had only done my duty as a human being and regretted not being able to rescue more people. I would have accepted on the second or the third proposition but we were forcibly separated when the fire brigade carriage came right at us with firemen and members of the public running behind. I lost sight of her and made my way home.

As in the case of the Palais Benedictine fire, I asked myself the same damned question. Who, from the other side, was born that year?

The German Navy was the answer.

Three days after the fire, on May 7th, the Greek-Turkish war ended with the intervention of the Great Powers that had proposed George for king, saving Greece and my widow. Actually, it was the super-powerful British navy that ended the dispute when the British decided to act. One more reason for Wilhelm's envy.

Much as I would have liked to have seen my widow again, the opportunity to travel to Greece did not arise. The market was too small to justify a trip. So I headed to London.

I always had a wonderful time in London but Vienna was my usual destination and my favourite one. Far more cosmopolitan, far more glamorous and located in the heart of Europe. I was spending so much time there that I even thought of renting a house. But in the end, I found a very hospitable hotel in the centre of Vienna.

The Klomser Hotel in Herrengasse was located in the heart of the city in the very heart of Europe. I would pass the time of day in the *Central Café* on the corner of Herrengasse and Stauchgasse or in the *Landtmann Café* in Universitatstring. These two cafes were about three hundred metres apart and if you were to draw a straight line between them, you would find my beloved Klomser Hotel in the middle. Vienna was wonderful all year round but my favourite season was the winter.

Of all the capitals of Europe, Moscow was the one I never visited. Primarily because I never forgot what happened to Napoleon when he went there. What's more, Mr Le Grand wanted me to focus on central Europe where new trends were being born. He also considered Russia's elite to be few in number and that they drank too much vodka.

I continued to close deals for my wonderful product, supporting Dreyfus with the Dreyfusards and accusing him with the anti-Dreyfusards and commenting accordingly on Emile Zola's letter published in January 1898 in support of Dreyfus. Gina was the woman I had lost and London was always my favourite place to compensate for my losses. Wonderful!

This, too, would soon come to an end but without any mistakes this time. Mr Le Grand died on June 25th,

1898. This extraordinary businessman was sixty-eight years old.

It was certainly a great loss for the entire business, not just me, but I never imagined it would be responsible for the end of my life as I knew it. His heirs held entirely different views about doing business and there was nothing I could do about it. They decided that I should help organise the presence of the Benedictine Liqueur at the 1900 World's Fair in Paris.

"What about my customers?" I asked.

"Don't worry," they replied.

Alexandre Le Grand was made an Officer of the Legion of Honour, Captain of firefighters, a city councillor of Fécamp, a member of the general council of Seine-Maritime and a Knight Commander of the Order of St. Gregory the Great. This man wanted me to maintain close connections with my customers and they knew better than that?

I call it the Wilhelm syndrome. Otto von Bismarck, who also died a month later, on July 25th, made the whole of Europe dance to his tune; the Napoleon of diplomacy. No other leader achieved greater diplomatic and political success than he did. And you, ignorant young Wilhelm, dismiss him? Merci!

It was a boring job that I took on in Fécamp. The only positive outcome was my proposal for Louise Abbéma, the French painter, sculptor and designer to advertise Benedictine. She created an oil-on-canvas titled 'La Renommée de la Bénédictine', which was displayed at the *Salon* - the official Paris art exhibition - in 1899 and then at the World's Fair in Paris in 1900.

I did my best to ensure the company's best possible participation in this international exhibition but it was sad to think that from now on, my life would be reduced to this. I'd had similar feelings aboard the SS Alesia all those years ago.

In May 1899, I travelled to Algiers because my father was seriously ill. When I arrived, he had already gone. I didn't have the chance to see him, talk to him, touch his hands. The hands that used to throw me into the air, up into the sky…

I was a terrible son. Possibly a terrible person. An idiot who thought he knew everything.

I spent some time with my brothers and their families and on May 29th, 1899, the SS Alesia docked at Algiers with her cargo of sulphur on fire. She was on a voyage from Palermo to New Orleans. I couldn't believe my eyes. It was as if my wish had come true but twenty years later. The ship's cook had been killed in the fire.

It could have been me if I'd stayed on board and if I'd stayed on board the SS Alesia, I wouldn't have experienced those wonderful years in Paris and Vienna. What's more, I would have been dead.

The mysterious fellow stared at me continuously. Although surprised at first by the awkward question the man repeatedly asked, it didn't take me long to understand.
I was thirty-seven years old, no longer a child and had been doing business for quite some time. I was not Le Grand or de Couperdin, but I had achieved a lot thus far.

I had survived cholera, conquered the antiquities market, spoken up against the Sicilian Mafia, sold Europe a small lake of the Benedictine liqueur and survived two catastrophic fires. I knew what he wanted. I figured he must have overheard me talking to my Dreyfusard and anti-Dreyfusard clients.

I stared back at him and remained silent.

I know what you are doing and I am not giving in to you. I don't give a damn about Dreyfus and his affair. I'm just getting on with my business.

He continued to stare at me sternly and after an awkward silence, he said something that took me by surprise.

"Mr Aguillon, I would like you to work for me. I believe we could work very well together."

At Benedictine S.A. I had done the job I was required to do. That part of my life was now over. After Mr Le Grand's death, the good times were gone for good. When the Expo was over, I had no idea what duties I would be assigned next.

There was another factor that made my decision easier. As previously explained, I had been tasked with the responsibility of presenting the Benedictine Liqueur at the Expo and was certain it would earn the distinction it deserved. However, the rival 'Micheline', a liqueur that no one had ever heard of was crowned 'Queen of Liqueurs', by the idiots who had organised the fair.

The story behind it was one of fraud. A man called Michelin Boato, a so-called alchemist, developed a *fountain of youth* in his secret laboratory. He disappeared along with his discovery which eventually reappeared and was created into a liqueur according to his secret recipe.

Who on earth would believe such nonsense? If you are going to tell a lie, make it feasible at least. Don't bring brilliant alchemists into it. Who the hell would ever believe you?

"I prefer Benedictine," said the big fat fellow with the Russian accent, who was standing nearby.

"Thank you, my friend."

"Cigarette?"

"No, thank you. What kind of cigarettes are they?"

"Russian," he replied.

"Edward Aguillon. I'm French!" I held out my hand.

"Baron Nikolai Hartwig," he said and we shook hands. "Ha! You need a cigarette in times like these. It helps. Excuse me, but I overheard your conversation. Is she your boss?"

"Yes."

And what a boss! A boss that shows no respect is no boss at all. So the newly-awarded 'Micheline' meant that all my efforts had been in vain?

We sat down for coffee and she blamed everything on me, making it sound like it was the end of the road for the company.

It's the Wilhelm syndrome. Bismarck said it loud and clear. 'The crash will come twenty years after my departure'. That's how long any Wilhelm lasts.

"I liked the Russian pavilion. Very impressive."

"Thank you. Everyone in the Foreign Affairs department did their very best."

"And you are one of them?"

"The most important."

"Your French is very good."

"I am a diplomat, Edward."

"I find myself in a very difficult situation, Nikolai. I have a new job offer. I'm thinking about it but it's difficult to decide. You know. To make the move."

"What does your wife say?"

"I don't have a wife"

"Then you are free. Do it, Edward. Get away from that woman who calls herself your boss."

"I think I will."

"We are in a similar position. I was promoted to Director of the Asiatic Department last month."

"Congratulations, my friend."

"Thank you. My wife and daughter were very excited. It may sound strange but I thought about it a lot before accepting it."

It was very strange indeed. He didn't seem like that kind of person.

"You seem ambitious, though. Take it as a compliment!"

"That's why I have to be doubly careful. A smart enemy will use your ambition to trap you."

"But you accepted."

"Yes. I went to my favourite city, Vienna, for five days. It was a kind of self-isolation. I always sleep well when I visit this city and return revitalised.

"I walked the streets, enjoyed good food and drank coffee alone. I read an interesting book by Saint Nikodimos called 'The Prison of the Five Senses'. It was very good indeed. I even read poetry and, believe it or not, it was during a simple moment like this that I decided to move on.

'But I shall undo my vest
And thrust out my chest to the moon,
With outstretched arms, I shall revere
The spreader of light upon the earth!'

"That sounds like a nice poem."

"Yes. It's by Soselo."

"Soselo?"

"It's a pseudonym. Soselo is a promising young poet from my birthplace, Gori, in Georgia. If you could read his poetry in Georgian, you'd like it even more. Absolute purity of rhyme and language."

"With outstretched arms, I shall revere… I've made my decision, my new Russian friend! I'm getting a new job.

"I would like to invite you to dinner at Maxim's, Nikolai. It's been refurbished recently by the 'Ecole de Nancy'. Graceful murals, mirrors set in hand-carved mahogany frames and curvaceous copper-and-brass decor. Absolute purity of rhyme and taste, as you say. I would also like to take you to other places with absolute purity of rhyme and vision but you are a married man. What was that book you mentioned?"

The offer of a new job came just at the right time. I was in a position to leave with my reputation still intact. The main advantage was that I would be constantly underway in Europe, free to develop my business. My new boss would be very busy too and we would communicate by letter and meet face to face at the Zurich Savoy Hotel in Switzerland once a year. Without a doubt, it was the perfect job and it was thanks to my friend, Alfred Dreyfus, that I found it. Thank you, Alfred!

And by the way, in my new position, I would be selling…

Guns.

PART THREE

When things go wrong, you curse the damned details that were responsible in the first place; the minor, insignificant, foolish things that forced you in the wrong direction. A petty decision, a missed turn, a wrong word…and there I was, locked in a room, alone for long. Sometimes I cried, sometimes I laughed, sometimes I just cursed.

When I had finished cursing my minor decisions, I cursed my major ones. If it weren't for those stupid decisions, everything would be different. Everything!

I'd be a different man. Maybe I'd have lived in a beautiful house in Fécamp and played with my kids on the beaches of Normandy.

It was a huge fair. There were so many people all over the world. Why did I run into this particular man? But I loved the work. I loved it from the very beginning.

I could have been attending to my vineyards in Algiers.

My God! I didn't even see my father before he died. What kind of a son was I?

Yasmine! What if I'd taken you to America before all this began?

Would I survive the current situation? If I did, I would never forget those times, that damned May of 1913.

But would I live to forget? Nikolai mentioned a book: 'The Prison of Five Senses'. I found it but it was in Russian so I couldn't read it. Maybe it was finally time for my release. Maybe I had nothing to fear, after all.

Damned…!

An hour and a half before dawn on May 25th 1913, the night manager walked up to the second floor of the Klomser Hotel in Vienna to wake the occupant of room number one. He had received a call from army headquarters instructing him to get the occupant out of bed and have him come to the phone for urgent business. The manager knocked on the door several times but was met by silence. The lack of a response and orders from a superior authority led him to open an unlocked door. What he discovered was shocking in the extreme. The body of a man in his fifties lay dead on the floor. Blood, brains and a pistol lay next to his cold, limp body.

That day, I was released from prison. I was set free.

"Edward, I'd like to ask you something," said my boss looking at me.

"Yes, boss?"

"You've successfully introduced me to these new markets so I assume there are people you trust, is that right?"

"Yes, that's right."

When I was hired, my business included the private sector only. Duels were common and there were quite a number of gun hobbyists. Militarism was a great advantage for any gun seller. But I moved on from that. When you start a new job, your eyes are opened up to a whole new world. New opportunities, new focus areas, new fields of knowledge. You see what was out there but you never really noticed, or look at it differently.

Associating with various institutions, clubs, duelists and other peaceful sectors of European society, I now began to look at everything from the point of view of the gun. That is to say, the historical aspects.

What rifles, pistols and cannons did Napoleon use? How far could his battery shoot? Did the mud of Waterloo make cannonballs ineffective?

What kind of rifles did the Prussians use while fighting in Sedan?

What did Mr Nobel's invention mean for the weapons industry? How did it affect gun powder as a raw material or as a product, shall we say? Everyday news would catch my attention in a somewhat awkward manner.

What type of gun did the anarchist Leon Czolgosz have hidden under his white handkerchief when he assassinated American President William McKinley on September 6th, 1901?

I would sit in a cafe and skim through *Le Figaro,* skipping all the details about the place, the murderer, and the victim to find out what kind of weapon was used. Manufacturer, model, etc.

It was a .32 calibre *Safety Automatic* revolver manufactured by Iver Johnson's Arms & Cycle Works, serial number 463344, produced by an American firearms, bicycle and motorcycle manufacturing company established in 1871 by the Norwegian-born Iver Johnson.

He qualified as a gunsmith in Bergen in 1857 and ran a weapons business in Oslo before immigrating to America. The particular model was called *Safety* because of the *Hammer-the-Hammer* transfer bar safety system, and *Automatic* because of the automatic ejection of cartridges upon breaking open of the revolvers. I didn't know whether Czolgosz's revolver had a double or a single post latch system. He had purchased just it four days earlier.

Do you see what I mean? And here is another example.

The South African Boer War between the British and Dutch settlers known as the Boers, or farmers, lingered on and on. Although I had read a lot about this war and Kitchener's awful tactics of capturing families, I could only focus on the *Mauser* and *Martini-Henrys* rifles, and the *Lee-Metfords* or *Enfields*.

The Boers were armed with the latest repeating bolt-action rifles, which fired smokeless powder cartridges. They had previously used their rifles for hunting and were excellent natural marksmen, who specialised in long-range shooting. Time and time again, particularly in the battles of Modder River or in Magersfontein, they were able to not only inflict heavy casualties on the invading British but also contain large numbers of troops for hours, thanks to the *Mauser*, a bolt-action, five-shot, repeating rifle. Damned German guns! It was similar to the *Dreyse* needle-rifle that was decisive in the Danish-German war.

My vital question was always the same, however. The one that any good salesman asks.

Who sold those guns? Who was selling the ammunition? Why them and not me?

My boss cut the deals with the official state armies but what about the rebels, guerrillas, outlaws and even the anarchists? Why not them? They all belonged to a dark, yet familiar category that no one had considered and the market was fair game for anyone who claimed they could conquer it. Multiple options existed for the eager salesman in the stable Europe of the time.

One of them was Sicily's Mafia, and I already had 'connections' there. Ok, they weren't exactly connections, but almost. We were surrounded by twenty men with guns that day. Why shouldn't I be the one selling guns to such Italians?

On the Balkan Peninsula, various groups were fighting against each other and against the Ottoman and Austro-Hungarian Empires.

What type of gun did the anarchist Leon Czolgosz have hidden under his white handkerchief...?

They were supplied by their supporting states, of course, but why not sell directly to them?

With the anarchists, however, it wouldn't be as easy because there was no central supply chain, but many of them were hiding out in Morocco, where there was a huge French presence. Tribes and Sharifs also existed with a constant need for my merchandise. It couldn't be that difficult to find the right people.

How naïve could I have been? Naïve enough to think there was a market for me in those narrow streets of ugly houses. A dirty place full of outlaws, anarchists, tribesmen…

I was taken to a village, thinking I'd be meeting a leader of a tribe in need of guns. Instead, I was being held in a small, filthy room and couldn't understand a word they were saying. Again.

Earlier, I'd spoken to a Moroccan who sold knives in a dirty shop. He introduced me to a neighbour who sold baskets and sent a young boy to inform two other Moroccans who were also interested, I assumed. They came, we spoke in broken French and they took me to a village. I thought I was on the right track, but once I got off the horse…

What was I doing in that room? Who had tied my hands? How long had I been there? Why did I have a headache?

The two idiots had taken me there with something else in mind. The door opened after nearly five hours of imprisonment and whom did I see?

"Frenchman!"

"Moroccan!"

It was my good old friend from the Bella Messina. Mighty Moroccan!

He was angry with the idiots when he saw me. Judging by their faces, a meeting between friends was the last thing they expected.

Moroccan, who deserved to be called Mehdi in Morocco, was now one of outlaw Mulai Ahmed el Raisuni's men. I knew Mehdi had been hiding at sea for many years as one of the crew aboard the Bella Messina. Now, he was hiding in the hills as one of the men of the *Sultan of the Mountains.*

"We left you in Normandy…"

"Tell me the news. What happened after that?"

"Yes, we were down to four men."

"You mean five."

"Moffa doesn't count."

"Who did the cooking?"

"Capitano."

"Was he any good?"

"Not as good as you, but good enough. When we arrived in Morocco, I decided to stay, to hide inland."

"Mehdi, I've never asked you this before, but… what were you… what are you hiding from? What have you done?"

"I never saw Capitano again. Now Raisuni is my boss," said Mehdi. It was obvious he wouldn't be telling me his secret.

His new boss extorted tribute from villagers in territories controlled by his followers. He also maintained a small fleet of boats and was a seafaring pirate from time to time. He was less successful in this field, however. He mostly kidnapped Moroccan military and political officials, beginning with the abduction of *Times* correspondent Walter Burton Harris, the only European he had kidnapped so far. The two idiots had taken me there as the next kidnap victim, either courting Raisuni's friendship or repaying old debts.

"You're dressed like someone important and they thought they'd make my boss happy."

"I sell guns, Mehdi. That's all."

"You are very important, Frenchman," said Moroccan, surprised.

"Get me a *Colt* M1900."

"Why would I do that, Guido?"

"Because I'm going to introduce you to my boss."

"But I know Conte Cucinotta anyway. I can contact him myself. Why would I bother you for that?"

"Because of our old friendship?"

"Come now, Guido!"

"Ok, listen Frenchman. Conte Antonio may be the buyer, but I'm the user and if I'm not satisfied…"

"A *Colt* M1900 it is, then. Do you want a *Mauser* C96, too?"

"The Broomhandle? No, too big. But if you insist, I'll take it because we're old friends."

"It's alright, Guido."

"No, I mean it. I know you didn't like me back then. Well, nobody liked me but we still had a good time in London with those English girls, didn't we?"

"Those were great times, Guido! Great times!"

"To tell you the truth, I wasn't the best sailor and I knew it. How could I be? I'd killed this Greek man who yelled at me," said Guido in a rare moment of self-criticism. He took me by surprise.

"But he was your supervisor. He was the boatswain. He was doing his job, Guido."

"That's nonsense, Frenchman! Anyway, I started thinking about it when Capitano rescued me after that fire broke out…"

"What fire? In the Palais Benedictine? It…"

"No! Aboard the Bella Messina. Don't you know what happened?"

"Know what?"

"Big fire Frenchman, big fire!"

"Tell me about it!"

"We were approaching Marseille with a consignment of sulfur. It was late and I was asleep…"

You were asleep most of the time.

"…when Capitano came and woke me. He was very anxious. He covered me with a coat and dragged me to the safety of the boat as the Bella Messina went up in flames around us. Berhane and Tafari were already there waiting. They were fighting because Tafari had forgotten his medallion. Anyway, he dived into the sea and swam back. He was crazy. No one else would have made it."

"Oh, my god!"

"It was hell! Capitano covered me with his coat as burning debris fell around us and crazy Tafari swam back to get his medallion. Can you believe it?"

"What about Berhane?"

"He went after him."

"When we were at a safe distance, I watched the Bella Messina go up in flames as she entered the port of Marseille."

"What about the brothers?"

"They both vanished."

"Poor things!"

"And all for the sake of a medallion!"

"The medallion of death," I said, remembering the other one hanging around my neck inside my expensive Viennese shirt.

"I'd be dead if Capitano hadn't remembered me in the panic of the fire. He had to keep me safe because he was responsible for my protection but in a situation like that… I couldn't… you know… I appreciate it, no matter what."

"What happened to him?"

"Capitano? Well, he'd lost his ship and had a very difficult time of it…"

Moffa went to Sicily with Capitano. By the time they got there, the Mafia had already heard the news but Conte Cucinotta wanted to hear it from his man on the scene, Guido Moffa. That's why Capitano saved him and protected him in the first place.

Capitano, now without a ship, was Antonio Caporaso again and begged the Mafia, and Conte Cucinotta in particular, for a loan to buy a new ship so he could continue his business. Conte Cucinotta denied him any help.

"I am sorry for your loss, Caporaso, very sorry."

He revelled in the fact that Antonio Caporaso was a man with no ship, no job, no family and no future. Capitano stayed with his brother for a while but a month later could take no more. He left Sicily poor and ashamed. He had neither the money nor the youth to sail to America. A merchant ship took pity on him and took him as far as Genoa. And no one has seen him since.

"How is your Capitano doing?"

What was the answer to that? Should I tell him I was sorry about my old boss's bad fortune? That I wished he was alive and healthy? That I would really like to find him and help him? Being neutral was the sensible thing to do.

"Guido told me about the fire aboard the Bella Messina. I had no idea."

"Didn't he tell you himself? I heard Caporaso is in France. You are his Frenchman, aren't you?"

"I haven't seen him since I left the crew in 1892, Conte Cucinotta."

"When did you start selling guns?"

"In 1900."

"We will help you, Edward."

His initial cruelty scared me once again but as the conversation continued he was more polite and open to doing business. Scary or not, it was good for my business. Like the Moroccan tribes, he recognised the value of a reliable gun supplier and I was slowly beginning to recognise it too. As for the quantities I shipped to the Mafia, they were double what I shipped to Morocco. Surprisingly enough!

What's more, once I'd started supplying my new clients with the merchandise, the need arose for its safe delivery. The only people who could secure my deliveries were the Mafia, who had the know-how from transporting lemons. Thus, we cooperated once again with the transportation of my 'black lemons', expanding their business even further. They cost my boss a lot of money but their reliability was second to none.

Once I'd taken an order, all I had to do was agree on the port to deliver it to. Everything else was covered. We delivered our order to a 'capitano' and the customer was guaranteed to receive it as long as he waited at the agreed port. We could even ship small orders, offering a service that had never been offered before in that sector of the market.

"Things are easier in Morocco and Sicily, boss. They trust me. In the Balkans, nobody trusts anyone."

"How did you manage to get in?"

"To the Balkans?"

"Yes."

"I am French and the French are good."

"Come on, Edward, tell me the truth."

"I tell everyone the truth."

"Which is?"

"That I sell guns and that's it. I ship my weapons to anyone who needs them and can pay. I don't care whether he's an outlaw or an army officer. I don't give a damn if he's Serbian, Greek or Bulgarian-friendly."

"What about the authorities, the Ottomans and the Austrians?"

"We don't speak to each other."

"Ha! And if you did?"

"I am a French journalist. I always carry *Le Figaro* with me as proof. I have no samples of my merchandise with me, no other papers, nothing. I simply take orders and write them in a code only I understand."

"Where do you write them?

"On the newspaper."

"You are very good…"

"I think when you speak to a customer logically, he understands, no matter what he thinks."

"… but… I mean, how did you approach your… logical customers?"

"Come on, boss. I'm sure you are better at that than me."

"Please tell me, Edward."

He is definitely going to ask me a favour…

"Well… in Serbia for example, I went to the military academy and asked for the best sniper to get his opinion on some of my rifles. To improve them, of course. I was nothing more than a weapons expert doing some research. Anyway, everyone was talking about this young officer called Vojislav Tankosic.

"The kid was pleased to help us, you know - the French gunmakers - with some improvements we were thinking of making. This Tankosic is an excellent shot, by the way. I never imagined a man could shoot like that. He's probably the best sniper I've ever seen. Well, you get the point. We became friends, he took a preference to my….our guns, and if Vojislav Tankosic uses our guns, he must know better. The others just follow their leader."

"This is the man you wanted the free samples for?"

"Exactly."

"And you converted the whole of the Serbian army to Francophiles, just like that?"

"Yes… it helped a lot that Serbia favoured French ammunition over any other."

My boss got straight to the point. The favour I assumed he wanted.

"How difficult would it be for you to initiate the use of their weapons?"

"I don't understand?"

"Look, if someone in Europe buys a weapon, he can only use it in a duel or for shooting practice, correct?"

"Yes."

"On the other hand, in the market sectors you move in, weapons make history, my boy!"

Oh, how I loved that expression!

Pierre de Couperdin, here I come.

"I was wondering if we could participate in the making of history. Those young Serbian officers carried out a coup d'état and the weapons you sold them killed the king six months ago."

"And the queen," I said half-enthusiastically. "The last queen died two years ago."

Queen Victoria died in 1901. Of natural causes, though eight assassination attempts had been made on her life by then. There would be no more, for sure!

"A limited use of weapons..." A minor detail. The coup d'état meant the end of an Austrian-friendly Serbia. "...now use your imagination, be creative and introduce some upheaval to this small sector of the market of yours. A bonus equal to the size of the upheaval you create will be paid into your bank account after our meeting at the Savoy next December."

Now you're talking!

"Edward, I wish to make it clear that I'm not asking any favours here. A small upheaval created anywhere in the neighbourhood helps me make bigger deals, so you ought to have your share. Do you understand, Edward?"

"Yes, boss."

"What do you say? Can you do it?"

"Of course! And I will make history, boss."

"So you're telling me the Bella Messina was totally destroyed in the fire?"

"Totally, my friend. And the Tana brothers didn't make it either."

"Is that true? Bad news but let's move on to getting a better price so we can buy more guns."

Of all the men I sold guns to, the man I trusted most was my good friend Moroccan. He was a very cruel man, however. Tafari and Berhane were good friends of his and when he heard of their deaths, he showed no emotion. He didn't even ask about Capitano. A cruel man, indeed!

"Moroccan, how can we talk about money when…", but he was a very good client so I seized the opportunity to make a daring proposition. "…you are sitting on a gold mine?"

"What do you mean?"

"You kidnap men, right?"

"Yes."

"So why don't you kidnap a foreigner and ask for a ransom?"

"What? Who?"

"Come on, this is the gateway to the Mediterranean Sea. Surely you can stop a rich man's boat and kidnap someone. A Frenchman, an Englishman, a German? Sultan will pay to keep his territory clean and avoid making an enemy out of a great power."

"Frenchman, you are a very dangerous man."

On March 15th 1904, the first thing I did was write a telegram to my boss. Two words.

'Watch Morocco.'

Fortunately, on April 8th 1904, the Entente Cordiale was signed between the United Kingdom and France. It was a series of agreements, the most important of which was a feature that recognised the United Kingdom in full control of Egypt, (although we constructed the canal), and likewise, France in full control of Morocco. I had no idea about that but imagine my boss getting a telegram revealing Morocco as a potential focal point!

I didn't wait for feedback from my friend but luckily, Raisuni loved the idea and knowing the weaknesses of his fleet, he decided to kidnap a foreigner living in the state of Morocco using the army and not his inferior - for a Berber - piracy skills.

Giving it no more thought, he decided to kidnap Mr Ion Perdicaris.

He couldn't have made a more colossal mistake. America was not one of the *Great Powers*. Why pick a man who had chosen to live in a dangerous country? That was his fault. Why pick a Greek?

Greece wasn't one of the *Great Powers*, either. Even if you lived there 2500 years ago, they wouldn't have sent a trireme to your rescue.

And who was this Ion Perdicaris?

A playboy. A dilettante.

It was in the spa town of Malvern in England in 1871 that he met Ellen Varley and they fell in love. Ellen was married to the well-known telegraph engineer Cromwell Fleetwood Varley, however. As his name implies, he was a proud descendant of the English generals Oliver Cromwell and Charles Fleetwood. The couple had four children, two sons and two daughters. That year, on his return from a trip abroad, he discovered that his wife had absconded with Ion.

The divorce was granted in 1873 and Ion settled with Ellen and her children in Morocco. He built a house in Tangiers in 1877, known as the 'Place of Nightingales'. He owned a menagerie of exotic animals.

As you probably realise, Ion was a very wealthy man. His father, Gregory Perdicaris, was sponsored as a young man in 1826 to study in the United States. Perdicaris became a naturalised citizen of the United States and married the daughter of a wealthy family in South Carolina. In 1837, he returned to Greece, serving as the American ambassador. He had a son in 1840. When Ion was six years old, the family returned to the United States and settled in New Jersey, where Gregory Perdicaris made his fortune as one of the founders of the Trenton Gas Company. In 1862, Ion travelled to Greece, intending to acquire Greek nationality to avoid confiscation of his family's property or being drafted into the Confederate States Army. In the end, he wasn't able to protect his property and left Athens.

After the war, Perdicaris lived in Trenton with his father and later moved to England to study electricity, where he met Ellen and, fascinated by Moroccan culture, he moved there and wrote several books on the country. He became the unofficial head of Tangier's foreign community, maintaining business interests in England and the United States at the same time, and making frequent visits to New York. He helped gain permission for the construction of a modern sanitation system for the city, which was his greatest achievement.

I didn't know whether to laugh or cry about this blind and idiotic selection of a victim. I'd hoped they'd kidnap a French- or Englishman so I could return to my boss.

Can you see what I had done?

There was instability at the gateway to the Mediterranean Sea. A citizen of one of the *Great Powers* was in danger. France needed to gain ground in Morocco. How would the other players react?

Would England support France? Would it support the Entente Cordiale?

Interesting questions.

At the same time, Raisuni would find the money to buy more guns… from me.

It was just a big, fat bluff. The only thing that could save the situation was if his stepson, Cromwell, were to be kidnapped with him, which was what happened in the end. Thank God, there was an Englishman on board and there was a small window of hope.

Cromwell Jr did not rescue the situation, however. So what did?

Democracy. That's correct. The amazing system of government where the people have the authority to choose their governors and regularly hold elections to select their representatives. In democracies, the period before an election is a time when anything is possible. Candidates make almost supernatural efforts to become elected. Fortunately for me, the United States was a democratic country.

Do you remember when the anarchist Leon Czolgosz killed President McKinley with a *Safety Automatic* in 1901? McKinley's vice-president was a man named Theodore Roosevelt, who took over the presidency after the president's assassination. I was even more fortunate because elections were imminent and President Roosevelt was running for reelection. The president recognised an opportunity in the Perdicaris affair. Or more precisely, he decided to make political capital from the incident.

That's how democracies work and I loved it.

Thank you, Theo, much obliged! Thank you Greeks, I love democracy!

Now see what happened, and I'll tell you in some detail. It was my first job and people are always proud of their first achievements. It's natural to be enthusiastic about such things, even when you know you're becoming slightly boring. But please be patient. I promise not to be as descriptive about my other jobs.

On May 18th 1904, Perdicaris and Ellen's son - the Briton, Cromwell Varley - were abducted from their summer home, the 'Place of Nightingales'. The ransom was set at $55.000.

The following day, the United States ordered Admiral Chadwick to dispatch a ship from the South Atlantic Squadron to Tangier.

On May 20th, the British dispatched a torpedo ship from nearby Gibraltar to the city.

On May 21st, representatives of the Sultan were sent to begin negotiations with Raisuni, but by May 25th, negotiations had achieved nothing at all. That was good. On the same day, Admiral Jewell was ordered to dispatch three more ships. The armoured cruiser USS Brooklyn and the cruiser USS Atlanta reached Tangier on May 30th and Admiral Chadwick took part in a conference with the

THE PERDICARIS INCIDENT.

The Sultan of Morocco being "persuaded" by Uncle Sam

I had brought half the American fleet to Morocco. It was my first big job.

Sultan's representative. The following day, the gunboats USS Marietta and Castine arrived and we - the French - as official rulers of the sea, assured the United States we would do everything in our power to rescue the hostages.

On May 30th, Secretary of State John Hay was informed that Perdicaris was no longer an American citizen, having taken Greek citizenship. Roosevelt's resolve weakened but he decided to continue with the negotiations as Raisuni believed that Perdicaris was an American citizen. Roosevelt tried to get Britain and France to join the U.S. in a combined military action to rescue Perdicaris. Things couldn't get better.

The two countries refused. Instead, they were covertly recruited to put pressure on the Sultan to accept Raisuni's demands.

On June 1st, as Raisuni followed the issue of great multinational interest, the ransom was increased to $70.000. Admiral Jewell arrived with the USS Olympia, Baltimore and Cleveland bringing the total of American ships in Tangier to the magic number of seven, manned by various marine corps commanded by Major John Twiggs Myers.

At the time, it was the largest gathering of American ships in any foreign port. And even if nothing transpired, it was a tremendous success as far as I was concerned. I had brought half the American fleet to Morocco. It was my first big job.

The marines were ordered to delay their involvement, as it was considered action by them would lead to the death of the hostages. The United States planned to use them to seize the customhouses of Morocco only if the Moroccan government did not fulfil their demands. This was serious, as the customhouses supplied much of the nation's revenue. It was made clear that the Sultan should make the concessions necessary to persuade Raisuni to release Perdicaris and to attack Raisuni if Perdicaris were killed. Just four marines landed in Morocco carrying sidearms and were ordered to protect Mrs Perdicaris.

On June 2nd, the Italian cruiser Dogalli arrived at the port and tensions grew to the point that fears of an uprising arose in the city.

On June 6th, the Spanish battleship Pelayo and the Spanish ironclad Numancia arrived, due to fears that the United States might force Morocco to assign them a port. In response to the request of the British minister in Morocco, the HMS Prince of Wales left Gibraltar on June 7th.

That same day, President Roosevelt received confirmation that Perdicaris had registered in Athens as a Greek citizen. The whole American fleet had sailed to Morocco for a… Greek citizen.

What a colossal mistake!

However, the president had gone too far to be able to withdraw. Negotiations continued and on June 15th, Raisuni increased his demands to be given control of six, rather than two districts of Morocco. Obviously!

On June 19th, the Sultan accepted Raisuni's demands. On June 21st or 22nd, the ransom was paid.

Was this the happy end?

No! On June 22nd, Raisuni demanded another district to control. He probably counted the American ships and asked for one district for every American ship that arrived in Morocco.

On the other side of the Atlantic, the message was by now very clear, as the Secretary of State, John Hay dispatched an ultimatum to the Sultan of Morocco demanding 'Perdicaris alive or Raisuni dead'.

'Roosevelt and Hay know what they're doing. Our people like courage. We'll stand for anything those men do', exclaimed a Kansas delegate.

Finally, on June 24th, Perdicaris was home, tanned and much thinner, features that were appreciated later that century. Raisuni was appointed Pasha of Tangier, Governor of Jibala province and all his imprisoned followers were released. He used the money he'd gained to build a palace for himself, nicknamed the 'House of Tears' but more importantly, he ordered such a large quantity of rifles that he was now my best customer, surpassing Sicily's Mafia. Mehdi was gaining ground in the hierarchy.

Poor Mr Perdicaris. I never knew whether you were a Greek or an American citizen but if your ancestors had not invented democracy and if the Americans hadn't applied it, you would still be living in the mountains.

As for me, I earned the admiration of my boss as a successful employee at our annual December meeting at the Savoy Hotel in Zurich.

"Edward, I knew we would work well together but you have exceeded my expectations. The Perdicaris affair was handled to perfection; the timing, the people, the place, everything! I am amazed. Keep up the good work, Edward!"

The following day, I was surprised to find an unbelievable amount of money in my bank account. My boss was more than satisfied with the upheaval I'd caused.

"You think you can fool me, Edward?" said my boss with a bitter look on his face. He was walking around the table.

"Excuse me?"

"You think you can fool… ME?"

"Why, boss? Why would I do that?"

"You have to work hard to earn your money, you know. There are no short cuts when you work for me."

"What's the matter, boss?"

You know what bosses are like.

One minute you're the king of the world and the next you're a lazy lizard living at the expense of his business. Especially when it comes to sales. Alexandre Le Grand was the exception to the rule, of course. He would never have talked to me like that. He knew how to guide and oversee a good salesman.

Rest in peace, Mr Le Grand. You were as grand as it gets.

These harsh words were spoken to me by my boss a year after my Morocco job had amazed him. It was devastating.

But why was he behaving like this?

At the beginning of the year, I had been invited to dinner in Vienna by my favourite banker, Baron Victor von Kalchberg. On January 22nd 1905, I visited his beautiful home.

Just being there meant I'd succeeded in life. We'd met by accident at the entrance of the Klomser Hotel while I was making my way to the *Central Café,* just after Christmas, 1904. He had invited me for good reason, of course. I had introduced him to Mr Le Grand almost a decade before and Benedictine S.A. was now a customer of Lloyd Bank.

Imagine all the Benedictine that flowed throughout Europe and the cash that flowed to Lloyd Bank from Benedictine S.A. Also, imagine Mr Le Grand moving a large proportion of the money to the Lloyd Bank accounts of the contractors responsible for the construction of his new palace.

"Von Kalchberg, thank you very much for the invitation!"

"You're welcome, Edward, we'll have a wonderful time tonight."

I didn't know many people in the room but enjoyed making new friends among the Viennese aristocrats present. But that night, something extraordinary happened.

A wonderful surprise awaited me as I enjoyed the sumptuous feast.

"Mr Aguillon. C'est vous!"

Who is that woman calling me with such enthusiasm?

I turned around and saw Maria, the Italian woman I had 'rescued' from the flames of the catastrophic fire at the Bazar de Varieté eight years before.

Maria Beccadelli di Bologna, the daughter of Domenico Beccadelli di Bologna, Principe di Camporeale and Laura. You can imagine how happy and humbled I was when the woman I'd accidentally rescued greeted me at such a gathering and described how wonderful I had been in front of all those important people. I was the most popular man of the evening. All the women's eyes were upon me but I feigned humility.

"Edward, you are full of surprises," said our host, proud to have me as a guest at his dinner party.

"Mr Aguillon, you saved my wife's life and I have never had the chance to thank you," said a handsome figure with Germanic features and a strange accent. He was not Italian, for sure.

"I did what anyone would have done in the same situation."

"Your humility is what I admire most, Mr Aguillon. You lay low to avert our gratitude but tonight you cannot avoid it. My family owes you everything. Thank you, my friend! I am Bernhard von Bülow, Chancellor of the German Reich. Your friend forever."

Did you hear what I heard?

Maria Beccadelli di Bologna was the wife of Bernhard von Bülow. The Otto von Bismarck of the era.

Von Bülow was of Danish origin. He was fluent in both English and French having learnt both from his governesses as a young child. His father spoke French and his mother spoke English, which was common in Hamburg society. I won't refer to his military service during the Franco-Prussian War for obvious reasons.

In 1873, his father became the Secretary of State for Foreign Affairs of the German government, serving under Bismarck. Young Bernhard entered the diplomatic corps. His first short assignments were to Rome, St. Petersburg, Vienna and Athens.

In 1884, he hoped to be posted to London but became First Secretary at the embassy in St. Petersburg instead. On route to his new assignment, he spent a few days at Varzin with the Bismarck family, being a good childhood friend of Bismarck's eldest son, Herbert. The mighty Bismarck told him he considered relations with Russia more important than those with Britain, which was why Bülow was posted there.

Please remember that. The super grandmaster of diplomacy has spoken. The importance of a good relationship with Russia. Take note and never forget it. Otto von Bismarck has spoken. He knows, and you are lucky to learn from him.

Just like young Prince Philip, (the third son of King Amyntas and held hostage in Thebes), who was lucky to receive a military and diplomatic education from the greatest generals of their era Epaminondas and Pelopidas, who revolutionised the art of war and defeated the unbeatable Spartans.

Twice!

Fortunately, Philip took note and later built an army of his own according to their teachings. Von Bülow did not, however. To be fair, he wasn't the one who failed to renew the alliance with Russia, leaving the door wide open for France. But in 1897, when he, like his father before him, became State Secretary for Foreign Affairs, he didn't or couldn't make use of Bismarck's notes. The new secretary's main task was to build a world-class fleet capable of taking on the British.

I repeat. Bismarck considered relations with Russia more important than those with Britain. In 1897 however, relations with Russia were dead so it was time to kill relations with England, too, by building a navy. Bismarck was an old man when he heard this news and though confined by illness to his estate in Friedrichsruh, near Hamburg, he predicted a confrontation in twenty years. The same year I had rescued von Bülow's Italian wife from the catastrophic fire.

"It's an honour to meet you, sir."

"The honour is all mine."

"What a surprise for you, Edward! You saved the Chancellor's wife. Many would like to be in your position," said von Kalchberg.

"Well, I am surprised, as…"

"Many Italian women are married to Germans, Edward," said the baron, interrupting me. "There are many such couples because Italian beauty and finesse are always in demand."

"Especially by the Prussians," said von Bülow, laughing.

"Only one Italian woman has escaped us so far," said our host, adding intrigue to the conversation.

You got Gina, that's all I care about, damned Prussians!

"And who would that be?"

"Who? Tell us, Victor."

"I'll give you a clue… The French have her."

"The French?"

"An Italian woman in France?"

"Paris…"

"Is she famous?"

"The most famous Italian woman."

"Mirra Principi."

"No."

"Lydia de Roberti?"

"No."

"Tell us, Victor. We give up."

"Lisa Gherardini."

"I don't know her. Who is she?"

"The wife of Francesco del Giocondo. Otherwise known as Lisa del Giocondo. The one and only Mona Lisa."

"Oh!"

"Difficult, that would be very difficult."

"We should have taken her after the Franco-Prussian War. Wilhelm I was proclaimed Emperor of Germany in the Hall of Mirrors at Versailles; it was the perfect opportunity to take the ultimate Italian woman, the Mona Lisa."

"So why didn't we?"

"Because we moved her to the Brest Arsenal," I, the cowardly Frenchman, said. I was suffering inside, and recalling the Dreyfus affair, and that I was a guest of the baron, and that Baroness Raffaella von something or other was looking at me quite promisingly, and that… that's all.

I should have burnt to death in there with Maria Beccadelli.

"A brave Frenchman like the one with us here tonight deserves to have her and I am sure Leonardo Da Vinci is happy for her."

Bernhard von Bülow can read my mind, I'm sure.

Despite the quips, the evening went well with the Bülows and the baron expressing their gratitude at every opportunity and spending most of their time with me. Von Bülow was particularly grateful and made no secret of it.

We spent a lot of time together that evening, talking about various things. Eager to impress the chancellor, I mentioned my stay in Morocco a year earlier during the Perdicaris affair. For no particular reason, I mentioned the American, French, Spanish and British ships that had gathered there, for the sake of one man.

I was about to refer to the weakness in a democracy that led a candidate to behave in such a way but was interrupted by a more serious chancellor, who told me about the impressive navy Germany was building and that the German fleet was superior in many ways.

All Mr Bülow had registered was the absence of a German fleet from the Perdicaris affair gathering of ships. I hadn't intended to raise the issue, and quite honestly, it had never occurred to me.

Did I seize the opportunity? Of course, I did!

"The Sultan and I have mutual friends. I know from firsthand experience that he would be grateful for a way out of this mess. At the Berlin Conference, it was made clear that Morocco is independent. I don't think it will come about, though. Even Jean Jaurès…"

He loved what he was hearing, I could see it in his eyes and it was obvious he was piecing things together in his mind. All I did was plant a seed. A powerful seed that would bring Morocco to the centre of European affairs in a few months' time. It came to be known as the Morocco Crisis. A crisis so great that last year's Perdicaris incident was just that… an 'incident'.

I mentioned Mr Jean Jaurès, as you might have noticed. Remember that name. This man was so important, so clever, so damn right that I felt guilty about what had to be done.

That night, I returned to my room at the Klomser Hotel with Baroness Raffaella von Schneider. Baron Hugo von Schneider had died of cancer three years previously. He smoked a lot.

There must be a connection between cancer and smoking.

That same Sunday in St Petersburg, unarmed demonstrators led by Father Georgy Gapon were fired upon by soldiers of the Imperial Guard as they marched towards the Winter Palace to present a petition to the Czar. It was the famous 'Bloody Sunday'.

The following day, I left for the good old boiling Balkans and was so busy there that I forgot my conversation with Bülow. Next, I travelled to Sicily to visit my good friends and after that, I found myself with a beauty from Marseille, enjoying coffee and chocolates at the *La Maison Auer* in Rue Saint-François de Paule, in Nice.

La Belle Epoche!

It was March 15th and out of the blue, a newspaper article caught my eye. It told of French admiration for the Kaiser's yacht, the *Hamburg*, in Biarritz.

The first thing that came to mind was the meeting between Napoleon III and Bismarck before the Multi-Names-War. But when I read it was bound for the Straits, something else flashed through my mind.

He will pass Morocco on his way to the Straits!

I abandoned the lady from Marseille and the Belle Epoch chocolates and hurried to the post office to deliver a telegram. How would I claim my bonus if I didn't send a telegram?

'Watch Morocco again.'

I sent the telegram to my boss on March 15th, 1905. I knew he'd laugh because he'd probably kept the telegram I sent him a year before on exactly the same day. This time, however, my information had not come from outlaws and gangs but from the opposite end of the scale. The elite. The aristocracy.

I needed the money badly. Sorry, but I was greedy. What's more, I enjoyed the game and wanted to impress my employer even more. When he told me to keep up the pace, I desperately wanted to do as good a job. But it's not every day you find a Moroccan with connections and it would show weakness to cause a similar upheaval.

Anyway, let me briefly explain about the latest Morocco crisis I so handsomely created.

On the last day of March in 1905, the Kaiser arrived at Tangier and conferred with representatives of the young Sultan Abdulhaziz, who had paid the ransom the previous year. Wilhelm toured the city on the back of a white horse and declared he had come to support the sovereignty of the Sultan, thereby directly and provocatively challenging the French influence in Morocco. He returned to his ship in less than four hours. But four hours were enough.

We, the French, proposed a set of government reforms to Abdulhaziz, which he subsequently rejected and instead invited major world powers to give their advice on necessary reforms.

"Listen, Edward, if you think you can take the credit by reading the newspapers and selling old news to your boss, our cooperation ends here. Trust is what makes good business. Without trust, it's over. Now get the hell out of here and sell your nonsense to someone else," said my boss, walking up and down the cafe at the Savoy Hotel. He refused to sit down.

It was then I realised that sending a telegram would not get me paid. But I didn't expect it to get me fired either. Mr Elazar taught me something I would never forget. Always respect your boss and always tell him the truth. So I told him my version of the truth.

"You think I sent you the telegram because I'd read about the Kaiser's visit to Morocco in the newspapers?"

"I am sure of it. And we are only talking now because of the same telegram I received exactly a year ago. Otherwise, our cooperation would immediately have come to an end and we would never have seen each other again, Edward!"

"Oh, boss!"

"This minor detail allows you to explain yourself."

"Ok, then. Just listen. After our meeting last Christmas, I went to Vienna. There, I was invited to a dinner party where Bernhard von Bülow, the chancellor of…"

"I know who von Bülow is," said the boss, finally taking a seat. I took it as a good sign and continued.

"I mentioned that I happened to be in Morocco during the Perdicaris incident when the American, Spanish, French and English fleets gathered there and that the German navy was absent. It successfully triggered a conversation. We talked about the Sultan's situation, the Berlin conference, Jean Jaurès and so on. As a Frenchman, it was hard to make myself believable. And that was it. I know that the Prussians…"

"The Germans!"

"Whatever…want a say in Mediterranean key issues. Suez, the Straits and Morocco. The three keys of the Mediterranean Sea. Weltpolitik whar."

"Whar?"

"It's ancient Greek. The word comes at the end of the sentence and it means…er… 'that's why' or 'because' or 'for this reason'.

"Anyway, while talking to von Bülow, I was, in fact, inciting him to make a move over Morocco though I was unsure how long it would take the Prussians to act."

"The Germans, you mean!"

"…the Germans to act. Anyway, I didn't think it was necessary to tell you about this meeting because something or nothing could have come from it, and boss… er... now how can I say this…?

"I appreciate your trust and the freedom you give me in each situation. I think it would reduce the level of cooperation and our overall relationship if I were to bother you with the minor things I do to expand our business. I respect both your time and mine. You are paying for my time, after all."

I knew he was listening but couldn't tell whether he believed me or not. I continued with the necessary sincerity. No more, no less.

"To tell you the truth, I was trying to find out about any Pruss… German moves that would indicate progress, but with all the rest of the business and communication problems with the Balkans, I forgot my conversation with von Bülow. Sometime in March, I found out about the Kaiser's visit to the Straits, but I wasn't sure if Morocco was on the agenda so I decided to wait for more accurate information."

"From whom?"

"I would normally tell you, boss, but the honour of a married woman is sacred. As a man of honour myself, I must respect this."

He neither agreed nor disagreed and made neither positive nor negative gestures. I continued my explanation.

"On March 15th, my information was still unclear but there were signs the Kaiser would make a stop in Tangier. So I took my chances, wanting to surprise you exactly one year after my first Moroccan telegram. I thought you would find it amusing and if the Kaiser went directly to the Straits, I would have explained at our next meeting that it was without impact. But to be honest, even if nothing happened, I wanted to take the credit and prove I had met the 'Bismarck' of our times.

"And one last thing. I honestly cannot say whether the Kaiser's visit to Morocco was a result of my efforts. Maybe it was planned months before, maybe it was a last-minute decision by the Kaiser. Nobody knows, other than the Kaiser and Bülow, or any other damned Prussian. I simply did my job and I am not expecting a bonus because I cannot prove it."

Of course I wanted that bonus, but I was certain a man like my boss could find out the details if he wanted to. Eventually, I would be paid the bonus I deserved due to sheer good fortune.

You probably noticed how I failed to mention that the meeting with von Bülow was accidental, and of course it was by chance that I caught sight of the newspaper headline on March 15th. A married female informant was a good excuse any gentleman would support, don't you think? However, everything that was proven or could be proven was true. My truth, as Mr Elazar would say.

Now I had made my point, I was at my boss's disposal. He looked at me as he had on the first day we met and had asked about Dreyfus. A few critical seconds passed. Then, he stood up, intending to leave.

"Take a break. We'll talk again," he said.

"One more thing before you leave, boss!" I wanted the last word, no matter what.

"Yes?" he said turning to me.

"Can I just concentrate on selling guns? War will happen anyway. I don't think you need me to cause any more upheavals."

"Weltpolitik whar?" he said with a smile.

"Weltpolitik whar," I replied, returning it. I sat for a while and enjoyed my coffee before going for a walk beside the lake in Zurich.

I was certain he had the means to discover what really happened. Why the Kaiser had chosen to visit Tangier, I mean. There was a strong possibility it was a last-minute decision, totally irrelevant to my conversation with Bülow. Even if that was the case, I had made myself clear and our meeting ended on a positive note.

Now, this is what really happened, and when I say really, I mean it. Historically real. No nonsense. And how do I know?

"The Kaiser never planned to visit Tangier," said my good friend Hartwig, lighting one of his big, Russian cigarettes.

"Are you sure, Nikolai?"

"Absolutely. I mean… I don't need to talk to anyone to know that. Morocco is full of anarchists, Edward. What logical, royal human being would walk its narrow streets, even for an hour?"

"You know more, don't you?"

"I always know more, but who cares?" My good friend the Russian desperately downed a glass of wine to accompany his desperate words. "Who cares, after all?"

It was the end of May 1906 and I was in Vienna. I was still angry about the unfair words my boss had spoken six months earlier and my friend was in Vienna to recover from unfair treatment from his superiors some days before. We were at the *Maxim* once again, but this time, the 'Ecole de Nancy' décor was somehow dull.

On May 11th, the position of Foreign Minister of the Russian Empire changed hands and among many other candidates, Nikolai was the odds-on favourite to win as he had established a close friendship with the retiring Foreign Minister, Vladimir Lambsdorff. Actually, it was Lambsdorff who had promoted Hartwig to the position of Director of the Asiatic Department in 1900, when we met at the Paris Fair. Now, six years later, it was time for one more step. The most critical step. However, things didn't go as expected, so he came to Vienna to think and… curse.

"Damned Izvolsky! Damned Alexander Petrovich Izvolsky."

"Come now, Nikolai, maybe it's for the best. Soon your time will come."

"It is my time, Edward. But it's not just that," he said, pausing for a while. "Izvolsky will give me a minor post, an unimportant post, to be precise. I can't believe it! Izvolsky will outrank ME!" "But you have connections, you have ways of accessing information, right? No one knows the game better than you."

"Do you know what? Lambsdorff compared Russia's standing in Europe to 'that of a rich bride, whom no one wished to see fall into the arms of another man'. Multiple games are being played in Europe at the moment and I just have to get involved. I must be involved. I was born and bred for that.

"I see the way that German von Bülow acts and it drives me insane. And look at our Izvolsky! I'll give him two to three years, at the most. The 'rich bride' Lambsdorff left behind will be the ugly discarded bitch, like Germany at the Algeciras conference."

Almost two months earlier, the so-called Algeciras conference had come to an end. The conference to which Abdulhaziz had invited world powers to enlighten his administration in Morocco. It began on January 26th and, for the Prussians, it was a *Belle Alliance*, to put it politely. The only state to support them was Austria-Hungary. France would remain the key player in Morocco as the Entente Cordiale had decided, and it was, in fact, the main outcome. The Entente Cordiale was strengthened.

I seized the opportunity.

"Why… why do you say that about von Bülow?"

He looked me in the eye, took a sip of his wine and a serious conversation began.

"It was entirely due to pressure from von Bülow that the Kaiser landed in Tangier. Do you know why? He wanted to show his master that he knew the answer to your Entente Cordiale with the British. To show diplomatic action in the field of the…sea, so to say. He wanted to weaken the agreement by showing the English he could annoy the French and, believe me, if it weren't for the Kaiser's ever-growing naval fleet, he might have made it."

"Why?"

"Why? You really don't understand, do you, Edward?"

"No, I don't."

"Well, to simplify things, try comparing this, as Lambsdorff did," said Nikolai, as if he was teaching his young daughter the difference between left and right. "Imagine an Englishman sitting at a table drinking coffee with a French woman. If a handsome German baron approaches their table, the Englishman feels threatened, right?"

"Right."

"But, if instead of a German baron, a beautiful German baroness approaches them, the Englishman is happier and will use it to his advantage. He would even use the presence of the baroness to make the French woman jealous. In that case, the French woman feels threatened, right?"

"Right."

"Now listen carefully!

"A great German power with a strong navy is like the baron but a great German power without a strong navy is like the baroness. Got it?"

"Got it," I said, enlightened.

"Do you remember the 1900 Exposition, Edward? When we met?"

"Yes, of course."

"When I visited the German pavilion I…"

"You saw that German crane that could lift…" I interrupted, full of enthusiasm.

"No, no. That crane was in the Palace of Electricity. The Germans had exhibits all over the Exposition."

"Ah, yes! It could lift twenty-five tons. Amazing, wasn't it?"

"Indeed it was but you missed the most important message the Prussians made that year."

"And what was that?"

"*Fortune's star invites the courageous man to pull up the anchor and throw himself into the conquest of the waves*"

"What do you mean?"

"Didn't you see it?

"There was a large panel in the German pavilion on which the Germans had painted a stormy sea with huge waves and sirens blaring."

"I don't remember…"

"You were selling liqueur at the time, that's why you didn't notice. The motto I just quoted was written on the panel exactly as Wilhelm had ordered.

" 'Fortune's star', 'courageous man'… these were the Kaiser's words. Three years earlier, he had started building his navy. When I read this motto, I knew the Germans had chosen a dangerous path. A path I was relatively sure would get them into trouble with the British. Good for Russia."

"And France."

"Well, my friend, the crane might have stood there tall and proud but it was the navy that gave them 'masculine' power."

Hartwig was a very clever man, born to be a diplomat. What had really persuaded von Bülow to insist on this visit and neglect the aforementioned truth, however, was a Frenchman called Edward Aguillon.

That's correct. But I mentioned nothing to Hartwig about my role in this incident.

It's impossible to describe the warm welcome I received from my boss at our annual meeting at the Savoy. It was December 20th, 1906.

"Edward, I am so happy to see you again!"

"Me too, boss!"

"Those Italians of yours are an extremely good market. They have increased orders significantly."

"Indeed, they've even surpassed the sum of the Moroccan and Serbian markets."

"Good! Very good!"

"There is one thing I think you should know, though. They send a lot to America. I don't know if they sell it, but…"

"Thank you for telling me but I don't think they could sell guns there at a better price than mine, Edward."

"Oh!" I said as if I didn't already know that another Edward was selling guns in America. I paused while my boss shared his news.

"I assume you heard about the conference."

"The Algeciras conference, you mean?"

"Yes."

"That was almost a year ago. I read something about it," I said casually.

"You caused it and all you did was read something about it? It was your conference, my boy! You made it happen, Edward!"

"Are you sure, boss? The target was obviously the Entente Cordiale between England and France. The Prussians wanted to cancel this agreement by coming between them. The Kaiser wanted England to realise that they were on their side and they shouldn't let the French take Morocco."

"Yes, indeed. That is true. But the awkward way they went about it was down to you. I know that firsthand, Edward. Von Bülow did as you indicated. Wilhelm did not want to be there. He strongly resisted but then gave in, which he clearly regretted. It took time for him to realise that the British would never trust a country that builds a navy as powerful as their own."

"But diplomacy can achieve anything."

"Diplomacy can also ruin things, as in our case, and once that happens, generals become more trustworthy."

"And place more orders."

"Exactly!"

I knew I had the upper hand now, so I started to joke. "Bismarck would have persuaded the English that they don't really need a navy, wouldn't he?"

"Ha-ha! You can say that again! The Iron Chancellor would never have built such a navy in the first place. Wilhelm read Alfred Machan's book called 'The Influence of Sea Power upon History' and overreacted with his navy. Sadly, the German army is losing money because of this navy but the Kaiser still plays an important role in the growth of our market."

"I can imagine him as a child, visiting his grandmother in England and seeing the English fleet. Now he wants to play games of his own."

"I have no idea how he persuaded the Bavarians to pay for his navy though."

"Themistocles persuaded the Athenians to build a large navy, you know."

"How did he do that?"

"He introduced them to a familiar enemy they could actually see and be threatened by. Aegina, a rival city-state on an island opposite the Athenian port of Piraeus, twenty miles away."

In 483 B.C., an enormous new seam of silver was found in the Athenian mines at Laurium. Themistocles proposed that the silver should be used to build a new fleet of two hundred triremes, while his main rival, Aristides, suggested it should be distributed among the Athenian citizens.

"So why did Themistocles really want the navy?"

"Because of the Persians. But he knew that after the Battle of Marathon, the Athenians were too confident and the Persians too distant to scare his countrymen into action. Hence, the Aeginitans."

"Aha! So you are saying that…?"

"It wouldn't have been difficult to persuade the Bavarians to support a powerful navy because the German Reich is surrounded by the French and the Russians, who are in close vicinity and supported by the British, who are like the Persians."

"I don't think your analogy is correct. The Aeginitans are more like the British supported by the French."

"And the Persians?"

"Weltpolitik, I suppose."

"Maybe so. Countries too far away, the Prussians too confident in their army. Probably. Anyway, the Kaiser doesn't have to persuade anyone, he just gives orders, right?"

"It's thanks to him that the Entente Cordiale was signed in the first place. You are now friends with your eternal enemies. And the Algeciras conference strengthened that."

"Bizarre! The Prussians achieved the impossible. He did even better than Jules Verne."

"Where does Jules Verne come into this?"

"He died seven days before the Kaiser visited Morocco. But never mind that, it's complicated."

"Whatever you say. Edward, I would like you to continue this upheaval-making effort! Both attempts in Morocco had incredible results. You are gifted, my boy."

Bosses! Bosses! Bosses!

"Thank you, boss, but I don't think it's a very good idea. Don't misunderstand me. In the next two or three years, war will be upon us anyway, whether I do anything or not. Besides, we are already in the middle of a war."

"Which war?"

"The Pig War!"

The Pig War was a trade war between the Austro-Hungarian Empire and Serbia that began in 1906. The Empire unsuccessfully imposed a customs blockade on Serbian pork.

After the coup of May 1903, Serbia attempted to reduce its economic dependence on the Austro-Hungarian Empire. In 1904, it began to import French rather than Austrian munitions, and in 1905, it established a customs union with Bulgaria. Needless to say, their preference for French munitions was mainly due to my intervention with some of the key influencers. I had established the trust of the French, you see, because I stood close to the customer, as Alexandre Le Grand had always insisted.

Economically, however, it was still attached to the Habsburgs. Its major export was pork, most of which was bought by the Austro-Hungarians. When Serbia began to establish links with other countries, the Hungarian government decided to punish the Serbians with economic sanctions.

This was the so-called 'Pig War'. No bullets, no guns. Just pigs.

"Edward, please!"

"Ok, not the pig war, but the Balkans, the Kaiser, the colonies, Alsace, revanchism… It's obvious.

"Boss, I beg you! Release me of this duty or I'll cause the greatest war the world has ever seen just by reading the newspapers."

My boss laughed. Obviously, I couldn't forget what he'd said a year before. He was my boss after all, but now he had recognised, or even better, validated my worthiness, I had to make sure he remembered it. I wanted him to know I was aware of how valuable I was to him and protecting my honour was more important than any bonus.

"Oh come now, Edward, you're still angry about what I said the last time we met," he said, refilling my glass with whisky. It was probably an introduction to the money he was about to offer me.

"No boss, I was afraid of being fired from a job that I love and losing my dignity."

"The money you'll be paid will be enough to live on for years."

"Thank you, boss. I appreciate that but it's not the money I'm concerned about, and as I said, war is closer now than ever. You know that better than I do."

I didn't mean a word of it, of course, because I truly hoped for peace, tranquillity and calm and for my upheaval causing services to be appreciated even more.

"Edward, I achieved success in life by leading the events, not reacting to them."

"Boss, all you have to do is seize the opportunity. Three years, at the most."

"Ok, Edward. I respect your point of view. Honour whar!"

"Honour whar!"

"Continue selling my guns, my boy."

And that's exactly what I did. I continued selling his guns and expanding my network in a Europe filled with peace, tranquillity and calm.

In January 1907, I was once again invited to a dinner in Vienna by my favourite baron. Bernhard von Bülow and Maria Becadelli hadn't been invited and it was not the Vienna elite that stood out that day, but the elite of Graz.

I had just swallowed the last drop of my Benedictine when the guests looked in a certain direction. I turned my head and saw her enter the room. My heart began to beat like a Grand Armée drum.

'Gina!'

The only woman I ever wanted to marry. She walked around the room in all her glory and stopped near me. She was not accompanied by her husband. Oh my god! I must have been destined to meet her that night in Vienna. She had not seen me so I moved in her direction.

"Gina!"

"Good evening, beautiful lady!" An old man in a military uniform flanked her from the left, obscuring my view. He was short and thin with a large moustache and thick, spikey hair.

Naturally, Gina spoke to me first. "Edward! What a pleasant surprise!" I politely turned to the man and Gina was obliged to reply to him. He dismissed me completely.

"Virginia von Reininghaus!"

"Conrad von Hoetzendorf! Marshal of the Empire. Pleased to meet you, Madame Virginia!" He arrogantly introduced himself and kissed her hand.

"My pleasure, von Hoetzendorf! This is my old friend Edward Aguillon."

"A Frenchman? What do you do for a living, Frenchman?" His French was basic.

"I sell guns."

"Meet me tomorrow morning at the *Landtmann* for coffee. At ten o'clock," he continued in French. He grabbed Gina's hand and pulled her away from me, acting as if they were married.

I couldn't believe it.

Who is this unbelievable person?

The rest of the evening was awful. He behaved like her husband and didn't leave her alone for a second. Gina was being held hostage and was begging to be rescued. I could tell.

That evening, I realised how cowardly I was. I made no attempt to approach her. Why? Because she was the mother of six children and there were single ladies and widows among us. But she was still my Gina!

You are a coward, Edward Aguillon. A coward!

Even worse, I went to the *Landtmann* the day after to drink coffee with the Marshal of the Empire. An old man in a uniform. But business is business.

Shame on me!

"Time is short, so get on with it!"

"You are the one who invited me here for a coffee, von Hoetzendorf!" Having risen from my bed at the Klomser Hotel much earlier than usual, I was rather annoyed. Luckily, the *Landtmann* cafe was minutes away.

"But you're the one who sells guns. You used that wonderful lady to approach me. So what do you wish to sell to my army?"

You must be the biggest fool in the whole of the Austro-Hungarian Empire.

I don't normally do business with state armed forces so why should I sell anything to the awful man who destroyed my one-in-a-million opportunity with Gina?

"I don't wish to sell you anything, von Hoetzendorf. Nothing at all."

"What do you want from me, then?"

...the biggest fool in the world.

"I came to discuss the technological progress of weapons over the last few decades and how you think it might have changed the strategy of war."

He seemed flattered and didn't want to know why I had asked.

Did it ever cross your mind that I wanted to talk to Gina, too?

An unbelievable monologue on the importance of flanking the enemy began. He used the word flanking more than fifty times.

I didn't interrupt. All I could think of was not being able to speak to Gina the night before because of this strange old man.

At some point, von Hoetzendorf, pleased that I was still listening, changed the subject to his personal life and spoke of his depression, which worsened after the death of his wife two years earlier and his doubts about his fitness for office. He was a lonely, fifty-five-year-old man trying to get along with four sons and a demanding job.

The famous psychology professor, Sigmund Freud, was sitting at a table nearby and had heard the monologue. He probably realised that drinking coffee with a friendly listener was as beneficial as a session with a psychiatrist.

Conrad seemed relieved after talking about his troubles and ordered me to go for a walk with him. I obeyed without question. We left the *Landtmann*, walked along Löwelstrasse and continued to Augustinerstrasse. He was full of energy and didn't hesitate to mention his careful diet and multi-language skills.

When we reached Backgasse, we turned right, though I'd have preferred to have gone left in the direction of my hotel. Just before Universitätstring, we came across a young street painter, who was working on a painting of the beautiful Burgtheater building.

"Very good job, young man," said Conrad.

"Thank you, sir!"

"Tres bien!"

"Are you French?" The painter was happy to hear me speaking French.

"Oui."

"I like Paris. I was born in the same month the Eiffel Tower was opened to the public."

"You should visit Paris and paint it, young man."

"I will, someday, I will."

"You'd better hurry then because in two years' time, they're going to pull it down."

"When will it be ready?" asked the general. "The Burgtheater building, I mean."

"In two weeks."

"Take this money and in two weeks, I'll send someone to pick it up."

"Thank you, sir. Thank you!" The painter was surprised by Conrad's trust and generosity.

"Are you sure he'll be here in two weeks?" I asked as we moved on.

"Edward, it doesn't matter how advanced the latest weapons are. Whether a war is won or lost depends on the soldier and his leader. This is a man of honour. I can see it in his eyes and tell by his talent. What kind of a leader am I, if I don't know my men? Of all the things I have said today, this is the most valuable lesson."

"You know better, von Hoetzendorf," I said. I'd had enough of his psychotherapy. We continued our walk through the Rathauspark before reaching the town hall.

Conrad then made his final statement and voiced his innermost thoughts.

"I enjoyed our discussion, Edward. I like speaking French. When I awoke this morning, I wasn't feeling well. After dinner yesterday evening, I thought it best to leave Vienna immediately or this woman would shape my destiny. I am fond of her but I am fifty-five years old and have four sons. She is twenty-eight and is married with six children. What's the point? But after our discussion this morning, I think she's actually worth pursuing."

After our discussion? What discussion? I barely opened my mouth! Mr Freud certainly has a point!

"You obviously know better, von Hoetzendorf."

Exhausted by all the listening, I headed to my hotel to rest. Psychiatrists deserved every penny they made, I was sure of that.

As for Conrad, he pursued Gina intensively by visiting and writing her letters. She rejected him repeatedly but it didn't stop him from trying. A married woman with six children and half his age!

"You suspect your wife is cheating on you?"

"I know she is."

"Are you sure?"

"I'm absolutely positive."

"Do you have children?"

"Yes."

"You are a lucky man."

"Are you crazy? Stop playing with my…"

"No, my friend. I mean it."

"Look, we are the same age, right?"

"You are forty-five?"

"Forty-four."

"I am one year older than you."

"Well, I was born on the very first day of 1863 so…"

"Anyway, what's your point?"

"You are in a much better situation than me. I have never been married, I don't have children and I go to the cabaret every night."

"And?"

"You can do that too, and you already have children. But me? Maybe I will never have children. So who's better off?"

"But I love my wife."

"You used to love her. Now you are hurt. Look at all those beautiful women over there. Another bottle of wine?"

"It hurts so much. You'll never understand."

"Maybe I won't, but look at Chloe over there. You like her, don't you?"

"She is very beautiful."

"Tonight, she will make you forget your troubles."

"But do you know what's really difficult, Edward?"

"What?"

"I never look through other people's things, and certainly not my wife's, but on Monday, I found some letters… I just… the bastard!"

"I'd rather not know, my friend."

"I accidentally knocked over a box of her things and as I was putting them back… the bastard!"

"You saw the letters?"

"I read them too. Never in my life have I felt worse. She was… you know… my one and only."

"Chloe will make you feel better tonight."

"…and the bastard is well-known and much older. How on earth…?"

Chloe came over, kissed him and he succumbed. I had excused myself earlier to visit the bathroom and told her about the poor fellow. I noticed how he looked at her when we came in. She welcomed us and helped us with our overcoats.

I paid her in advance and she deserved the money. I spent that night with Charlotte, a beautiful Belgian brunette.

The following day, as I was leaving for Zurich, I realised the overcoat I was wearing was not my own. It was similar but in the inside pocket were the letters the famous bastard had written. It was December of 1907, and it seemed that every ten years, I would save someone's life.

At this time every year, I looked forward to the annual meeting with my boss. We talked about sales, commented on current affairs and how life was going. I said nothing about war or 'upheaval', and enjoyed not doing so, and he was obviously too proud to ask me.

Three years passed after my foolish, blind prediction, and on October 6th 1908, something happened that would make my boss happy and probably confirm my prediction. So what happened that day?

Conrad's boss, Emperor Franz Joseph, announced the annexation of Bosnia and Herzegovina, territories formerly within the sovereignty of the Ottoman Empire. The Bosnian Crisis, also known as the Annexation Crisis, also known as the First Balkan Crisis, had just begun.

Bosnia and Herzegovina were handed to Austria-Hungary by the Ottomans in 1878 when the Treaty of Berlin laid the foundation for this move. Under Article 29, Austria-Hungary received special rights in the Ottoman Empire provinces of Bosnia-Herzegovina and the Sanjak of Novi Pazar. The Sanjak of Novi Pazar separated Montenegro from Serbia and prevented the geographic and political union of these two states, which were often closely aligned.

The Austrian occupation of the Sanjak was also significant because it provided Austria-Hungary with a staging area for possible future expansion towards the Aegean port of Salonika in Ottoman-controlled Macedonia. However, by 1897, under the new Czar, Nicholas II, the Russian Imperial government had withdrawn its support for the Austrian annexation of Bosnia-Herzegovina.

This issue arose again when on July 2nd 1908, the Russian Foreign Minister Alexander Izvolsky sent a letter to the Austro-Hungarian Foreign Minister, Alois Aehrenthal, proposing a discussion about reciprocal changes to the 1878 Treaty of Berlin in favour of the Russian interest in the Straits of Constantinople, and Austro-Hungarian interest in the annexation of Bosnia-Herzegovina and the Sanjak of Novi Pazar. Both powers stood to win from the agreement.

I'm sure you remember Alexander Izvolsky. Not only was he chosen instead of my friend Hartwig but he posted him to the depths of Asia, too. You might also remember the keys of the Mediterranean Sea that I mentioned to my boss. One more key was up for discussion here. The Straits of Constantinople.

Diplomats Aehrenthal and Izvolsky exchanged letters and held a secret meeting on September 16th.

Guess who hosted that meeting.

My old friend Leopold Berchtold, the lawyer I had coffee with at the *Stella Polare*. The one I mistakenly invited to the Messina with the banker baron. He joined the Austro-Hungarian Foreign Service in 1893, two years after that fatal meeting in Trieste. The same year, he married Countess Ferdinanda Károlyi, the daughter of one of the richest aristocrats in Hungary.

He served at the embassies in Paris, London and St. Petersburg and at the same time, built up an impressive collection of antiquities.

Leopold hosted the secret meeting between the two diplomats at his castle at Buchlau in Moravia. The so-called Buchlau Bargain was the result. The problem started here, as no minutes were taken during these private meetings, which lasted a total of six hours.

Izvolsky accepted the task of writing up the conclusions of the meeting and forwarding them to Aehrenthal. On September 21st, Aehrenthal wrote to Izvolsky asking for the document. Two days later, Izvolsky replied that the document had been sent to the Czar for approval. The document, if it ever existed, was never seen by anyone.

It appeared there was a misunderstanding and on October 6th, Emperor Franz Joseph announced to the people of this Ottoman territory, his determination to recognise and grant them an autonomous and constitutional regime under his authority as their annexing sovereign. This was quite a surprise for Izvolsky and the Czar himself because for that to happen, the Straits would have to be dealt with.

Serbia mobilised its army on the very next day and the Serbian Crown Council demanded the annexation be reversed or, failing that, Serbia should receive compensation. It was defined on October 25th as a strip of land across the northernmost portion of the Sanjak of Novi Pazar.

Understandably, it reeked of war, and Bismarck's words would come true. It seemed that finally, the war would begin over a foolish matter in the Balkans and I wouldn't make any money out of it.

My boss was happy at our annual meeting in Zurich that damned December.

"You were right again, Edward. You said it would take three years, and here we are. We finally have a war."

"...I'll paint you and your friend walking in front of the Opera House, ok? You'll see yourselves every time you look at the painting."

"Yes, boss," I replied, showing how happy I was my prediction had come true.

"Russia will back Serbia without a doubt and obviously won't allow Austria-Hungary to fool her like that. Serbia mobilised first."

Always close to the customer, I travelled to Serbia. Some five thousand volunteers had been organised there by my good friend Vojislav Tankosic, contrary to Serbian government policy. This was important for me.

I have already mentioned Tankosic. He was a Serbian military officer and member of the Black Hand, who participated in the May Coup of 1903. He was one of the most important Chetniks and my very good client and friend. Bold and rude, he would shoot apples from the heads of his Chetnik fighters. He was now a graduate of the military academy in Belgrade and was awarded the Order of Karađorđe's Star. He was, without a doubt, the best advertiser for my high-quality guns.

Austrian and Hungarian newspapers reported a thousand bands in Serbia with twenty well-armed fighters in each, and that each fighter gave one of his two guns to Bosnian rebels. Note here that I had sold them the guns. Do the calculations and see if it was worth it. If financed by the Serbian government, I'd have sold nothing, unlike my boss and his rivals because this was their market but at the time, I was pocketing a generous commission so it was profitable for my boss anyway. Tankosic, of course, got his personal weapons for free.

Luckily, diplomacy had worked a miracle once again. The British opposition to amending the Treaty of Berlin over the Straits left Russia empty-handed. Izvolsky and the Czar considered the annexation and Aehrenthal's manoeuvres to have been made in bad faith. Furthermore, Izvolsky was considered responsible for the failure of Russian diplomacy and was forcibly ousted.

On March 26th 1909, Austria-Hungary provided Britain with the negotiated text of Serbia's declaration committing Serbia to accept the annexation. Later that day, Austria-Hungary decided to partially mobilise its armed forces. Happily, not a single bullet was fired in 1909 and the Eiffel Tower remained standing as it had proved to be valuable for communication purposes. Honestly!

"Nikolai, I never thought we would meet again like this."

"Thank God I'm out of exile," he said taking one of his big, Russian cigarettes.

"Come now, you were the ambassador of Persia. Persia is important for Russia."

"It was a diplomatic exile. And a fatal one. I should be the one talking to Aehrenthal. I don't think he would mess with me. The pseudo aristocrat Jew! Damned…"

"It was undeniably a very dirty game he played."

"And now the Czar is forced to accept Sergei Sazonov to replace Izvolsky."

"Who forced him?"

"Pyotr Stolypin, the chairman of the Council of Ministers."

"Why him?"

"Why him?" He was being sarcastic. "Because Sazonov is married to his daughter. That's why! He is Stolypin's son-in-law. Completely and utterly controllable."

"From Izvolsky, the 'King of the Bosporus', to Sazonov, the 'son-in-law'. Ha! Anyway. Here we are in Belgrade. How are sales? Going well? Better than the Benedictine?"

"Well, sales are sales. There's no big difference."

"Will you be talking to the Serbian generals here?"

"No, I don't sell to the army. Just the private sector."

"Who are your Serbian clients?"

"My biggest clients are army officers but I cover their 'private' needs."

"Edward, I didn't exactly succeed Izvolsky but I was not posted here by accident and I won't just be warming the ambassador's chair here in Belgrade. I have great plans for the region. It would help if I had an indication of the 'private sector' in Serbia, Bulgaria and Greece. I place my trust in our old friendship!"

"I'll help you any way I can, my friend."

I told him all I knew about the Chetniks, Komitaj, Captains, Greek, Serbian and Bulgarian leaders in the Macedonian area.

"What about the Albanians?" he asked.

"Never been there. They are closer to the Ottomans, so there is no business there for me."

"What do you think, Edward?"

"About what?"

"About the general situation in the Balkans."

"It's complicated, very complicated."

"Come now, tell me… anything… anything that comes to mind… about this complexity, I mean."

"Ah, yes… let me think… well look…"

"Go on."

"I can tell you this. It was something I came across four years ago in Monastir, a Macedonian city. I was walking in the city when suddenly, Ottoman policemen came running down the road. A convict had escaped and was hiding in the city's narrow side streets. There was a huge commotion.

"Eventually, they caught him and led him to the execution platform that had been set up in 'At Bazaar' square. I couldn't believe my eyes. The man asked for his hands to be released, mounted the steps of the scaffold alone, put the noose around his neck, shouted 'Long Live Greece' and with no hesitation, kicked the box from under his feet."

"A brave man!"

"So why am I telling you this? He shouted 'Long Live Greece' in Slavic, and until 1900, he had been cooperating with the Bulgarians against the Ottomans. Then, he turned against them."

"What was his name?"

"Captain Kottas. A Greek Slavophone, who spoke Bulgarian, too. He was initially a member of the Bulgarian IMRO, the Internal Macedonian Revolutionary Organisation."

"You sell to the IMRO?"

"Yes, I do. I sell anywhere I can. It's my job. Do you get my point, Nikolai?"

"Do you sell to the Ottomans, too?"

"The Kaiser provides the Ottomans with all the weapons they need."

"They have a German officer, don't they? Leman or something."

"Liman. General Otto Liman. He's the number one in Constantinople, modernising the Ottoman army along European lines."

"The Kaiser wants to be seen as the protector of the Muslims, which means he wants a place in the sun and now that the Ottoman Empire is on the decline, he has his eye on a colony."

"England and France were the first to occupy the world so he must seize all the opportunities he can get."

Peace prevailed. My professional pride was intact and I couldn't wait for the next meeting with my boss at the end of the year.

"Listen, boss, regarding the Bosnian crisis. It didn't go well as far as business is concerned but Russia is now behaving like a wounded dog. It will bite if somebody tries to…" I tried to sound optimistic.

"No one knows, Edward. Another diplomatic victory will soon heal the wound… I was so sure this time."

"Talking of diplomacy, the new Russian ambassador in Serbia is a good friend of mine. Nikolai Hartwig." I mentioned Hartwig to cover his actions later.

"Anyway business is good so no problem."

No problem, he said. Of course, there was a problem. He was just trying to hide his bitterness.

Next December, you'll be on your knees begging me to restart the upheaval business if 1910 is as peaceful as 1909 was.

And 1910 was peaceful, thanks to me. Thanks to Edward Aguillon.

I was drinking coffee at the *Central Café* in Vienna. Over the last few years, I had often seen Mr Levi Bronstein there. He was a Russian revolutionary figure, who wrote articles for various Russian and Ukrainian newspapers under a variety of pseudonyms. He had been in Vienna since Conrad met Gina in 1907. His hair was like a lion's mane and he wore peculiar round glasses. He was a calm and peaceful person.

This time, I was sitting at a table quite near the back of the café, quietly reading my *Petit Journal*. I happened to exchange some words with the waiter in French. I was about to leave for Sicily but the discussion I overheard that day led me to Bosnia.

At a nearby table, a man sat alone reading his newspaper. Later, he was joined by another.

They were speaking Serbian and I paid no particular attention to them. It was quite normal as I spoke some Serbian myself and understood it relatively well.

I continued reading *Le Petit Journal* and kept a low profile. It became difficult, however, when I realised the two fools were talking about me in an offensive way, trying to find out whether I understood Serbian. I was the only person nearby. I turned the pages of my newspaper, pretending not to understand.

It was fun!

Once their ridiculous method had assured them I could not understand their language, they continued to speak but more quietly. I was still able to hear them.

One of them was Rade Malobabic, a Serbian military intelligence officer who was freshly stationed in Austria.

I couldn't believe my ears! They were discussing a plot to assassinate the Emperor. Franz Josef had announced he would visit Bosnia and Herzegovina on June 3rd, 1910 and according to the conspirators, the volunteer was ready. In other words, the person they had found to kill him was determined to carry it out. He was ready to kill and commit suicide and was waiting to receive his gun.

Bogdan Zerajic, whose identity they did not attempt to hide, was a law student at the University of Zagreb and the city of Mostar was where the assassination attempt would take place. I turned a page of the *Petit Journal* now and then to make it look as if I didn't understand what they were saying. It was becoming increasingly difficult.

After discussing the details of how they would get the gun to the student, they paid for their coffees and made their way out of the café.

"Bonjour monsieur!" said one of them sarcastically as he passed my table.

"Dobro jutro idiote!" I desperately wanted to reply and scare the life out of them but held my tongue instead. "Bonjour monsieur!" I replied and smiled like an idiot.

I had to meet someone in Zagreb.

I knew if the young lawyer achieved his goal a great upheaval would begin. A great war even. I didn't know how serious that war would be but it would make my services obsolete. What's more, my boss would happily tell me how right I'd been that war was inevitable.

On the way there, I seriously considered the option of killing him but I did not want to harm a young man. He was twenty-four years old and came from a poor family that lived in the town of Nevesinje, around forty kilometres east of Mostar. He had studied law but found work as a primary school teacher in Serbia.

Austria had made things worse by completely annexing Bosnia. Firstly, for the Muslims, who were now ruled by a Christian emperor, and secondly, for the Serbian Christian population - who saw their dreams of autonomy drifting away - not to mention the atheists and communists who read the works of Nietzsche, Mr Bronstein's articles and an abundance of Russian socialist and anarchist literature. And yet Bosnia was still the poorest part of the empire by far after the annexation; a forgotten area somewhere to the south. Aehrenthal's diplomatic victory was quite impressive. Eventually, the political situation in Bosnia and Herzegovina triggered Bogdan's conscience. If anyone wanted to kill Franz Joseph now, all he had to do was put a gun in the young man's hand.

But I was also seriously considering another option; one that would solve all my problems at once. One that could even elevate me to the nobility of the Austro-Hungarian Empire. Becoming Edward von Aguillon was now a serious possibility. My future could turn out to be similar to that of an Austrian… butcher.

Ten years before I was born, Franz Joseph Karl was a thirty-three-year-old king. On February 18th 1853, the young king was taking a walk along one of the city's bastions, wearing, as always, a suitable uniform for the occasion. He was accompanied by one of his officers, Count Maximilian Karl Lamoral O'Donnell. O'Donnell was of Irish descent.

Suddenly, a man armed with a knife approached them from behind and stabbed the emperor in the neck. Count O'Donnell struck the attacker with his sabre, and with the help of a man who was standing nearby, overpowered him.

The assailant was a Hungarian nationalist named János Libényi, who, after standing trial, was executed. Count O'Donnell was promoted, while the lucky man who helped neutralise Janos was elevated to the nobility by the emperor. His name was Joseph Ettenreich, an everyday butcher who became Joseph von Ettenreich.

As you can imagine, the idea of identifying the young student, following him at close range and saving the emperor from certain death was very charming indeed. It would earn me titles, make me rich, and I would gain admiration. Why ever not?

Naturally, my boss would fire me. I would explain to him that I'd tried to save Franz Joseph, because Archduke Franz Ferdinand, his heir, was a renowned pacifist. I wasn't sure if he'd believe me, however.

Not that it mattered. Von Aguillon wouldn't care about that. One thing, however, made me give it second thoughts.

At moments like this, anything is possible, anything can go wrong. In the assassination attempt of 1853, the emperor's life was actually saved by an unusual aspect - the imperial uniform with its high collar that almost completely enclosed the emperor's neck. The collars of the royal uniforms of that era were made of very sturdy material exactly for this purpose; to protect the emperor from this type of attack. Though wounded and bleeding, the emperor's life was saved by his collar and two men who happened to be nearby were given titles. Without such a collar, these two men would have been considered incapable of good such a deed, or even traitors and the reign of KFJ would only have lasted five years.

Do you see what I mean? The risk was high.

The dilemma gave me a headache and in the end, I decided to do what was best to keep my job and persuade him not to go ahead with his plan.

I am a Frenchman, not a 'von...'.

I located his house and threw a message attached to a stone while he was home. I will not go into detail about what I wrote to make Bogdan change his mind. Suffice it to say, he was still absolutely determined to attempt the assassination of Franz Joseph. In fact, he came within touching distance of the emperor, outside Mostar railway station.

And I was within touching distance of Bogdan.

Sorry, I couldn't resist! I was five seconds away from becoming a *von.*

He didn't reach for his pistol, however, and eventually gave up. I'd probably persuaded him not to go ahead with it by putting doubts in his head. He hesitated for some unknown reason. I was that unknown reason. Europe was safe. People would still require my services and I would never be a *von.*

My words had no lasting effect on him, however. Some days later, he changed his mind after reading an article written by the journalist Risto Radulovic, who argued against dispiritedness in the public life of Bosnia and Herzegovina. An event that would unite them into forming a revolutionary movement was needed and someone had to do something. Thus on June 15th, the day of the start of the Austro-Hungarian Campaign in Bosnia, Bogdan Zerajic attempted the assassination of General Marijan Varesanin, the governor of Bosnia and Herzegovina. He fired five shots but missed. With his sixth and final bullet, the young student killed himself.

If the article by Radulovic had been written before Franz Joseph's departure, either the emperor would have been dead or I would have become a 'Von'. It was amazing how a newspaper article could change the fate of a royal. Unfortunately, it was also a newspaper article that had changed the fate of the emperor's wife Elizabeth twelve years before.

Luigi Lucheni, a twenty-five-year-old Italian anarchist, had gone to Geneva intending to kill Philippe, Duke of Orléans, the heir to the throne of France. The duke, however, had left Geneva earlier than planned and Luigi missed his opportunity. Disappointed by his bad luck, Luigi grabbed a Geneva newspaper and accidentally caught sight of news of interest to anarchists who wanted to kill royals.

The newspaper gave details of a woman under the alias of 'Countess of Hohenembs', who was staying at the Hôtel Beau-Rivage. She was, in fact, the Empress Elisabeth of Austria. She had travelled to Geneva incognito but someone from the hotel informed the newspaper that the Empress of Austria was a guest there. Luigi couldn't believe his luck. His business trip would pay off.

On Saturday, September 10th 1898, while the Empress was walking along the shore of Lake Geneva with her lady-in-waiting, the anarchist stabbed Elisabeth with a four-inch-long sharpened needle inserted into a wooden handle.

"1910 ended peacefully. 1911 is a new year and will be a good year, Edward."

"It surely will, boss."

"Edward, you will make it a good year."

"I hope so, boss."

"You don't understand, Edward. You will make it a good year."

"Sales will increase, I can assure you of th…"

"Don't talk nonsense, Edward. You know what I mean."

I would have loved to have seen him beg me but he was still my boss so I changed my attitude.

"If I understand correctly, boss, you want me to cause an upheaval?"

"Do you know what happened at Fashoda in 1898?

"France was one step from war with England…"

"Yes, and?"

"…and they didn't go to war."

Let me remind you of where the Tana brothers came from. The Blue Nile flows from Lake Tana to join the White Nile, and Fashoda is located on the White Nile, around five hundred kilometres to the south before the rivers merge.

"'A war for so miserable and small an object is what I could hardly bring myself to consent to', Queen Victoria said."

"She was right, but that was not the problem. After that, they started talking and began to understand each other. That was more of a problem."

"Which, with the help of the Prussians, led to the Entente Cordiale."

"We're afraid this Fashoda business might happen again. Are you married, Edward?"

"No, boss."

"A couple who fight every day will eventually face a crisis in their marriage, just like Fashoda. If they are afraid to divorce because of their children, backlash from society or for whatever reason, they risk sticking it out forever and thus grow old, sleepwalking through a miserable, boring life and die knowing they were too afraid to escape their monotonous relationship.

"A new equilibrium is created. Do you understand?"

"Like an Entente Cordiale?" Of course I understood but I was determined to investigate any possible problems. "Come now, boss, the Prussians would never enter an Entente or accept an equilibrium. They're Prussians, after all."

"Edward, Hugo Stinnes told me…

"The industrialist?"

"Yes. He said that after six to seven years of peaceful progress, Germany will be the uncontested economic master of Europe. Culture and politics will follow. He is already investing in France and England. He is right. Once your Prussians reach that point, my line of business will be difficult, if not obsolete."

Something occurred to me and I paused. My boss picked up on it immediately.

"Of course your share will grow accordingly. It won't be just a bonus."

"What will it be?"

"A fortune."

"But how, boss? It'll surely take time."

"Don't worry about the time. Continue to do what you do and don't bother with next year's meeting. You'll have funds to support your effort."

"Ok, boss!"

"Good."

"So this is my priority, now? Sales, I mean..."

"Your only priority, Edward Aguillon."

Handed an amazing project like this, it was a good idea to show my boss I was ready and able to deliver.

"This time, I won't send a telegram, boss, but there is one thing."

"And what is that?"

"Watch Morocco again."

"Ha! You're quite a man, Edward. Ha-ha-ha!"

I'm sure I surprised you, too. With my readiness, that is. It was simple enough. After work came to a halt in 1905 due to my boss's mistrust, I continued to plan possible upheavals and connect with the right people. I knew he'd come back to me and so every year before we met, I had a proposition to make. Except in awful 1908, when the Bosnia crisis took place, or to be more accurate, the Aehrenthal-Izvolsky crisis.

For this meeting, in particular, I wanted to be as well prepared as possible. I knew it was imminent. In October, I had visited Morocco, where I sold guns and met my friend, Mehdi, who was now in a much more powerful position. I knew firsthand how bad the situation was and with a little help, I could make it happen.

Now was the time to deliver.

As usual, I spent a few enjoyable days in Vienna before setting to work. Now please pay attention and find out what it means to be a hard-working salesman in 1911.

I arrived in Morocco before the end of February. Remember young Abdulaziz, who was forced to pay Raisuni a lot of money to free Perdicaris? He lasted until 1909. From 1909, his brother Abdelhafid was the Sultan and a very cruel Sultan at that. That made things easier for me. All I had to do was pay my friend the right amount of money and promise him more once the rebellion was underway.

And why did I believe a rebellion in Morocco would be fruitful? The answer is simple.

Because of the damned Prussians!

Whenever I visited Sicily, I always thought about the crew of the Bella Messina and Capitano. Where was he now, what might have happened to him? He would probably be angry at me for doing business with his life-long enemy.

I, on the other hand, was grateful for my dealings with the Sicilian Mafia. I could never have safely transported large quantities of guns without Conte Cucinotta's support. My "black lemons" had expanded the Mafia's business even further. I had made them more powerful.

I arrived in Sicily in the middle of February and had the privilege of meeting Conte Cucinotta himself. Usually, I would have talked to one of his men. Regardless of how much our cooperation had grown, regardless of how big business had become, and despite him now being an old man, he always asked the same question.

"How is my friend Caporaso? Is he ok?"

"I haven't seen him since the great fire at Fécamp, Conte Cucinotta. If he is alive, he will return to Sicily someday and you will be the first to know."

"He never came back."

"He is a ruined man. At his age, it is hard to start over and, to be honest, I feel sorry for him. I was the cook aboard the Bella Messina for four years."

"Edward, who is in a position to watch all the ports of the Mediterranean Sea and make sure your guns are delivered?"

"You are, Conte."

"No, Edward. I am too old now. It's the fear. It's always the fear." He paused for a while and looked at the familiar naked Greek in the corner of the room, the reason our cooperation had begun. Now, he stood in a corner of his beautiful house.

"I never did that again, you know," he continued.

"Did what?"

"After the Messina, I never asked if anyone was cheating on me." He paused again and then stood up, walked over to the Kouros and continued. "Nowadays we do our research, let them get on with it and after that, no matter what day it is, whether it's night or day, or whether they are asleep or awake, after that, Edward, they are dead."

The old man me scared once again, as you can imagine. I had no idea why he was telling me this.

Was it the unknown fate of Caporaso?

Was it something he had found out about the Messina antique business?

What was it?

Whatever it was, it chilled me to the bone. I almost died of fright.

"So Edward, business is good. Why did you want to see me?" He sat down.

"Yes, Conte Cucinotta, business is good and I'm working hard to expand it even more."

"You are a good salesman."

"Thank you, Conte Cucinotta. I was in the Balkans and now I'm on my way to Paris."

"So you've come out of your way."

"Yes, I wanted to talk to you. I appreciate our cooperation and your help and I wanted to share some information that might help you. For the last ten years, I have travelled throughout Europe, the Mediterranean Sea and North Africa. I come across people, situations, and organisations and lately, I have begun to realise that knowing things in advance is very important.

"The thing is, Conte Cucinotta, the situation in the Balkans is not good. The Christian populations under the Ottoman Empire are at boiling point. Gangs and rebels are rising up. Greece, Serbia, Montenegro and Bulgaria are rapidly promoting their interests."

"That is not something I don't already know, Edward."

"It's not the same as in the past. Soon, there will be a major confrontation."

"So?"

"I am sure the Italian government would be interested to know that."

"Why?"

"The Prussians already have their eyes on colonies in the Ottoman-controlled areas and the Mediterranean Sea. Why shouldn't Italy benefit too, and in advance?"

"You still hate the Prussians, Edward."

"I do."

"Again, I don't understand why you are telling me this."

"I am simply sharing this information in case it helps you and your relationship with the Italian government, Conte Cucinotta."

"Are you aware of Sicily's history, Edward?"

"Some of it."

"The Phoenicians, Greeks, Romans, Arabs, Lombards, Jews and Normands are all our forefathers and have influenced Sicily. The Italian government can't even protect the poor lemon growers. The Italian government needs me, I do not need them."

"It is not a bad thing to need you more, Conte Cucinotta. Fifty years have passed since Italy's unification. It's a good year to try for something better," I said. His eyes sparkled, just like they did on the day I told him about the Mafia's global expansion.

I continued to show off my knowledge of history.

"Garibaldi started out from Sicily and I'm telling you, guns will soon be used here in the Sicilian neighbourhoods. The Italian government is struggling to show who's in charge in the area. Morocco, Algiers and Egypt left long ago. Other Ottoman territories are waiting. I can hear the bells ringing. The Sicilian Vesper is about to start."

"Ah, the war of Sicilian Vespers." He stood up and walked about. "On Easter Monday in 1282, at evening prayers at the Church of the Holy Spirit outside Palermo, a Frenchman, a sergeant by the name of Droue assaulted a married Sicilian woman. Her husband killed him with his knife. When the French soldiers tried to take revenge for their friend, the Sicilian crowd at the church killed them all. They were your people, Edward. This war lasted for twenty years."

"No one should touch another man's woman, Conte Cucinotta. I have a decent amount of money to support you, you know."

"Who do you work for, Edward?"

"Alsace and Lorraine."

We drank the last of the Benedictine I had brought him as a gift, talked the usual talk about our "black lemons" and I was done.

Before I left Sicily, I sent a telegram to my boss.

'Mare Nostrum'

My next destination was Serbia. Not that I needed to do anything there. Hartwig had already made a move, I was certain of that. All I needed to do was evaluate the situation and send a telegram to take the credit.

I left Sicily at the end of February and at the end of March, there was already extensive reference to Libya throughout Italy. In newspapers and nationalist societies, the air of Italy's colonial rights was everywhere.

I have already mentioned the Congress of Berlin in 1878. Italy's claims over Libya dated back to verbal discussions at the time. France and Great Britain had agreed on the occupation of Tunisia and Cyprus respectively, both part of the ailing Ottoman Empire. When Italian diplomats hinted at their government's possible opposition, the French replied that Tripoli would have been a counterpart for Italy. In 1902, Italy and France had signed a secret treaty, which accorded freedom of intervention in Tripolitania and Morocco. The time had come. The invasion was described as little more than a 'military parade'.

I couldn't have been more fortunate. Hartwig was the best man to help with my 'project' without knowing about my secret goal. We had common goals anyway.

"You smoke a lot, Nikolai."

"Not while I'm asleep, though."

"How are things in the neighbourhood?"

"Peaceful."

"The greater area is not so peaceful."

"The Prussians?"

"Damned Prussians. Remember Morocco, Nikolai?"

"Oh yes, what a crisis!"

Here, I made a fatal mistake and was too enthusiastic. Or maybe I just wanted to impress my friend. It was one of those mistakes you regret as soon as they're made.

"I am sure there'll be another similar case soon. I sell guns in Morocco and a rebellion is about to start there, I know."

"There were problems two years ago when the new Sultan took over and Abdulhaziz was cast aside. Nothing happened then so why now?"

Instead of giving a general answer and changing the subject, I elaborated. I was grateful for my friendship with Hartwig and got carried away. He was indeed the best man to help me with my 'project', but I should be more careful.

"Think. Two years ago, Bülow was still in power and all of Europe was talking about Bosnia."

"Aehrenthal's tricks. Correct."

"Now the Kaiser has new men in place and they will obviously want to prove themselves."

"What?"

"Bethmann, the new chancellor and Kiderlen-Wächter, the new head of the Foreign Office will surely seize any opportunity to act and succeed where their predecessors failed."

"You seem pretty sure of that, Edward," said Nikolai with a sarcastic smile.

At that point, I knew I had said enough.

"Hypothetically speaking, of course." An experienced salesman, I changed the subject immediately.

"But as far as the Kaiser is concerned, it's a fact and I know it happened. Six years ago, when the Kaiser visited the Sultan, he took him a gift. A German rifle. When he showed it to him, do you know what happened? The Sultan took cover because he thought he was going to assassinate him."

"The Sultan! The Ottomans almost conquered the whole of Europe two centuries ago, and now this! It's the only thing we can thank Austria for. Twice, they stood firm against the Ottomans. Did you know that the croissant was invented in Austria, Edward? Austrian bakers had heard of the tunnel the Turks were digging and made bread in the shape of a half-moon to celebrate their victory against the Ottomans, whose flag depicted the half-moon."

"I thought croissants were a French invention."

"No."

"But you know why the Ottoman flag bears the star and the crescent, don't you?

"It's the Islamic symbol, isn't it?"

"No, it's the symbol of Hecate an ancient Greek Goddess, who protected the city of Byzantium the Greek colony of Megareis, which was later named Augusta Antonina by the Roman Antonino…"

"…and later Constantinople by Constantine the Great. I do know some history, Edward."

"Ok. The thing is, Hecate became a kind of cult figure in Byzantium from the time it was founded. She originated from Thrace and was considered the patron goddess of Byzantium because she was said to have saved the city from an attack by Philip, the father of Alexander the Great, by the appearance of a bright light in the sky."

I admit I exaggerated a bit to make my friend forget about the Moroccans and the Prussians. But Hartwig was not just an ambassador, you know. He was an extremely clever man and a very experienced diplomat. I thought I had successfully changed the subject but as you will see later, Hartwig was too smart not to have understood about my new crisis in Morocco, the so-called Agadir crisis, which went unbelievably well. He understood my dark role better.

I sent my boss a telegram from Serbia and left for Paris

'Nikolai Hartwig'

When the rebellion began in the middle of April, the Sultan was besieged in his palace in Fez. The French prepared to send troops to help put down the rebellion under the pretext of protecting European lives and property by dispatching a flying column at the end of April. Morocco again.

Once my three areas of focus were complete, I returned to Paris. I needed to rest and have fun. And oh Lord, were there options for that! I made the most of our wonderful cabarets, restaurants, cafés, brasseries, bistros, bouisbouis, caboulots, mannezingues, boussingots, mastroquets, bouchons…

Take that, Bismarck!

We, the French, are very specific when it comes to liquid refreshments, food and indulging in the five senses. A dictionary and a private tour would be handy to understand the small but crucial differences between these establishments. The *Belle Époque* in Paris, after much hard work, was particularly revitalising, especially for a forty-eight-year-old man. Good wine, good food, gorgeous women. June of 1911 was wonderful! I had prepared the ground and expected to reap the benefits in the most beautiful city in the world.

The Champs-Élysées or the Elysian Fields - the place for dead heroes was the best place for living heroes like me. The avenue is almost two kilometres long and connects the Place de la Concorde and the Arc de Triomphe. The Arc had been commissioned by Napoleon after his victory at the Battle of Austerlitz but ironically, it was not finished until Waterloo.

Once, I was walking near the Place de la Concorde and came across some students protesting about Alsace Lorraine. It was the 'Ligue des Jeunes amis de l'Alsace-Lorraine' (League of Young Friends of Alsace-Lorraine), a nationalist student group, founded that very same year. Good customers, I thought.

I was very moved and protested alongside them. I promised to support their effort and offered them all the financial help they needed. It was a generous promise, considering they had three thousand members. I even had a moment of glory by giving a short speech.

"My grandfather died in the Battle of Ligny and I lost my brother in the Battle of Sedan. The wounds of my brother's loss have never healed and seeing you, young men who weren't even born when the damned Prussians stole Alsace and Lorraine, I feel lucky to live in such a great country. In each of you, I see the brother I lost. I see the leaders of tomorrow, who will lead France once again to Napoleonic glory. To a new Austerlitch! A new Jena! Alsace free! Lorraine free! Vive la France!"

I had never felt better than on that day. Honestly!

At the same time, on June 8th, the Spanish army occupied Larache, and three days later, Alcazarquivir.

On June 20th, France agreed to start negotiations. After ten days, they still had not responded. It was then that Kiderlen-Wächter, the new head of the Foreign

Office, asked the Kaiser for permission to send a gunboat to prove himself. Typical of the Prussians!

And just as everything was going to plan, disaster struck and my work, my dreams, my personal Parthenon were ruined.

Apollo had not forgotten.

He didn't forget Pericles and he hadn't forgotten me. Twenty-four years after I stole those statues from his island, my Nemesis had come and now I would have to deal with it.

Democracy! Damned democracy!

Any fool can decide, any ignoramus can vote. How can you leave a country's future in the hands of the average gullible person? Don't parents care about their children's futures, the future of tomorrow's… ignorant citizens?! The ignoramuses of the future?!

Democracy!

On June 27th, Joseph Caillaux was elected the fifty-seventh prime minister of France. He was the leading radical politician and a so-called 'realist', who believed that France and Germany would both benefit if they cooperated. Cooperation with the people that occupied Alsace and Lorraine.

How on earth was this possible?

A classic traitor.

When I heard the news, I couldn't believe it. Now that he had been elected, I was certain a policy of conciliation with the Prussians would follow during the rising crisis in Morocco.

This is why democracy cannot be counted on. It is unpredictable. Sometimes it is helpful like it was with the Perdicaris affair, and sometimes it can ruin your dreams as it did that year at the end of June. I hadn't seen it coming and now it was too late.

Four days after the election of this traitor on July 1st, the German gunboat SMS Panther arrived at the port of Agadir under the pretext of protecting German trade interests. The larger Bremen-class cruiser, the SMS Berlin, arrived days later, replacing the gunboat.

Germany, envious of Theodore Roosevelt, wanted a Perdicaris of her own, and so employed the German civilian Hermann Wilberg, who was sent to Agadir on behalf of the German Foreign Office to provide the pretext for German intervention in Morocco's affairs, which resulted in the Agadir crisis.

However, his journey was delayed and he did not make it in time to be 'rescued' by a German gunboat, when he arrived in Agadir on July 4th 1911, three days after the SMS Panther. He was thus dubbed as the 'Endangered German' for posterity.

The British were worried about the Panther's arrival in Morocco. The Royal Navy had their naval base in Gibraltar, south of Spain. They believed the Germans' intention was to turn Agadir into a naval base in the Atlantic. Britain sent battleships to Morocco in case war broke out. As in the first Moroccan crisis, British support for France demonstrated the strength of the Entente Cordiale.

On July 7th, the German ambassador in Paris informed the French government that Germany had no territorial aspirations in Morocco and would negotiate for a French protectorate based on 'compensation' for Germany in the French Congo region and the safeguarding of her economic interests in Morocco. Caillaux agreed to give the Kaiser a portion of the French

Congo in exchange for a German withdrawal from the port of Agadir. The traitor!

I was furious, angry and distressed and felt betrayed by democracy. Please consider my situation.

The rebellion in Morocco had started in the middle of April. I had successfully used Morocco twice before in 1904 and 1905. The first Moroccan crisis was in 1904, the second in 1905 and the third was underway in Morocco in 1911. This 'Agadir crisis', as you saw, was a combination of my two previous Moroccan jobs - the Perdicaris incident and the first Moroccan crisis. All of my Moroccan jobs took place in the summer, so I decided not to cause another because even a future idiot might suspect something. You don't need to be as clever as Hartwig to realise that someone met with his boss at Christmas, worked on the project over the next few months and brought it to fruition in Morocco in the summer.

Three times over.

That was it. I couldn't use this card again.

And here comes Joseph Caillaux, sent by Apollo to neutralise the ground I had laid. It's a good job I didn't steal more statues from Delos, because the wrath of Apollo would have been even greater, making my attempts in Morocco fade into insignificance, though no bullets had been sold in either instance. The great significance of this crisis was that it was Germany's turn to feel humiliated, after Russia in 1908. The Prussians took some parts of Congo but the Austro-Hungarians would not diplomatically support their ally.

'We can't follow you to Agadir,' said Aehrenthal, politely. As politely as he could.

Please remember this quote. It is crucial. 'We can't follow you to Agadir'. This is how diplomacy works. We can't follow you to this 'miserable and small object'.

One of the reasons the Caillaux pro-German policy made me even angrier was that I hadn't seen it coming. If I'd known, I'd have been more proactive and neutralised him earlier. I had stumbled upon proof that he'd had an intimate affair with a married woman. I should have exposed him before he was elected but was too busy that year. Causing him damage now would have been unnecessary revanchism, and eventually, the unnecessary neutralisation of a valuable tool.

Now, I had to do something radical.

The Place de la Concorde is where executions took place during the French Revolution. King Louis XVI, Queen Marie Antoinette and most importantly, as far as I was concerned, Antoine Lavoisier, the father of modern chemistry and the brain behind the Du Pont industry. Lavoisier was a formative influence in the formation of the Du Pont gunpowder business because he trained Éleuthère Irénée du Pont in the making of gunpowder. Du Pont stated that his gunpowder mills 'would never have been started, but for his kindness to me'.

This gunpowder, as well as Nobel's dynamite, was the core of my merchandise. Guns, bombs and batteries are simply transfer boxes that deliver the powder in variable forms and quantities. I had already sown the seed for the powder in three areas that year but as things turned out, some extra work was needed. It was possibly the most important of all my jobs so far. Additionally, it would prove to my boss that I was working and not relaxing, by capitalising on the successful, but unlucky, third Moroccan crisis, which I had so much hoped to do.

I sent a telegram to my boss. Two words again.

'Mona Lisa'

You are probably wondering what the point of this telegram was.

As already mentioned, I had taken time off in previous years but I never stopped plotting, and a possible event with an Italian woman in Paris had often crossed my mind. Let me explain.

Do you remember the discussion I had with von Bülow and the Prussian elite about Italian women and Prussian men? Please also remember that Baron Victor von Kalchberg had said that they should have taken the ultimate Italian woman - the Mona Lisa - after the Franco-Prussian War. That was a good joke!

Imagine then, that the Prussians not only occupied Alsace-Lorraine but kidnapped the Mona Lisa as well. In that case, revanchism should always be written with a capital R, in my opinion.

Do you agree? And please don't tell me she was Italian! I've already told you the history of Leonardo Da Vinci and King Francis, le Père et Restaurateur des Lettres.

Furthermore, after eight years of selling the Benedictine liqueur, which, as we all know, King Francis so enthusiastically approved, I felt a certain connection with this painting. I don't know why. It nourished my soul. My dream. My goal.

The Prussians didn't take the Mona Lisa while they had the chance, but it's never too late.

Do you understand what I mean?

You are probably asking yourself why on earth I would risk my pride, my job and my whole life to add one more spark and kindle a war.

Now that years have passed, I would agree with you, but that summer, I felt unbeatable. The election of

Caillaux had angered me and I was certain if the French discovered that the damned Prussians had stolen the Mona Lisa, just as we were about to hand over Congo, a short, sharp war over Alsace-Lorraine would be justified. The Russians would support us from the east and the English would support us with their Royal Navy. Hartwig would seize the opportunity and keep the Austro-Hungarians busy in the Balkans, and Aehrenthal would tell the Prussians they were unable to follow them because of the Mona Lisa. I thought the war should last less than thirty-eight minutes, breaking the record of the Anglo-Zanzibar War.

I was doing my job while serving my country. I was blessed.

Another important point is that I didn't feel I was taking a risk. Some months before, the director of the Louvre, Theophile Homolle, had proudly stated that the Mona Lisa couldn't be stolen from the Louvre.

I spent a lot of time inside the Louvre and noticed that the guards were asleep most of the time. Actually, they were old men; retired policemen just biding their time. At the same time, workers in uniforms carried paintings to the labs, for conservation, I assume. At the time, the Mona Lisa hung on a wall in a room called the *Salon Carré* with other paintings. Hung, that was it. I checked one day while I was there alone.

All I had to do was observe the movements inside the museum. My only concern was the painters who made copies of the Mona Lisa, but I could handle that. I just needed to choose the right time of day.

And one more thing.

Who is the director of the Louvre once again?

Theophile Homolle, the man who directed the excavation at Delos before I set foot on the island, twenty-four years before.

After what Apollo did to me I have the right to strike back. This was meant to be.

Stealing the Mona Lisa was not the extraordinary, breath-taking event, the stuff of which movies are made, as you will see.

On Sunday, August 20th, just before the museum closed, I walked down the nearest service staircase, hung up my overcoat and put on one of the white smocks the museum employees usually wore. I slowly walked to the room where the painting was hanging and carefully lifted it off the four iron pegs that secured it to the wall. I even asked the guard to help me and he was more than willing to do so. I thanked him and he greeted me as his shift had come to an end.

I went down the service staircase, took off the uniform, removed the protective case and frame, - as Mr Elazar had done with his painting of the month - attached it to my body and hid it under my overcoat. Then, I made my way out with the last of the Sunday visitors. Unusually, I was wearing an overcoat in August but an overcoat is always useful, as we learned from the brave Prussian General Blücher. Damned Prussians!

The next day on August 21st, the museum was closed. When it opened again on Tuesday, August 22nd, no one noticed a thing, to begin with. At around eleven o'clock, Louis Béroud, a painter who made copies of the Mona Lisa for sale, came to the Louvre to sketch the 'Mona Lisa au Louvre', which is exactly what it was. The Mona Lisa had hung in *Salon Carré* with the other two paintings but instead of the famous La Joconde, he found four iron pegs.

Béroud contacted the section head of the guards, who assumed the painting was being photographed for marketing purposes. A few hours later, Béroud checked with the head of the museum, and it was confirmed that the Mona Lisa was not in the hands of the photographers. At midday, we - the French - froze when we heard that the Mona Lisa had been stolen. Theophile Homolle was forced to relinquish his position.

The greatest art theft of the century thus came about. My part in the theft, however, was not nearly as impressive as the action of the police that followed. That was indeed a unique piece of work. A once in a lifetime job that would never be repeated.

The mastermind behind it was the one and only Louis Jean-Baptiste Lépine, the Préfet de Police. In the past, through wise diplomacy and carefully organised policing, he had managed to avoid the worst of the consequences of the Dreyfus Affair.

Lépine acted with his usual decisiveness, ordering the museum to be closed for a week whilst forensic analysis was carried out. The country's borders were also closed. Lépine had no idea, of course, that the reason I had stolen it was to blame the Prussians and start a war. He probably thought some crazy rich collector had stolen it, or a thief who planned to sell it. Anything was possible, but he was a man of measure and he certainly measured up.

Should I have been worried because the guard had seen me and even helped me take the Mona Lisa? I wasn't because I knew he would take this secret to the grave otherwise the whole of France or the whole world would tear him apart. It's as simple as that.

The impact of the theft was quite astonishing. Millions of people saw the image of the Mona Lisa for the first time in newspapers and magazines. For the first time, queues formed outside the Louvre to see the empty space where the painting had hung. The historical four pegs.

On September 7th, some progress was made. Police arrested and jailed the French poet and art critic Guillaume Apollinaire on suspicion of aiding the theft of the Mona Lisa and several statuettes from the Louvre.

When Apollinaire was questioned in custody, he was compelled to reveal the link to his friend Pablo Picasso, which led to Picasso being questioned. The two were interrogated separately. Picasso was so afraid, especially of being deported to Spain, that he denied ever having seen Apollinaire, who at the time was his closest friend. In fact, it was he who had introduced Apollinaire to his partner, Marie Laurencin in 1907.

Indeed, they were guilty of stealing art from the Louvre. Ancient Iberian statue heads stolen from the Louvre in 1907 by Apollinaire's secretary, almost certainly commissioned by Picasso himself, who may also have assisted in the theft, were found hidden in Picasso's dresser. He used the statue heads as models for a painting at the time. He called it 'Les Demoiselles d'Avignon'.

Picasso was set free the same day but Appolinaire was held for a week and became very depressed. He was devastated by the whole affair and the way he had been treated.

While we're here, I should also tell you that a large proportion of Parisiens believed the thief was a rich American collector, and another large proportion believed that the Germans were responsible and did it to ridicule the French. The second group was much closer to the truth - my truth - and it was my mission to reveal this truth when the timing was right, but for the moment, I hung the Mona Lisa in my apartment in Paris, had a glass of Benedictine and waited for the fuss to die down. I knew it would cause a great upheaval - that's why I did it - but it surpassed all my expectations.

As I was about to move on to implicating the Prussians in the theft of the Mona Lisa, a stiletto changed my plans. Unexpectedly, the 'Mare Nostrum' affair was the first to bear bullets… Sorry I mean, fruit.

Conte Cucinotta had acted swiftly.

The Italian government was initially hesitant but in the summer, the preparations for the invasion were finally carried out and Prime Minister Giovanni Giolitti began to probe the other European major powers about their reactions to a possible invasion of Libya.

An ultimatum was presented to the Ottoman government on the night of September 26th. The Ottomans, through Austrian intermediation, replied with the proposal of handing over control of Libya without warring, maintaining a merely formal Ottoman suzerainty. This suggestion was comparable to the situation in Egypt, which was under formal Ottoman suzerainty but was actually controlled by the United Kingdom. Giolitti refused, and war was declared on September 29th, 1911. The Italian stiletto policy was a fact.

On October 15th, nine Italian aeroplanes and eleven pilots landed in Libya. On October 24th, the Italian pilot Captain Riccardo Moizo carried out a reconnaissance flight in Tripolitania, reportedly the first-ever strategic reconnaissance by aeroplane. On November 1st, another Italian pilot, Gavotti, dropped four 1.5 kg bombs on Ain Zara, pulling the pins with his teeth. This was the first aerial bombing in history. A new era had begun. On November 5th, Italy declared its suzerainty over the whole of Ottoman Libya.

The first bombing in history had taken place and Hartwig was making preparations in the Balkans.

"Congratulations, Edward! It's unbelievable what you have achieved in one year. You are the Da Vinci of war."

"What are you implying, boss?" I said, smiling with pride.

"Hahaha! Edward! 1911 was your best year ever. You are amazing!"

"Thank you, boss."

"Your third Morocco project was a marvellous success. The Italians are unstoppable and the Mona Lisa is still missing?"

"If it weren't for the Italian stiletto, the Mona Lisa would have been found…"

"Where?"

"… in Prussian hands."

"The Prussians stole it to humiliate the French, you mean?"

"Exactly."

"So how are you going to proceed?"

"Not how, boss, but when. The timing is crucial."

"You know better. I trust you, Edward."

"Thank you, boss."

"I hear that Balkans are at boiling point. Your Hartwig is quite a man."

"He's the real boss of the Balkans."

"You already knew him, didn't you?"

"From the time I sold Benedictine."

"What's his secret?"

"What do you mean, boss?"

"Everybody has a secret. What's his?"

"Hartwig is a remarkable man, boss. If he were foreign minister instead of Izvolsky, there wouldn't be a Bosnian crisis for the Austro-Hungarians to deal with. And he did not become foreign minister because Stolypin gave the position to Sazonov, his son-in-law."

Piotr Stolypin, the prime minister of Russia, was assassinated on September 14th, seven days after Picasso was arrested. The day Apollinaire was released. Just for the record.

"Come now, Edward. The ambassador is acting as if he's the Czar. He must have a secret."

I shouldn't have answered the question but I couldn't resist giving him an honest answer. He could have been trying to find out if I wanted to take credit for my friend's work. I couldn't believe he would do such a thing after a year of European disruption caused by me. Anyway, he was the boss.

"His wife is extremely well connected in Russia."

"Aha, I knew it. I knew it! You are next to the right person, Edward."

"That's true, boss. The only reason a war in the Balkans has not started is that he has to synchronize four states - Serbia, Bulgaria, Greece and Montenegro. Otherwise, the Italians would come second."

"You can't be sure. Maybe it's because I still have orders to deliver. I should congratulate you separately for

Italy. You arrived there in February, and in March, all the newspapers were talking about Libya."

"Just doing my job, boss."

"So what does this year have to offer, Edward?"

"Once the Balkans get involved, the big players will get involved too."

"So I believe."

"I have one question though, boss."

"After a month or two of their involvement, peace will prevail and I'll be out of a job."

"Edward, tomorrow you will be paid five times more than you expected."

"Good," I said, knowing I deserved it.

"You deserve it. And if the big guns come into play, you will be able to retire with a billion francs in your bank account in Zurich."

"A billion?"

"Come now, if you find the Mona Lisa, you'll get fifty thousand francs."

I loved the way the boss said 'retire'. I'll make sure I retire for good.

"Please give this to Mr Nizetas, Mr Nikon Nizetas. He'll pass by later to pick it up. Thank you."

He hadn't seen me sitting at the table in the reception of the Klomser Hotel, so I had the opportunity to play games with him. I put on a rough Greek accent and started talking loudly.

"You have me waiting here for three hours, Mr Hartwig. Nobody has ever done that to Nikon Nizetas before. We the Greeks gave you civilisation. Where is my envelope? I am Niko Nizet…"

Nikolai swiftly put his hand over my mouth without laughing and rushed me to the door. He clearly did not like my joke.

"Sorry, my friend, I was just happy to see you and wanted to make you laugh. What's the matter, my Greek accent wasn't good enough?"

"I suffer from insomnia and my head is still pounding. Let's go somewhere for a strong coffee and smoke a cigarette. We are in the most beautiful city in the world, Edward!"

"After Paris, you mean."

"No! However much I hate Austrians, I must confess that Vienna is the most beautiful city in the world, with the most beautiful women, the most beautiful buildings and the best cafés. Let's walk for a while.

"How are the preparations, going?"

"You already know, so why do you ask? Tankosic told me you were there in March."

"You knew?"

"I know everything."

"He is very strict about selection. Out of two thousand candidates, he has chosen only two hundred and forty-five volunteers. I think you need the numbers."

"No, with the new weapons you are selling, we need good men. Numbers are not as relevant anymore."

"You know better."

"You want more men to sell more guns, Edward?"

"It's my job."

We walked quite a distance until we came to the Vienna State Opera House. There, I saw the young painter who had impressed Conrad with his bright eyes four years before. He was so focused on his painting that he jumped when I attempted to speak the German language.

"Hello, young man. How are you?"

"Well sir, thank you," he said. He did not recognise me.

"I have good news for you, young man. The Eiffel tower is still there, still waiting for you."

"Ah, I remember you. The Frenchman with the general. It was four years ago. I haven't been to Paris yet but I will make it, someday. I would very much like to paint it. You speak German?"

"A little. This is my good friend Hartwig. He is from Russia."

Hartwig nodded his head.

"Russia? That's a big country! A lot of space!"

"But very cold, young man. You wouldn't like it," said Nikolai flatly.

"What are you painting?" I leaned over his easel. "Of course! The Opera house! What a wonderful painting. Just like a picture. So many details. Did you study painting?"

"No sir, I was rejected by the school of fine arts. They said I should focus on architectural design, but I am an artist," said the young painter with much distress.

"I don't believe it! I would like to buy this painting, young man. When will you have it ready?"

"By the end of next week, sir."

"Do you paint portraits?"

"The truth is, I'm not very good with people."

"Ok, I 'll pick it up next week, then."

"You know what, sir? I'll do something for you. I'll paint you and your friend walking in front of the Opera House, ok? You'll see yourselves every time you look at the painting."

"Lovely idea!"

"What a wonderful idea!"

"But be careful young man, if you paint me as fat

… and another large proportion believed that the Germans were responsible and did it to ridicule the French.

as I am, I will hunt you down and make you pay for it," said Hartwig, bluffing seriously.

"What's your name?" I said to lighten the atmosphere.

"Adolf, sir."

We left the young painter after I'd paid him a deposit and continued our walk.

"Nikolai, why were you so cruel to the young painter?"

"I wouldn't give this man a single franc."

"But he is a good painter."

"A photograph would do a better job. I didn't like his style."

"At least he makes his living in a nice way."

"Edward, you are a good salesman but as a diplomat, you would share Izvolsky's fate. You honestly cannot see that the young man was an imposter?"

"How could you tell?"

"I could see it in his eyes. I know. He had exactly the same look as the late Aehrenthal. He could even be his younger brother."

"Aehrenthal is dead?"

"Yes, Alois Lexa von Aehrenthal died suddenly last month. On Saturday, February 17th."

"Really? What did he die of?"

"Leukaemia, I think."

"How old was he?"

"Fifty-seven."

"He was undeniably a great diplomat, we have to agree."

"I think not, and not because I am Russian."

"Why then?"

"Because Edward, my friend, his 'diplomatic victory' in 1909 was the reason I was brought out of exile, the reason that in a few months' time, four countries will shoo the Ottomans from the Balkans before Austro-Hungary 'diplomatically' makes its way to the Aegean Sea."

"But no one knows what will happen. Who will take his place?"

"Leopold Berchtold."

"Are you sure?"

"I'm positive. Maybe I knew before Franz Joseph."

"I know that man."

"How do you know him?"

"He collects antiquities. And many years ago, I used to sell antiquities."

"Ok, I'm paying for your coffee."

"Come now, Nikolai."

"You are my most valuable friend right now, Edward."

"Do you believe a great war will spread over Europe because of the Balkans? Bismarck said that…" I seized the opportunity to find out if he also believed the coming war in the Balkans would start a great war, as my boss did.

"I know what Bismarck said about some damned foolish thing in the Balkans that would start a great European War. He said it a year before he died. He also predicted the timing."

"Really?"

"What did he say?" I acted as if I didn't know.

"Come now, you are French, he was Prussian," said my friend teasingly.

"Please tell me."

" 'Jena came twenty years after the death of Frederick the Great. The confrontation will come twenty years after my departure if things go on like this.' "

"Bismarck resigned in 1890, didn't he?"

"Wilhelm stood him down him on March 18th that year."

"So we have a gap of two years, Nikolai. That was in 1910 and now it is 1912. My only explanation is Joseph Caillaux."

"Your prime minister?"

"Our traitor-six-month-ex-prime-minister, you mean. In January, he and all his ministers were was forced to resign."

"I heard about it."

"The bastard! He had secretly negotiated with Germany without the knowledge of the president."

"Remind me of the name of your president?"

"Armand Fallières."

"Democracies!" Nikolai nodded his head, disapproving of the best failed political system to date.

"Last October he married his second wife, you know."

"Armand Fallières?"

"No! The traitor. Joseph Caillaux. The one who gave the Kaiser a large portion of the French Congo, as if Alsace and Lorraine were not enough."

"The Balkans are upon us now. Twenty years have passed. The war will begin, Edward, just as Bismarck said. We'll march from here and you'll march from Alsace-Lorraine and we'll meet in Vienna."

"Berlin! A new Jena is upon us! Marshal Davout's single corps defeated the Prussian main army in Jena you know, Nikolai and…"

"Now you're talking."

Whenever I talked to Hartwig, I became a little wiser. This time, however, it was a revelation. Now I understood why my boss was so sure the Great War was upon us. It was… Bismarck.

I was certain that without my intervention, the war would have started in 1910 after the assassination of Kaiser Franz Joseph. After my return to business, it should have started in 1911 but thanks to democracy, it would be after that. The Balkans were encouraged by the Italians, who were encouraged by me and my third Moroccan crisis. What took place in Morocco was undeniably damned and foolish. We, the French, persuaded the Sultan to ask for help three weeks after we had been there… helping. The German Perdicaris rushed like mad and arrived three days later than planned to be 'rescued'. Damned and foolish indeed!

'But not in the Balkans. Not in the Balkans!' I hear Bismarck sarcastically saying.

I must admit, however, what Hartwig had said about the Bosnian crisis and the dark Aehrenthal role also helped. Thank God, Franz Ferdinand, the heir to the Austro-Hungarian Empire, was there to stop Conrad!

Believe it or not, Gina had got a divorce and was now with him. He wrote her a letter every day but still, he couldn't marry her because the emperor wouldn't allow such a marriage. It would be foolish.

If the Bosnian crisis was the cause of the war, Bismarck was right once again. My services would not have been needed and I wouldn't have made so much money over the last few years. It seemed that Bismarck was always right. Damned Prussians!

I looked for the young artist to pick up my painting at the end of the following week but, much to my disappointment, I didn't find him. Conrad was wrong and Hartwig was right. Hartwig was right again.

But all was not lost. I drank my liqueur and stared at the Mona Lisa in my Paris apartment. I planned to return it to the museum once the war started but needed a glamorous way to do so. And maybe earn the fifty thousand francs, too. Until then, I kept my cards close to my chest. You never know what might happen.

In the summer of 1912, Italy commenced operations against Turkish possession in the Aegean Sea after approval from the powers that wanted to end a war that had gone on for much longer than it should have. Italy occupied twelve islands in the Aegean - the so-called Dodecanese - and the Austro-Hungarians finally realised that this could fuel the ambitions of the Balkan nations, causing unbalance in the already fragile Balkans.

Indeed, the Balkan war began in October. Well done, Hartwig!

Everything went to plan and the war came about but without the expected interference of the big players. Had something gone wrong with the formula?

What had Bismarck missed?

'Not damned foolish enough, my friend!' I hear Bismarck sneering.

The Balkan wars were creating a new crisis in Europe and the great powers became involved, threatening and bluffing once again.

Russia mobilised to show the Austro-Hungarians that this time, no Aehrenthal nonsense would be accepted.

As usual, I met my boss before Christmas in Zurich. I always enjoyed our meetings at the Savoy Hotel. We talked for almost two hours about current events, the new Balkan situation and how good business had been. Finally, we came to the purpose main of the meeting.

"Edward, I was wrong."

"In what way?"

"I thought the Balkan war would cause a great war."

"The Balkan wars are still in progress. Wait and see, boss."

"No, Edward. I know. They will go to conference. It's over. The spoils are good and they'll soon find a solution. England will arrange it. The ambassadors of the great powers will meet in London. Representatives of the Balkan nations will also be present. They'll have a good time."

"What about the Prussians?"

"They will cooperate with Britain to bring the crisis to an end. Wilhelm's new hobby is archaeology. He spends his time in Corfu and the heir, Franz Ferdinand, is clearly against war. He dreams of unifying the states of Austria-Hungary and magnetising the neighbouring states. Very dangerous for our business. If he succeeds, even the Bavarians will join him as Wilhelm's naval expenses are driving them mad and the Persians are nowhere near."

"Are you afraid of the Fashoda effect, boss?" He looked desperate.

"The Fashoda effect, Franz Ferdinand's plans and more, a lot more than that. Believe me, our business has never been in greater danger."

"How is that possible? Tell me, boss."

"There is a man," he paused, obviously concerned, "from the other side of the Atlantic… an American." He paused even longer.

"…and?"

"We'd better watch out for him. No one knows anything. He is very clever. He hasn't told anyone about his plan." He paused again.

"Anything about what?"

"Well, there are the Pacifists - Jean Jaurès, Suttner, Carnegie and the Carnegie Organization and all that. You know about them. We know about them. I'll come back to them later." He paused again.

"I don't know Suttner."

"She is a writer and was awarded the Nobel Peace Prize in 1905."

"Big money!"

"She's the person who persuaded Mr Nobel to establish the peace prize in the first place."

"Clever money!"

"This American is more dangerous than all of them put together."

"More dangerous?"

"As far as our market is concerned. He could knock us out of business."

"How? …but why?"

"He thinks a war will not be good for business and the world…"

"We must be the only business that disagrees with him."

"Unfortunately!"

"And what can he do about it? What is he going to do?"

"He's coming to Europe to 'persuade' the kings of Europe to agree to ever-lasting peace and understanding, I suppose. We don't know the details.

"We do know, however, that he is capable of anything. He can persuade anyone to play his game. He has done it in the past. Once he sits down with the kings, he will work his magic and peace and stability will spread throughout Europe."

"Come now, boss, we're in the middle of a war in the Balkans, and this man will bring peace and stability to Europe? You must be exaggerating!"

"I told you, Edward, the Balkans will not give us our great war. Forget it. And our long-term future is coming to an end because of this damned American."

I have to admit I had never seen my boss like that before. What kind of a man was this super American? Probably a man who would steal the Mona Lisa and keep it in his basement to admire it alone while drinking whisky and smoking a big cigar.

"Boss, even if he is capable of such a thing, I'm sure that if he talked to the Kaiser today, the Kaiser would think he'd been sent by the British to stop him improving his navy. If he were to talk to the Czar, the Czar would think that the Kaiser had sent him because he had started to fear. If…"

"We know that and he knows that."

"So?"

"This businessman from across the Atlantic specialises in gathering parties together and persuading them to cooperate."

"And how would he do that?"

"This year, on May 24th, the Kaiser's daughter is getting married. All the kings of Europe will be there. Cousins, uncles, sons and daughters. Only dead kings will not be present. The last time they gathered like that was at the funeral of King Edward in 1910."

And because of me, he was the only king who died that year. Natural causes.

"If this American is present at the wedding, we are out of business, Edward."

"And you want me to arrange for the American not to be there?"

"Or cancel the Kaiser's daughter's wedding," said my boss.

Many questions were still unanswered but I realised any doubts I had about this American's capabilities were of no use.

"Ok boss, just one more thing. It's probably too late, but I think I could arrange for the *Great War* to come out of the Balkan War, even now."

"I don't think that's possible any more, Edward."

"I'll give it a shot and if it doesn't work, I won't spend any more time on it."

"And how will you do that?"

"That's what I said, I'll give it a shot."

"Ok, but give me one more clue."

"Hans Christian Andersen."

"The fairy tale writer from Denmark?"

"Yes! Now, this dangerous American. What's his name, boss?"

As usual, Mr Bronstein was sitting alone, reading and writing notes. Last September, he had been sent to the Balkans by the Kiev newspaper 'Kievskaya Misl' as a war correspondent to cover the Balkan Wars in Serbia, Bulgaria and Romania.

I ordered a coffee and began to contemplate my challenges for the coming year. At some stage, a short man of about thirty entered the cafe. He was thin with pitted, greyish-brown skin. His peasant's moustache was quite characteristic and he carried a plain, wooden suitcase. He was looking for something or someone and seemed to have found it when he saw Mr Bronstein. He approached him slowly and greeted him but there was no indication of friendliness in his eyes for the loyal customer of the *Central Café*.

He introduced himself as Koba and sat down, putting his suitcase on the floor next to him. His Russian accent was exactly like my friend Hartwig's thick Georgian accent. He took out his passport and showed it to Mr Bronstein, who read out his name.

"Sta-vros Pa-pa-do-pou-los?"

"It's a Greek name," said the newcomer.

The Russian was using a Greek name as a cover. Stavros Papadopoulos.

At this point, two young men in their twenties entered the cafe. One of them stumbled on Koba's wooden suitcase.

"Hey, what's all this? Why did you leave your suitcase there, are you trying to kill me?" said the man looking at Koba, who remained silent.

"Come on, Josip, let's go. You aren't hurt, we are ok," said the man's friend.

Josip persisted. "Get that suitcase out of the way or you'll kill someone."

Mr Bronstein intervened to prevent a fight.

"Stavros, pass me the suitcase, please!" Koba took it and passed it over the table. "Be careful, you don't want to kill me too!" he continued.

Josip looked angrily at Koba, who remained silent while staring into Josip's eyes. He was unwilling to apologise.

"Hey, Tito, come on, you're keeping us waiting." A group of union members were waiting in a corner of the *Central Café*. "Come on, we have work to do. Let's go!" said his friend, grabbing him by the arm.

"Watch it Sta… whatever your name is, just watch it!" Josip left to join his companions.

The two Russians were now alone and could continue conspiring in Russian. It was like listening to my friend Hartwig. The man with the suitcase was Georgian but that was of no interest to me. I needed to focus on the American that had scared my boss to death with his capabilities and secret plans for global peace.

The man admired Napoleon even more than I did. He was enthralled by his victories over the kings, his strategic thinking, the Napoleonic Code and the like. He even owned Napoleon's watch. Not a copy, but the original Napoleon had worn. He probably paid a lot of money for it, too.

I like this man already. How could I possibly do him harm?

I have a painting from Napoleon's bedroom so we have something in common, at least.

Maybe I could give him the Mona Lisa because Napoleon had kept it in his bedroom. In return, I could ask him to go back to America and leave us alone.

He also owned one of Leonardo Da Vinci's notebooks and a five-page letter that belonged to George Washington. Judging by his collection, he had a mission in life. How could you not admire such a man?

He drinks a lot and smokes big cigars and the breakfast he eats would probably kill a horse. With habits like these, it would be a miracle if he reached the age of seventy.

They say that when you look into his eyes, it's like watching the headlights of an oncoming train. He is 1,88 meters tall, by the way.

I'm two centimetres taller and I got the Mona Lisa for free, Mr American Emperor!

There was no way I was going to touch this man. I had persuaded Bogdan not to kill Franz Joseph by mentioning the emperor's age. Now I needed to prevent this American Napoleon from attending the wedding or to cancel the wedding of the Kaiser's daughter.

Who is she marrying, by the way?

Ernest Augustus, Duke of Brunswick, the heir to the Kingdom of Hanover, which had been annexed by the Kingdom of Prussia following the 1866 Unification War.

Please notice my use of the correct name for the damned occasion.

Their engagement would take place in Karlsruhe on February 11th.

Do I have time?

On my way out of the *Central Café,* I saw Adolf, the young painter, with a friend. They were talking about the mayor of Vienna...

"Hello, Adolf!"

"Hello, Mr Frenchman! You didn't show up and I sold it to someone else," he said, smiling.

"Oh really?" *The liar!* "Have you been to Paris to paint the Eiffel tower yet?"

"No, not yet, but soon."

"I'll pay you in advance for the painting!"

"Haha! Don't worry, I'll paint you the picture I promised. In two weeks," he said. He took a seat at the table I had vacated next to the Russians and opposite Bronstein and Koba or Sta… or whatever his name was.

I arrived in Salonika at the beginning of February. They were very difficult times for the city. I wasn't going to be spending time and resources on that effort, so I went to the port of Salonika, where I found my old friend Alexá drinking in a tavern.

He was in a very poor state.

I told him I'd thought about what he'd said when we met in Athens in 1896, that many years later, I had seen come true. He was right and I was beginning to embrace his ideas. I even told him I was a member of an organisation based in Germany dedicated to change in Europe. We were currently planning assassinations, bombings and coup d'états across the continent to get rid of the kings and create a new order. A new reality.

He was stunned by the amount of information I gave him. I could tell he knew nothing but was very excited. Finishing up, I asked him the classic question to give an illusion of freedom.

"Do you want to be part of our organisation?"

He accepted, of course, and I imagined he would do the job I had in mind for him without any hesitation. When I showed him the gun, however, he was very scared.

I tried all the usual stuff about courage, guts and honour but he was too afraid to follow his ideas.

"The Cretan police are all over the city. They are extremely tough and I'm not joking."

It was true. Greek prime minister Venizelos ordered Cretan Gendarmerie units to be sent to the city having foreseen the problems with law and order that would arise after the liberation of the city and knowing the Bulgarians and probably the Austrians, would seek to promote a picture of chaos. The Greek state was incapable of imposing order. Once the Greek army arrived in Salonika, a one hundred-and- fifty-strong Cretan police force was sent to the city. As soon as they disembarked, a wave of discipline, law and order came over the city. Soon, the entire body of the Cretan police force followed. Forty-five officers, fifty senior non-commissioned officers, and 1.371 junior non-commissioned officers and constables serving in the Cretan Gendarmerie.

Until then, Salonika was a multinational city comprised of Greeks, Jews, Turks and some Slavs. The populations of the suburbs and rural areas surrounding the city were Greek, however.

In the city centre, the Jewish community was the largest. When Mr Elazar's ancestors were driven out of Spain, a large proportion of them arrived at this port. Much of Mr Elazar's correspondence was to and from Thessaloniki. To begin with, and for commercial reasons, the Jews would have preferred an Austrian administration or the internationalisation of Salonika, which was practically the same as the Austrian solution. So at first, they followed the orders of the Austrian ambassador, who refused to offer buildings to the Greek army but gave many of their buildings to the Bulgarians. Soon, they changed their minds.

Now you know why I thought I could still bring about a bigger war. The Austrians annexed Bosnia in 1908 and went to a lot of trouble with Novi Pazar to be closer to the port. Now the Aehrenthal effort - dirty or not - was buried for good, unless…

The population of the city had almost doubled due to the war. Also present were the Greek army, the Bulgarian army, gangs of Komitadji-Bulgarian irregulars, and the crews of British, Russian, Austrian and French warships in Salonika to protect their citizens. Their own private Perdicarises.

How could I forget my first 'job'? My first Moroccan crisis.

There were also the Turkish troops, who, according to the treaty, had freedom of movement. The Turkish Gendarmerie and police were also there, and according to the treaty were not disarmed. Also present were a large number of Turkish armed deserters, who wandered the streets begging for food and money. Finally, there were Muslim refugees, who had gathered in the city as a result of Bulgarian atrocities against the unarmed population. They wanted to make it look like a city of anarchy or appear that they were in control. The unarmed population assembled in cemeteries and on squares creating unacceptable conditions of hygiene and the immediate risk of the spread of epidemics throughout the city.

When I arrived, the chaos was obvious but under control. In a short period of time, Salonika was fortunate to witness peace and order. The presence of the Cretan Gendarmerie patrol always drew the attention of the crowd.

Alexandros was right. With these men in the field, the job would be difficult to carry out so I decided to leave. Just before, I thought I would give it one more try, as promised to my boss.

"Alexandros, I have to leave to organise other regions now. I will leave you the gun and two hundred German marks." I took out the cash and watched my old friend's eyes light up. It was an encouraging sign so I continued. "If you do what we ask of you, you will be paid five thousand German marks and I will take you to Vienna as my assistant."

"Who do you want me to kill?"

This is where Hans Christian Andersen enters the scene.

As previously mentioned, while at the Olympic Games in Athens, I had much in common with King George I. He was a prince of Denmark and became King of Greece in the same year his father fought the Prussians. He was not far ahead of the Germans, unlike his son Konstantinos, who studied at the Prussian War Academy in Berlin and married Sophia, Wilhelm's sister.

The Kaiser's sister was the wife of King Christian IX. Yes indeed. Sophia was also the granddaughter of Queen Elizabeth but that was quite common within the royal circles of Europe so it doesn't count. In the world of science, they say 'all things being equal'.

The Germans had all the right motives to kill King George and have a more favourable king in Greece, the country with the important port of Salonika. It was from here that my guns were distributed to the Balkan

Peninsula. Furthermore, Wilhelm could show his personal friend the Sultan that he was helping in any way he could.

I assumed once that had happened, King George's younger sisters would be angry. As you already know, one of them was the mother of Great Britain's king, and the other, the mother of the Czar. If you remember their names, I admire you. Alexandra was the mother of Great Britain's king and Maria the mother of the Czar.

Young George, Maria and Alexandra grew up listening to the wonderful stories of Hans Christian Andersen, the greatest storyteller in the world. Now if young George was dead because of the Germans, I assume that mothers would be upset about their king's sons, George V and Nikolai III. These two kings were identical, by the way. The new King Konstantinos was also a cousin of the Czar and the British King but they were both also cousins of the Kaiser. 'All things equal' was deeply integrated into the Belle Epoch.

Imagine the combination of the Prussians killing King George, stealing the Mona Lisa and at the same time, their allies, the Austrians, supporting the chaos and the Bulgarians in the Greek city of Salonika. How would a conference move things on, I wondered.

"You want me to kill the king?"

"I want you to kill the 'enemy' of the people. The crown that gives commands, kings who are unfair. You will set an example for those who are suffering and those who do nothing to improve their social circumstances.

"The main thing is to shoot and run. Even if you miss, don't fire a second shot. Just run and hide. I will arrive by ship to collect you. First, we will go to Paris and then Vienna. You will be a rich man, Alexandros. It will be like America, but much better. If you are caught, don't panic, I will rescue you. But don't mention me to anyone, in the name of our old friendship, ok?

"Ok."

At the end of February, I left for Rome.

Cancelling the Kaiser's daughter's wedding was somewhat difficult so I decided instead to neutralise the super-American who wanted to maintain peace by manipulating kings, just like Napoleon.

Once I'd found out a bit more about him, I was certain of the danger our sector of the market faced. There was no doubt about it. I was also certain that my boss had unsuccessfully tried to 'neutralise' him already and now was my chance to prove to him what I was capable of once again.

This American Napoleon had already succeeded twice in doing what he was planning to do in Europe at the Kaiser's daughter's wedding.

The first time was in 1882 when the competition between two major railway companies would destroy the promising market of the American economy.

Exactly!

It was like the naval competition between the Germans and the British, like the arms competition between the Germans and the Russians, like the Balkan competition between the Russians and the Austro-Hungarians, and most of all, like Alsace-Lorraine…

No! Alsace-Lorraine was not a competition; it was an illegal occupation by the damned Germans! But the others could have destroyed the promising markets of wellbeing, technology, the Belle Epoque and everything else.

In 1882, the Pennsylvania Railroad company competed against the New York Central Railroad company. Both were trying to dominate the same areas and as a result, their profit margins dropped dramatically. Investors were running away.

To get a better idea of the situation, it's worth knowing that $1.5 billion had been invested in American railways by British investors, and as a result of this crazy railroad war, investors were pulling money out of the market at a rate of twenty-five million a year. Please remember that the railway business accounted for two-thirds of all publicly traded companies. A lot of money was at stake and after the bankruptcy of a powerful railway company, it was obvious that the collapse of the infant American economy would follow by domino effect.

Clearly, a solution needed to be found before the catastrophe developed but George B. Roberts, the president of Pennsylvania Railroads, and Chauncey Depew, the president of New York Central Railroad, were determined to keep up their rivalry to the end, no matter what. It is easy to understand why they both were so stubborn. Each was confident in their company's superior strategy, strength, and ability to adapt in this super-competitive environment, and were destined to dominate competitors, and so on…

This list could go on forever inspired by Darwin's theory of evolution and the stupidity of mankind, whereby humans adapt to social, economic, political, business and any other sector where competition exists. As if civilisation, art, love and creativity have nothing to do with the human soul. Just as kings and rulers are confident in their army's superior strategy, strength, and ability to adapt in a super-competitive environment, and are destined to dominate competitors, and so on…

You get the point.

Times were hard and investors in the know were deeply worried. If the situation didn't change soon, a disaster could happen and even those who weren't worried would face the consequences. Material suppliers, ordinary workers, small business owners, unsuspicious housewives, kids with unemployed fathers, and every human being not brought up with catastrophe and disaster like I was.

It was time for the American Napoleon to step in. And he did. His main objection was to protect his credibility with the British investors who had trusted him by investing in American railways and New York Central Railroads in particular.

In the summer of 1885, John Pierpont Morgan invited the two railway presidents on a cruise along the Hudson River aboard the unique *Corsair*, a luxurious yacht built by Marvel of Newburg and at 185 feet, it was one of the largest yachts constructed in America. It could be propelled by steam or sail and even boasted a fireplace in its luxurious interior salons.

Morgan invited them as guests, offering a beautiful and distraction-free environment where they could negotiate and reach an agreement to end this cruel and destructive competition. He neglected to inform them, however, that the *Corsair* would continue cruising until an agreement was reached. Thus, they were imprisoned until they agreed on a deal not to kill each other.

The cruise started early in the morning and Morgan left the presidents to negotiate alone under an awning on the deck. He made sure they enjoyed first-class meals, beverages and a large supply of Havana cigars. Finally that evening, the presidents came to an agreement to end the rate war, swap their duplicative lines and keep out of each other's territories. Hands were shaken and the 'Corsair Pact' was realised. Morgan's no-exit negotiating strategy was applied with tremendous success. His reputation in the City of London was now safe and he made a $100.000 commission and a million in profit from his rail bonds. A good pact!

Later in 1907, he repeated his magic formula, saving the American economy from collapse. In October of 1907, a funding scheme attempted to manipulate United Copper Company stock. It was a copper mining company, as the name implies. The speculation failed, which led to runs on the banks that had lent money to the scheme and later spread to affiliated banks and trusts causing the bankruptcy of the brokerage house, Gross & Kleeberg, and the Knickerbocker Trust Company - the third-largest trust in New York City. Earlier in June, a recession had begun due to the San Francisco earthquake the previous year, which had initiated a liquidity crunch. It was a recipe for disaster and the 'panic' began.

Morgan was now seventy years old. As the main financier of America, he had engineered the mergers of companies such as U.S. Steel, General Electric and American Telephone and Telegraph. As you can imagine, he was the equivalent of minister for steel, telecommunications and electric power, super-minister of America, and prime minister or emperor, all in one.

He was attending a church convention in Richmond, Virginia when chaos knocked on the door of New York's banks. He was called back by his partners. He arrived in New York City on Saturday, October 19th. The following morning, he received visits from the presidents of all the banks and trusts in his library at Madison Avenue and 36th Street. He gathered information about chartered working groups to get the facts and over the next several weeks, deployed the information to organise successive rescues of the major institutions.

The 'Corsair' scenario was repeated in this library and on the morning of Saturday, November 2nd, Morgan called an emergency conference to save Moore & Schley, the largest of the exchange's brokerage firms, which had borrowed heavily using shares of the Tennessee Coal, Iron and Railroad Company as collateral. Morgan could use U.S. Steel to save Moore & Schley but by the evening, an agreement had not been reached and the meeting was adjourned.

By this time, around fifty bankers had gathered at the library to discuss the crisis. The presidents of the clearing-houses gathered in the library's East room and the trust company executives in the West room. At the same time, the executives of US Steel, Moore & Schley and Tennessee Coal gathered in the librarian's office. Morgan stated that he would agree to save Moore & Schley only if the trust companies would work together to bail out their weakest brothers. He locked them in and pocketed the key, making it clear they could only go home once a deal was reached. He was alone again and played solitaire, his favourite card game while waiting for a result that this time, was much more difficult and complex to reach.

At three in the morning, the bank and trust company officials were still locked in the library. Morgan entered the talks and advised the trust companies to provide a loan of $25 million to save the weaker institutions. The trust presidents were reluctant to act even though it would otherwise lead to a complete collapse of the banking system.

At around 4:45 a.m., they were sleepless and exhausted. They signed the agreement and Morgan allowed them to go home. Job done. Just like the 'Corsair Pact'.

This man was about to perform the same magic with the rulers of Europe. The Kaiser's daughter's wedding was the perfect opportunity and Morgan probably considered it his greatest and most important 'pact'. Like his eternal hero, Napoleon Bonaparte, the outsider who was not invited to intervene a century before, he wasn't either. 'I have come down to Washington to see the president and I'm going to stay here until I see him', he stated during the Great Depression of the 90s, when he had a plan to restore America's gold reserves and President Grover Cleveland refused to receive him at the White House. This American emperor was looking for an opportunity to prove his Napoleonic capabilities.

No one knew what he was planning to say to the kings of Europe or how he would lock them in no-exit negotiations to stop them playing with fire, or rather, dynamite. A second Austerlitz was imminent, for sure.

The previous year had been very difficult for Mr Morgan. He was commanded to appear in front of the Pujo Committee, a committee formed to investigate Wall Street bankers and financiers who exerted powerful control over the nation's finances. The so-called 'money trust'. Although many bankers were investigated, it was evident that John Pierpont Morgan was the main target of the investigation.

Finally, among other things, the report identified over $22 billion in resources and capitalisation controlled through 341 directorships held in 112 corporations by members of the empire headed by John Pierpont Morgan, an emperor who, in many ways, was controlling almost two-thirds of America's Gross Domestic Product. Suddenly, he was portrayed in the newspapers as a greedy businessman, an evil monster. In his finals years, it was clear that his legacy was targeted. That was serious.

At the same time, as part of a bigger evil plan, the seventy-four-year-old magnate was struck another blow. A year before on April 15th, one of his investments through the International Mercantile Marine Company, the mighty *Titanic*, sank. Incredibly, it was due to a slight change of plan that Mr Morgan was not on board the *Titanic* with his multimillion-dollar art collection. He cancelled at the last minute, choosing to remain at a resort in Aix-les-Bains in France. Good country, good choice!

'Monetary losses amount to nothing in life. It is the loss of life that counts. It is that frightful death', said John Pierpont Morgan in response to the sinking of the *Titanic*. I was going to meet him to talk about the latter.

I knew of his love of solitaire so I rented a room at the Grand Hotel Plaza, found a good table at the bar and played my own game of solitaire. I placed my big Havana cigars on the table, drank my Benedictine liqueur and read my newspapers. I followed this routine all day every day.

On March 20th, I read in the newspapers that on March 18th, King George had been killed.

Like in Athens, George went about his business in Salonika without any real protection. While out on an afternoon walk near the White Tower on March 18th, - March 5th according to the old calendar - he was shot in the back at close range by Alexandros Schenas, who was said to belong to a socialist organisation and declared when arrested, that he had killed the king because he refused to give him money. George died instantly when a bullet penetrated his heart. The Greek government denied any political motive for the assassination, saying that Schenas was an alcoholic vagrant.

To my great surprise, Alexandros succeeded as far as the optional criteria were concerned but failed to carry out the obligatory. Killing King George was optional but he did it. Escaping was obligatory and he blew it. Once my job was finished, I would have to return to Salonika I thought to myself and took another sip of my liqueur.

At some stage, the notorious John Pierpont Morgan arrived at the hotel.

From the moment he arrived, he noticed me playing solitaire and one evening, on Sunday, March 30th, he approached my table.

"Have you anything to suggest, Mr Morgan?" I asked.

Although, in poor health and having suffered two titanic blows in the past year, he was still vibrant. There was a twinkle in his eyes and I was certain he would hit back in May. The Kaiser's daughter's wedding would undeniably be his masterpiece. His own Austerlitz.

That is precisely what we do not want you to do, Mr Morgan.

Mr Morgan's friend, the millionaire Andrew Carnegie, had founded the Carnegie Endowment for International Peace, the so-called CEIP, three years before. It was an organisation dedicated to advancing cooperation between nations and promoting active international engagement by the United States. It had offices in Washington, Moscow, Beirut, Beijing, Brussels, and New Delhi. Think tanks, meetings, discussions, reports… My boss couldn't have cared less.

Mr Morgan took a different approach to the Corsair or Library Pact (gather them together, lock them in and get a deal) with his friend Carnegie. This approach scared my boss to death.

The two magnates had long discussions while smoking cigars and drinking Benedictine under the enigmatic gaze of the stolen Mona Lisa. They respected each other, as together, they had made the greatest economic transaction ever. More than a decade previously, Carnegie had approached Morgan to sell him the Carnegie Steel Corporation as he had decided to retire from business. Carnegie wrote on a piece of paper the amount he was willing to sell his business for and delivered it to Morgan. The banker gave it one look and agreed on the spot to pay $480 million for a company that was making $40 million every year. The biggest business deal ever made was decided in seconds.

Carnegie was amazed and was now the richest man in the world. Later, while both were celebrating the deal, he remarked that he should have asked for an extra $100.000. Morgan responded instantly once again.

"If you had, I would have paid it."

Do you see the difference? Carnegie assumed that Morgan would call his advisors to gather the data and information necessary to go ahead with such a great deal. Meetings would be held, calculations would be made, market analysis, economic threats…

Morgan didn't need it. He knew what he had to do and at what price. He also knew what the kings of Europe had to do. He explained to his millionaire Scottish friend that organisations and institutions could help by studying the aftermath of war, but for a great war not to be triggered by an inkling, only a strong, decisive lockdown could do the job.

A Royal Wedding Pact!

On the other hand, as we sat there at the Grand Hotel Plaza, the Carnegie Endowment sent a mission of

Austrian, French, German, British, Russian and American representatives to gather information and produce a report on the Balkan War.

No one would try to stop them. Why would they bother?

The real danger lay behind the great moustache with the man who was sipping my liqueur and puffing on my Hercules Cigars. He smoked dozens of them a day.

He could easily have stolen the Mona Lisa.

We had much in common. During the American civil war, he financed the purchase of five thousand rifles from an army arsenal at $3.50 each, which, after a minor modification, were resold a month later to a field general for $22 each. I admired him, but business is business.

The following morning, he was found dead, exactly as Berhane had said it would happen. It was widely announced that on Monday, March 31st, the great John Pierpont Morgan died in his sleep. He was seventy-six years old. There was no way he would attend the Prussian princess's wedding in May so my boss could now relax.

His body was returned to America aboard the *SS France*, a French Line passenger ship. Flags on Wall Street flew at half-staff, and in an honour usually reserved for heads of state, the stock market closed for two hours when his body passed through New York City.

By that time, I was back in Salonika, trying to work out what to do with my friend, Alexandros Schenas, who was having a rough time in prison. Obviously, my options were few and I was annoyed to see the Cretan policemen. Various problems still existed but in the time between my departure and my return, they had successfully established an air of greater control and security. Not exactly what the Austrians and I had expected, especially after King George's death. And in

Europe, the impact of the assassination was not what I expected either, though everyone knew it was the damned Prussians who had killed the king.

The situation was unique and it was better to take no more risks. It was the money and the hope of a luxurious life in Europe that gave Alexandros the motive to kill the king and it would be money that gave him the courage to kill himself.

I found out where one of the chief guards lived and one day, while he was home, I threw a large packet of German Marks with a note in Greek through his kitchen window.

'If he remains silent forever and his written confession is burned, you will receive ten times more.' Signed by 'The Kaiser'.

On May 6th, Alexandros Schenas, my old friend from New York, committed suicide, falling to his death from the central police station window. Later, when the paperwork was taken to Athens, it was burned by accident on the ship that transported it.

No more German Marks were thrown through his kitchen window, however. The guard was rich enough as it was. Had I remained in Salonika, I probably would have thrown him some more, but soon after disposing of the first packet, I left.

I had told my boss I'd give it a shot but I was also thinking of other things to try out. I was a workaholic. With all the upheaval and my presence in the Balkans, the opportunity to play my Mona Lisa card hadn't presented itself. It was pointless now anyway.

My first thought was to kill King Ferdinand of Bulgaria, who was of German origin and had anti-Russian sentiments. His father was Prince August, whose first cousin, Albert, had married his other first cousin, Queen Victoria.

His aunt, Queen Victoria, was strictly opposed to him becoming a king, but it was his mother's intrigue that was responsible for it.

Princess Clémentine of Orléans had married an ordinary duke and put all her effort into making her children kings. Her favourite son, a descendant not only of Louis-Philippe but of the Sun King, deserved to be a king somewhere, wherever it was.

Ferdinand was fluent in several languages and took great interest in the natural sciences and nature, all of which, Clémentine believed, would make Ferdinand an excellent king. When the time came, Clémentine actively lobbied for Ferdinand's election as Prince of Bulgaria. Agrippina had made Nero an emperor by lobbying, too.

The Kaiser liked the idea of replacing the Balkan region under the Ottomans with a German- friendly Bulgaria. So if 'Foxy Ferdinand' as he was known, was assassinated, the Kaiser might be upset. Of course, the assassination would be viewed as revenge for the assassination of the anti-German King George of Greece. So now they would be quits. This project would deliver ambiguous results and needed much preparation, for which I no longer had the time.

My second thought was to leave Salonika, not by boat, but to ride through the burning Balkans as a French journalist or something, to the area that caused the 1908 crisis, the well-known Bosnia. There, I could maybe encourage the Bosnians to rebel against the Austro-Hungarians. On the borders, their Slavic brothers - the Serbians and Montenegrins - had successfully dismissed the Ottomans and taken the precious Novi Pazar that the Austro-Hungarians so badly wanted. Even an incident between Conrad's soldiers and the Bosnians or Serbians could bring about the result I so badly desired.

The time was right for a Bosnian revolt to take place, I thought. It would give Conrad the reason he badly needed to disobey Franz Ferdinand and confront the Serbians, and at the same time, earn the privilege of marrying Gina, literally with his sword. On the other hand, my good friend Hartwig would have the opportunity to develop Serbia even more. It seemed feasible enough, and best of all, it was on my way home. I am a good salesman, am I not?

"Hartwig, you made it. Congratulations!"

"Thank you, Edward, but what are you doing here?"

"I came today from Salonika."

"And what were you doing there?"

"I arrived on the French ship that came to protect the French population of the city. It's nice to experience these historic events!"

"You should have stayed there. Travelling through the Balkans is dangerous, Edward. Unnecessarily dangerous."

"Nikolai, I have sold guns in Morocco, Sicily and in every volatile state. The Balkans were always my favourite market."

"Well, I am always happy to see you, my friend," he said, taking out one of his big Russian cigarettes. "How are things in Salonika?"

"Bad, very bad, but the Cretan police are doing a fine job."

"They didn't protect their king though, did they?"

"These anarchists are unpredictable, you know, like the man who killed Queen Sissy."

"Come now, Edward. That was the Germans."

"It's quite possible, I suppose."

"If the Serbians had taken Salonika, I'd be there now, you know."

"And this anarchist would have killed you too, right?"

"Why kill the Russian ambassador?"

"You are undeniably the King of the Balkans, my friend. Everyone knows that. And not only in Serbia!" And I didn't say that just to make him feel good. He had brought Serbia and Bulgaria together and strongly supported Greece's entry into the Balkan League.

"Oh, thank God General Putnik didn't join the race to Salonika and headed west instead! I'd be the dead King of the Balkans, otherwise! Ha-ha!"

"The Bulgarians are still trying, you know. And the Austrians are helping them any way they can," I said, knowing I was touching on his favourite subject - the damned Austrians.

"Damned Austrians! I should… I should…, anyway. I predicted it from the beginning. As far as I am concerned, the first phase of this war is over. And the second phase starts here."

On hearing these words, I tried very hard not to reveal my excitement. '*I need to send a telegram*', I thought.

"Bosnia?" I asked, full of hope.

"Bulgaria. I was suspicious of their territorial aspirations in Macedonia from the beginning. Foxy Ferdinand imagines himself in Constantinople, ruling the whole of the Balkans. Venizelos knew that, too. That's why he sent his super police force there. I brought Serbia and Greece together to teach the damned German a lesson."

"Damned Prussians!"

"Ah, Edward! We are tortured by the same demons."

"Nikolai, wait a minute. The Austrians are playing games in Salonika. Surely they'll seize the opportunity to attack from the west and reach the Aegean Sea once the Bulgarians have been taken care of in the east."

"If they haven't done it so far, why do it now?"

"To protect the foxy German king."

"That means Russia would attack the Austrians."

"And then the Prussians would attack Russia."

"And that means you, the French, would attack the Prus… Germans."

"Together with the English navy."

"I can't count on that, but listen. Nothing like that is going to happen," said Nikolai, killing all my dreams.

"Why not?" I asked, desperately disappointed.

"Because the Kaiser always declares his support for Austria in all circumstances. He is not ready for war. Not yet."

Indeed, at the German Imperial War Council on December 8th, 1912, the consensus was that Germany would not be ready for war until at least the middle of 1914, and passed notes to that effect to the Austrians. Of course, no one knew but the Council and probably, some Russian spies.

If I were Austrian, I would take it as a declaration by the Prussians that they want a war in the middle of 1914 and I could help with that. Just joking!

Suddenly, something occurred to me. I was now certain that Nikolai Hartwig had played a major role in the Russian intelligence service. What was his role at the expo of 1900? Wait a minute! He approached me after I'd spoken to my boss. He knows who my boss is. Ah! He was expanding his network. Why would he waste time with a liqueur salesman?

Maybe he was gathering information and recruiting spies. How could a fanatic Panslavist, who hated the Austro-Hungarians, so passionately consider Vienna the most beautiful city in the world? And why was it always his favourite destination? He was clearly going to be there at every opportunity. He visited Vienna far more often than Moscow and never mentioned visiting his birthplace of Igor in Georgia.

Ok. I never visited my birthplace of Algiers, either. Maybe that's what we liars do.

I understood his sentiment. Vienna is full of beautiful gardens. He is an admirer of those beautiful little flower poems that the young poet from Igor named Soselo wrote. It makes sense.

> The pinkish bud has opened,
> Rushing to the pale-blue violet
> And, stirred by a light breeze,
> The lily of the valley has bent over the grass

As a man who reads such poems, it makes sense to like Vienna. But after a while, it's odd.

Maybe there is a woman involved, but probably not. He is a happy family man. His daughter Ludmilla adores him. That means he has a good relationship with his wife. A daughter always hates a father who does not treat her mother well.

Talented at making friends and winning people over, he was perfect for the job. All those years, I thought I was learning from him but maybe he was learning from me, too. The information I gave him about the IMEO and Komitaj and all those guns I sold in the Balkans were vital to him. My God! Maybe he acts like a good friend to all his 'informers'.

Hartwig was 'a sedate bearded Muscovite of deceptive bonhomie', Leopold Berchtold had said. He was deceptive for sure. Oh, Lord! What a fool I had been.

"Are you all right, Edward? The Kaiser has a lot more ships to build until he can take on the British navy. The Prussians are still behind, my friend," said Nikolai. I remained silent. It was like I'd been hit by a flash of lightning. He lit another cigarette "However, you could have a point about the Austrians because of this… this… what's his name? Co... Conrad von something? He hates us as much as I hate them. It is possible to seize the opportunity without thinking of the consequences. He would even try to reach Thessaloniki if the ambassador there encouraged him to do so. Let's call the city by its proper name from now on, shall we? Thessaloniki. Venizelos told me the correct name."

"Yes, Thessaloniki was the name of Alexander the Great's younger sister. Nike is the word for victory, *niki* in Greek. And *Thessalo* is from the area of Thessaly. Philip probably wanted to remember a victory in Thessaly."

"Ok, you're better at history than me, I know that."

"Anyway Nikolai, I never sold a single gun to the Bosnians. My guns reached that far but only because of Tankosic. And I can assure you if I ever got that far, I could start a Serbian Vesper."

"Why would you do that, Edward?"

"Alsace and Lorraine."

"Alsace and Lorraine?"

"I am fifty years old, Nikolai. Soon, I will be an old man and I can't bear to die knowing the damned Prussians… who killed my brother… who killed my grandfather… will keep Alsace and Lorraine forever, just to remind us of the crimes they committed.

"And if I had the opportunity to help my country and stop this torture now, while the Prussian navy is still under construction, it would be a shame not to try."

"You know something, Edward? I'll be honest with you.

"At this stage, I don't want a great war to take place. A war that would give you Alsace-Lorraine. I'm sorry. But I do need the Austrians to be occupied in the territory they illegally annexed in 1908. 'Greece can provide 600.000 men for the war effort. 200.000 men in the field and the fleet will be able to stop 400.000 men being landed by Turkey between Thessaloniki and Gallipoli', was what the Greek ambassador to Sofia said while negotiating Greece's entry into the League."

"It was a victory of the sea, sea is *thalassa*. Thus, Thalassoniki. Right? Ha-ha!"

"Whatever…but if, by your efforts, you can keep Conrad busy inside Bosnia, your service to this second crucial phase will be just as valuable, my friend. The general there is a man named Potiorek. Oskar, I think… Oskar Potiorek."

Who was fooling who, you might be wondering?

Or to be more accurate, you know Edward Aguillon is talking nonsense but what about Nikolai?

I was now one hundred per cent certain that he had used me in the past, was using me now and would do so in the future. But we were still good friends, of course. In fact, this is what good friends usually do, but it takes years or decades to find out.

He had never made a single, even minor mistake that would expose his true intentions. Until today that was. See what happened next.

Nikolai had said the Germans were not ready yet. This indicates he has inside information. He realises his mistake immediately.

Then, he continues to explain that the Prussians are lagging behind in the naval race, when a minute earlier, he said he didn't think the British navy would back us up.

So first, he tries, unsuccessfully, to hide his mistake, going against his own words, and then, he continues to tell me what I wanted to hear. Furthermore, he pretends not to remember the name of Conrad von Hoetzendorf. Who? Nikolai Hartwig, the man who knew the poems of Soselo by heart. Finally, he starts the nonsense with Salonika and Thessaloniki, trying to change the subject.

I needed him to believe I knew nothing of it, of course. That's why I interrupted by emphasising and encouraging his deluding technique. I needed him to relax and it worked with the trivial *thalasso* nonsense I came up with.

He was suspicious of me because he knew all I wanted to do was sell, sell guns without borders. Even to Serbia's enemies. He was right once again.

The Austro-Hungarian army was already in place to protect its territory from the Serbians and Montenegrins and to attack if necessary. If, for example, the Serbians tried to make it to the Adriatic Sea again, or if the situation in Thessaloniki got out of order, or Foxy Ferdinand needed help, or Conrad needed Gina.

My feelings were mixed. I was excited about being so close to my goal. One more attempt was all I needed to get the job done. Hartwig was my only concern. He was certain that in this second phase, Serbia and Greece would destroy Bulgaria, as she would also have to face Turkey from the east and Rumania from the north. Foxy Ferdinand was clearly not Bismarck. That's probably why they called him Foxy.

I realised the moment I arrived in Sarajevo that there was nothing I could do. Austria-Hungary declared a state of emergency, implemented martial law, seized control of schools, and prohibited all Serb cultural organisations. Not exactly what I needed. They wanted Sarajevo to be the opposite of Thessaloniki. There we agreed, here we disagreed.

Wherever I went, wherever I looked, there were Austro-Hungarian soldiers. Their presence disappointed me at first and I thought about leaving straight away, but then I decided that for a man of my age, it would do no harm to lie low, get some rest at a decent hotel, take a walk by the river Miljacka, enjoy a good meal and then make my way to the centre of the Empire.

It was May 10th, and the weather, unlike the Austrian soldiers, was encouraging for long walks. After a long walk by the river, I stopped to get something to eat at the tiny *Moritz Schiller's Delicatessen.*

"Sir!"

"Yes?" I answered, turning to the table next to me. A young man was sitting there.

He leaned towards me and whispered secretively. "You were with Tankosic, last year."

"Sorry, I don't understand, young man," I said in poor Serbian and continued eating my sandwich.

He swiftly left his seat and came towards me.

"It was you!" he said enthusiastically.

"Vojislav Tankosic?" I asked.

"Yes, I was a war volunteer."

"Really? Why aren't you at the front?"

"Tankosic thought I'd be of more use here in Sarajevo," he said, looking down at the table. Of course, I knew that this was due to Tankosic's high standards. My hopes of creating an upheaval rose.

"What's your name, kid?"

"Gavrilo."

"I am Edward, nice to meet you, Gavrilo."

"Me too, sir."

"Let's go for a walk, Gavrilo."

This short young man had seen me speaking to Tankosic, the number two of the Black Hand. It was enough for him to naively start a conversation with me and trust a man who has connections with the top hierarchy. I realised that in this particular phase of the Balkan war and with martial law in Sarajevo, he considered my presence a sign of something big.

How could I let him down?

We left the delicatessen in Franz Josef Gasse, a small road vertical to the Appel Quai Street parallel to the river and I headed left across the road to walk by the river.

Gavrilo grabbed my sleeve. "Better to go through the side streets."

"You're right," I said, rather embarrassed.

Once we had walked about fifty meters, I asked with some authority how many of them were in Sarajevo.

"There are many of us, but we of the Young Bosnia group are five."

My hopes dived over the Latin Bridge and fell into the Adriatic Sea.

"They are Christians like you?"

"I'm not a Christian."

"Gavrilo is the name of an angel."

"I know, my mother wanted to name me after her late brother Spiro but I was named Gavrilo because of the priest. He said that the Archangel Gabriel would help me survive."

"And you did."

"Not for much longer, I suffer from tuberculosis. We don't believe in God, anyway. God is dead."

"Ok, but where are you registered?"

"We are all Yugoslav patriots."

Five atheists cannot bring about 'Serbian Vespers'. Orthodox Easter was on April 27th, and now it's May 12th. Not enough force, too much Nietzsche, too late. Boss, you were right. Too late!

But I was a workaholic.

"Gavrilo, is there a safe place we can meet tomorrow with your friends?"

The next morning, on May 13th, I woke up in a cell at the Austro-Hungarian police station in Sarajevo. My head hurt and I couldn't remember what happened.

I remembered greeting Gavrilo, walking alone by the river and later returning to the hotel. I remembered greeting the receptionist, a very polite Bosnian woman, and then taking the stairs. Did I get to my room? I honestly don't remember.

After an hour of anticipation, the door of my cell opened and a big man in a police uniform came in. His moustache was smaller than mine, but I don't think that was the reason for his anger.

"My name is Edward Aguillon and I am a French citizen. I demand an explanation." I said in basic German.

He led me to another room with a chair and a table. I waited there for another half an hour.

Suddenly, I heard a stern voice calling my name in a rather sarcastic way. A thin man slowly entered the room and sat at the table in front of me.

"French citizens also have accidents, Mr Aguillon."

It was then I remembered that someone had hit me over the head from behind when I entered my hotel room. I assumed I'd been followed from the time I entered the Empire. In such times, it would be unusual not to be followed. When you go from Serbia to Sarajevo and walk side by side in conversation with a Young Bosnian, you are asking for trouble.

I honestly don't know what shaped my next moves. Maybe it was the sense of danger. Maybe pure fear. Maybe the irony of the Austrian policeman with the stupid voice, the strange spelling of my name, the way he sat at the table, and the whole situation triggered a reaction in me. It put me in a certain frame of mind, like the time I was faced with the Sicilian Mafia leaders and a Kouro. This time, however, I would put my life in even greater danger by risking everything.

"What is your name?" I asked calmly looking him in the eye.

"You can call me Edmund."

"Edmund, please call General Oskar Potiorek. I must speak to him as soon as possible."

"That is not possible."

Naturally, I didn't expect him to do such a thing. I wanted him to sense something else was going on. By asking for the general, I had nothing to fear.

"Edmund, can I tell you something in private?"

Edmund nodded at the giant, who left the room unwillingly. Having made sure he'd left, I turned to Edmund and whispered.

"Edmund, I cannot tell you my real name and I cannot reveal anything about my mission. All I can tell you is that if I do not pass important information to the general today, our army will be in great danger and the responsibility will be all yours."

"You expect me to believe you are an Empire spy?"

"I don't give a damn what you believe. I must pass on crucial information to the general, today."

"I will do it for you."

I looked at him suspiciously, indicating it was difficult for me to trust him.

"How long have you been here in Sarajevo?" I asked.

"Two years."

I looked at the empty corner of the room and sighed a huge sigh. I looked at the closed door making sure no one was there and whispered slowly. "I will give you a name. Give it to the general and tell him that somewhere in Vienna, is an envelope addressed to this name. Get this man, no matter what."

"Somewhere in Vienna? That's very funny, Edward."

"Look, if you hadn't put me in here, I would have found exactly where. You have no idea how important this is."

"You are lying. It's obvious, my friend."

I was furious. "I've worked for the HaHo for fifteen years. I've been trying to catch this asshole for the last four. Two men died on the job before me. And now, because Edmund in Sarajevo is too busy to write down a name, it was all for nothing?" I whispered through gritted teeth.

Good lies require specific numbers, specific acronyms, anger, fast-talking and an imposing glare.

"What is the HaHo?"

"HAbsburgs HOhenzollern secret intelligence service," I said. Edmund flinched at the sound of the Austrian Imperial family next to that of the Kaiser.

"Never heard of it."

"And you never will. The central powers needed a joint effort to take on the strategic encirclement by Russia, France and England. We would be fools not to work together. Only Conrad von Hoetzendorf knows of our existence." I was suddenly more reliable.

"Why are you here?"

"For the same reason the army is here. The same reason the Serbians and the Russians want to be here. There are gaps in Russian intelligence."

"I see."

"Now, find this man, even if Vienna has a thousand post offices. Find him!"

"Who?"

"One more thing."

"What?"

"You must not reveal your source. The army must say that the spy was revealed due to specific anti-spy procedures. No connection must be made with the Sarajevo police or the army, otherwise, my organisation and I will be exposed. And we don't want that to happen."

"Give me the name."

"Nikon Nizetas."

How did I come up with a name like that?

A year earlier, Hartwig had given an envelope to the receptionist of the Klomser Hotel with this name on it. If you remember, he shut me up when I pretended to be Nizetas by saying he hadn't slept the night before. I paid no attention to it then but once I figured out he too was in the information business, I was sure that Nizetas was a pseudonym or a code name for a spy. Furthermore, the Hartwig I met in Paris was proud of his wonderful, revitalising sleep, and what's more, he didn't seem tired in the least that day in Vienna. Last but not least, the Russian in the *Central Café* with Mr Bronstein also used an undercover Greek name. Greek names were probably fashionable for Russian spies at the time.

I was certain that once the Balkan war had started, he was unable to travel to his favourite city built by the Austrians he hated to gather information and pay his source. So he must have used the post office.

You may believe it was risky but if you think about it, there was no risk at all.

What would happen if no envelope was found?

First, it would be because Edmund got in my way. He blew it and would now be on the HoHa or HaHo's blacklist.

Secondly, and most importantly, Edmund's subconscious mind was to blame for the matter. Once he'd dispatched a large number of the soldiers to search for Nizetas and been exposed to General Potiorek, he'd be mentally obliged to convince himself he'd done so for a good reason. And that good reason was me. His self-defence mechanism would convince him he had access to a valuable spy. Why else would he go to the trouble to create an upheaval with Vienna's entire postal service?

The longer it took and the more resources committed to finding Nizetas, the more reliable I was as a source. It was as simple as that.

I'm sure I don't have to explain what would happen if the envelope was found.

I gave Edmund the name on May 13th. I was having the worst time of my life in a small prison cell with no information about what was happening. At first, I considered a delay a good sign. It meant that something or other was in progress. Furthermore, I knew the delay would give Edmund more time to believe in the importance of the spy he was holding.

But gradually, alone in that dark prison cell, I was going mad. I was in what seemed like a never-ending dark zone. The humidity, the rats, the absence of light. Why was this happening to me?

I had been naïve once again, and now I was paying for it with my life.

At some stage, I heard the door open. I had no idea what day it was or whether it was day or night. How long had I been in this hole? The burly man came in and told me to take my jacket and follow him. They were probably be moving me somewhere else. He took me to the room with the table where I'd met Edmund thirteen days earlier. Edmund, the chief of the police, was waiting there with an Austrian army general. It was General Oskar Potiorek. There was a knife on the table.... Oh my god!

Now let's look back and see what happened in Vienna or any other goddamn place while I was cursing my fate in prison. It may help you understand what happened next.

On May 13th, Edmund gave the name to the general, probably bragging about the continuous efforts of the local police force under his direction.

The general immediately passed the information to his headquarters, bragging about the continuous efforts of his regiment under his direction.

Such information from a city under martial law and close to the borders during the Balkan war was more than crucial. Remember that after the annexation, Austrian and Hungarian newspapers reported that there were a thousand bands in Serbia with twenty well-armed fighters in each.

The following morning, Vienna's post offices were extensively searched. By midday on May 14th, there was an outcome.

Fortunately, they had found a *post restante* letter at the main post office, which arrived on May 9th and was waiting to be collected. 'Post restante' is a service where the post office holds the mail until the recipient collects it. It is a common method for receiving mail when a person is unable to have their mail delivered directly to them because they are underway in a particular location or because he or she is a spy.

Police detectives were assigned to monitor the post office and follow whoever claimed it. Unfortunately, the claimant hadn't turned up to collect it. Finally, on Saturday, May 24th, he appeared to collect the goddamn letter. The two detectives, fed up of waiting at the post office that day, saw the suspect but sadly, lost track of him. He did something very clever that took them by surprise.

He took a taxi.

Now you understand why the Austrian-Hungarian Empire had big problems! While the super-detectives stood there wondering what to do or how to explain to their superiors that they had lost track of the suspect, the taxi that Nizetas had taken returned. Fortunately for me.

The detectives took the taxi and asked to be driven to the address that the previous customer had been taken to. Unfortunately, the taxi driver took them to the Klomser Hotel. Yes, the renowned hotel of my preference in the heart of Vienna, with hundreds of people coming and going and thousands walking about on the corner of Shenkenstrasse and Bankgasse.

Nizetas was lost forever.

No! Fortunately, they discovered the sheath of a pen-knife in the taxi on their way to the hotel. The suspect had probably used a pen-knife to open the envelope and dropped the sheath. An unnecessary luxury, you might say. There was hope for the Empire, after all!

When they arrived at the hotel, there was only one thing they could possibly do. They told the management to ask the guests if anyone had lost the sheath of a pen-knife and waited in the lobby.

Imagine you are a spy and you have just received proof of your espionage. Everything had gone well. You went to the post office in disguise. No one recognised you and you left again. You went to a hotel room in the centre of one of the biggest cities in Europe with no one following you, and now safe and secure, you continue happily with your life as a spy.

Now imagine someone knocks on the door of your room. You are scared but you have to answer it.

"Who's there?"

"From the reception, sir. Have you lost the sheath of a pen-knife?"

"No, I haven't," you answer immediately. Maybe you realised you dropped the sheath, maybe you didn't. Who cares?

Or imagine that no one knocks at your door. You make your way out, and while passing the reception, the receptionist asks you a question.

"Have you lost the sheath of a pen-knife, sir?"

"No, I haven't," you answer immediately. Maybe you realised you dropped the sheath, maybe not. Once again, who cares?

Isn't that right?

As my luck would have it, Nizetas appeared at the reception to claim his precious pen-knife sheath. The two detectives were waiting in the lobby, paying more attention this time.

Why did Nizetas act that way?

Because he had been doing so for many years. He had been recruited in 1901, and since then, had been well-paid by the Imperial Russian government for his services.

He was the ninth child of a family of fourteen children. His father was an officer in the Austrian Army but in 1851, at the rank of lieutenant, he switched careers because, for officers of the Habsburg Army, the job did not pay well. He started work on the railways and moved to Galicia where he earned a decent salary, which included pay rises but not analogous to the growth of his family. The super-spy was born in 1864, in Lemberg or Lviv, the Lion City, and six more children followed.

Growing up in a city where people spoke Polish and Ukrainian in their everyday lives and German at school, he became a masterful linguist. Thus, it was easy for Nizetas to navigate a multi-ethnic empire and a multi-linguistic society, where each ethnic group had its own language, customs and cultures.

He loved luxurious cars and expensive clothes but never had a family because he was a homosexual. The Russians gave him the money he badly needed along with their promise not to reveal his secret. In those days, it would have meant his downfall. He had gradually built up a lifestyle far beyond what a normal salary could pay but no one ever suspected him.

After twelve years in the spy business, Nikon Nizetas acted by default knowing that nothing was going to happen. That no one was going to seek him out.

This time, when the mysterious man came to claim his sheath with no disguise, the two detectives were surprised to see their former boss, Colonel Alfred Redl, Chief of Staff of the 8th Army Corps and former head of Military Counter-Intelligence of the Austro-Hungarian Imperial and Royal Army.

Russian military intelligence had found out about Colonel Redl's homosexuality, information that was used to blackmail him into revealing classified information. In 1902, he officially began his career by passing a copy of Austro-Hungarian war plans to the Russians. The Austrians discovered the leak and General Arthur Giesl von Gieslingen, the head of Austro-Hungarian military intelligence, delegated Alfred Redl to investigate the source of this leak.

The Russians realised that Redl was invaluable and were now willing to sacrifice other lower-level informants as Russian spies to protect Redl and enhance his reputation for efficiency within the Austro-Hungarian army. Thus, in consultation with his Russian contacts, Redl was able to reveal several Russian spies, impressing his superiors and making a name for himself. From then on, Alfred Redl was Russia's leading spy. And some spy he was, too!

He betrayed secret agents of the Austro-Hungarian Empire in Russia. He would either send Austrian agents into Russia, only to reveal them afterwards, or betray Austrian agents within the Russian Imperial Staff. They were either hanged or forced to commit suicide. He even informed Russia about various Russian officers, who contacted Austro-Hungarian intelligence. He was clearly worthy of his salary, you see, and the Russians never stopped supplying him with enormous amounts of money.

He passed information about mobilisation plans and important details about fortresses in Galicia. He sold Austria-Hungary's most sensitive military intelligence to the Russian Empire. His treachery included providing the enemy with Plan III, the high command's invasion plan to attack Serbia, if ever necessary. The information in Plan III would turn out to be invaluable to the Empire's enemies.

In 1912, Redl became chief of staff of the VIII Corps under his old commander, General von Gieslingen. He knew how effective Redl was. When he left the counter-intelligence service, Redl even trained Major Maximilian Ronge, who succeeded him.

The super-spy was subsequently confronted in room number one of the Klomser Hotel by a party of military officers. He admitted his actions and to having sold military intelligence to a foreign power. Conrad von Hoetzendorf ordered that Colonel Redl was to be left alone with a loaded revolver. That luxury pen-knife sheath had proved fatal. The luxury he desperately needed for all his gadgets had betrayed him. It was May 25th, 1913.

Next to the knife was a fork, a soup spoon and a teaspoon for the sweet, and a wonderful-smelling dish of chicken and potatoes, accompanied by a hearty salad, bread and cheese. There was also a bottle of wine and glasses, all carefully positioned on a beautiful tablecloth.

"Edward, or whatever your name is, it was an honour to work for the HaHo and it is my honour to dine with you," said the general.

If it wasn't for the meal, I wouldn't have believed him but now it was obvious my shot in the dark had found its target. Now I was the boss.

"That was a delicious meal and the wine was particularly good. Now, General, I need two things from you. I assume Edmund informed you that I, your source, must not be revealed."

"Yes, we took care of that. We agreed that the spy was found by instigating the common practice of checking suspicious mail such as a *post restante* to be returned unclaimed. One suspect envelope was found to contain a large sum of money as well as references to known espionage cover addresses. Thus, when a duplicate letter with money was posted to the same undercover name, we followed whoever claimed it. Satisfied?"

"Brilliant!"

"And what is the second thing you need, sir?"

"I need someone to give me one or two kind punches."

"You are a real professional HaHo agent, sir!"

That very same day, on May 25th, 1913, I was set free. I was released from prison with blood on my clothes, which were in an awful condition. I looked very bad indeed. Thank God my Young Bosnian friends took care of me and helped me get out of Sarajevo. I was going to Paris to rest. No war this year. The burning Balkans would no longer be my market.

That same day, two more spies were released. The imprisoned British spies Captain Stewart and Captain Trench. They were pardoned and released by the Kaiser as a favour to the United Kingdom. Can you guess why?

Because on the same Saturday that Alfred Redl had claimed the letter from Vienna's main post office, the Kaiser's daughter, Victoria Louise, was married to Ernest Augustus, Duke of Brunswick. All the kings of Europe were in attendance. The wedding was the largest gathering of reigning monarchs in Germany since German unification in 1871 and one of the greatest European royalty social events. Attendees included Wilhelm's identical cousins King George V and Czar Nicholas II. The wedding feast included more than a thousand guests. The most important man was absent, however. If John Pierpont Morgan had been there, he would probably have found an opportunity to perform his miracle. He would have successfully closed the most important deal of... humanity.

Anyway, I had fired my final shots and the dangerous Mr Morgan had faded into the distance. It was time to get serious and focus on my next crisis. No nonsense this time!

PART FOUR

I did the job! I finally did it!

I rolled the Morocco dice three times. I had roused Italy's 'Mare Nostrum', fired up the Balkans… with the help of the late Hartwig, and last but not least, the assassination in Sarajevo would never have taken place if it hadn't been for me.

I had started this dead-end game alone and now the game was over. Death was here for good. The late Jean Jaurès was absolutely right but no one listened to him. Now it was too late.

My boss didn't show up at the December 1914 meeting. We were supposed to meet before Christmas but he didn't come. As usual, I was staying at the Savoy Hotel. I waited for days but he didn't appear. It was a huge disappointment. I wanted to ask him when he thought the war would end. It was four months old already and millions had died.

There must have been some kind of plan.

Three days before Christmas, an astronomical amount of money appeared in my bank account. I nearly threw up. Was it because he was pleased or because he wanted to burden me with all the responsibility? I left the money where it was.

I left the bank feeling sick. I needed to walk. To get away. When I reached the lake, I walked along the River Limmat until I came to the coast. Lakes can be very dull sometimes. They're nothing more than restricted water holes. I ambled along as there was nothing to do and nowhere to go. The world I loved had come to an end.

Suddenly, I saw an old man looking at me. He was tall but hunched over by his advanced age. He was expensively dressed and looked like a wealthy, high-ranking aristocrat. He had long white hair and a beard like Jean Jaurès. For a moment, I thought it was a transformation of him. Maybe he'd returned to take revenge.

I thought it better to walk on and pay him no attention but then I heard an old, but familiar voice calling out to me.

"Frenchman!"

I turned and went up to him. I knew I had never met this man before. He came towards me. His walk was very familiar but still, something wasn't right.

I looked into his eyes but they were hidden behind his Trotsky-type glasses. He stepped forward, removed his hat and brushed back his long, white hair. He looked like a former pirate.

Who is this man?

He took off his glasses and when I looked into his eyes, I couldn't believe it.

You are alive?

Five days after I was released from prison, the Treaty of London was finally signed. The so-called London conference had begun at the end of 1912, just as my boss had said.

He was right from the beginning!

The Balkan War could not produce a Great War. Quite the opposite. It would eventually become the Fashoda of the new century. As you realise, it was a very long conference. Austria-Hungary wanted to support the new state of Albania so that Serbia would be kept away from the Adriatic Sea and a new protectorate would be in place for the Empire to annex sometime in the future. I mention this because the disagreements on the Albanian borders, and specifically the fate of the small town of Scutari, could have brought us the war we were hoping for.

However, just like Queen Victoria's 'miserable and small' Fashoda, the British Secretary of Foreign Affairs, Edward Grey, had said it was 'unreasonable and intolerable that the greater part of Europe should be involved in a war for a dispute about one or two towns on the Albanian frontier'.

Furthermore, and quite typical of a conference of this era, three of the ambassadors were cousins. Austria-Hungary's Count Albert Mensdorff, Russia's Count Alexander Beckendorff and Germany's Karl Max Prince Lichnowsky. Cousin ambassadors, cousin kings. It was no surprise that Franz Ferdinand was planning to revitalise the League of Three Emperors. Kings attending weddings, cousins attending conferences, spies being released, treaties being signed. This only served to complicate things. It wasn't looking good for my career.

One month later, on June 29th, Foxy Ferdinand launched a pre-emptive attack on his former allies, Serbia and Greece. Not so foxy. Hartwig was prepared and the Romanians and the Ottomans entered the game. In the end, the Balkan War only produced a miniature second Balkan War. They were the final convulsions of the Dying God of War, however. Franz Ferdinand strongly supported peace and on August 10th, 1913, the Treaty of Bucharest was signed.

The God of War is dead, my dear Nietzsche.

In the first week of December 1913, I was at the Savoy in Zurich for my annual meeting with my boss. Our last annual meeting as it would turn out to be.

Following my imprisonment in Sarajevo, I did nothing at all, as you have probably guessed. You know me by now. I was determined to do nothing even if the Kaiser stood for president in the French elections. I simply enjoyed Paris with its wonderful cabarets, restaurants, cafés…you know. Good wine, good food, gorgeous women. I gained ten kilos in a few months;

French cheeses whar, but regular long walks that September saved me from gaining more.

"I still find it difficult to believe that I created more upheaval by kidnapping Perdicaris than by killing King George. Isn't it tragic?"

"Like another tragic Prince of Denmark."

"Who?"

"Hamlet."

"Shakespeare's?"

"Yes, *The Tragic History of Hamlet, Prince of Denmark*."

"To be or not to be?"

"Anyway, Edward. It was the timing."

"The timing, democracy, the Cretan Gendarmerie."

"Timing in a democracy is a crucial factor."

It was obvious that from the middle of 1914, any timing would be right for the German machine but I said nothing because if my boss knew that, he wouldn't appreciate my work. The Kaiser's archaeological adventures on Corfu were a problem but a minor one.

"What are you planning to do with the Mona Lisa?" he continued.

"I believe the Mona Lisa should be used in conjunction with another event."

"Louis Lépine has retired, you know."

"Really?"

"Yes, on March 29th."

"I was in Italy at the time."

"When Mr Pierpont Morgan passed away, right?"

"Right…" I felt sad about what I had done to this rich fellow. "It feels strangely sad that the great Louis Lépine has retired without having found the famous Mona Lisa. He has many achievements to be proud of, though."

"Don't be sad. He is now an elected member of the Académie des Sciences Morales et Politiques."

"And the Mona Lisa is safe right there on the wall in my apartment. It must be destiny. It hung in Napoleon's bedroom from 1905 but he was away fighting and campaigning all over Europe most of the time. Now, it's hanging on the wall in my apartment and I am away causing fights."

"Except for the last few months," said my boss with a firm expression on his face.

"I have no specific plan yet, boss but I'm nearly there." I was anything but.

"Don't worry Edward, I understand…" He softened his stance.

My boss is insane.

"Perhaps that's why the Mona Lisa wears a black dress, Edward."

"What?"

"Because you are always away."

Totally insane!

"Oh, of course! But I often wonder why the wife of a silk merchant is wearing such a simple black dress," I said, trying to lighten the atmosphere.

"You should be wondering why so many damned foolish things have taken place and more than twenty years later, disaster is yet to come."

Damned Bosses!

"Bismarck lied too sometimes, boss."

"And he wasn't the only one, you know. An English lord said that the Entente Cordiale would eventually mean war with Germany and he said it on the day the Entente was signed."

"Which lord was that?"

"Archibald Philip Primrose, Lord Rosebery. A British Liberal statesman…and it's becoming increasingly more difficult to understand why a single German shot hasn't been fired yet. Not one!"

"Maybe it's because France is financing Russia, which holds the Germans back, boss."

"Bismarck had good reasons to keep Russia close at hand and the League of the Three Emperors, encouraged by Franz Ferdinand will do the job. Edward, if I didn't believe in your talent I'd be quite desperate."

"Thank you, boss."

"And without effort, our business will be confined to duels and hobbyists. The summer is always productive after our meeting here in December, Edward, and I'm sure this year will be no different. What are your plans for the coming year?"

"I told you, boss, I have no specific plans yet."

"But you said you are nearly there, didn't you?"

It was a foolish thing to say. All I've done for the last few months is enjoy the food and wine. Now it's time to come up with some more convincing tripe.

"Well, boss, I'll tell you my thoughts." I leaned forward in earnest. "What we need is the 'Pope effect'. That should start a big war."

"Interesting. What do you mean, Edward?"

I wish I knew myself. I'll just have to buy some time until something else comes to mind.

"Do you know the story of Pepin, the father of Charlemagne?"

"No."

"Well, Pope Stephen II was having problems with Aistulf, King of the Lombards. He crossed the Alps and visited the Kingdom of the Franks to ask for assistance against Aistulf. At the time, the King of Franks, Pepin the Short, father of Charlemagne, was away to the north fighting the Saxons. He was happy to learn that the pontiff was travelling north to meet him bearing gifts and was even happier to help him. And why?

"Not because of the gifts but because desperate Pope Stephen ingratiated Pepin to his cause by bestowing on him and his son the title of 'Patrician of the Romans'.

"And Charlemagne was his son, right?"

"Indeed, he was.

"So in the spring of 755, Pepin and his army crossed the Alps, fought the Lombards and defeated them and forced Aistulf to return all the papal lands he had occupied. A treaty was signed between Aistulf and Pepin and the Frankish army went home. When Pepin returned, Aistulf broke the treaty and besieged Rome again.

"What could the Pope now do? He needed Pepin but had nothing more to give him. He had played the 'Patrician' card too early. How could he persuade him to fight again now?"

"What did he do?"

"Nothing. Pope Stephen did nothing."

"So you're telling me you won't be doing anything to cause an …upheaval?"

"Let me finish, boss."

"Ok."

"St Peter sent a letter to Pepin."

"What?"

"A personal letter."

"Really?"

"Really!"

"And what were the contents of that letter? What did St Peter say?"

"He said a lot but briefly, he told Pepin that if he didn't return to help the Pope, he and his people would never go to paradise."

"Ingenius!"

"Exactly."

"Did it work?"

"Of course it worked, boss. Pepin hurried all the way back. His soul was at stake. The souls of his children were at stake. We're talking about St Peter here. No joke!"

"He could hardly do otherwise, I suppose. So, what's your point?"

"Honour."

"Please, be more specific."

"In short, clever men are a danger to our business. I need men with honour. They're easy to manipulate. All you have to do is connect their honour to the outcome you require and sit back. Just like Pope Stephen did. Capito?"

"Capisco."

He knows I'm deceiving him! I need something more credible! A number, a name, a… That's it.

"My first step will be to neutralise our ex-prime minister."

"Who?"

"The man who ruined my last Morocco Job. Joseph Caillaux. He's a danger to my plans. I was intending to destroy him politically in the next few months."

"You know better, I suppose." He had his doubts but it looked as if I'd fooled him.

"So, how are sales going, boss?" I said trying to change the subject again.

"Good, very good! Better than ever, to be honest, but you know what Anton Chekhov said."

"The Russian writer?"

"Yes, the Russian writer. 'If there is a rifle hanging on the wall in act one, it must be fired in the next act. Otherwise, it has no business being there'."

"Ahaa!"

"I look forward to your telegram, Edward." He looked calm and relaxed and left without another word. He probably realised I was lying.

Damned bosses!

I served ten days in a Sarajevo prison, killed a king, a menace and an old friend because of you. For the past ten years, Europe has been dancing to my tune.

Perdicaris, Morocco. After the Bosnian crisis, you all but begged me. Morocco, Libya, The Balkans, and now you're looking forward to my telegram?

Looking forward to it?

You pay me good money but have some respect!

Thank God I used the Caillaux card!

Sales! Who wants to work in sales, anyway? Alexandre Le Grand knew how to show his appreciation. But he was grand. LE Grand.

I'm done with sales! I'm too old. I know too much to be able to agree with anyone anymore.

On December 13th, I returned to Paris. I got off the train at the station and, for the first – or second - time in my life, I experienced what it was like to have your dirty deeds exposed. It was like being struck by a bolt of lightning.

A newspaper boy selling *Le Petit Parisien* ran in front of me and all I saw was a picture of the Mona Lisa with the huge headline: *LA JOCONDE EST RETROUVÉE.*

Oh, no!

How naïve I had been to leave it hanging in my apartment. What a fool! I thought I was clever but I was just a lucky fool. A complete fool! My boss was waiting for a telegram and now this!

I froze with fear then broke into a sweat. I hurried from the station carrying my small suitcase, looking around as I went. If I were to die of a stroke, it would be here in the streets of Paris. And if I'd got back on the train, I'd have died of shock already. Moving kept me alive.

I had lost everything because I was so self-assured.

How was I supposed to explain to the police that I'd stolen the Mona Lisa to blame the Prussians and start a war to take back Alsace and Lorraine but the Italians acted too quickly with their stiletto policy so I kept it?

Maybe I should say I saw Joan of Arc in my sleep…

Idiot, foolish, naive Edward Aguillon! You are responsible for the theft of the Mona Lisa.

What had I done? Suddenly, I regretted everything I'd done in my life. Again. The Mafia should have killed me twenty years ago. I wouldn't be going through this now if they had. When I was captured in Sarajevo, I knew I was innocent. Now I was guilty.

Apollo was taking revenge.

It was obvious. A thief broke into my apartment while I was away. He saw the painting and took it to claim the reward. Wait a minute…wait a minute! I could say I bought it as a copy. I had no idea it was the original.

But who would believe me? No one. Whom did I buy it from and what did it cost? Maybe I just found it and thought it was a fake! So I hung it in my apartment and didn't return it to claim the reward because I thought it was a copy. And I was stupid enough to hang it on a wall I hardly looked at. I didn't need fifty thousand francs. I was often away and…

Maybe my boss was to blame because I'd been lazy for the last six months.

No! No way!

Lost in my thoughts as I madly paced the streets of Paris, a voice from what seemed like outer space called my name.

"Mr Aguillon! Mr Aguillon! It's you!"

They've found me!

Red-faced, I turned and saw a young man calling me from the other side of the street. He was not a policeman. But who was he? I slowly raised my left hand to politely greet him. The unfamiliar man crossed the street, full of enthusiasm.

"Mr Aguillon, I haven't seen you for a very long time. You don't come to our meetings anymore," he said. "Oh my god, what's happened to you?" he added seeing my bright red eyes and the desperate look on my face. "It's me, Raoul Villain, from the 'League of Young Friends of Alsace-Lorraine'. You do not look well."

Suddenly, I remembered him. He was a student. He was standing next to me when I gave that heroic speech some years ago when the *Ligue des jeunes amis de l'Alsace-Lorraine* was founded. He was one of the few people in Paris who would believe without question that Joan of Arc had appeared to me in a dream and told me to steal the Mona Lisa, but at that point, despite my angst, I was hard-wired to display a different reaction.

"Raoul, of course I remember you, but I am in a very difficult situation. Our cause is in great danger, young man. I wouldn't want to get you into any trouble."

"Mr Aguillon, you know me, I want to help. Tell me what's going on. Please!"

"Ok, let's go somewhere safe."

Raoul studied archaeology at the École du Louvre, an institution of higher education located in the Aile de Flore of the Louvre Palace. It was dedicated to the study of archaeology, art history, anthropology and epigraphy. He lived in a small student apartment, two blocks from where we met. We hurried on in silence but I sensed he was excited to see me and become involved in a top-secret spy situation. Meanwhile, my brain was inventing the necessary nonsense to feed his naive enthusiasm.

"Listen to me, Raoul. What I am about to tell you must remain between us. The Prussians have spies everywhere. Everywhere, my boy! If you speak to the wrong people, our fight for Alsace and Lorraine will be in danger and so will your life."

"Mr Aguillon, I am a man of action, not of words and spectacle. Please tell me how I can help."

"Once you find out, there is no going back, son."

"I would be more than happy to give my life for Alsace and Lorraine."

"Three years ago, I started travelling throughout Lorraine, supposedly for a wine business. In reality, I was an arms dealer."

"Wow!"

"Our organisation was formed eight years ago when the Prussians tried to kick us out of Morocco. We signed up around ten patriots in Fécamp. Men of honour! We swore on oath that if a Prussian bullet ever took us down, our blood would seep into the soil of Lorraine.

"Or Alsace."

"Or Alsace! We'd had enough of diplomacy and cowardly notions of peace and a harmonic way of life so we decided to form a secret organisation to free the sacred land where Joan of Arc was born. And set it free with guns, the only medium the Prussians could relate to."

"What is the name of the organisation, Mr Aguillon?"

"*Mona Lisa*."

"Why not Joan of Arc?"

"So as not to give ourselves away, brave Raoul. Not to give ourselves away."

"Ingenius!"

"*Mona Lisa* smuggled around three thousand guns and five thousand bombs into Alsace. I moved half of those guns myself. Our connections saw to it that many of them are now in Lorraine.

"*Mona Lisa* gradually won over more supporters. We are now more than seventy men. Do you remember the Dreyfus Affair, Raoul?"

"Of course I do. My parents almost divorced because of it."

"There are moles everywhere, Raoul. Your best friend or even the founder of the *Ligue des jeunes amis de l'Alsace-Lorraine* could be a mole."

"Do you think Dreyfus was a mole, Mr Aguillon?"

Smart enough not to answer that question, I continued in a whispered voice.

"There is a mole in *Mona Lisa* and I am the only one who knows. You are now the second one to know about it."

"Do you know who he is?"

"Yes."

"Do you want me to kill him, Mr Aguillon?"

"No, Raoul. Killing him would be easy enough but will not solve our problem. I want him alive because he might not be the only mole among us. Until today, I thought they were unaware that I'd figured it out."

"What happened today?"

"I came on a train from Zurich. Next to me sat a man called Louis from Bordeaux, or so he said. Opposite me was a man who remained silent. At Basel station, the man opposite me stood up and prepared to get off the train but before he did, he turned to me. 'The *Mona Lisa* will be the death of you, lousy Frenchman,' he said in a German accent and pulled a knife on me.

"Shocked, I stood up to grab him. Louis from Bordeaux grabbed his hand and took the knife but he got away. Damned Prussian coward! It was then I realised that the mole wanted me dead.

"Louis was shocked and wondered what was going on. Naturally, I told him I didn't know. He kept asking questions and eventually I realised he, too, was a Prussian spy.

"When we arrived in Dijon, I took out my knife and held it to his throat. He was scared to death. He told me that France was full of German spies who would bring us to our knees, no matter what. In England alone, there were five thousand spies working as waiters. There were even traitors who worked for the government. He said I didn't have much time because they would kill me but first, they would destroy my integrity. I threw him out of the train in Dijon.

"When I arrived in Paris, there were men, waiting for me."

"How did you know that?"

"One of them checked his gun under his coat but I cleverly escaped them.

"Now you can appreciate why I'm so upset, my boy. I have no idea what those damned Prussian spies have in mind. How will they destroy me? I would gladly give my life, Raoul, but I'm afraid they'll destroy our organisation by instigating dirty lies about the patriots of *Mona Lisa*. After all our efforts for so many years! We were so close, so close," I said, shaking my head in desperation.

"Do you want me to contact the members of *Mona Lisa* you trust?"

"That's very brave of you, Raoul, thank you. But the man I trusted most is the mole. Who am I supposed to contact now?"

"What are we going to do, Mr Aguillon?"

"We?" I said, touched by the willingness of this young man to help a fellow patriot. "I'm very lucky to have met you, Raoul. God sent you to save our patriotic struggle."

"I am lucky to be able to serve my country."

"But I can't just sit like a duck and wait for them. The first thing I must do is leave Paris secretly."

"Where will you go?"

"I don't know but it must not be by train because they will find me. Marseille is the best option."

"I can arrange a seat in a carriage going south. You can change there and they'll lose track of you."

"You were born a spy, Raoul! Orleans will be fine."

"May I ask why you choose Marseille, Mr Aguillon?"

"The mole's family lives there," I replied, though I planned to head west after Orleans and go to Brest. There, I hoped to find a ship bound for America. I desperately wanted to see the Statue of Liberty again.

"Can I come with you, Mr Aguillon?"

"No, son. You're in big enough trouble as it is. Once I find out the information I need, I'll contact you if I'm still alive. Now you are one of us. A member of *Mona Lisa*."

"Thank you, sir, I won't let you down. I'll arrange the carriage for you. You can rest here today and leave tomorrow."

"You are doing your country a great service, Raoul. Here, take the money for the ticket. Use the name Jean Amsallem for the reservation."

"Make yourself comfortable, I'll be right back, sir."

How did you like my story? Not particularly fascinating but it did the job. As far as this young man was concerned, I was a hero. When he sees my name in the newspapers it will be the ultimate success for a spy who knew the Prussians blamed a patriot for the theft of the Mona Lisa. Hopefully, by then, I'd be safely on my way to the new world.

"Mr Aguillon! Mr Aguillon, where are you?" shouted Raoul to no reply.

He searched the house but neither I nor my belongings were anywhere to be seen. Disappointed, Raoul sat down and put the ticket on the table. Seconds later, I opened the door.

"Sorry, Raoul, I had to make sure no one followed you." The moustache I had proudly sported for decades, like many of the Belle Epoch era, was gone.

"I used your razor; I hope you don't mind, Raoul."

"You leave for Orleans tomorrow morning at nine, Mr Aguillon."

And soon after, for New Orleans, I thought, picking up my ticket.

Raoul was as happy as a lark. What a story he'd have to tell his grandchildren!

"Tell us about the Mona Lisa spy, again, Grandpa. Please!"

The following morning, I travelled by carriage to Orleans, bouncing up and down with six others. How lucky we were to have trains. If Napoleon had travelled by train, he would have conquered Russia!

Having recovered from the initial shock, the only thing that mattered was to get out of Europe as quickly as possible and never to be seen there again. If a reward of fifty thousand francs was to be given to the man who found the Mona Lisa, imagine how many years the man who had stolen it would be sentenced to. As for money, I had plenty in the bank so I honestly didn't care. I remembered what the late Mr Morgan had said and adapted it to my situation: 'Monetary losses amount to nothing in life. It is the loss of freedom that counts. It is that frightful jail.'

In jail for eternity. Oh my god! I realised how naive I'd been to steal the Mona Lisa. Bad deeds always carry risk. I was a wanted man and for no reason at all.

After Orleans, I headed north-west by any means I could, avoiding the large cities and trains. Throughout the journey, I was forced to rest in any hotel I could find due to the uncomfortable ride and its effect on the posture of a fifty-year-old man.

One cold December night, I reached the beautiful town of Brittany in the Finistère region of northwestern France. Morlaix was a small city and as these were probably my final days in France, I decided to spend more time there at a nice hotel in the centre of the peaceful town. It was called the *Hotel de l'Europe.*

I honestly don't remember if I arrived before or after Christmas. The hotel was festively decorated and people exchanged seasonal greetings but I avoided looking anyone in the eye for any length of time. I was given a room in the hotel loft.

I spent my time in my room, mostly, and walking, which opened my eyes to the beautiful French countryside for the first time. The bay, the bridge, the houses, the landscape; all the elements I had never appreciated and would now miss, leaving them behind forever on my voyage to the new world.

Time passed, a new year had begun and one day, I decided to take breakfast at the hotel restaurant rather than in my room for the first time.

While I was eating breakfast, I saw a copy of *Le Petit Journal* on a nearby table. There was a picture of Leonardo Da Vinci showing the Mona Lisa to King Francis. They got the nose right.

It was the December 28th, 1913 issue. In the bottom left-hand corner was a picture of me running away with the covered Mona Lisa in my hands. That wasn't exactly how I did it but they got the moustache right. In the bottom right-hand corner was another sketch of the crowd admiring the painting.

Next to *Le Petit Journal* was a local newspaper, *Le Courrier du Finistere.* The headline read: 'After a tour of

Italy's greatest museums, the Mona Lisa is back at the Louvre today.' It was dated January 4th. A Sunday.

It didn't make sense. I tried to stay calm and indifferent and finish my breakfast. It became increasingly difficult to do so.

Why did they send it to Italy in the first place?

I abandoned my croissant and grabbed the damned *Courrier* and hailed the beautiful Breton waitress who was serving breakfast.

"Miss! Black coffee, please! Strong, black coffee! Here! Thank you, thank you!"

As I began to read the article, I realised I was the first man on earth living in a parallel universe, decades before the theory of parallel universes became known.

The article stated that sixty thousand Italians had said goodbye to the Mona Lisa at Milan railway station. It had been found when an Italian had tried to sell it to a gallery in Italy.

Ok, now it made sense. My apartment had probably been burgled by an Italian. I was back in the real universe. America, here I come.

I dropped the local newspaper and grabbed the *Petit Journal* with its front-page pictures. It was definitely a more reliable source of information since my moustache was right.

I read it from cover to cover.

No! No way! No, no, no!

The Italian, a former employee of the Louvre, had stolen Leonardo's masterpiece single-handedly almost two years ago because he wanted to compensate Italy for Napoleon's looting of treasured artwork. Damned Prussi…talians!

I returned to my parallel universe.

"Miss! More coffee, please! Black!"

CE FUT SOUS UNE BLOUSE QUE MONA LISA FUT ENLEVÉE

LA RECONSTITUTION DE L'ENLÈVEMENT DE LA "JOCONDE"

"...this means that the theft of Mona Lisa is an Italian guy... with poor history knowledge..." said the police director

I read the article three times. In detail. And one more time, backwards. I cross-checked *Le Courrier du Finistere*. There was definitely something wrong with this place. The *Hotel de l'Europe*, I mean.

The building that housed the hotel was very old and had originally been the private residence of Count Claude Haudeneau de Breugnon. He died in Paris on September 6th, 1792 without descendants and the residence was divided into sections. The part nearest the town hall, known as *la maison neuve* or *la grande maison*, was rented to a merchant and in 1806, it was sold to Gabriel Bourdoulous.

The part of the building along the Aiguillon Bridge and Rue du Pavé was leased to Antoine Maillard. At the end of the eighteenth century, it became the *Hotel du Grand Turc.*

The French revolution caused delays with the inheritance, which was finalised in 1813 - one hundred years earlier to be precise. It was a chilling thought.

The property was divided between three families: Saliou Chef du Bois, Le Bihan de Pennélé and de Coëtlosquet.

In September 1816, a new manager by the name of Pierre-Charles Lardet changed the name to *Hotel de l'Europe* and in 1923, changed it again to the *Hotel de Paris* after having bought a third of the building from Baron Jean-Baptiste de Coëtlosquet.

In 1846, Monsieur Lardet changed the name of the establishment back to *Hotel de l'Europe.*

The hotel never changed its name again.

One thing was certain. The name of the hotel had changed about as many times as I had swapped universes while eating breakfast. I had no idea what kind of person Count de Breugnon was but when the owner of such a property dies with no descendants during the French

Revolution, there is bound to be trouble. French counts, lawyers, inheritance claims!

Or maybe there was a broader issue with the city of Morlaix. The bay, the bridge, the houses, the landscape; they were all odd. Later, I talked to some of the Morlaixeuse. They all approved of the newspaper.

Have I lost my mind? Is Edward Aguillon going mad?

It appeared, however, that I could walk the streets of Morlaix carrying *Le Petit Journal* without anything to be afraid of. It was my old familiar copy, which I continued to read on a regular basis.

My Paris apartment was occupied by an innocent man who had nothing to do with the Mona Lisa. I was a decent man who paid his bills, took long walks, ate at the few city taverns, took breakfast at the *Hotel de l'Europe* and had innocent conversations with the beautiful Breton waitress serving black coffee.

It was in these strange times in that innocent universe that I decided I would only leave with a solid plan in mind. A plan for the job I needed to finish. Once I had carried out this plan, I would return to Paris by train carrying my newspaper and make my way to my apartment. Whatever the circumstances, I would take a bath, get some rest and then visit the Louvre. Once everything was in place, I would execute my other plan. The plan *de l' Europe*.

My plan would cover all the details according to the affordable tools at my disposal. It would have to be feasible. Honour and intelligence had to be taken into consideration. It would use men of honour as leverage to move things in the right direction and it would eliminate, or at least reduce the number of clever men who could, and would, cause obstacles. Ideally, it would fulfil the prophecies of wise men of the past. Their words of wisdom would always be my guide. It was like the chicken and the egg dilemma. Which came first?

Nonsense!

There was no such plan and Sylvie, the beautiful Breton waitress, as well as offering me very fine coffee, offered me very fine kisses. Soon after and without a plan, I left for France, maybe for a new universe, but always with my precious copy of *Le Petit Journal.*

1914 had arrived. Happy New Year to all parallel worlds out there!

After taking my bath, I lay on the couch and looked at the empty wall where I had hung the Mona Lisa on that Sunday in August. The Mona Lisa I had stolen from the Louvre. During all my short stays in Paris, she had been good company. Now the wall was empty and it was as if she had never been there at all.

Finally, years later, I felt I had something in common with Mr Elazar and his Months or any American menace who hung a painting in his private space for personal enjoyment. The Mona Lisa, the woman in the painting, was like a mother figure to me; the mother I had lost as a child.

I lit a cigar, served myself a glass of Benedictine and took out my *Le Petit Journal.* The letters had started to fade after carrying it around for so long. I dropped it on the table with a huge sigh. *Le Petit Journal* reported the same damned, or for some, blessed, news and it was not the only newspaper to do so. I had bought numerous issues of other newspapers. *Le Figaro, L'Intransigeant, La Croix, Le Temps, Le Petit Parisien, Le Matin* and one more issue of *Le Courrier du Finistere.* They all referred to my case and agreed with each other but not all had such extended articles, at least not in these issues.

Le Figaro was mainly concerned with the minister of finance and ex-prime minister, Joseph Caillaux. You know about him already. I'd promised my boss I'd neutralise him. Damned…!

He was back in town as minister of finance and wanted to introduce the principle of income tax, progressive taxation and other such things. He'd campaigned intensively for this principle and now he was paying the price. *Le Figaro* extensively claimed he'd used his official position to facilitate speculation on the Paris Bourse and that three years earlier, as prime minister, he'd tried to influence the director of public prosecutions to delay the course of justice regarding a corruption case, known as the Rochette case.

Caillaux was the first part of my non-existent *plan de l' Europe.*

It was clear that *Le Figaro* didn't like innovative matters such as income tax and demonstrated its disagreement. It couldn't go very far with its campaign, however. It couldn't really do any damage to Caillaux. It needed help and I was there to provide it.

As far as my Mona Lisa was concerned, however, we all agreed. Even Caillaux.

The Italian's name was Vincenzo Perrugia. The owner of the art gallery in Florence was Alfredo Geri. Another man named Giovanni Poggi, director of the Uffizi gallery, was also involved. The Mona Lisa was exhibited in five museums throughout Italy. Sixty thousand Italians greeted it in Milan. Dates, names, facts, numbers. All the ingredients of a good lie.

Why is my wall so empty? Where is the Mona Lisa? How on earth is it possible on this earth?

Come on Edward! Who are you afraid of? You have nothing to fear right now.

You talked to so many people on the way to Paris, far away from the Hotel de l'Europe. Far away from Morlaix! The people on the trains agreed with the newspapers. The people in the restaurants agreed with them. Other newspapers are carrying similar news.

So why you are drinking liqueur and smoking cigars and staring at an empty wall when no one is looking for you? Why? How can this be possible?

I went into the bedroom and took out *my* painting, *my* Mona Lisa. The one I had single-handedly stolen to blame the damned Prussians.

I took it out of its dust sheet and carefully hung it back on the wall. There, where it belonged. Opposite my couch to keep me company.

Earlier that day when I entered my apartment, I was so happy to see her smiling at me. Then I looked at the damned *Le Petit Journal.* I even verified its extensive article and I don't know why, but I was terrified! She was hanging there just as I left her, despite the reality of the situation. Terrified, I grabbed the painting, covered it with the dust sheet again and stashed it under my bed, as if I, or she, were being hunted down.

The next day, I was the first person to enter the Louvre. I hurried in and headed to the *Salon Carré*. I stood before the four pegs from which I had dismounted the Mona Lisa. Seeing the empty wall frightened me again. The Mona Lisa had gone, yet thousands of people had come to the Louvre to see those four pegs since she had been stolen.

But now it should have been there. Oh my god! *Le Petit Journal, Le Courrier du Finistere,* all the newspapers…

Of course it's not there because it is hanging on the wall of your apartment. Idiot! This is a trap. The brilliant Lépine has set a global trap to make the real thief return. He's as sly as a fox. Foxy Lépine! The best detective the world has ever seen. He's retired but still carries on. And he did it. He made me return. Maybe he even tricked us into thinking he's retired.

I tricked an old guard but that doesn't mean I can trick Lépine. He let time pass, lulled me into a sense of false security and now look! Oh my god!

Scared stiff, I looked around but all I could see was a beautiful woman looking at the beautiful roof of the *Salon Carré* and a young guard looking at the beautiful woman.

With my head down, I started walking calmly but faster than usual. I made sure no one was following me. A long queue of people had gathered outside another room inside the Louvre.

I hurriedly made my way out, unwilling to make the same mistake as Alfred Redl in the Klomser Hotel, which had cost him his life.

They could be giving money away for all I care.

As I walked past the ever-growing queue, a sign on the wall caught my eye. An arrow was pointing in the direction of the queue.

PEN-KNIFE SHEATH, it said.

I walked on because, unlike Alfred Redl, I wasn't going to go looking for a pen-knife sheath and get caught like a rabbit in a trap. I'd been stupid enough to come here in the first place and I wasn't going to make any even bigger fool of myself. Not me. Not Edward Aguillon!

Suddenly, a young guard stopped me.

"Sir?"

"Yes! What? Is there something wrong?"

He can't possibly have recognised me. I shaved my moustache off this morning.

"That exit is out of use for security reasons. Use the other exit, please!"

"Ah… ok. Thank you, young man!"

Heading in the other direction, I noticed the many signs and arrows pointing in the direction of the… 'Sheath'. Now they were obvious but I certainly hadn't noticed them on my way to the *Salon Carré* when I entered the Louvre that morning. They were all over the place!

'MONA LISA'.

Like Colonel Redl, I couldn't resist. It was my destiny, I suppose.

So I queued. I actually queued.

By tomorrow, I'll be found dead in my room with my brains blown out. It's destiny. 'All who draw the sword will die by the sword.'

In our case, it was the sheath of a pen-knife, dear Alfred.

Calmly and patiently, I entered the room and was surprised to see her dress and her face from a different angle. Other visitors scrambled to see her.

It took another ten minutes, which seemed like an eternity, to get close to her, stand in front of her and witness her beautiful, enigmatic smile.

Hello mother. What are you doing here?

Let's go home, mother!

I cried. On Wednesday, January 28th 1914, I cried for the first time in many years.

Parallel lines never meet. They never intersect. But if they do, everything doubles.

It's the same with parallel universes, I suppose. But a great achievement or a supernatural event could probably force those parallel universes to intersect at some point in time. It was clear at this particular intersection that everything would double.

Everything?

Maybe not everything because that would be catastrophic. Maybe just the achievement that caused this unlikely deviation from those parallel lines.

The Mona Lisa.

At this intersection of two universes, the achievement - the masterpiece, would double.

Was I living in a world born out of a deviation that produced two Mona Lisas, or not? Had I been living at the intersection of two parallel universes since I arrived in Morlaix?

Damned city!

Damned Count!

Jean Theophile Homolle had rushed back from his vacation shocked to hear that one of Leonardo Da Vinci's paintings had been stolen. He had been the director of the national museum since 1904 but was now forced to resign. He would have resigned anyway. That was the easy part.

The hard part was that he would have to live the rest of his life as the man who lost the Mona Lisa. He would be a disgrace to the art world. It was an enormous responsibility. He should have insisted on professional security. He had neglected a very serious matter. All those old men asleep in the museum…under his direction.

How could he have been so naive?

Mr Homolle recalled the loss of the antiquities on the island of Delos. No one knew about it because no one had seen the treasures. And no one ever would. The security of the Louvre was a different matter, however. He should have insisted and if they ignored him, he should have threatened to resign.

Now it was much too late. The Mona Lisa had gone for good. And if that wasn't embarrassing enough, he now had to face Louis Lépine, Préfet de Police, who probably considered him a suspect too. It was already rumoured to be the case.

Mr Lépine was extremely responsible and professional. Sixty detectives commandeered and sealed the museum. They spoke to everyone who had a connection with it. Maybe Lépine would find the Mona Lisa by taking advantage of the newly available technology to uncover evidence that would previously have escaped him.

But now what? Would he spit in his face because of his inadequacy? Mr Homolle was terribly ashamed of himself.

"Bonjour Mr Lépine," said the former director, rather scared.

"Bonjour Mr Homolle. Come in, please, and take a seat."

"Thank you."

"Things must be very difficult for you at the moment."

"I…I…just…" The former director could hardly speak and almost burst into tears.

"It's ok, I understand, I understand."

"Is there any chance of finding it, Mr Lépine?"

"Well, to tell you the truth, it won't be easy. Whoever stole it did an excellent job. Many detectives are working on it at the moment and we still don't know what the investigation will reveal."

"We'll have to wait and see, then."

"You realise I must ask you, Mr Homolle, do you have any suspicions? Do you have any idea who would commit such a crime? Who would like to have the Mona Lisa in their possession? What do you think?"

"I know of many gallerists who'd like to have it but I don't think they'd ever risk stealing it. A rich collector, maybe? But they are so many of them throughout Europe and America, it would be almost impossible to track them down."

"Yes."

"But if you have any clues, I would be glad to help with any additional information."

"As a matter of fact, Mr Homolle, I do need your help. And right now!"

"I'm more than happy to oblige."

Louis Lépine got up from his desk and slowly walked around in circles.

"May I call you Theophile?"

"It would be an honour, Mr Lépine."

"Call me Louis.

"We're facing a national disaster, you know, Theophile, and it is my responsibility to deal with it. You probably know that I am a man who gets results. When I was hunting down the 'Bonnot Band', I ordered the building to be blown up with dynamite and shot Jules Bonnot in the head myself.

"Those are results, Theophile!

"You will also remember, I believe, the great flood of Paris in 1910. Results there, too."

"Results indeed," repeated Theophile, nodding in agreement.

"In this particular case, what is our main aim?"

"To find the thief, I suppose."

"Actually, no! I don't give a damn about the thief.

"As Préfet de police, I will have succeeded if the Mona Lisa is returned to the Louvre tomorrow morning, even if we never find the thief. We will have achieved a result…A result!

"Of course, I would happily shoot him in the head, as I did with Bonnot, but that's irrelevant. Results… no matter what!"

"Results. I agree."

"A hundred years from now, we will both be dead and no one will remember whether the thief was found or not, whether he lived or died or spent his life in prison or as a free man.

"What's more important is that future generations will have the privilege of admiring Leonardo Da Vinci's painting as we did, rather than just read about a unique work of art that was lost forever because we were incapable of protecting it." He chose his words carefully and specifically to offend his new friend, Theophile.

"Of course," replied the poor former director of the Louvre.

"As you know, the police are focusing on finding the thief to retrieve the Mona Lisa. If we don't find him, however, we'll need a contingency plan to get the results we need, no matter what."

"I...I don't understand, Louis...Really!"

"Allow me to explain. Two separate plans will be carried out at the same time. Firstly, there will be an in-depth investigation which will lead us to the thief and, eventually, to Leonardo Da Vinci's painting. Secondly, we will take all necessary action to return the Mona Lisa to the Louvre where it belongs, no matter what."

"Good!"

"Do you understand?"

"Well, to be honest, I find it rather difficult to…I mean, I can't see the difference between the two."

"You may think they are the same but they are not. Please listen carefully because I will not repeat myself. Perhaps I should rephrase it to clarify the distinction.

"Two teams will work simultaneously. The goal of the first team will be to find Leonardo Da Vinci's famous La Gioconda. The goal of the second team will be to hang the famous La Gioconda on the wall at the Louvre, no matter what.

"No matter what, Theophile! Results, no matter what!"

"Ok, but wait a minute. If you find it, why will you need a second team to hang it on the wall?"

"Because it must be hung there, even if I don't find it."

"What? I don't believe it! I honestly don't believe it! You're going to…m…make a copy and fool the whole world, you mean?" Homolle was furious.

"No! I repeat. It is my job to make sure that future generations will have the opportunity to admire the Mona Lisa. And I don't mean a copy."

"What? How?"

"A detailed and precise reproduction of Leonardo Da Vinci's work, that's what I mean."

"Louis, you are unbelievable! You're willing to fool future generations with a detailed, exact copy simply to achieve success?"

"No, Theophile, no! I knew you would think that but it's not the case."

"Oh yes, it is! I know it is. And you know it is!"

"Calm down and listen. I'll be retiring soon. If my first team do not find the thief I'll have to retire without solving the case. Correct?"

"Correct."

"But if in two or three years' time, the Mona Lisa is found, will I take any credit for it? What do you think, Theophile?"

"No."

"For future generations, my friend. I'm doing it for them.

"I'm an old man, Theophile, a distinguished man, who needs no further appraisal in life. I'll be happy knowing the younger generation will come to the Louvre without having to discover that the great painting which used to hang on those four pegs is not there now because we were unable to protect it.

"You are an old man, too. Two years younger than me, I think."

"That's right."

"You don't want to be remembered like that, do you, Theophile? The man who lost the Mona Lisa."

"What about the art critics and specialists?"

"I couldn't care less."

"Over the years, cracks have formed on Da Vinci's painting as they do on all paintings. They are unique and impossible to reproduce no matter how good the artist is. It's impossible, I tell you. I repeat. Impossible!"

"Listen, Theophile.

"When I set out to reorganise the flow of traffic in the centre of Paris by introducing one-way systems and roundabouts, they also told me it was impossible.

"I introduced forensic science to detective work.

"I introduced the police to criminology and examining the psychology of criminals.

"Under my direction, fingerprinting became established as a method of identification. People were always telling me things.

"Those cracks you mentioned are much like the fingerprints of a painting."

"I couldn't agree more."

"And you have photographs of the Mona Lisa in the museum?"

"Yes, but they are not the only ones. There are many photographs of the Mona Lisa all over the world," said Homolle.

"Good."

"Listen, I honestly don't know how you came up with this ridiculous plan but if you try something like this, one day, someone will find out. Someone will talk."

"Who's going to talk?" Lépine took slow, short steps around the room as he spoke.

"I don't know. A member of your second team, maybe?"

"You are the only member of that team, Theophile"

"Oh!"

"If you agree, of course."

"And who will paint this painting?"

"That's where you come in. You are the only person in the world I trust to find the most talented man for the job."

"Yes, but what if he is talented but unreliable?"

"That's why I am also a member of this team, Theophile. You show me the man who can reproduce a detailed and accurate masterpiece and I will make him the most reliable man in the world."

"And once it's ready, we just drop it off at the door of the Louvre?"

"No, of course not!"

"Ok, I suppose we have time to think about that later, Louis."

"Not at all."

"What? So what do you mean?"

Louis Lépine finally sat down next to his new friend and explained. "When I introduced one-way systems and roundabouts to the movement of traffic, flow control was very important."

"Flow control?"

"Yes. Flow is controlled when there is a target ahead. A target to be reached, no matter what. And this target has to be known in advance to plan ahead."

"So?"

"The theft of the Mona Lisa was an inside job. I have already studied the profiles of all the employees of the Louvre. Our man had a good knowledge of the area and did it for idealistic and psychological reasons."

"What kind of psychological reasons?"

"A Frenchman who admires Napoleon and wants to get his hands on a painting from the wall of Napoleon's bedroom, or a German who hates the French because his father died in the Franco-Prussian War, or an Italian who wants it returned to Italy because Napoleon stole it."

"But the Mona Lisa was not stolen by Napoleon. King Francis bought it directly from Da Vinci."

"I know, but the poor Italian is clueless about history. The nationality of the thief depends on our…"

"Our? Our…? Our what…?"

"Our…target.

"That's the other reason you are on this team.

"You have many connections in the art world and I would like you to find me an honest gallery owner, anywhere in the world, who will receive a letter telling him to buy a painting and when he realises it is the stolen Mona Lisa, he will not keep it but deliver it to the Louvre instead."

"Alfredo Geri. He owns an art gallery in Florence."

"Florence? That's where Da Vinci painted the Mona Lisa, isn't it?"

"Yes."

"You seem pretty sure about this Geri. Are you quite positive?"

"Absolutely! I trust him more than any other French gallerist I know."

"Excellent! That means the thief who stole the Mona Lisa will be an Italian…and clueless about history, as we agreed," said the police chief. He went over to his desk, carefully noted the name of Alfredo Geri and grabbed a pile of papers from his desk.

"This is the Italian pile. We have many Italians here, mostly from the north of Italy, in search of a better future," he continued.

"I divided this pile of Italians into two sections. One for Louvre employees and one for subcontractor employees. Which of them have any connections to the *Salon Carré* or the Mona Lisa?"

"I am extremely impressed by your methodology, Louis," said Homolle, unable to hide his respect for the mastermind.

"Louvre or subcontractor, Theophile?" repeated Lépine waving a pile in each hand.

"Some years ago, a subcontractor changed the frames of our paintings. I think La Gioconda was among them."

"Subcontractor it is!" said Lépine like an enthusiastic auctioneer and dropped the papers in his left hand on his desk. He gave the other pile to Mr Homolle. "For each employee, there is also the name of the subcontractor. You name our man."

"Ok it was a carpentry company, I think…" said Homolle. Suddenly, he threw the pile onto Lépine's desk. "No! I cannot do it. I cannot destroy the life of an innocent man," he said. He stood up and went over to the window. "I cannot participate in this. I am sorry, Louis. It is a moral issue. I cannot allow myself to do this."

"Theophile, Theophile didn't you hear what I said?" Lépine smiled. "The man you choose did it for idealistic reasons. And he is a very lucky man, as I will personally secure his future. A worry-free future. And this is possible because he will have stolen the Mona Lisa as an Italian patriot, who, like all his compatriots, innocently wishes the painting to be returned to its place of origin.

"This poor Italian, who could even be a relative of Da Vinci's, lives a life of poverty in the city of lights and is regularly subjected to the arrogant behaviour of the French, who enjoy economic prosperity, colonial expansion and cultural innovations. They consider him and all Italians inferior but display Da Vinci's masterpieces in their museums at the same time.

"Stealing the Mona Lisa was simply a peaceful protest.

"I have good connections with the *carabinieri*, but I don't think we'll need them. He'll be a loyal Roman soldier. An Italian hero. A patriot."

Homolle, satisfied by Lépine's explanation, took the papers and after sifting through the profiles, found the perfect candidate. He handed it to the Préfet de Police.

"This man was in the group that changed the frames in the *Salon Carré*."

Lépine took the paper from Homolle and held it at arm's length. "Vin-cen-zo Pe-rug-gia." His eyesight was failing him. "I admire him already," he enthused, looking at his team.

"Is that it, then?"

"You've forgotten something."

"What's that?"

"You must find me a man capable of reproducing a detailed and accurate masterpiece. This…" Lépine took the paper from his desk again, "…Vincenzo Peruggia…

will take it by train to Florence and give it to this… Alfredo Geri…in two or three years from now, if the first team doesn't come up with the…"

"Results."

"We are a great team, Theophile," he said, extending his arm to him. "Alors, have you got a man for the job?"

"There is only one man I know who is talented enough to carefully and accurately reproduce the work of Leonardo Da Vinci.

"He is a young painter and lives here in Paris, about thirty years old. He experiments with new, modern things but he is very talented, I can assure you of that. He's Spanish."

"What's his name?"

"Pablo Picasso."

So that's your explanation!

I mentioned earlier that Lépine was determined to get results, no matter what. Remember the dates, please. It's important!

On August 22nd 1911, the alarm sounds. On that day, Lépine decides to create two teams that will work simultaneously. He knows no one would risk losing a great masterpiece once they got hold of it.

I agree!

A few days later, the secret second team becomes official and Lépine must make Picasso a reliable 'reproducer'.

On September 7th, the young painter in question - Pablo Picasso - trembled with fear in the interrogation room.

It took him sixteen days.

Oh, how I admire Lépine!

I must tell you the details because Louis Lépine deserves it.

Stop clapping and sit down!

Honouré Joseph Géry Pieret, Apollinaire's former secretary, had noticed how easy it was to steal from the Louvre many years earlier.

"I'm going to the Louvre, Madam, do you need anything?" he said to Apollinaire's spouse, Marie Laurencin, as if he were going shopping.

Once the Mona Lisa was stolen, he presented himself as Baron Ignace d'Ormesan at the headquarters of the *Paris Journal,* bragging about how easy it was to steal from museums and as proof of his audacity, he handed over a recently stolen statuette.

Why did he do such a thing?

Was he looking for profit?

Or hoping for a moment of fame?

No! This was the beginning of Lépine's effort to ensure the young Picasso was at his disposal and that no one would ever suspect them if they saw them together.

How did he find Géry Pieret?

As you know, he widely bragged about his accomplishments at the 'free-for-all' museum of the Louvre. Lépine soon heard about him and knew he could connect him with the Spaniard. He pursued him but Géry Pieret had delivered the statue to the *Paris Journal* to avoid being accused of the theft of the Mona Lisa. Or so he thought.

When Apollinaire read the *Paris Journal* particle, he panicked, informed his friend Picasso and just as they were about to throw the stolen statuettes into the River Seine, they changed their minds and decided that

Apollinaire should also take them to the *Paris Journal* offices.

He tried to do it anonymously but was arrested and sent to jail. Little did he know that Lépine would have caught him anyway because of his connections with the Spaniard. Thus Picasso was brought in for questioning.

Lépine entered the scene with an appropriate introduction. To begin with, he had to ensure his detectives would frighten the life out of Picasso, simultaneously facilitating two famous tricks for the first time in history.

First, the prisoner's dilemma, (developed decades later in game theory), describes how two completely rational individuals might not cooperate, even if it appears it is in their best interests to do so.

Apollinaire and Picasso were put into separate cells. Picasso was terrified about what his friend might reveal. The detectives accused the young painter of serious crimes. Maybe his poet friend would accuse him of everything, simply to evade conviction. Maybe even of stealing the Mona Lisa. He was confused and knew he couldn't trust anyone. He denied having ever seen Apollinaire.

Apollinaire! His closest friend in all of France!

Now, it was time for the second part of the scheme.

The famous 'good guy-bad guy' technique.

Lépine instructed his evil, angry detectives to scare the life out of Picasso. They rolled up their sleeves and laid into him mercilessly, verbally at least. Picasso, alone in a cell, and terrified about what might follow was threatened with the reputation of name, his paintings and his life.

The detectives did an excellent job.

Orders from higher up, however, stated that physically, he wasn't to be touched. Lépine knew how precious the prisoner was to him.

The detectives thought they were looking for the thief of the Mona Lisa. Please remember that. They were members of Lépine's first team. They had no idea about any second team and the real objectives of their superior. The second team consisted of just two members - Lépine and Homolle.

When the members of the first team had done their job, it was time for the second team to take action. The door of the small cell opened and the notorious Lépine entered in all his glory and ordered the detectives to leave him alone with the suspect. The detectives obeyed out of respect for their prestigious superior. Now they were alone. The Préfet de Police and the Spanish painter.

Picasso was released the very same day.

It is worth knowing that 'Les Demoiselles d'Avignon' of 1907, the painting for which Picasso used the stolen statue heads, is widely considered to be the first great work of Modernism.

Modernism, using three-thousand-year-old stolen models! Incredible! Apollinaire wrote the preface for the first Cubist exposition outside Paris the very same year. In Brussels, at the VIII Salon des Indépendants, he described Cubism as a new manifestation and high art.

After leaving prison one week later, unlike his lucky friend who was released on the same day, the poor poet was expelled from his apartment. His lover, Marie Laurencin, and her mother offered him refuge in their home. A year later, their liaison ended. Picasso's involvement in the theft, however, was hardly known, despite the so-called *affaire des statuettes* making international headlines.

Well done Lépine, well done!

With Picasso otherwise engaged, Lépine concentrated his efforts on poor Vincenzo Peruggia, a thirty-two-year-old Italian, who happened to have worked on changing the frames of the paintings in the Louvre. The approach in this case was much simpler.

In August, Peruggia had received a visit at his dingy apartment from a detective of the first team, who, incidentally, never stopped looking for me, but obviously, nothing was found.

This time, the second team paid him a visit.

"I've found the Mona Lisa, Mr Peruggia."

"I am happy to hear that, Mr Lépine. I was very sad to hear it was stolen. One of your detectives came the other day…"

"We know, Mr Peruggia. We know."

"King Francis bought the painting from Leonardo Da Vinci and it is a great honour for us Italians…"

Homolle and Lépine looked at each other before Homolle interrupted the friendly Italian fellow who appeared to know his history. "We have found the Mona Lisa, Mr Peruggia, but we can't have it back yet."

"Why?"

"It's complicated," said Lépine.

"Who is the thief?"

"A German spy."

"Why did he steal it?"

"He wanted to start a war. He is dead now, but diplomacy takes time. You know how these things work."

"We'll get it back soon but need your cooperation in another matter."

"I'd be glad to help, Mr Homolle."

"Good. The whole world is talking about the Mona Lisa but no one knows that she was Italian, dear Vincenzo, and that is very concerning."

"She was from Florence!"

"Exactly, son," said Lépine.

"Whenever I mention this to journalists, historians or critics, they simply ignore me and regard it of no significance." Homolle was very good. A precious member of the second team.

"And that is not fair, son. Not fair at all."

"I agree. Everyone thinks she's from Paris," said the Italian.

"We would like the Mona Lisa to return from Florence to Paris once again for the whole world to understand."

"To be educated, son."

"What a great idea! How can I help?"

"However much we promote this return journey, no one will take any notice if we don't make it into an adventure. The Mona Lisa, you see, hung in the Louvre for many years and no one was interested in her. Now the painting has been stolen, people all over the world are talking about it.

"They even visit the Louvre to look at the empty space in the *Salon Carré* where she once hung."

"That's true."

"We'll leave it for a while and when the time is right, we'll announce that the Mona Lisa has been found at its place of origin, in Florence. It will be displayed in the greatest Italian museums and then brought back to the Louvre."

"And why do you need me?"

"To transport it from here to Florence by train."

"It's only a sixteen-hour journey, son."

"We'll pay for your ticket, hotel and expenses and you will be paid one hundred francs."

"It would be my pleasure!"

"There is another option, however."

"Yes, Mr Lépine?"

"We will guarantee you a good job with a decent income for the rest of your life in France and at the same time, you'll be considered a hero in Italy, if..."

"If?"

"If you pretend it was you who stole it in the first place and returned it to its place of origin because Napoleon stole it from Italy," added Homolle.

"But Napoleon didn't steal it. King Francis..." replied Peruggia.

Homolle interrupted.

"Ok. To take revenge because he had stolen the Horses of Saint Mark from Venice to mount them on the Arc de Triumph..." he added.

"Those horses are a product of theft, anyway. The Crusaders stole them from Constantinople in 1204 during the..."

"To take revenge and compensate Italy for Napoleon looting their artwork, for God's sake!" Lépine was annoyed by Peruggia's knowledge of history.

"Wait a minute, you want me to say that I...stole the Mona Lisa?"

The second team remained silent.

Lépine considered this the most difficult part of his team's effort to return the Mona Lisa to the Louvre.

Homolle thought it was even more difficult than reproducing the cracks in Da Vinci's painting.

"Yes!" they said in unison, looking as innocent as possible.

The thirty-two-year-old Italian sank his head and couldn't believe what he had been asked to do. He remained silent long enough for the two notorious older men to reconsider their indecent proposal and feel guilty, Homolle in particular, about initiating and participating in an evil plot to deceive the whole world, which would force an innocent man to confess to such a terrible crime.

The Italian raised his head. "The whole world will think that I, Vincenzo Peruggia, have committed the greatest theft of the century?"

"We realise that, son…"

"Unbelievable! My friends in Milan will be amazed! I'll show them what I'm really worth…they thought I was just a bookworm…" Peruggia laughed enthusiastically and broke into the beautiful Italian language, imagining the glorious times ahead.

Louis Lépine and Theophile Homolle were speechless… and done.

Although Peruggia was instructed to say nothing to anyone, the young man couldn't believe his luck and couldn't resist sharing his enthusiasm with his father. On 22nd December 1911, four months after the theft, he wrote that Paris was the place 'I will make my fortune and it will arrive in one shot.'

The following year, while the Italians were taking the Dodecanese, he wrote another letter. "I wish you a long life and hope you enjoy the surprise your son is about to bring about for you and all our family."

Everything else went as planned and as reported in *Le Petit Journal*, which gave me doubts about my sanity.

Pablo Diego José Francisco de Paula Juan Nepomuceno María de los Remedios Cipriano de la Santísima Trinidad Ruiz y Picasso, a Spanish painter born on October 25th 1881, completed his reproduction in absolute secrecy in two years. Cracks whar!

He made an amazing job of it, Picasso whar!

Vincenzo Peruggia, an Italian carpenter born seventeen days earlier than Picasso on October 8th 1881, wrote a letter to the gallerist from Florence, Alfredo Geri, who called in Giovanni Poggi, director of the Uffizi Gallery, to authenticate the painting. After his sixteen-hour train journey with all expenses paid, they met at a hotel. After reclaiming the painting, Poggi and Geri informed the police, who arrested Peruggia at his hotel.

Geri and Poggi stated that Peruggia asked for money. The fact that he gave them the painting so easily, however, weakened their argument. But it wasn't important because it was not the thirty-two-year-old Italian 'thief' who was tested from now on, but the thirty-two-year-old Spanish painter.

Picasso passed the first test easily and if you would like to admire his work, you can visit the Louvre whenever you like.

At Peruggia's trial in Italy, the court agreed, to some extent, that he had committed his crime for patriotic reasons and he was given a lenient sentence. He was sent to jail for one year and fifteen days but was hailed a great patriot in Italy and served just seven months.

With no logical explanation and still in tears after seeing the Mona Lisa at the Louvre, I wrote a letter to *Le Figaro*; the best newspaper in Paris and probably, France. I addressed it to the editor, Gaston Calmette. While at the post office, I remembered my stupid boss looked forward to receiving a telegram so I sent him one. This time, it was single-worded.

'Franz'

That year, I had missed my trip to Vienna and needed to justify it. Sending the telegram was like rolling a dice.

This is probably my last year in this, or any, job. Might as well enjoy it!

Heeding to my fantastic 'plan', I decided to concentrate my efforts on the centre of Europe. It was where the Central Powers lay; the Austro-Hungarian Empire, essentially.

At the centre of this empire was Emperor Franz Joseph Karl. In the past, he had often been the target of the *Black Hand* and it would be a shame if they acted, finally, and I didn't take credit for it. Besides, I'd saved him in 1910. He was eighty-three years old but with no 'brain', the *Black Hand* was just that - a hand. An old man with lumbago already has one foot in the grave. The Grim Reaper expects him to die of natural causes and will likely get angry if he dies by other means. Then there was the heir, Archduke Franz Ferdinand Carl Ludwig Joseph Maria. We happened to be the same age. He repeatedly denied Conrad a war over a five-year period and would probably continue to do so, unless someone persuaded him not to do such a terrible thing.

Furthermore, he would soon have the opportunity to apply his insane ideas by creating his 'united states' of Austro-Hungary, handing out privileges to the southern Slavs and Hungarians. If that ever happened, my unrealistic *plan de l' Europe* would be obsolete.

As you probably realise, it was thanks to him that I'd made my fortune because if I hadn't stopped Conrad in the past, my boss wouldn't need me anymore. The war would have started in 1908 because of Bosnia and Herzegovina. If he'd had the opportunity to enforce his ideas, a war of any great scale would have been light-years away because the Kaiser was too busy with his archaeology on Corfu. It would cost me money. There was an obvious intersection here. Franz was the reason I was here, but what brought me here wouldn't get me there, if you know what I mean.

Now before I tell you about the third Franz – yes, there was one more, you need to know about the House of Habsburg.

Franz Ferdinand was born in Graz and was the eldest son of Archduke Karl Ludwig of Austria, the younger brother of Emperor Franz Joseph. In 1875, when both Franz and I were eleven years old, his cousin, Francis V, Duke of Modena, died, naming Franz Ferdinand as his heir on condition that he added the name 'Este' to his own. Archduke Franz Ferdinand of Austria-Este thus became one of the wealthiest men in Austria.

Lucky fellow!

Fourteen years later in 1889, his cousin and heir to the throne, Crown Prince Rudolf, committed suicide at his hunting lodge in Mayerling. Franz Ferdinand's father, Karl Ludwig, was therefore left as first in line to the throne but he died of typhoid fever in 1896. Thus, Franz Ferdinand was groomed to succeed the throne.

Four years later in 1900, and while I was changing careers, he married Sophie Chotek, who, according to the old emperor Franz Joseph, was not blue-blooded enough. In the Privy Council Chamber of the royal Hofburg Palace, Franz Ferdinand was thus forced to swear an oath that his children would not succeed him as emperor.

Franz Ferdinand had a younger brother called Otto, who died in 1906 at the age of forty-six. Otto had a son, named Charles Franz Joseph Ludwig Hubert Georg Otto Maria, who was now the next in line after Franz Ferdinand. This was my third Franz.

On June 13th, 1911, as my Agadir crisis shook Europe, Charles announced his engagement to Princess Zita of Bourbon-Parma to the Austrian court. They were married on October 21st the same year at the Bourbon-Parma castle of Schwarzau in Austria. Picasso was already working hard on his Joconde.

The eighty-one-year-old Emperor Franz Joseph, Europe's longest-serving monarch, (my first Franz and Charles's great-uncle), attended the wedding and was relieved to see an heir enter a suitable marriage. He was so happy, he proposed a toast at the wedding breakfast. It was particularly significant and you can imagine how happy he was when Archduchess Zita gave birth to a son - Otto Junior - on November 20th, 1912. Meanwhile, Picasso was still working hard on the Mona Lisa.

Finally, just to surprise you, there was one more Franz. The unseen Franz number four was something of a fourth ace up my sleeve, the ultimate horse in this race. Franz Xaver Josef Conrad von Hoetzendorf, the field marshal who was in love with Gina, had urged for war thirty times and uncovered the espionage activities of Colonel Alfred Redl the previous March, thanks to me.

The problem, as far as I was concerned, was that after he'd revealed Alfred Redl, he'd probably have to abandon his army's plans because the enemy knew about them. He would now have to develop and organise a new plan which would take much time and effort. He would need at least two years for that, I thought.

I had accidentally proffered peace. The night he ordered Redl's suicide, he was probably relieved that war hadn't yet taken place. Delaying a war was a problem for him now, too. He needed a war as soon as possible to get Franz Joseph's permission to marry Gina, a divorcee with six children. I met Conrad once, as you remember, but I had no idea if he was mad enough to risk a war with an enemy that knew his plans. At the same time, I was unable to tell whether he had lost his mind to Gina. If that were the case, the *Black Hand* and Conrad had too much in common.

Now you realise why my four Franzes had much going for them and I was planning to use their multi-dimensional relationship to create an upheaval. A central upheaval always rumbles the perimeters. In this case, the Hungarians and the Slavs.

In Hungary, however, was a very smart man - István Tisza, the prime minister of the Hungarian

Parliament. He was two years older than me and a champion duelist, like George Clemenshau. I thought I could use his only weakness; his devotion to Emperor Franz Joseph.

On the other hand - the *black* hand – with the Slavs in Bosnia, there was much hope. Serbia, under Hartwig's influence, would steal any opportunity and was still keen after the Balkan victories.

I hadn't spoken to my friend for a long time but I was afraid to contact him because he had lost his best spy while I was in a Bosnian prison and any connection would be fatal. And eventually was fatal.

Once I had sent my one-word telegram and the letter to *Le Figaro*, I bid farewell to my Mona Lisa and packed for Vienna. You can guess which hotel I stayed in.

I didn't want last year's tragic events to influence me. Location is very important!

On my first morning in Vienna, I went for a coffee at the *Café Central*. Lev Davidovitch Bronstein was sitting in his usual place, wearing the same glasses and sporting his eternal lion's mane haircut. He had maintained this habit of writing and idea-forming while drinking coffee for many years with patience and passion.

My boss had no patience, however. It was my job to devise the plot. Franz, Franz, Franz and…Franz. And now that I've explained the 'Four Franzes' argument, surely it's clear what I had to do or pretended to do, to cause instability.

First of all, let's leave Franz Joseph out of this. I am not the *Black Hand* and I have explained his case already. The only reason I would consider doing something would be if he dismissed Franz Conrad or allowed him to marry Gina. Both of these actions would neutralise my best partner.

If Conrad were dismissed, I could at least hope for a new intimidating field marshal but if Conrad were to marry, it would be a catastrophe. The marshal in command would enjoy spending time with his beloved wife and preparing his new invasion for the next decade or so, and no one could argue with him.

"Are you crazy? Alfred Redl betrayed all our plans. How dare you suggest a war with an enemy knowing exactly how we plan to outflank them! It's like sending your children to certain death. I am a strategist, not a butcher. We're working hard on our new plans and by 1920, we'll be ready. And that's final!"

I would have to kill him myself.

Putting aside Franzes numbers one and four for the moment, we are now left with the heirs.

Franz Ferdinand swore that his children would not be kings. However, he swore it while in love and without children. Now he was married with children - two sons and a daughter. Could his attitude have changed? Maybe, maybe not.

Franz Charles knows he is next in line and that his son, Otto, will follow him. All he had to do was have more children, enjoy life and wait. I didn't think he'd be in any hurry with the problems the Empire was facing.

"I'll leave my dear uncle to experiment with his ideas and then see. Time is on my side."

Franz Conrad didn't have time, however. He was already sixty-five and Gina, all but thirty-five. He first proposed preventive war against Serbia in 1906 and did so again in 1908 and 1909, in 1912 and 1913, in October 1913, and in May 1914. Between January 1st, 1913 and January 1st, 1914, he had proposed war against Serbia twenty-five times and he continued to do so even after the Redl affair, as you know.

Gina had made him lose his mind. It was obvious.

He would even have killed Franz Ferdinand, who stopped him. I had found my victim and I had found my killer. Let me buy you a coffee with Mr Bronstein. Black?

Just kidding! Conrad was faithful to all the Franzes so I had to turn to the other brainless entity and ask if they could give me a hand. A 'black' hand!

The days went by very quickly. Mr Bronstein continued to write articles for the newspapers and I continued to read all the newspapers I could get my hands on, sometimes at the *Landtmann Cafe,* sometimes in the *Central Cafe* or in the Klomser Hotel lobby. I kept myself informed about every little detail that could help me justify my… 'Franz'.

In March, two important pieces of news developed. Not one, but two.

Suddenly, the God of War returned from the land of the dead. March justified its name, being named after Mars, and wars usually started in March, the first month of the calendar in the ancient world.

It seemed that while I was in Vienna, the *Le Figaro* articles about Joseph Caillaux had continued and the finance minister was paying for it by being faced with a daily, bitter campaign about his odd decision to introduce progressive tax.

On March 13th, 1914, the newspaper published a personal letter the finance minister had written thirteen years previously revealing that he and Berthe Gueydan, then a married woman and later his first wife, were having an intimate affair. The letter mostly confirmed a number of political double deals made by Joseph Caillaux and I had nothing to do with it. My letters were far more serious.

On March 16th, the editor of *Le Figaro*, Gaston Calmette, entered the newspaper offices at around six o'clock in the evening with his friend, Paul Bourget, a novelist and five-time nominee for the Nobel literature prize. Calmette was informed that a woman had been waiting to see him for more than an hour. She was Madame Henriette Caillaux, Joseph Caillaux's wife, wearing a fur coat and with her hands in a muff to keep them warm, probably. The fashion had been popular in the previous century and had now returned.

Gaston agreed to see her in his office, although his friend thought he should avoid her. When Madame Caillaux entered Calmette's office they exchanged a few words but then, she took out the pistol she was hiding in her fashionable accessory, a .32 automatic Browning, also fashionable at the time. The popularity of the gun cannot be overstated.

She fired six shots and only two of them missed their target. Henriette Caillaux remained calm and made absolutely no attempt to escape while a doctor and the police made their way to the scene. She even refused to enter the police van. Instead, she insisted on being driven to the police headquarters in her car, by her chauffeur, who was waiting outside. So it was done.

The fifty-six-year-old journalist died six hours later. He should have listened to his friend, Bourget. Five Nobel nominations must have meant something. Joseph Caillaux resigned his post the following day, on March 17th.

And what was the second important piece of information?

The whole world had known about Franz Ferdinand's visit to Sarajevo since March. I came across it on the same day I read about the Caillaux affair, but even if I hadn't, I'd have got to have known about it anyway.

Everyone at the *Central Café* had been talking about it from the time the visit was announced.

"He's going to inspect the army in Bosnia."

"Do you know why?"

"Why?"

"Because it's the only way he and his wife can ride in an open carriage together."

"What?"

"It's because of his oath. The emperor does not allow Sophie to share the rank or splendours of an archduke or sit next to him on any public occasion."

"I know. And her children will not succeed him. That's cruel!"

"However, when he is acting in a military capacity, she is allowed to enjoy her husband's recognition."

"Our soldiers can expect a lot of army inspections, then."

"You can be sure of that."

… sometime later at the *Landtmann Café.*

"The trip to Sarajevo is cancelled."

"Why?"

"Come now, because the emperor is ill, of course. How can the heir be absent if the emperor is ill?"

"Is it serious?"

"Well, when you are more than eighty years old, everything is serious."

"He's eighty-two, isn't he?"

"He'll be eighty-four in August."

"Aha!"

"You should know better. He's your emperor, after all."

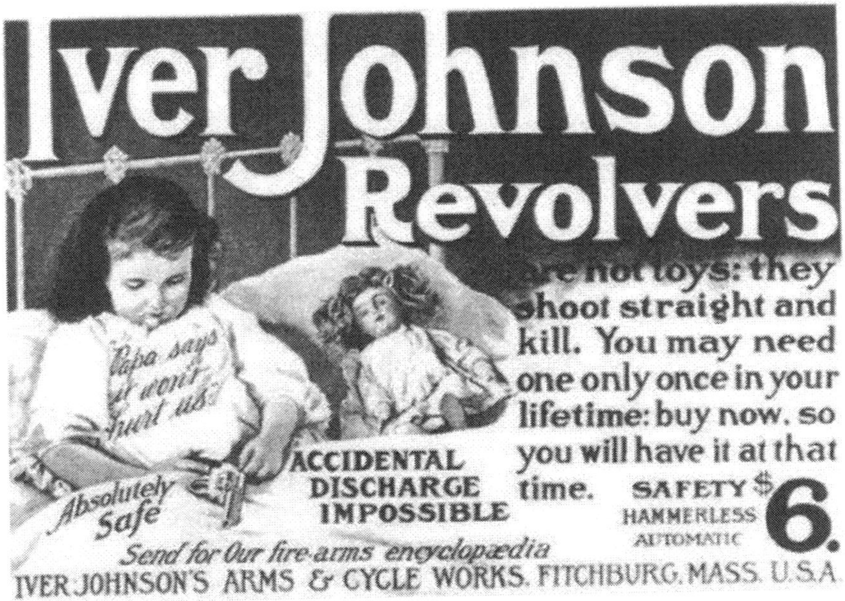

"Are you ready to kill for your country?" I said putting a revolver on the table. It was classic and reliable and safe enough for a young man to handle.

… later, at the *Landtmann Café.*

"The archduke is going to Sarajevo, by the way."

"When?"

"On June 28th. It's his fourteenth wedding anniversary. It's a Sunday, too."

"The 28th? So it's the 28th minus thirteen days. That's June 15th, according to the Julian calendar. Not a good day."

"Why not?"

"It's a Serbian national and religious holiday. On that day in 1389, the battle of Kosovo against the Ottomans took place. The Serbians call it the Vidovdan."

"So what?"

"The Sultan was assassinated in his tent by a Serb. And it's… wait a moment…. 1914 minus 1389… 520 … no… 525 years ago. Exactly!"

"For goodness sake! Don't you know how old Franz Joseph is? He's your emperor! And you know all that other stuff. What are you? A Russian spy like Colonel Redl?"

"A Serbian spy, you mean?"

"It's the same thing."

I sent a telegram to my boss the day I found out.

'Ferdinand'

The date was March 15th. For the third time. My bonus was now guaranteed and maybe I'd secured another year in the job.

Almost three months later on Tuesday, June 30th, I found myself in Belgrade. I'd always hated carriage journeys but now it was worse. I got to my room at the Moskva Hotel and went straight to bed. A great opportunity had been missed. It was over.

This time, there wasn't much for me to do. It was up to the Young Bosnia organisation now. I had simply shown them the way.

I was experienced enough to know that there would be an assassination attempt on the archduke. I had prevented Bogdan Zerajic's attempt four years earlier, on June 3rd, 1910 and he was now considered an idol by many Slav students.

Last year, the city was under martial law because of the Fashoda Affair in the Balkan War. The pro-Serbians were very despondent. That year, a brilliant royal mind assumed it should be widely known that Archduke Franz Ferdinand would visit Sarajevo on June 28th. Maybe it was royal protocol.

"Please prepare your guns and bombs! Especially the students who tend to leave everything until the last minute. Remember Bogdan Zerajic, practice your shooting and be consistent."

Bogdan Zerajic shot at Varesanin five times and missed. With the sixth and final bullet, Zerajic killed himself. If he'd used a .32 automatic like Madame Caillaux, he'd have succeeded, you can be sure of that. She scored four out of six and the Young Bosnian, one out of six.

This time, I had no concerns about finding an assassin and there was no need for preparations. I was simply there to make things easier for whoever the prospective assassin was.

Younger professionals may find it strange but it's true with any new job, especially in sales or account management. At first, you travel a lot, work long hours, are kept away from home to get to know your market sector and find reliable customers to bring you…results, as the unique Lépine would say.

The years pass and you develop a name for yourself, knowing how things work and the key elements that bring maximum results with minimum effort. You know whom to talk to and what to expect.

In my case, all I had to do was turn up in Sarajevo a week or two before the archduke and talk to my friend Oskar for five minutes in private.

"The HaHo forces have a large presence here in Sarajevo you know, Oskar."

"What? Where?"

"You'll never see them out and about, and if you do, you won't recognise them."

"Wow!"

"I just wanted you to know, so you can relax. You must be very stressed because of the archduke's arrival next Sunday. We have everything under control. I just thought I'd inform you because we're old friends."

"Thank you, Edward!"

"Just relax, don't worry and don't say anything to anyone."

"Much obliged! You have no idea how many things I had to do. I was very nervous. It wasn't just me either. The whole police department is in the same position. This Young Bosnia organisation causes big headaches. I haven't been able to sleep since it was announced but I'm relieved now that the HaHo are here in Sarajevo."

"We're just doing our job, Oskar. See you around."

That's all I did. Honestly. Nothing else. And it worked. It worked like magic.

Governor Oskar Potiorek's only concern from now on was the wine that would be served and the music that would be played at the official reception. His biggest task was to greet the archduke's wife, Sophie, with full imperial honours because everywhere else, she was denied it.

He also had the opportunity to show what a great ruler he was and refused to use the army to guard the streets of Sarajevo because he had pacified the mischievous pro-Serbians and when the local military commander, General Michael von Appel, proposed that troops line the intended route, he was told that this would offend the local population.

So, thanks to the HaHo, the road was now clear for anyone to aim and take a shot. Things didn't go to plan, however.

On Sunday, June 28th, the imperial couple arrived at Sarajevo railway station and were met by a car manufactured by Gräf & Stift. It was a sports car with its top folded down. The governor, the mayor, the chief of police and other officials were also there and met by other cars.

I stood among others near the Appel Quay beside the River Miljacka. As the motorcade approached, a young man, free from any obstruction, threw a bomb at the car carrying the archduke and his wife. It was around ten o'clock in the morning. The bomb bounced off the car, into the street and exploded under the car behind wounding several passengers and bystanders, around sixteen to twenty people in total. The car carrying Franz Ferdinand and his wife arrived at the town hall as planned.

It was difficult to tell if the driver had seen the bomb and accelerated or if the impatient, inexperienced student eager to get rid of the bomb was to blame. More importantly, the job was done and there would be no war that year.

I immediately took a carriage and left for Belgrade. It wasn't safe to stay in Sarajevo.

I didn't cause a war for my boss but he will soon find out about it and appreciate my efforts. An upheaval will definitely be caused.

The Franz Ferdinand telegram was justified.

While eating my breakfast and drinking coffee in the *kafana* of the Moskva Hotel, I heard a waiter discussing an assassination in Sarajevo with another guest. They seemed concerned so I asked what had happened.

"Archduke Franz Ferdinand was killed in Sarajevo on Sunday."

"No, no! Don't believe everything you hear. They tried to kill him but failed. He's quite well, don't worry." I appeared relaxed and assumed that journalists had distorted the truth.

"Are you sure?"

"I was in Sarajevo. I saw it with my own eyes. A bomb was thrown but it missed the archduke's car and exploded under the car behind. There were a few injuries but that's all. He and his wife continued safely in their car and the man who threw the bomb fell into the river. They caught him in the end."

"These newspapers! Lies, lies, lies!" said the waiter.

"But everyone is talking about it and they say that the archduke is dead," said the other man.

"Believe whatever you like," I said and continued eating my breakfast. "Could I have some more coffee, please?"

"Are you sure, Nikolai?"

"Positive. Why would I have celebrated otherwise?"

"It's simply not possible."

"Why isn't it possible?"

"Because I was there, I saw the police arrest the young man who threw the bomb."

"What bomb? He was shot."

"Where?"

"On Apple Boulevard, next to the river."

"But I saw him safely pass that road on his way to the town hall."

"I have two questions for you, Edward."

"Ask away!"

"First. Why did you leave immediately after the incident?"

"Because I had planned to do so. I would have left earlier but I got up late and thought I'd watch the commotion. I told the carriage to wait for an hour."

"...and what were you doing in Sarajevo in the first place?"

"Nikolai, you know what I do. Guns!"

"…and bombs."

"Exactly. And I have a large supply of old, secondhand guns to push. They won't sell in Paris and Vienna, you know that."

"Ok Edward, but look, one sure thing is certain right now: he is dead. I don't care about the details and we'll meet again in the next few days, if you're still here, of course. Now, excuse me, please, I'm in rather a mess. I'm in urgent conversation with Alexander at the moment to get Serbia through this crisis."

After the failed bomb attack, the archduke arrived at the town hall for the scheduled reception. Officials and members of the archduke's party discussed what to do next. It was proposed that the couple remain at the town hall until troops could be brought into the city to line the streets.

Of course! What else would they do?

But no! Oskar refused the obvious because soldiers coming directly from manoeuvres would not be wearing the appropriate dress uniform. Appropriate dress uniform!

Can you believe it?

"Do you think Sarajevo is full of assassins?" He was quite firm.

Naturally! Someone had probably told him about the HaHo spies, giving him a false sense of security. Even now?

In the end, the semi-royal couple decided to visit those wounded by the bombing in hospital. To ensure the archduke's safety, General Potiorek decided the imperial motorcade should travel directly along the Appel Quay to

Sarajevo hospital to avoid the crowded city centre. It was a very wise decision. As wise as it could be.

One minor detail. The drivers were never informed because Potiorek's aide, Eric von Merrizzi, was in hospital. The archduke's aides asked my friend, Edmund, to inform the drivers of the new route but he forgot. Actually, only the driver of the first car needed to be informed and the others would follow. They couldn't have missed him because they were the only three cars in the city.

At 10:45 a.m, the couple returned to the motorcade with Potiorek, once again taking the third car. It was a big mistake. The governor should have led in the first car to scrutinize the area. In the appropriate dress uniform, of course.

When the first two cars reached the Latin Bridge, they turned right into a side street, leaving the Appel Quay. It was where I'd bought myself a sandwich a year before and met the young Bosnian, Gavrilo Prinzip, who got me into trouble. *Schiller's Delicatessen.*

It seemed that Gavrilo had a special preference for this deli as he was having a bite to eat there with a Belgian-made pistol in his belt. He was probably disappointed that his friend's bomb attack had failed.

The archduke's driver naturally followed the first two cars and took the turn. Only then did Potiorek realise that they had taken the wrong route.

"Stop!" he shouted.

'For me, it is a relief from a great worry'.

Who might have said those words?

You probably think it was me when I'd verified that the assassination had taken place or maybe, it was my boss. Or my friend Hartwig, at his party for the occasion.

It may take you by surprise but the above words were quoted by Franz Joseph Karl to his daughter, Marie Valerie, when he learned about the assassination, expressing his greater confidence in the other Franz - the new heir presumptive, his grandnephew Archduke Charles, who had a son called Otto.

Any of the other three Franzes could also have said these words. Conrad and Charles had reason to do so and you know why. But I tended to lean in Conrad's direction and hoped my horse would run to the final mile dragging the other Franzes with him.

You'd think it would be difficult for the emperor to be dragged into war after expressing his relief but the opposite is true. Due to his difficult relationship with Ferdinand, he was obliged to show the others he would honour his heir and wouldn't let it go. Charles too. A very important detail. Honour!

Also, it was quite common in those days for anarchists to kill royals. The citizens of Vienna continued to drink their coffee and talk without thinking about the possibility of war. It was the same all over the world.

"If there is a poisonous adder at your heel, you stamp on its head, you don't wait for it to bite," said Conrad. He was writing to Gina that the time had come. That the poisonous adder knew he planned to stamp on its head thanks to a mole, however, had not occurred to him at all.

Berchtold, as ever, was undecided. He didn't disagree but wanted to ensure that public opinion was ready for it. The only person who could spoil everything now was István Tisza, the prime minister of Hungary. The clever one.

He had predicted a war with Serbia would trigger a war with Russia and therefore, a European war in general. He was also well aware that the war with Serbia would only cause problems. If it were won, there would be thousands of men like Gavrilo within the Empire's borders. If it were lost, it would be a tragedy. Furthermore, a strong Serbian population would weaken Hungarian power. So the Empire and the Hungarians would only be disadvantaged by such a war, even if Russia never entered it.

Honestly, if I could have, I would have arranged or facilitated his assassination, too.

Franz Joseph stated that his attitude would depend on the Kaiser's support. "If Germany supports us, will we go to war?" asked Conrad with incredible diplomacy. He wished to entrap the peaceful old emperor like a woman who needs a favour from a man.

The ageing emperor nodded. That was crucial. Now all that was needed was the support of the Kaiser. But support for what?

For a sudden attack, for a war to burn Serbia to the ground, for a war to annex Serbia, or for anything that came along?

The chef de cabinet, Ludwig Alexander Georg Graf von Hoyos, a diplomat in favour of war, went to Germany on July 5th to deliver a letter from the emperor and returned with a promise for support to any justified reaction by the Empire. In fact, he returned with a top-secret 'blank cheque'.

The disadvantage was the cheque's expiration date. The Germans considered it immediate but the Austrians took it to mean eternal. This famous blank cheque was obviously too unspecific. If the Austrians had attacked immediately, even the Czar would have considered it natural, being a royal.

Conrad said it was harvest time and the soldiers were in their fields. But what about the 'poisonous adder at your heel', Conrad?

Tisza, trying once more to avoid war, proposed an ultimatum be sent to the Serbians and Leopold Berchtold, now on the same side as Conrad, committed to sending an ultimatum that would never be accepted, so that war would undoubtedly break out.

When he took over his position after Aehrenthal's sudden death a year before, he was advised not to be influenced by Conrad because Conrad would be in favour of all kinds of wars and a great 'hurrah' policy to conquer the Serbs and who knows what else. Tragically, this advice was given by Franz Ferdinand, who was not around anymore to remind Leopold, once again. Tragically enough!

"I'm telling you, Edward, this is the most difficult situation I have come across in my entire career as an ambassador."

"Come now, Nikolai. Anarchists kill royals all the time. Queen Sissi, King Umberto, King George, to name but a few."

"Especially, when you're around!"

"What? What do you mean by that?"

"What do I mean by that?" said Nikolai sarcastically. He looked at the ceiling and took out one of his big Russian cigarettes. "Last year, when King George was killed, you were in Thessaloniki and this year, Franz Ferdinand was killed while you were in Sarajevo."

"And in Vienna, I drink coffee at the same cafe as Mr Bronstein, the *Pravda* journalist. I was also in Italy when John Pierpont Morgan died in bed."

"You see what I mean?"

"I arrived in Thessaloniki some days after King George's assassination and I left Sarajevo before Franz Ferdinand was killed."

"Why were you in prison in Sarajevo last March?"

"Because they saw me talking to a Young Bosnian. We began a conversation in the Schiller deli. I told him where to stand and how to shoot. I told him when the Governor says 'stop' and the driver puts the car in reverse gear, there will be enough time to shoot the archduke at close range. But not his wife, though."

"So they put you in jail because you had spoken to Gavrilo Prinzip?"

"Yes."

"And this year, Gavrilo was free to walk about while an attempt to kill Franz took place?"

"Austrians!"

"When did they set you free?"

"Once I committed to spying for them!" I said smiling. "Satisfied Mr Hartwig?"

"Edward, how long have we been friends?"

"Since the beginning of the century."

"I ask you in the name of our old friendship, what else do you do other than sell guns?"

"You've finally got it, Nikolai. I'm a spy."

"For whom."

"For Alsace and Lorraine."

"I see. I have work to do now, Edward. Sorry, but you have to leave. Today I have a meeting with the Austrian ambassador, Mr von Gieslingen."

"They haven't attacked yet so they won't attack at all."

"I have asked for French ambassador Descos, your fellow countryman, to be replaced and I will prove to the Austrians and the Germans that a French gun seller is playing dirty games in the region."

"That's all right with me but what has he done?"

"He said that a Serbian military party was involved in the assassination and other such lies."

"I understand. So in order to cast doubt on the Austrians, you're throwing false accusations at your friend."

He got up and went to the office of his aide to confirm his appointment with the Austrian. While they were talking, I sat alone with his cigarettes, his Benedictine and my gold medallion. The one you already know about.

"Have you heard the news, Goran?"

"What do you mean have I heard the news? I'm going to his funeral tomorrow."

"Hartwig, Hartwig, Hartwig!"

"God rest his soul!"

"God rest his soul, indeed! He was a great man. A truly great man."

"Do you know what happened, Grigorije?"

"They killed him, Goran."

"Who?"

"The Austrians! They took revenge for their heir."

"But why kill Hartwig?"

"Because he was the real king of the Balkans. He organised the wars and doubled the size of Serbia. He destroyed the Austrian effort to annex the rest of us and get as far as the Aegean Sea and…"

"Grigorije, keep still while you're talking or I'll injure you," said the barber who was cutting Grigorije's hair. Goran was sitting next to a man who, so far, had remained silent..

"The Austrians! They took revenge for their heir."

Illustration taken from the cover of 'Die Neue Zeitung'. July 10th 1914. © /oenb/anno/Austrian National Library

"Ok, Danilo," said Grigorije to the barber. The important thing though, is the way they killed him."

"How did they do it?"

"They summoned him to the Austro-Hungarian Embassy. There, they have this special chair that kills anyone who sits on it without leaving a trace. They brought it from Vienna exactly for this purpose."

"Really?"

"Yes. Von Giesl, the ambassador, sent a carriage to fetch Hartwig's daughter Ludmilla and a doctor but when Ludmilla called a policeman, the Austrians invoked the embassy's rights and sent him away."

"Really?"

"You see, Goran? They had something to hide."

"Maybe they used poison?"

"So the Austrians killed our king just twelve days after we killed their heir," noted the barber.

"Excuse me. We didn't kill Franz Ferdinand. Gavrilo Prinzip is not Serbia's ambassador, is he?" said Goran.

"Hartwig was not our king either… Grigorije, don't move your head."

Grigorije gestured accordingly.

The man sitting next to Goran remained silent. He remembered very clearly what happened last Friday in his office.

Nikolai Hartwig didn't accept the coffee that he offered him but from the time he entered, he didn't stop smoking his favourite Russian cigarettes. He formally offered his condolences on the death of Franz Ferdinand and reassured him that the rumours about a bridge party he had hosted that Sunday, the day of the assassination, were absolutely false. He also urged him to ignore the lie that the Russian embassy had declined to fly its flag at half-mast during Franz Ferdinand's funeral.

He thanked Hartwig, considering everything settled, and then the extremely overweight Russian ambassador came precisely to the point.

"I ask you in the name of our honourable friendship to answer as explicitly as you can. What will Austria-Hungary do with Serbia and what has been decided in Vienna?"

"I can assure you that the sovereignty of Serbia will not be infringed and that with the goodwill of the Serbian government, a solution can be found to this crisis that will please both parties," he answered diplomatically.

"Thank you very much, my friend, thank you," said Hartwig and collapsed from a sudden heart attack.

Baron Giesl von Gieslingen, the Austro-Hungarian ambassador, waited patiently for his haircut, paid his bill and left without revealing his identity. The previous day had been a Sunday and he met his Italian counterpart. From their conversation, he realised that Hartwig had lied to him on Friday about both the bridge party and the flag. Maybe this special chair from Vienna kills anyone who lies or hears something about an ultimatum. No one knows.

On Monday, July 13th, the day Baron Giesl had his hair cut, I intended to leave for Paris. However, when I learned that Hartwig would be buried in Belgrade at the request of the Serbian government, I postponed my journey until the next day.

It was the second time I had waited for a baron outside a Serbian Orthodox Church. Many years before, I had waited for Baron von Kalchberg outside the Church of San Spiridione in Trieste. This time, it was the right church but the baron was dead. I prayed for the soul of Baron Nikolai Hartwig at the Cathedral of St. Michael the Archangel with more than a hundred thousand citizens of Belgrade, all prominent members of Serbian political, military and cultural life, as well as the entire diplomatic corps.

I followed the funeral procession towards the new cemetery along Terazij Street in central Belgrade. There, among the massive crowd, I noticed a camera pointing in my direction. It was very rare to see a camera in those days and after the fire at the Bazar in 1897, which broke out because of one of those devilish machines, I rather disliked them. I realised, however, that it would be the second time my image would be immortalised. The first time, it had been captured by the young painter in Vienna, I was with my friend, Nikolai, then too.

I had expected him to die in his sleep like J.P. Morgan. The poison works as Berhane had said, but the cigarettes and obesity had probably beaten the poison to it before Hartwig went to bed. Rest in peace, Nikolai!

"Mr Aguillon!!!"

"Good morning Raoul."

"Please come in. How are you? I thought I 'd never see you again."

"I didn't recognize you with that beard."

"I haven't shaved since the day I became a member of *Mona Lisa*."

"Oh, my friend, the last seven months have been the toughest period of my life. You are alone, I assume?"

"Yes, Mr Aguillon. No one else is here."

"Good. There is something very important I need to tell you."

When I arrived in Paris I had no idea about the 'blank cheque' the Germans had given to the Austrians and the ultimatum Leopold was preparing for the Serbians. Once I found out about the ultimatum on July 26th, I knew the next two days would be decisive and I was too old and too tired to let anything go wrong and miss this great opportunity.

For Russia to back Serbia, it needed support from France. Only one man could stop France from supporting Russia, thus war from spreading, thus my plans from being fulfilled. Without it, the conflict would be just a small, local fight between the Empire and the Kingdom of Serbia. A Serbia however, that had just emerged from the victorious Balkan Wars and had thoroughly prepared its army to face the invasion Plan III of the Empire's high command.

"They're hunting me down, Raoul. They're everywhere. Everywhere, my friend!"

"How can I help?" asked Raoul, excited that I once again featured in his anti-Prussian world of espionage.

"You are very brave, Raoul!"

"Do you know something, Mr Aguillon? The day I became a member of the *Mona Lisa* organisation, the painting of the Mona Lisa was found. It had been missing for more than two years. For me, this was a sign. A sign for my destiny, for our organisation, for Alsace and Lorraine."

Do you know what Aristotle said about young men?

They have exalted notions because they have not been humbled by life or learned its necessary limitations. Moreover, their hopeful disposition makes them think themselves equal to great things. They would always rather do noble deeds than useful ones. Their lives are regulated more by moral feeling than by reasoning. All their mistakes are linked to doing things excessively and vehemently. They overdo everything. They love too much, they hate too much…

"I couldn't agree with you more," I said, looking him in the eye. "And it's not by accident that you are our final hope, Raoul. The final hope of Alsace and Lorraine."

"Final hope? Me?"

"Yes, you, Raoul Villan!"

"Why?" He was happily surprised and unable to hide his enthusiasm.

Poor, naive young man!

"Because you are the only member of *Mona Lisa* that the enemy is not aware of. I have not told anyone about you and if you have kept your mouth shut, there is a great chance that…"

"I haven't spoken to anyone, Mr Aguillon. From the mom…"

"I know, Raoul. I know." I pacified him. "That's why I am here."

"Thank you for your trust, Mr Aguill…"

"You can call me Edward, my friend."

"I'll try Mr Agui…Edward."

"Look, Raoul. Soon they will catch me. They've already killed our leader and they will kill me, too."

"They've killed our leader?"

"Yes. The most important founding member of *Mona Lisa* and our leader."

"How? Who was he? Can you tell me?"

"The greatest tragedy of all, young man, is the way they did it. They sent us a message at the same time. We will kill you publicly and will not be punished at all. No one will notice a thing.

"He was well-known and the damned Prussians killed him, making sure the whole country knew about it and, at the same time, nothing would be revealed.

"Do you realise now who our leader was?"

"Er, no… I…," he murmured, guilty about his ignorance.

That's the whole point, naive Raoul. Be ashamed, young man!

"It's because you are innocent, Raoul. Your heart is brave but your mind is kind so it is difficult to see the obvious even when it's right in front of you…"

"Mr Aguillon, I…"

"Gaston Calmette."

"Whaaaat?"

Are you surprised by my lie? I'll give you some more information to help you understand.

The Caillaux affair shook Paris and the whole of France, especially while Henriette Caillaux's trial was in progress. It started on July 20th. . You may find it strange but in the July of 1914, the assassination of Gaston Calmette was much more important than the assassination of Franz Ferdinand. On the other hand, it wasn't that strange because the cold-blooded murder of the editor of *Le Figaro* in the heart of Paris by a woman with a .32 automatic has far more hidden secrets than the murder, somewhere in the Balkans, of Austria-Hungary's heir by a young anarchist using a .380 semi-automatic FN 1910 Model. Both guns were designed by John Moses Browning and were produced by the Fabrique Nationale in neutral Belgium, by the way.

What's more, she was defended by the prominent attorney Fernand Labori, who tried to persuade the jury that her crime was not a premeditated act but her uncontrollable female emotions had resulted in a crime of passion. Is it possible for someone to perform a crime of passion and remain instantly calm about it?

Yes, if that someone is a woman.

But how is that possible when, at the same time, the attorney tries to prove his client is innocent because women are not as emotionally strong as men?

To avoid any misunderstanding and because it was a far more complex case, you should take into account that Fernand Labori was the attorney of Alfred Dreyfus, Emile Zola and other famous defendants. His speeches were regarded as masterpieces of forensic eloquence and I was certain this time he would achieve his client's acquittal. Thus, brave Raoul would be even further persuaded of the damned Prussians' plot to eliminate *Mona Lisa.*

The interesting part for most people was that Henriette was Caillaux's second wife. She was born Henriette Raynouard and at the age of nineteen, she married a thirty-one-year-old writer named Léo Claretie. She had already given birth to two children when in 1907, she began having an affair with Joseph Caillaux.

What a year! And it was also the year that Conrad began pursuing Gina.

In this case, however, they were both married but still, they were closer in age and Henriette had only two children. Not six. A year later, she divorced the writer but Caillaux encountered great difficulty divorcing his wife. When he finally did so, they got married in 1911, almost two months after the Mona Lisa 'came into my possession'. They were probably one of France's wealthiest couples with their fortune being estimated at around one and a half million francs.

Money, power, illegal affairs, pistols, famous lawyers, notorious members of French society including the president of the republic!

How on earth was it possible for Gavrilo Prinzip to be measured against all that?

The defendant believed that *Le Figaro* would publish private letters which would expose her and her husband for having a relationship while the former prime minister was still married to his first wife.

She remembered that her first husband, Léo Claretie, had found some of these letters and that she never got them back. She also remembered he told her he had lost them because he mistook his coat for someone else's. Mine.

Writer's lies!

As you know, Calmette was in the possession of some private love letters the Caillaux couple had written while their relationship was illegal. I sent them to him personally, but we would never know if *Mona Lisa*'s leader would ever use them.

It was time for guns to be bought and used. Joseph Caillaux would either challenge Gaston Calmette to a duel or Madame Caillaux would protect her husband by doing what she did.

I have told you enough already for you to understand the dark role of the Prussians in this case and it all had to do with Mr Caillaux himself. As prime minister during my second Moroccan crisis or Agadir crisis, if you like, he had worked very hard for a peaceful solution. Also, he strongly opposed the enlargement of the French army that three years of compulsory military service would ensure. It's no surprise that *Le Figaro* called the former prime minister particularly insulting names: 'Germany's Man' or the 'Shady Financier'.

"So now your eyes have been opened to all this, my boy," I said. I could see how amazed Raoul was to hear this top-classified spy news.

"I don't believe it! How could I not have seen it before? It was so obvious."

"Do you understand how deeply dangerous this is for our nation?"

"They killed the leader of *Mona Lisa*, Gaston Calmette, a true patriot, and no one understands their sinister plots. She should be sent to the guillotine."

"She is not the only one, Raoul. Even if she were convicted, ten more like her would appear out of nowhere."

"What about her husband? The *Germany's man*?"

"There is someone above him, Raoul. I tracked down their main coordinator. It wasn't easy, but eventually, I found him."

The truth was that Joseph Caillaux would also have been a great obstacle to my goals as a voice of moderation that would keep France out of the imminent war but now, after this enormous scandal, he was totally destroyed. Thus, with the help of brave Raoul, I would try to destroy the strongest voice for peace.

"I discovered the leader of the Prussian espionage in France."

"Who is he?"

"You won't believe it, my boy. He is a well-known man. A famous man. He managed to fool us. He talks about peace and how awful war will be, making millions of our patriots forget about Alsace-Lorraine and accept defeat.

"His main purpose, however, is to trick us so his bosses - the damned Prussians - can seize more of our fatherland."

"Those Prussians are very clever. They have excellent cover. Thank God *Mona Lisa* is here! Who is the bastard?"

"Before I tell you, I need to ask you something."

"Yes?"

"Are you prepared to do your duty for France? Are you ready to kill for your country?" I said putting a revolver on the table. It was classic and reliable and safe enough for a young man to handle. I saw the fear in his eyes as he looked at it, however. He was probably the wrong horse.

Le Petit Journal

ADMINISTRATION

5 CENT. SUPPLÉMENT ILLUSTRÉ 5 CENT.

ABONNEMENTS

25me Année —44— Numéro 1.219

DIMANCHE 29 MARS 1914

Tragique épilogue d'une querelle politique

Mme CAILLAUX, FEMME DU MINISTRE DES FINANCES, TUE A COUPS DE REVOLVER M. GASTON CALMETTE DIRECTEUR DU " FIGARO "

"… We will kill you publicly and will not be punished at all…"

"Can't we just expose him and make him suffer?"

You are a coward, Raoul! You are afraid of using a gun and you think you can make him suffer?

"There's no time for that, son. The Prussians and the Austrians will march east and when they are done, our turn will come. We mustn't be caught napping."

"I'll do whatever it takes. Who is he?"

"Do you have a pocketbook?"

"Yes."

"Take these notes and copy them. These are some of his habits, everything you need to know about him. He's in Brussels at the moment. If I wasn't on the run, I'd do it myself.

"If something goes wrong, I'm counting on your patriotism and integrity. Keep *Mona Lisa* safe, Raoul. You are the only one who can reverse the situation."

"I am ready to give my life, Mr Aguillon."

He was anything but ready but that was the best I could do. I had done my job. Now I had to wait and see. The days passed and nothing happened. My words were soon forgotten, it seemed, as they were in Bogdan Zerajic's case.

At the same time that France's attention was distracted by this sensational case full of passion, bullets and income taxation, the situation in Europe was improving day by day. On Thursday, July 23rd, Baron Giesl von Gieslingen, sporting a recent haircut, presented an ultimatum to the Serbian government. Prime Minister Nikola Pasic was absent at the time so the ultimatum was served to the Serbian Minister of Finance, Lala Pacu, a chain-smoker. Serbia would have to respond in forty-eight hours if she accepted the obligations of the ultimatum.

On Saturday, July 25th, Baron Giesl von Gieslingen still looking great in his new haircut, burnt the entire contents of the embassy including the special killing chair and left Belgrade, despite the Serbians having accepted all demands but number six.

According to obligation number six, Serbia should bring to trial all accessories to the archduke's assassination and allow Austro-Hungarian delegates and law enforcement officers to take part in the investigations.

If my friend Nikolai Hartwig had been alive, he would have persuaded Pasic to agree even to that term, giving the Austrians what they wanted…and more. He would have internationalised the investigation calling on Russian, French, English, German, Spanish, Italian, Belgian, Greek, Bulgarian, Norwegian, American, Mexican, Ottoman, Persian and Bolivian delegates and law enforcement officers from every single country in the world to humiliate the Austro-Hungarians diplomatically. He would have enjoyed playing his ambassador game and taken revenge for the annexation crisis of 1908 that wounded his loyal enemy Izvolsky so badly.

If only!

"So after all…" said the old emperor, "continuing to argue that breaking off relations does not necessarily mean war, does it?"

"Well, yes…." Leopold was unclear about it and couldn't remember what Franz Ferdinand had said.

They were in Ischl in Austria that Saturday when, at 6 p.m., the war ministry informed him that relations with Serbia had been interrupted. As Baron Giesl von Gieslingen left Belgrade, Franz Joseph signed off full mobilisation against all intuition, logic and will.

The first king had fallen.

"But that eliminates any reason for war. Serbia has capitulated in the most humiliating way. The few reservations that Serbia has about various points can, in my opinion, surely be cleared up by negotiation," stated the Kaiser after reading Serbia's reply. It was Sunday, July 26th, and he was cruising in the North Sea. However, his Chancellor, Bethmann Hollweg, excluded the parts where the Kaiser had told the Austrians not to go to war when he forwarded his message. Germany could easily state they couldn't follow through on number six, even though a blank cheque had been given.

"You no longer have control of the affair in your own hands," said his Conrad, implying that the army would stage a coup d'état and depose Wilhelm in favour of his hawkish eldest son, Crown Prince Wilhelm, if he continued to work for peace. However, this king hadn't fallen. Not yet.

Damned Prussians!

"The monarchy is at stake," said the real Conrad and on Tuesday, July 28th at 11:00 a.m., Austria sent a telegram to Serbia declaring war, while in the Paris courts, the acquittal of *Germany's man*'s second wife was declared. When I met the desperate Léo Claretie on that December night in 1907, he was ready to jump into the Seine but I never imagined that by helping him, I would accidentally gain access to *Germany's man*'s personal correspondence. In democracies, such things can change the course of history or even influence it.

"I will not be responsible for a monstrous slaughter," stated Czar Nicholas on Wednesday, July 29th, having exchanged messages with his German cousin Willy and denied his generals a general mobilisation, ordering a partial one against Austria-Hungary instead. It was a form of diplomatic pressure similar to that used during the Balkan wars when he tried to avoid a diplomatic defeat analogous to that of Alois Aehrenthal during the Bosnian crisis.

On Thursday July 30th, his Conrads insisted but the Czar was totally against it, honouring his German cousin, Willy.

The Foreign Minister, Sergei Sazonov, met his ruler at three in the afternoon and after an hour of arguing in favour of the war and without success, he finally used a familiar tactic that always brought results.

No, he didn't give him a letter from Saint Peter claiming that his soul would be saved if… No!

"A war with Germany is the only way you can save your own life and protect the throne for your son," said Sazonov.

From 1613, the House of Romanov had ruled Russia. The three-hundred-year-old glorious reign of the Romanov Dynasty was now at stake as that of the poor Habsburgs had been. Very similar to the 'Pope Stephen approach', don't you think?

The second king had fallen.

The following day was Friday, the last day of the busiest July humanity had ever seen and the day the Russian general mobilisation began. On hearing the news, the Kaiser felt betrayed by his cousin Nicky and I was feeling betrayed by brave Raoul. So far, he had done nothing. He was cowardly and immature after all! I would have done it myself but eventually, the Gavrilo inside Raoul came to life.

By late that Friday evening, Jean Jaurès had been assassinated. At last!

He had been dining with friends at the *Café du Croissant*, in Rue Montmartre. At 9:40, Raoul Villain walked up to the restaurant window and fired two shots into the socialist leader's back. He died five minutes later.

I was there and saw Raul getting caught but it didn't bother me. I was also there when the ambulance came for Jean Jaurès. Many people had gathered and were watching the upheaval…my upheaval.

Pictures were being taken with those devilish machines. Damned photographers!

Jaurès was supposed to attend an international conference on August 9th to attempt to dissuade the belligerent parties from going ahead with the war. He never made it. With Jean Jaurès absent and Joseph Caillaux neutralised, posters went up throughout France the following day announcing general mobilisation.

Rest in peace Jean Jaurès! War has come.

The Third…Republic had fallen.

The night before, brave Raoul had walked up and down the pavement with his revolver but hadn't found the courage to use it. I somehow understood that. He was twenty-nine years old; not young and ignorant like Gavrilo Prinzip.

Do you know what gave him the final push and made him decide to act?

Henriette Caillaux's acquittal on Tuesday. Raoul Villain was persuaded that day that he should use his revolver and take revenge for the leader of *Mona Lisa* and destroy the Prussian spy system by killing the top man. He even admitted intending to murder Henriette Caillaux afterwards and you know why! He wanted to send a signal to all the *Mona Lisa* members out there.

I understood his initial hesitation. It's not easy to take the life of another human being. Aristotle was right. Young men's lives are regulated more by moral feeling than by reasoning. All you have to do is link their moral feeling to the outcome you want.

Like Pope Stephen did with Pepin the Short.

Of course, the king was not a child and neither was he short, by the way. He was an adult king but a child where his faith was concerned. The Pope realised that and acted accordingly.

"Come and help me if you like but if you don't, don't. You are free to decide for yourself. St Peter says your soul is in danger here."

The same thing happened in July as I'd told my boss it would. I explained to him my version of the truth. People, and youngsters especially, can commit the most unbelievable crimes once the right outcome is connected to a specific action and other options are excluded.

On Saturday August 1st, Wilhelm ordered mobilisation and for the Prussians, mobilisation was no bluff, no diplomatic tactic, no game and no nonsense. It was war!

The third king had fallen.

'I can honestly say that I have never been more bitterly disappointed', wrote British prime minister Herbert Asquith on the first day of that cloudy August.

Naturally! He hadn't seen his young lover, Venetia Stanley, for a whole week and he was writing to her to let her know that he was very hurt. He competed with Conrad by posting, on average, three letters a day. Maybe there was something wrong with males born in 1852. He was just two months older than Conrad and thirty-five years older than Venetia. Conrad, on the other hand, was twenty-seven years older than Gina.

"We are within measurable or imaginable distance of a real Armageddon. Happily, there seems to be no reason why we should be anything more than spectators," he said, mentioning for the first time the growing crisis

The Third…Republic had fallen.

in continental Europe on July 24th. . Serbia meanwhile, was considering the response to the ultimatum.

On August 2nd, a secret alliance was signed between Germany and the Ottoman Empire and on Monday, August 3rd, Germany declared war on neutral Belgium and France according to the 'Schliefen plan' and Prussians follow the war plan, no matter what.

To be fair, the British tried hard to overcome this crisis diplomatically and had absolutely no formal obligation to enter the war. The Entente Cordial said nothing about offensive or defensive obligations. Edward Grey, the Secretary of State for Foreign Affairs, had done a good job keeping his hands free. That's why it was named the Entente Cordiale in the first place. It had a French name so that every Frenchman felt obliged to honour it, if necessary. The average British person, however, would accept it if his country could not honour an *An-Tant-Cordy-Al*, or whatever those French words meant.

The British were brilliant at such things and the Battle of Waterloo was not named the 'Belle Alliance', as von Blücher proposed. *Belle Alliance* was French and would always remind future generations of the decisive contribution of the Prussians. Waterloo is an easy English word, suitable to emphasise (when the right marketing tactics are applied) Napoleon's downfall and simultaneously mute any other…

Sorry, I forgot!

The British honoured their Friendly Agreement, however, and entered the war on August 4th because if Britain had decided to abandon its cordiality after the end of the war, a few weeks later, or so they thought, she would have found herself with no friends and with one major player on the continent. A new Napoleon. A new 'monster' but this time, there would be no option for coalitions against it. Britain was always uncomfortable when the continent was ruled by a single continental power.

And that is how a great war began because it began. 'We are here because we are here', sang the British soldiers as they set off on arduous marches a few months later. How right they were!

Does anyone remember an heir called Franz Ferdinand? Anyone?

And what about his wife Sophie, pregnant at the time? Gavrilo killed her while aiming at General Oskar Potiorek from a distance of two meters. If only Tancosic hadn't been so strict with his selection of volunteers the year before. If only!

The common denominator in persuading the three great kingdoms was the 'Conrads' effect. Powerful, bellicose generals.

"The monarchy is at stake."

"The House of Romanov is at stake."

"Your reign is at stake."

Or, "your soul is at stake," as St Peter would say.

Monarchs need good generals and powerful generals are always a threat to the king. All three kings of Austro-Hungary, Russia and Germany saw themselves in danger that July.

No monarchy is safe enough without a strong, faithful army. The last was in Constantinople after the death of Basil II Porphyrogenitus in 1025. The Eastern Roman Empire, known as Byzantium, was extremely powerful at its height, having eliminated all the dangers in the north, south, east and west because of Basil's continual wars. Constantine X became king in 1059 and feeling safe, he continued to severely undercut the training and financial support for the armed forces and fatally weaken the generals and defence. He thus dissolved the imperial army because it was no longer necessary and generals were always a threat to any king. It sounds simple, doesn't it?

It took just twelve years for the battle of Manzikert to begin. And Waterloo was Napoleon's Manzikert.

What's more, how could the Kaiser stop the armed forces when three years earlier, he'd been called insulting names by newspapers after my last Morocco job. 'Wilhelm the Sudden', they called him, for changing his mind so easily. Well, not any more.

"This time I shall not give in," he repeated three times while speaking to the industrialist Gustav Krupp von Bohle und Halbach, early in the crisis on July 6th. It produced an almost comic effect, according to Gustav. He had just delivered the blank cheque but he didn't want a war.

When little boys play with their tin soldiers, some plan the battle in their head and carefully line up their soldiers at exactly the same distance and look at them from different angles, taking note of their uniforms, the field and the flanks.

But the battle never begins.

Then, they carefully put the tin soldiers back into the box. Wilhelm was one of those boys. He didn't want to see his navy destroyed or even scratched. He preferred to watch parades and demonstrations, as he had done as a child in England.

Maybe this king had fallen first without even knowing it.

As far as democracies were concerned, or so it appeared, if you had access to personal correspondence and newspapers, you could do whatever you wanted. In my case, I used my accidental access to some personal letters by giving them to *Le Figaro*, thereby exploiting the newspaper to achieve my goal. But what if a world existed where both correspondence and information could be controlled?

It would be the Waterloo of free speech, of logos. It would be Waterlogos or Waterloogle. You get the point.

Anyway, the job was done. It was time to leave for Switzerland with my Mona Lisa.

"Capitano?" I said. I couldn't believe my eyes!

"Frenchman, you're all grown-up!"

"I can't believe it's you!"

"It's not me really. Come on, Frenchman, let's walk."

We walked along the River Limmat. It was the biggest surprise I could ever have imagined. I had come to see my boss and... I met my old boss, the long-gone Capitano Antonio Caporaso.

"Antonio Capodistria."

"A Greek name! You're not the first person I've met who uses an undercover Greek name."

"And not just any Greek name. It's the name of a diplomat, the unofficial Russian ambassador to Switzerland in 1913."

"So what?"

"Now there's something you don't know, Frenchman. You used to know so many things..."

"I am a bit rusty, I suppose."

"His mission was to disentangle the country from your dominance...from Napoleon. He personally facilitated the initiation of a new federal constitution for the nineteen cantons that were the component states of Switzerland with personal drafts."

"Really?"

"He secured Swiss unity, independence and neutrality, which brought prosperity."

"And why did you choose such a famous name? Isn't that dangerous?"

"Because that's the best way to hide. Don't you get it, Frenchman? No one suspects someone who's not hiding."

"I must admit though, I wouldn't have recognised you if you hadn't revealed yourself, Mr Antonio Capo… distria. You are so different. So different to the man I used to know."

"I know, I know!"

"I mean your…"

"Hair?"

"Yes, and your beard… and… I thought that you were bald, Capitano!"

"Don't worry. There are many Capitanos and I haven't heard that name for years. It's ok. This river doesn't go as far as Sicily. It flows in a northwesterly direction and doesn't reveal secrets…

"Anyway, back then, I shaved almost every day, Frenchman. Every day!"

"Why?"

"Because I was a slave! A slave aboard my own ship, Edward.

"I had all the responsibilities, the fears, the agony. I was a ship-owner, a captain, a sailor, an entrepreneur… taking all those risks, the sea, the… I… you have no idea, and at the end of the day, they were always there to deny me… my money, my future, my hopes, everything a courageous man aspires to. I was a slave. I felt like a slave and I was a slave. I should have bought a steamship after the '70s. I wanted to invest in one. A new Bella Messina.

"But they wouldn't let me. He wouldn't let me.

"I started shaving as a reminder. A reminder to break free someday. Later, I figured out it would also be useful if I had to go into hiding. I knew they would never allow me to quit with dignity and live a decent life.

"I thought the junk from the Aegean Sea would give me my freedom..."

"And I blew your efforts, Capitano?"

"No, Frenchman, no..."

"I blew it, Cap..."

"The opposite is true. You raised my hopes, Edward, with your talent for finding customers...and making deals, you... gave us wings. Not just me, all of us. We were all so excited. So excited about the potential. Moroccan used to tell me to protect you, Frenchman, because you were so precious. Moroccan! I wonder what happened .to him. They were great times, Frenchman. Great times."

"My best times, too."

"Remember Donna Julia?"

"Oohhh, Donna Julia. What a beautiful woman she was."

"Yes, very beautiful."

"What happened next, Capitano?"

"How did I survive? How do you think?"

"I think you saved a lot of money and after the fire in Marseille..."

"How do you know about the fire?"

I was going to tell him that Moffa told me but thought that would worry him unnecessarily. The sound of his name alone would spoil our wonderful walk by the river.

Pictures were being taken with those devilish machines. Damned photographers!

"The receptionist at the *Quatre Chats* in Marseille told me about the tragic demise of the Bella Messina."

"The tragic demise of the Bella Messina…?" Capitano smiled.

"Yes."

"Let me tell you the real story, the way it really happened.

"The Bella Messina entered the port of Marseille in flames. Moffa and I were there…"

He told me everything Moffa and Conte Cucinotta had told me and I pretended to hear it for the first time. The fire, Capitano's hard times in Sicily… everything. If he hadn't told me his tragic story himself, I'd have thought he had died alone somewhere in the port in Genoa and was fed to the fish.

"…in Genoa, I lived like a vagabond and begged for money. Sailors, captains, policemen… I even begged the Mafia's man for money. Their informer. Damned informers!

"I wanted everyone to see me in my dirty, tattered clothes, crawling through the mud of Genoa's streets. Once they'd seen enough, I left. I disappeared, never to be seen again.

"No carriage, no horse, no boat."

"How?"

"On foot, Frenchman."

"That must have been tough."

"No. It was more like a revitalising, long walk. Farmers helped me on my way, carriages too. I was safe, now.

"After a long journey, I reached Aix-en-Provence, about thirty kilometres north of Marseille. There, I met my old friend, Capitano Francois Lachat. He abandoned the sea for his love of wine and had a chateau there. He was the one who suggested this plan, many years before."

"It was a plan?" I already knew it was a plan but it was good to let an old man impress you with his story.

Capitano smiled. "Of course, it was a plan, my boy! Once I had rested at my friend's chateau, once I had drunk enough wine and enjoyed royal breakfasts, I made my way to…England."

"England?"

"I had to collect my insurance from Lloyds, you see."

"So this was…"

"…what I was doing while you and Di Batista and that little creep, Guido, were enjoying yourselves with those beautiful English girls.

"I bought fire insurance for the Bella Messina, the ship I owned outright and which would someday transfer a consignment of sulphur… and near the port of Marseille… you know."

"Now it all makes sense. But wait a minute. Berhane and Tafari burned to death aboard the Bella Me…"

"How did you come up with that, Frenchman?" said Capitano, disturbed by what I had said.

"..ssina, didn't they?" I made it sound like a question at the last moment. "You said you and Moffa…"

"Because I left the best part until the end."

"The best part of this happy end, Capitano?" I said, rather relieved. If he'd been younger, he'd have grabbed me by the scruff of the neck but when a man grows old, his reflexes, his perception of lies or sincerity are much weaker.

"I have no special interest in things, you know. In anything that is made of something, no matter how beautiful it is, how old it is, how…do you understand?

"But when it came to setting fire to the Messina, I just… I couldn't do it. The vessel was my home, my family. How could I set fire to it? What if Lloyds found an excuse not to pay me?

"Even if I'd moved on with a steamer, I still wouldn't have abandoned the Bella Messina. When my friend Francois explained the plan, he insisted this was the only way I could break free but I was adamant."

"How did you decide in the end?"

"When I saw the Palais Benedictine go up in flames and brave men like you naively dashing into the flames to rescue those precious items, when I saw you bring out Tafari under that shield…"

"I used it to help us breathe…"

"I don't care… but it was then that I figured a way to finally break free without… you know…"

"Oh, come on, tell me, how did you do it?" It was becoming clear, but…still impossible.

"It was all a matter of timing and pure… illusion," said Capitano, gesturing like a magician.

"I sent a message from Fécamp to my friend Francois in Aix-en-Provence. When we arrived in Morocco, Moroccan decided to stay there, while the Tana brothers, Moffa and I moved on. The Bella Messina was already loaded with a small quantity of inflammable sulfur I had bought myself to cover for our otherwise empty cargo hold.

"We stopped at the ports of Valencia, Barcelona and Montpellier. Moffa enjoyed himself and didn't have to think about loading and unloading. At the same time, Moroccan was on his way to Marseille to find Francois.

"In Montpellier, I received the telegram I was waiting for and we set sail for Marseille. We had to arrive there at night…"

"Because Moffa would be asleep…"

"…and it would be dark.

"Capitano Francois Lachat and Moroccan awaited us in the dark of night in an old, two-mast schooner fit for the scrapyard a mile or two outside the port of Marseille.

"Once we'd found each other, and believe me, it wasn't easy in the middle of the night, the Palais Benedictine Grand Master Illusion began… and boy, did we do well!

"We created smoke by burning torches and old fabric and once there was enough, I woke Guido and covered him with my coat to protect him. I put my arm around his shoulders and covered him so tightly he could only see the floor and led him to the boat. I kept him protected with his head down when Tafari dived into the water to swim back to the Bella Messina because he had forgotten his medallion. Berhane followed, despite me telling him not to, but what could I do? I kept hold of him so he would not do the same and go and help them."

"Ha! Guido?"

"Once we were safe and out of danger, I pointed to an old burning vessel slowly approaching the port of Marseille.

"I kept his head pointed in the direction of the port and looked back at the Bella Messina for the last time. Berhane and Tafari sailed away in the opposite direction with Lachat and Moroccan in the dark of the night. I could hardly see the Messina. My beautiful ship was safe and I was almost free."

"Unbelievable!"

"Guido was very touched that I had been kind enough to protect and save him."

"I'd have liked to have seen that!"

"You can imagine the rest. In Niche, Berhane and Tafari bought Capitano Lachat's old vessel, repaired it and named it the Blue Nile. I told them to buy a steamboat as soon as they could get a loan but I don't know what happened to them in the end. I am sure they did well."

"What about Moroccan?" I asked though I had met him too, of course.

"Moroccan must have stayed with them until they got a decent crew together. I never saw him again. Never.

"He told me he'd like to return to Morocco someday, though."

I was surprised that Moroccan hadn't told me anything about Capitano and the Messina. He'd kept it secret despite us doing business together. Obviously, he never trusted me.

Who trusts a salesman, after all?

"What was Moroccan hiding from, Capitano? Who was after him?"

"Oh, how I miss the sea! Oh, how much I miss my schooner, my Bella Messina," said Capitano as if he hadn't heard my question. "Berhane told me he gave you his medallion. Did he really?"

"Here it is," I said, showing it to him. I was disappointed that I was never going to find out about Moroccan's secret. "He gave it to me the day I rescued Tafari from the flames of the Palais Benedictine."

"Did he tell you what's inside?"

"Yes!"

"Mysterious people, those Amharas, aren't they?"

"Indeed."

"Can I see this mysterious root?"

I took my medallion from around my neck and gave it to Capitano. "I think Berhane would be happy to know it's in your hands now."

Filled with curiosity, Capitano opened the medallion. "Hey, it's empty!"

"Oh yes, the last time I opened it, it all fell out and I didn't want to touch it."

"I hope it wasn't while you were cooking!"

Indeed, I was cooking!

"So why didn't you go to America?"

"Frenchman, don't be so naive! It's not the best place to hide. There are many Italians there... ports...you know. I chose a city far from the sea but only as far as man on the run would normally do. Not too near, not too far..."

"...and you're not so much a Caporaso anymore either, are you?" Caporaso means shaven head.

"Ha, ha! That's true, Frenchman. I was no longer a slave. I was a free, rich man looking for a quiet life in the beautiful city of Zurich near the beautiful River Limmat and the lake. Only a damned war like the present one could destroy it all, Frenchman.

"Now, let's go and drink some wine. Where are you staying?"

"At the Savoy."

"The Savoy? That's an expensive hotel. Do have friends here? Or a woman?"

"No, no... I just have some business to finish."

"Hotels must be empty, these days."

"Surprisingly enough, I met another Frenchman here. His name is Paul Bolo and he has connections to an Egyptian Khedive."

"Stay away from him!"

"What? Do know him?"

"No, but the lady that cleans my house also works as a cleaner at the *Hotel du Saint Gothard* and she told me about a Frenchman by that name who met with some Germans there."

"Are you sure? A French-speaking person with Germans in Switzerland is not something..."

"Quite sure!"

"It stinks, for sure."

"I don't remember the German names but that French name is not one you forget. The French call him Bolo Pasha."

"Yes, Bolo Pasha. That's him."

"Stay away from him! Now tell me what you've been doing. I assume you've done well for yourself too, judging by your expensive hotel and clothes."

I didn't tell him about the real job that had made me a fortune. I simply mentioned the sales of Benedictine and guns for duels. How could I tell him about the terrible things I had done? My terrible recipes for disaster.

Some days later, I followed Moroccan's example by heading off to my birthplace. The Mona Lisa and I left for Algiers. It wasn't an easy journey during the war. It was quite a struggle to reach the Mediterranean ports.

Any port! Any port would do, and I eventually made it to the port of my destiny.

Trieste!

But it was a different Trieste, much different from the Trieste where I had met Gina with its Grand Canal, Piazza Grande, *Caffè degli Specchi* complete with mirrors and that wonderful lighting, the *Stella Polare*, Tommaseo, Cattaruzza and so many other beautiful cafes. They were all gone.

After Trieste, I arrived in Malta and from Malta, I left for Tunis and from there, I went to Algiers. I was home.

Another home! Another man! An evil man.

PART FIVE

Around twenty years had passed since the end of the war and Bismarck's magic number was within reach.

Shots that could have caused a war were taken, like the shots in Sarajevo on Sunday, June 28th. 928 shots, to be precise and once again, on a Sunday.

He was informed about the shots just as Franz Joseph Karl was informed that Franz Ferdinand Karl had been killed in Sarajevo. Unlike Franz Joseph Karl, however, he was not relieved by the news. He and his fellow citizens would face sleepless nights caused by fear instead.

Nine men took part in a meeting, like Franz Joseph's meeting with Berchtold, Tisza, Conrad, Charles, Hoyos and his cabinet. Only Franz Ferdinand was missing. Unfortunately.

The generals unanimously agreed that a full-scale attack and invasion was the only solution, as Conrad did. This time, it wasn't days but minutes that would decide who would win the war thrust upon them.

Less than a month before, he had explicitly promised his people he would act in a situation like this. It was a much stronger commitment than Franz Joseph Karl's promise to Conrad that they would go to war if the Kaiser supported them.

In both situations, a War of Pigs was involved.

Had the end of the world finally arrived?

Sorry, but it was inevitable.

Historians said the same about the Great War. My damned war.

On August 25th 1925, a young girl holding a notebook and pen ran into my shop. An old man in his seventies with a pointed beard and small, round glasses and two other girls followed.

"Barbara! Wait for us," shouted the girls.

"Please be careful, girls, don't touch anything," said the man as he came in.

I was reading Alexandre Dumas' historic book *Act of Corinth* when the small crowd entered and continued to do so, leaving my customers to browse the dusty items in my shop. The gentleman insisted on walking towards me, however, so I put my book down and sighed. He spoke first.

"Good morning, sir," he said in polite French.

"Good morning."

"Is this Mr Elazar Alsallem's shop?"

"It is."

"Do you know what happened to him? Is he…? Do you know where Mr Elazar is?"

"Mr Elazar?"

"Edward, it's you! You're back, my boy!"

"Uncle Elazar!"

We embraced in silence. Seeing the tears in his eyes, I almost cried, too. Like I cried when I saw the Mona Lisa in the Louvre on that strange morning.

As always, the shop was clean and tidy with the right mon… But wait, something was wrong! It was March and August was hanging on the wall. I almost criticised him for not changing the painting of the month but managed to resist. How could I tell an eighty-year-old man what to do?

We talked for hours and believe me, it was the best conversation I had ever had… memories, political analysis, judging facts, talking about books, telling jokes and laughing but I would never be able to match Mr Elazar's unique stories. I truly appreciated the wonderful, sacred time we spent together.

He didn't complain at all that I had stopped writing to him; he didn't even hint at it. He said how much my father missed me and how sad he was that I was not there.

"He was very hurt, my boy."

"I visited my brothers. They were happy to see me but equally happy to show how angry they were because they hadn't heard from me for so long. They're right. I'm a terrible person. I think it's time to leave for America. I was a terrible son, Mr Elazar." I bowed my head in shame and changed the subject. "I never married, Mr Elazar and it's strange to be called a boy when you're more than fifty years old."

"You're not that old yet. It's your fiftieth birthday on January 1st. And you should enjoy your fifties, my boy! You're in the senility of your youth and the youth of your senility." He stood up and went over to the vases, a sign that another story was about to begin. "There was this ancient Greek philosopher," he said and paused to make the story sound more important. "When he was a young man, his mother would often tell him to get married. 'Too early,' he said, 'not the right time'. The years passed and his mother

kept insisting but she always got the same reply. 'Not the right time.'

"The philosopher grew old and was still not married and when his ageing mother raised the usual subject, he replied, 'too late, not the right time.'

'Ha-ha! You see Edward, it's never the right time. We both say the same thing. Not the right time. Too early. Too late."

'How old was he?"

'Rumour has it he was fifty but they were only rumours."

'Ha! Ok, I see what you mean. There was one, Mr Elazar..." I paused, making it look as if I was trying to explain. Mr Elazar came to the rescue.

"There's always one, Edward. For every man, there's always one. And she is always very beautiful. And then, something happens. Some damned foolish thing. And life doesn't turn out as it was meant to be. And as time goes by, the missed oppor... the burden... becomes heavier and heavier. Sometimes, you catch yourself repeating her name in your mind like a prayer. And then..." he stopped and looked at August.

"Then?"

"Then... there are two kinds of men. Those who marry another woman and those who live their lives alone."

"Like you and me, Mr Elazar?"

"Revekka," he said with a heavy sigh. It took him a while to continue. "She was my third cousin and they came to visit us when she was seventeen years old. From the moment I saw her, I knew I wanted to marry her and be with her for the rest of my life." He paused again. "That night before I fell asleep, I told my older brother how happy I felt. He said nothing but the very next day, he spoke to my father behind my back... The arrangements were made... Noam married Revekka...Noam married Revekka... and... that was it."

"What did you do, Mr Elazar?"

"What did I do?" He looked at August again and mumbled, ashamed. "Nothing… absolutely nothing, my boy…but cry alone… and cowardly behaved as if it had never happened."

"Oh, Mr Elazar!"

"Have you ever wondered why I shared my most memorable moments with your father? With your family? I kept a distance from my family. I couldn't bear it. I couldn't be close to her so I stayed away from all my relatives. This was the result of my initial silence. Your father was a great friend to me despite being quite a bit older.

"My correspondence, my books and my collections compensate for losing her after that damned foolish moment of sharing my happiness with my brother."

"Were there ever any other women, Mr Elazar?"

"No, because every woman deserves a man that loves her and her alone. Nobody has the right to take that away from her, Edward. Nobody!

"So I belong to the second category of men."

"You are a great man, Mr Elazar."

"A great man now ready to take a great step, Edward. I'm leaving for Jerusalem and I honestly don't know if or when I'll be back. I would be very grateful if you would take over my shop and keep an eye on my house. If I come back, you'll be free to leave, if not, they are yours to keep and do whatever you like with. I'll arrange the paperwork with Levi, my lawyer, and after…let's say two years, everything will belong to you and you are free to do whatever you like."

"Mr Elazar, I don't know…you are doing me a…how can I…"

"Just say if you agree because time is going on. I'm in my eighties, you know."

"He went to Jerusalem ten years ago."

"Really? He mentioned it in one of his letters but I never thought he'd do it."

"Are you a friend of his?"

"Yes! Well, he was a friend of my father's but we used to get on well together, too," he said. He paused to speak to the girls in English. "Girls, please be careful now." Two of them were looking around the shop and the girl with the notebook was admiring a specific object. He turned to me and introduced himself. "Henry Morgenthau."

"Morgenthau? I remember that name! I used to collect Mr Elazar's mail when I was a child," I said and stood up to introduce myself. "Edward Aguillon."

"Lazarus Morgenthau was my father."

"A friend of Mr Elazar's is a friend of mine, too, Henry!"

"I visited Mr Elazar when I was much younger. This place was quite different then," he said smiling. He looked around and August caught his eye. "I see you kept his tradition with the paintings of the month. That's August on the wall there."

"I agree. It's a deal, Mr Elazar. And to show you my commitment, I'll replace August with March so everything is just right."

"Don't touch it, Edward," he said sternly.

"Why not?"

"Because last year, August drew his weapons and everything came to a halt. Millions of young men have died, my boy. You may change it only when the war is over and I hope that will be very soon."

"I'm very happy to hear that, Mr Elazar. I was surprised to see August but I thought you had forgotten to change it."

"I am more than eighty years old but I don't feel old, Edward. My shop is my business and everything in it is there for a reason."

"Mr Elazar stopped changing the painting when the war started. He wanted me to change it once the war was over but, to be honest, I never did."

"Why not?" asked the girl with the notebook, rather concerned. She'd been listening to our conversation while staring at the painting.

"Barbara! Maybe Mr Aguillon likes August," said Mr Morgenthau, trying to justify my actions.

"No! I'll tell you why, Barbara, because you deserve to know. How old are you?"

"I'm thirteen."

"So you were born in 1912."

"On January 30th."

"I was born in January, too, but many years ago, in 1863."

"Just like my grandfather."

"Mr Edward is younger. Seven years younger than me."

"So, Barbara, when you were two years old, a terrible war broke out and ended when you were six."

"I know. The Great War. I was on a small Italian boat when the Royal Navy's *Gloucester* fought against *Goeben* and *Breslau.* I don't remember, of course, because I was only two years old but my grandfather told me about it. We were going to Constantinople."

"Well done, Barbara, for remembering the names of the ships! Mr Elazar, who used to own this place, told me before he left that he'd refused to change it since August of 1914 because it was then that weapons were drawn, everything came to a halt and millions of young men died. I was only to change it once the war was over."

"I know, I heard you telling my grandfather."

"I didn't change it for two reasons. First, I keep it there as a reminder of all the terrible things those August weapons caused."

"Don't you want to forget about that?"

"No! No one must forget because if we do, another August will come along and make the same terrible mistakes. And if it ever happens again, I'm afraid August will draw much bigger weapons and kill even more people. We must never forget, young girl. Never!"

"I couldn't agree with you more, Mr Aguillon," said the grandfather.

"Please call me Edward!"

"And the second reason?" Barbara was curious to know.

"The second reason is more difficult to understand."

"I can try."

I looked at Mr Morgenthau and he encouraged me to continue.

"I'm afraid this *Great War* is greater than we think."

"What do you mean?"

"The war simply took a break and if we're not careful, it will start again very soon."

"But that will be another war, not the same one."

"I guess you're right, Barbara. So August is just a reminder."

"And who is this smiling lady, here?" Barbara pointed at the object she had been admiring.

"What do you think, Mr Elazar?"

"I've never seen the real Gioconda but the copy you bought is very good and quite old, judging by the cracks I see here. It's a good copy. Very good, indeed!"

"That's what I thought, too. Mr Elazar, do I have to ask your permission to hang this painting next to August?"

"Of course you have to ask my permission! But it will look very good here, over this shelf where it can be seen everywhere. Don't put it next to August, Edward. It won't look right there."

"It's the famous Mona Lisa, painted by the Italian Leonardo da Vinci many, many years ago." I was telling the truth. Nothing but the truth.

"It's the most beautiful painting I have ever seen."

"I have to agree," said Mr Morgenthau. "An excellent, almost perfect Gioconda."

I must confess that when Barbara asked why I hadn't replaced the Month when the war came to an end, I owed her a proper answer.

I asked some random questions to give myself time to think of something to say. I told her there were two reasons to make her think I was serious.

The *Mona Lisa* came into my hands in August 1911. August again. Initially, I wanted to use this as the second reason but when I began to explain, I thought it better not to. I didn't know this Morgenthau and any additional information could have ruined Lépine's great effort. When I realised, I covered it up with the nonsense about the Great War not being over but just taking a break. Would any rational human being, of this generation at least, think of starting another war after the hell the world had been through in the Great War?

To be honest, the first reason was also a lie. August wasn't there as a reminder of the war. Sorry, but what was I supposed to say? That I couldn't be bothered to change it or that Alexandre Dumas wouldn't let me? That it wouldn't look good?

As you may have realised, Mr Elazar did not come back that year or the year after. Or the year after that. He never wrote to me, either. He was probably resting in peace in Jerusalem, as he had always intended. I was now the owner of a decent business, living in a decent house nearby and with a great supply of merchandise under the shop.

Customers were scarce due to the war but I couldn't have cared less. If a customer appeared, of course, I would serve him or her to the best of my ability, as Mr Elazar did, and proudly tell stories about the items and how rare they were. But I spent most of the time reading my huge collection of books. A collection I had inherited from Mr Elazar and which had spread all over his house, my house.

Do you remember the two coffers? History came alive when I opened them. One was full of swords and the other full of military uniforms. French, English, Prussian, Austrian… Some were so old, I had to look hard to recognise their origin but they were well preserved inside the coffer.

The only thing I couldn't do was keep the shop clean and free of permanent dust. I never understood how Mr Elazar managed it. Sometimes, I even forgot to replace an item on a shelf. You can imagine the state of the shop with habits like that.

The years passed, and on November 11th 1918, Henry Nicholas John Gunther, an American soldier whose parents were children of German immigrants, was killed at 10:59 a.m. by a German machine gun. By then, eight and a half million men had been killed, twenty-one million had been wounded and eight million were missing or had been taken prisoner. These men should have been the protectors of their families, wives and children, who were now widows and orphans and many young women would never be able to have children. Cholera, typhoid and scurvy had even reached Hartwig's favourite city of Vienna. Vienna!

At 11:00 a.m., the armistice came into force and the damned war was over. Gunther was the last soldier killed. After the Great War, the Piazza Grande of Trieste would be known as the Piazza Unità d'Italia.

By then, my antique shop was full of dust. On the last day of war, a pleasant young gentleman came into the shop and wandered through the dusty pottery items, inspecting them with the help of his glasses and evaluating them while twirling his thin moustache.

I ignored him and continued reading Plato's *The Republic*. Suddenly, my Mona Lisa caught his eye.

"Oh, La Gioconda!" he said, getting as close as possible to the painting. "A half-length portrait by the one and only Leonardo da Vinci. An archetypal masterpiece of the Italian Renaissance!"

"Really?"

"Yes. The painting's novel qualities include the subject's enigmatic expression, the monumentality of the composition, the subtle modelling of forms, and the atmospheric illusionism."

"You seem to know a lot about it."

"The painting is likely of the Italian noblewoman Lisa Gherardini, the wife of Francesco del Giocondo, and is in oil on a white Lombardy poplar panel. It's believed to have been painted between 1503 and 1506. Leonardo may have continued working on it until 1517, however," he continued arrogantly.

"It took him all those years?"

"It was not widely known outside the art world but in the 1860s, a portion of the French intelligentsia began to hail it as a masterpiece of the Renaissance period.

"A nice copy you have here! Yes, a very nice copy indeed, but…" and with the enthusiasm of Archimedes shouting *Eureka,* "I can see some slight differences… yes, this lady is not smiling at all. The original is more ambiguous, as I mentioned before. Furthermore, this artist attempted to replicate Da Vinci's smoky effect but tried too hard, I think, and there is some asymmetry in the background. Yes, that's it! A nice piece of work, though." He was satisfied with his findings. He turned around and introduced himself; "Jean Armand, art critic, as you probably guessed."

"Of course," I said flatly. I pitied him.

Is he arrogant because of his ignorance or ignorant because of his arrogance? Maybe both.

"You have some fine antiquities here," he said, looking around.

Now it was my turn. I got up and went over to a tray with six small glasses on it.

Antiquities you see, antiquities you will buy. The customer is always right.

"My grandfather was Napoleon's cook's assistant. He came up with the Marengo recipe after the Battle of Marengo. Did you know that?"

"No."

"On June 14th 1800, Napoleon defeated the Austrian army at the Battle of Marengo in Piedmont. As usual, Napoleon was hungry after the battle and wanted a quick meal. He wasn't a patient man, you see.

"His chef was forced to comply with his wishes and ordered my grandfather to make something with the supplies at hand and so he could blame him later.

"My grandfather found a chicken, some eggs, tomatoes, onions, garlic, olives, some olive oil and Napoleon's brandy. He cut the chicken into pieces, fried them in olive oil, then made a thick sauce with the onions, garlic and tomatoes and simmered the chicken in it. He laced the concoction with brandy and added the olives. Then, he fried the eggs with crayfish for a side dish and served it with plenty of crusty bread.

"Napoleon was delighted, Chicken Marengo was born and the emperor demanded the same dish after every battle."

"That's amazing!"

"Now, I will show you something even greater, history in the making!

"While Napoleon was eating breakfast in a Caillou farmhouse on Sunday, 18th June 1815, he talked to his marshals about Wellington's capabilities as a general, how bad the British troops were and how the battle would be no more difficult than eating breakfast. He and his marshals made a toast to victory with this set of glasses here," I said, showing him the beautiful, dusty set on a silver tray.

"Impressive!"

"After Waterloo, my grandfather took them and kept them as a memoir of the greatest strategist of all time. It's the most precious item here. And even if that Mona Lisa were the original, I would value this family treasure more."

"Is it for sale?"

I continued as if I hadn't heard. "I put it on display because of this disastrous war but I hope no one ever buys it."

"How much are you selling it for?"

Lost in the pain of my bad fortune, I continued to ignore him. "As they made the toast, the bells of a nearby church rang out, taking Napoleon by surprise…"

"Three hundred francs, my friend!"

"…he was annoyed and asked why the bells were ringing. Glass in hand, Marshal Ney went over to the window and…"

"One thousand francs!"

"If you insist!"

No wonder there were no art critics in Plato's Republic.

Once I had found a new mission for my shop, or rather, the mission found me, I did what was necessary to make it a good antique shop, which was nothing. Absolutely nothing.

As usual, I let the dust settle and had a story for each and every object involving a specific owner or a tragic event. I didn't mention Napoleon or famous men too often because it would appear I was lying when all I was doing was inventing innocent myths. Later, I put some of the uniforms and swords on display in the shop. They gave validity to my stories.

Naturally, I was very careful with the locals, who rarely entered my shop. Sailors, travellers and anyone you would normally see at a port were all potential customers, as well as random strangers looking for a shop with exceptional rarities at the Mediterranean port of Algiers.

Rarities? This was the hardest part. Remember the tray of glasses used for Napoleon's toast? Mr Elazar had around forty sets in stock. And of course, I was always interested in a customer who wanted to buy something.

"Where are you from?"

"Where are you going?"

"How long are you staying in Algiers?"

Actually, I was more interested in when they were leaving. I would make a note of the date in a special book and bring out a similar set only after they had left. I wouldn't like Mr Armand to come in again and find that Napoleon had multiple sets of glasses in Le Caillou. It would make a Waterloo of the Belle Alliance.

Surprisingly, throughout the years, no one, apart from the ignorant art critic, noticed the Mona Lisa again. Millions of people queued outside the Louvre but here, I was the only person to admire it. Maybe it was because of the poor lighting or because it was just a copy among the other unique treasures with rare stories to back them up.

But today, a clever little girl was fascinated by the painting.

She noticed the smile.

She loved it.

"Where have you come from, Henry?"

"We were in France and are going to America. These young ladies are my granddaughters, my daughter's children. You met Barbara, this young lady is Josephine - she is fifteen - and this is Anne, who's eleven."

"Bonjour, Monsieur Aguillon!"

"Excellent accent, Josephine! Well done! Your grandfather must be a very good teacher."

"Ok, girls choose anything you like for a souvenir and let's go, otherwise the ship will leave without us."

Josephine chose a water glass with a ballerina on it, Anne a water carrier, but young Barbara was undecided.

"Barbara, please choose something, Mr Aguillon is waiting."

At that moment, I made what was probably the oddest decision of my life.

"No, Barbara doesn't have to choose, Henry," I said to Mr Morgenthau.

"Why not?" asked Barbara.

"Because you've already seen something you like. I'll pack it for you and arrange for someone to help you take it to the boat," I said. I took a chair and safely dismounted the Mona Lisa."

"No, Mr Aguillon, we cannot...," said Mr Morgenthau.

"Wow! Thank you very much, Mr Aguillon!"

"You're not leaving without this painting, Henry. It belongs to Barbara, now," I said, taking down the Mona Lisa.

"But we cannot accept such a wonderful gift. Edward, please!"

"Just give me a moment to pack it up safely."

As I carefully packaged the Mona Lisa, I was tempted to tell an amazing story about a painting stolen from the Louvre but held myself back.

"So, tell me Henry, what were you doing in Constantinople during the war?" I asked instead.

"I was the ambassador of the United States of America."

"Really?"

"Yes."

"It must be difficult being an ambassador during a war."

"During this war especially and in Constantinople, even more so. Turkey was a place of horror."

"I heard about the Ottoman massacre of the Armenians."

"By the end of the war, Edward, two million Assyrians, Greeks, and Armenians had perished, having been subject to a wholesale massacre by the Ottomans. Two million souls, my friend. People must never forget. Never! And I am dedicated to this purpose. It's my duty as a human being."

"Two million?"

"Talaat Pasha, the Ottoman interior minister, even demanded a list of all the Armenians insured by Life Insurance Company and Equitable."

"Why? To double-check if anyone was left alive?"

"Ha! Because now they'd been slaughtered the money should go to the Turkish state."

"Unbelievable!" *There are people worse than me.*

"Our people will never forget these massacres," said Henry Morgenthau.

"Grandpa, Anne wants to go," said Barbara.

"Wait a moment, Anne. We'll be leaving soon," he said and turned to me again.

"What can I say about your gift, Edward? It's... wonderful. An honour for us. An honour for Barbara."

"There are two things I would like you to know, my friend. Barbara, please listen!

"This painting is very important to me. I hardly knew my mother, you see. She died when I was a child. The painting is like a picture of my mother, honestly. I don't know why Leonardo painted it, but to me, the Mona Lisa is a kind of mother figure."

"Please keep it, Mr Aguillon. I could never accept it."

"Barbara, I am an old man. I have no children and I would like this painting to be left in the hands of someone who will take care of it and I know you are that person. Now listen carefully! I want you to take more care of this painting than you would of any copy of it or even the original that hangs in the Louvre in Paris. Do you understand? I know you will do this for me."

"Still, it's a very generous gift, Edward."

"Which brings me to something else," I said, looking at Barbara. "I am not giving it to you for free, Barbara."

"What do you mean, Mr Aguillon?"

"In exchange, I would like you to write a book explaining that the Great War began for absolutely no reason. Explain to people that those guns were fired in August for no reason. Believe me, I know what I'm talking about. It's the truth. Is that a deal?"

"But I am only thirteen years old, Mr Aguillon. They won't believe me."

"I'm sorry Barbara. I meant when you are older and go to university. Write it then, ok?"

"It's a deal," said Barbara, looking at her grandfather. "Just like you, Grandpa!"

I arranged for the painting to be transported to the ship and after bidding them farewell, I gave Barbara two books, including the one I had been reading.

"You're going to write a book so I'm giving you these. Mr Elazar had a huge library and would be happy for you to have these books. It's a gift from him, ok? This one, by Alexandre Dumas, is called *Act of Corinth* and the other is by Thucydides. Useful history to know."

Barbara turned to her grandfather, asking if she could accept them. I looked at him sternly and he smiled in agreement. I wished them a pleasant trip to America.

You're probably wondering how I could just give the Mona Lisa away like that.

To be honest, I didn't really think about it. As you get old, you start to worry about your precious possessions. If something happened to me, Leonardo's unique masterpiece would probably fall into the hands of a boring ignoramus like Mr Armand, who would find fault with it or hang it in a house where no one would appreciate it. In all her innocence, young Barbara had singled it out amongst a host of other items. I assumed my trust in her would make her extra careful with this particular painting. The Mona Lisa was safe now, I felt.

Half an hour later, the heaver brought me a small book. *Ambassador Morgenthau's Story, 1918* was the title. There was a dedication inside. 'Pour mon ami Edward, l' antiquaire le plus généreux du monde. Henry Morgenthau'.

The most generous antique dealer in the world? Who me? Little do you know, Henry!

I had gifted Dumas, Thucydides and Da Vinci and received a Morgenthau. An extraordinary day for the man who killed kings, ambassadors, politicians and magnates. An extraordinary day indeed! The enormous significance of the day, however, wouldn't be revealed until decades later. Peruggia and Picasso would be proud of their cooperation with Lépine to 'hide' the real Mona Lisa by giving it to young Barbara to keep safe.

Vincenzo Peruggia and Jean Theophile Homolle, the director of the Louvre, died in the same year that I gave the Mona Lisa to Barbara. Homolle died at the age of seventy-seven, on June 13th, and Peruggia died on his forty-fourth birthday, on October 8th, 1925. As Lépine promised, he had taken care of the young Italian the best he could.

Despite being sent to jail for a year and fifteen days, Peruggia was hailed throughout Italy as a great patriot and remained in prison for just seven months. By the time he was released, my *plan de l'Europe* had succeeded so he was forced to serve in the Italian army during my Great War. He later married and had a daughter called Celestina.

Lépine arranged for him to work as a painter and decorator in France in the town of Saint-Maur-des-Fossés. To avoid commotion, he used his birth name - Pietro Peruggia, probably acting on Lépine's advice.

It worked. No one paid any attention to him but two decades later, in 1947, when another Vincenzo Peruggia died in Haute-Savoie, they mistook him for the

Mona Lisa's Peruggia and obituaries were written accordingly.

On the day I gave away the Mona Lisa, seventy-three-year-old Conrad von Hoetzendorf took his last breath at a spa in Mergentheim, the headquarters of the Knights of the Teutonic Order from 1526 until 1809. His wife Gina was at his side.

Franz Joseph had finally given permission for their marriage in 1915. The following year, Franz Joseph died and the new emperor, Charles I, dismissed Conrad one year later in 1917. After the war, he was free to live peacefully in the Austrian mountains with his beloved wife, taking long walks with Foxy Ferdinand, ex-king of Bulgaria. He learned English, adding another language to the eight he already spoke and wrote a five-volume memoir, which detailed the responsibilities of his fellow decision-makers leading up to the Great War that killed one of his sons and led to the downfall of the Austro-Hungarian Empire. He denied any responsibility and hadn't even suspected it, unlike the Count of Hoyos, who attempted to commit suicide because of that awful July when he returned from Germany with the disastrous 'blank cheque'.

Later in 1925, after Conrad's death, a journal titled *Diary of my Sufferings* was found. The journal included more than three thousand letters written to Gina von Reininghaus. He wrote to her daily, even during the war. However, fearing a potential leak and the scandal that would ensue, he never sent the letters to their intended recipient but kept them private instead. Some of the letters were more than sixty pages long and detailed his great love for Gina.

Conrad was the last of the four Franzes.

Emperor Charles Franz lived to see disaster come about. He died in exile on April 1st 1922, on the Portuguese island of Madeira with his beloved wife, pregnant with their eighth child, and the nine-year-old former Crown Prince Otto at his side. A month earlier, he had caught a cold which developed into bronchitis and subsequently progressed to severe pneumonia. He was just thirty-five years old.

"Good morning sir," said the young man in English.

"Good morning."

"Can I look around?"

"Yes."

He was in his thirties and his accent betrayed him as an American. His moustache was similar to one I had sported in my youth and he wore glasses like Mr Bronstein's. He seemed a decent, educated man and judging by his warm smile, was not arrogant.

While he was looking around my shop, I noticed he was mostly interested in swords and military uniforms.

"Could I have a look at this sword, please?" he asked politely. I nodded.

After viewing some of the swords, he asked me a question.

"Do you know if any of these are Prussian army swords? I am of Prussian origin and would like to own a Prussian sword."

Ok, stay calm. Don't worry. Everything is under control.

You've probably noticed that I no longer had bad feelings for the Prussians. After all I had done, how would that have been possible? What's more, I had come to appreciate Bismarck as the greatest politician of the nineteenth century. Believe me. And it wasn't just because I was an old man. Bismarck introduced retirement plans, by the way, and I must confess, I sometimes wished I were Prussian because of those pension plans! And after the Great War, how could I not appreciate his diplomatic genius, especially now that Alsace and Lorraine were both free?

It seems, however, that Mr Ivan Pavlov had not won the Nobel Prize in 1904 by accident. He was the first Russian to be awarded it. According to his research, a neutral stimulus, for example, the Prussians, became a conditioned stimulus, when they occupied Alsace and Lorraine. A stimulus is a connection response that requires no learning and because of this so-called 'classical conditioning', when the young man said 'Prussian sword,' my response was conditioned.

I stood up and walked over to the uniforms and swords. I took down a very old black, patched military coat in terrible condition but pretended it was very precious to me.

"This overcoat is worth a million swords, young man. This coat defeated Napoleon!"

"How did it do that?"

"On June 16th 1815, three days before Waterloo at the Battle of Ligny, the brave Marshal Blücher faced the French. Towards the end of the battle, Blücher fell under his dead horse. The French Cuirassiers were advancing. Everything was lost…

"August Ludwig von Nostitz threw this coat over his commander to obscure Blücher's rank and identity from the cavaliers that passed over him.

"He survived. Once the French were gone, he escorted the Prussian commander from the battlefield…

"Without Blücher, the Prussian army would have retreated. Blücher, with this coat slung over his shoulders, headed to Waterloo to attack the French at Plancenoit, while Napoleon crushed Wellington.

And that was Waterloo, my boy!"

"Very impressive!" The young Pruss-American was amazed and carefully took the coat in his hands.

"After the Battle of Waterloo, at around 21:00, Prince Blücher and the Duke of Wellington met face to face at the *La Belle Alliance,* indicating the fighting had ended. It was then that Blücher gave the coat to Count Nostitz."

"Ah, there is a *Belle-Alliance-Platz* in Berlin. And how did this coat fall into your hands?"

"My grandfather was the owner of *La Belle Alliance.*

Count Nostitz told him the story in the morning and gave it to him as a souvenir before burning the Caillu farmhouse. That's where Napoleon spent the night before the battle. It was filthy dirty, covered in mud and blood and the significance it has today was not apparent at the time. Today, this coat is of great historic value, my boy."

"Would you sell it?"

"Many have asked to buy it but so far, I have declined."

"I'll give you fifty francs."

"It's not a matter of money."

"Two hundred francs!"

"We are only discussing it because of your Prussian roots, but my grandfather…"

"Five hundred francs."

"I am an old man and it wouldn't be right for something so important to be forgotten. Agreed."

"Thank you, Mr…?"

"And I'll tell you something else, young man. The battle should have been called La Belle Alliance but Wellington insisted on Waterloo."

"Really, Mr…?"

"Aguillon."

"Thank you, Mr Aguillon! You are an amazing person but before I leave, I would like to do you a favour."

"What favour is that?"

"I understand that, at your age, health is of some concern."

"The declining years certainly have their issues."

"Listen, I am a doctor and I'm sure you've heard about the great benefits of Radium."

"Yes, I have."

'Radiate Youth and Beauty', 'Radium Restores Health to Thousands', 'Remarkable New Radium Liniment Instantly Drives Out Pain from Aching Joints and Muscles!'

These were some of the advertising slogans I had heard but never took seriously.

"Most of the manufacturers of these products are lying to take people's money. Radium is in scarce supply and extremely expensive and the vast majority of radioactive products peddled by quacks in the United States do not actually contain radioactive ingredients at all. They are scams."

"Unbelievable! Scientists taking advantage of people's health!"

"*Bailey Radium Laboratories* in New Jersey produces an energy drink that is literally 'A Cure for the Living Dead'. It works like magic. I've seen it for myself. It cures impotence, diabetes and many other ailments. They call it *Perpetual Sunshine* because it revitalises the human body by stimulating the endocrine system. It cures more than one-hundred-and-fifty endocrine diseases, to be precise. It was developed by Dr William J. A. Bailey, the owner of the company and chief laboratory technician. I know him personally and he is a dignified professional with a thorough knowledge of his field. An excellent scientist!"

"That sounds impressive. A lot of progress has been made in America," I said, thinking how lucky I would be to sample this unique medication and live healthily for years to come. These things matter when you are old, you see.

"When my friend Dr Wendt learned of the benefits of Radithor, he asked for my help and that is the reason for my trip."

"Radi...?"

"Radithor! And I happen to have some with me," he said, taking a small bottle out of his bag to show me.

"How much does one of these cost?"

"As you can see, it is registered to the US Patent Office. It contains not only Radium but Mesothorium and the water is not once but three times distilled. These people are professionals. You know they're not just selling you plain water. Tiny amounts of radium are dissolved in the water, which is distilled three times. More specifically, it contains a minimum of one microcurie for each of the radium 226 and radium 228 isotopes. The results prove it. What do you think of that?"

"Do you have more bottles with you?"

"Yes, on the boat but I promised Dr Wendt and he is my friend. And it has one disadvantage, Mr Aguillon. It is very expensive."

"Of course, because it's magic. How many bottles do you have?"

"Damned Prussians!"

"What did you say, old man?" asked the nurse. She looked at the doctor. "His voice is very hoarse, I can't understand him at all."

"He is getting on, Marie. He is an old *Pied-Noir*."

"Damned doctor! I'm French! Don't call me...... my brother. Damned...!" I had to pause to clear my throat.

I hated to be called 'black feet' after the sailors who worked barefoot in the coal room of their ships. You know why, I'm sure. Their feet were blackened by the soot and dust. It made sense.

But why are you calling me Pied-Noir?

Some say it's because of the black boots the French soldiers wore compared to the Algerians who went barefoot. But why were they called after the black boots they wore and not the red trousers? *Pantalon Rouge* sounded much better.

Others say it's because of the black boots my father and the original settlers wore while working in the fields or riding their horses.

Which is true?

None of it! It's all nonsense and I should not be called by that name. Nevertheless, all Frenchmen born in Algeria were called by this name. Even worse, anyone of European origin who lived in Algeria was called by this name.

"Relax, old man. I'm sorry, Marie here will take care of you. She'll get you anything you need. I'll be back in an hour, ok?"

Marie smiled at me as if I were a silly young child. She was nice, though. She reminded me of the Breton I met at *Hotel de l'Europe* the year I… you know.

"Mr Aguillon, you did well to leave Algeria. We'll take care of you. Don't worry!"

She was lying. I had heard her talking to the doctor earlier. She couldn't understand why I'd bothered to leave Algeria at my age. I can't blame her. She was right. She was also right about my voice. My voice was permanently hoarse and it had been since I was outsmarted by that…

Distilled three times! I hadn't seen it coming. How could I? I was blinded by my fear of missing out. I thought it would make me young again, that it would give me a second chance. Why was I so naive?

It was all there. The numbers, the names, the rarity, the enthusiasm. All the ingredients of a good lie. And it was hard not to trust a doctor. A doctor is not a salesman. Why would he lie to me? It's natural not to trust a salesman, but a doctor?

Why did I believe he was a doctor in the first place? It took me a while to accept it. It also took me a while to accept the sound of my painful, croaky voice, the nights I couldn't sleep, whole days of vomiting, and the headaches that went on for hours on end. If he'd killed me and taken all my money, I'd have suffered less and he'd have earned more. Why? For God's sake, why? … Damned Prussian!

After five dark months, I was still alive and eventually figured out why. This time, it was for real. 'All who draw the sword will die by the sword'. It was my destiny. If you kill with sales you will die with sales. It was as simple as that. Now I could relate to Alfred Redl. He betrayed for luxury and luxury betrayed him. The doctor had tricked me. He had asked for a Prussian sword as if it was some kind of warning. The scoundrel! How come I didn't see through it? We were the same kind of people. No values. I bet he'd have agreed with me about the Dreyfus affair, too.

In the end and to my great surprise, I didn't die. The headaches gradually stopped, I could sleep again and I could eat soup without vomiting. Now I was just weak and in poor health, shuffling around my antique shop day in, day out and collapsing into my seat. I got up only to admire my old military uniforms and swords and recite fanciful stories about my merchandise to customers in my permanently croaky voice. Perhaps it was a reminder to stop the lies, though I never stopped telling the little white variety.

During my convalescence, I was troubled by other issues. Why didn't I die? Hadn't I suffered enough? Was there more suffering to come? What else was there to see? Did God want me to live through the extraordinary decade that was to come? What would happen in the thirties? Another war maybe?

Yes! And there was more.

In 1932, another professional liar, an American journalist called Karl Decker, whose pen name was Charles Duval, published a strange story in the Saturday Evening Post. Many years before, he had met an Italian called Eduardo de Valfierno, who confessed to the theft of the Mona Lisa. What a liar! Decker, I mean.

More specifically, Valfierno had paid a French art restorer and forger named Yves Chaudron to make six copies of the Mona Lisa. Not one. Six. The six forgeries were shipped to various places around the world to potential customers. Once it was all arranged, Valfierno commissioned Peruggia to commit the theft and the copies would then be delivered to the buyers, who lit up their cigars, drank liqueur and marvelled at the original Mona Lisa stolen especially for each of them. Ingenious, wasn't it?

And it gets better. Valfierno had made a fortune and didn't bother to contact Peruggia again after the crime. Why risk it? The Mona Lisa had disappeared and that was all that mattered. Eventually, the truth was revealed, the truth you already know. Peruggia was caught trying to sell the painting and it was returned to the Louvre.

A minor detail - Eduardo de Valfierno and Yves Chaudron didn't exist. Karl Decker had created a scenario that could have endangered the real Mona Lisa that was now in Barbara's hands. She could easily have assumed it was one of the six illegally produced copies and painted by someone called Yves Chaudron, not by Da Vinci or even Picasso.

How awful!

Luckily, her father, Mr Maurice Wertheim, was an art collector. His collection of Impressionist and Post-Impressionist works included many by famous painters - Edgar Degas, Édouard Manet, Henri Matisse, Vincent van Gogh and of course Pablo Picasso. Surely he would have been able to recognise a masterpiece painted by Da Vinci and keep it safe for young Barbara, who was now twenty years old.

The following year, the great, the undeniable genius Louis Lépine died at the age of eighty-seven. I'm sure he never believed Decker's lie. The size and weight of the painting were wrong in the article. I can imagine Lépine laughing as he read it.

Two years passed after this strange event and a new one rocked my already vulnerable world. I had just sold the gun that started the Great War to an American sailor. Yes, the one Gavrilo Prinzip used to kill Franz Ferdinand in front of the *Schiller Delicatessen*… but anyway.

"You know what, old man? An investigation has begun into the reason for the Great War," said the young sailor, happy to have come upon such a historic item.

"Wha…?"

"Yes, in the United States. The Special Committee for Investigation of the Munitions Industry has been formed. Senator Gerald Nye is determined to find out the truth. His courage and determination are inexhaustible. He'll dig deep. You know, *who* sold ammunition, *who* made money, greedy bankers and gun sellers, that kind of thing. He's going to find them and make them pay."

That's why I'm still alive. I'll have to pay. They'll find my boss and he will… No wait, he must be dead by now. But they'll find the payments. The bankers will point at me. I even killed a banker, but Morgan…

"Are you all right, old man?"

"Yes. I… the war, you know…"

"I understand. Goodbye, and thanks for the historic weapon."

"Goodbye, son."

For the next few days, I couldn't sleep. The Nye Committee would dig deep. It wouldn't be difficult to find me. A film-maker had captured me at Hartwig's funeral. A photographer had captured me after Jean Jaurès' assassination. A simple cross-check and I'd be fully exposed. Damned technology! The whole world would find out about my sinister occupation. I should have stuck to the Benedictine, got married, and lived a miserable life in Fécamp.

I was afraid that one day, the door would open and the HaHo would come and arrest me and there would be no Nikon Nikitas to save me this time.

My alter egos will come back to haunt me.

I thought about it and, logically speaking, no committee would take issue with a sick old man. And my judgment was correct. They were looking elsewhere.

Luckily, the Nye committee only investigated the financial and banking interests at the root of the United States involvement in the Great War. In America, during the 1920s, apart from a plethora of radioactive products, many books and articles were written about the high cost of war and some argued that financiers and arms manufacturers had manoeuvred the United States into entering the Great War. Obviously, a committee such as this couldn't be financed for very long and the investigation came to an abrupt end in early 1936.

That same year, Raoul Villain was killed in Ibiza by a small detachment of Spanish soldiers who came ashore at Cala de San Vicent. Brave Raoul had come to Ibiza via Mexico and was trying to live anonymously and be forgotten. When he was brought to trial after the end of the war in 1919, not only was he acquitted, but Jean Jaurès' wife was ordered to pay the court costs. In 1936, however, he paid for naively believing the words I had spoken. The words of a liar.

Two years later, a historian called Charles Callan Tansill wrote *America Goes To War,* exploiting the Nye Committee's report of testimony and evidence to develop and confirm the heavy influence exercised by Wall Street finance and the armaments industry in the process that led to American intervention. As if the war started in Europe for good reason and America was dragged into it due to greed! They didn't have a clue about the American Napoleon. I was safe.

Not that safe, however.

Remember the young painter in Vienna whose birthday was around the same time the Eiffel Tower was built? The one that I encouraged to visit Paris to paint it?

He took my advice too seriously and finally visited Paris on June 24th, 1940. He didn't paint the tower though; he just took some photographs.

You might also remember the young poet from Igor, Hartwig's birthplace. He was the one who visited Mr Bronstein in *Central Café* under the name of Stavros Papadopoulos - the one with the wooden suitcase. Two months later, on August 21st 1940, the poet sent an assassin to kill Mr Bronstein in Mexico. In 1902, Mr Bronstein had changed his surname to *Trotsky,* inspired by the name of a jailer at the Odessa prison where he had been held.

The painter and the poet had something in common. Their fathers used to beat the hell out of them. In the summer of 1939, they agreed to be friends, but as the poet was killing Mr Bronstein, the painter was making plans to kill the poet the following summer using his soldiers.

Remember what I said about little boys playing with their toy soldiers? There were two categories. The boy in the second category acts like Wilhelm, except for the final step. Once in position, the battle begins and he violently sets them against each other, destroying them, breaking them as if it's the last game he will ever play. The painter was in this category.

The poet did not belong to either category, however. He was in a category of his own, destroying his soldiers one by one or all together before the game of toy soldiers even starts.

These two men killed so many people that only Death himself could outdo them. The worst thing that ever happened to humanity was brought about by these two men with strange moustaches and that's probably the reason the trend was largely abandoned. 'Who, after all, speaks today of the annihilation of the Armenians?' said the painter who killed six million Jews.

Soselo killed twenty-five million people. The poet was beaten even by his mother, maybe that's why he killed more people. Soselo killed thousands of his own people and would continue to do so during the war in Poland.

Come to think of it, without my war, one of them would still be painting the Opera House in Vienna and the other would still be writing poems somewhere in Siberia. I deserve to be bathed in a tub of Radithor.

Talking of which, let's examine the situation from the other side of the Atlantic. It wasn't much better, in my opinion at least. During the war, William John Aloysius Bailey was the wartime manager of an electronic division of a company called International Business Machines.

Who was this man?

He was the mastermind behind the patented Radithor medication and a Harvard University dropout. He had absolutely no idea about medicine and was only interested in making money. This ignoramus had been convicted for other scams before he discovered the notorious *Bailey Radium Laboratories.*

In 1915, he was sentenced to thirty days in jail because he and two others committed fraud with the *Carnegie Engineering Corporation*, which incidentally had nothing to do with the famous magnate Andrew Carnegie.

Three years later, he was fined $200 for fraudulently promoting pills for male impotence called Las-I-Go. The pills contained strychnine, a highly toxic alkaloid, which causes poisoning and results in death by asphyxia. He was convicted once again but Bailey had finally made his way by selling whatever his empty head could come up with to revitalise the human body.

He also founded two other robust and ingenious companies, the *Thorone Company* and the *American Endocrine Laboratory*, producing medicinal cures and a neck harness that would solve all health problems. The *Radioendocrinator* was initially sold for $1000.

No one stood in his way and in 1925, armed with the know-how for medical scams, he proudly set up the *Bailey Radium Laboratories,* which produced his absolute masterpiece - Radithor.

Testimonials from patients and doctors accompanied by photographs of the careful extraction, high-level purification and strict testing of radium at the Bailey Laboratories were illustrated in glossy brochures and sent to registered physicians all over the United States.

The increase in sales this time around, however, was due to another monstrous tactic. For every bottle a doctor prescribed, Bailey would pay him 17% of the cost of the Radithor. It was called the 'professional fee' and so the 'professional' doctor, like the Prussian in my shop, earned an extra income.

Bailey Laboratories simply purchased purified radium from the American Radium Laboratory at wholesale prices, bottled it in distilled water and sold it, marking up the price by 500%. Correct. Five hundred per cent.

Why not reward the damned salesmen for their years of study, diligent efforts to understand the human body and the sacrifices they made to become doctors?

Surely they deserved it.

More than 400.000 bottles were marketed and sold worldwide between 1925 and 1930 and Bailey got rich. Unfortunately, I was on the receiving end of the scam in Algiers. Justice was served you might say, and I would agree. I was one of the first victims of 'fee-splitting quackery', as it was officially known and it was terrifying to live in a world where a doctor is permitted to prescribe medication under the notion of *one single death is a tragedy, but one death out of ten is a statistic.*

Soselo had said something similar and he was not an educated man, unlike the evil-minded doctors who came up with the scam.

The only person he never managed to kill was *Tito*, who stumbled over his wooden suitcase in *Central Café*. He repeatedly sent assassins to do the job but they failed. He stopped when Tito politely asked him to do so or he would send an assassin himself and there would be no need for more. He was a tough guy, this Tito.

Stalin, like Hartwig, died on March 5th, 1953. Everyone thought his heart was to blame but he was poisoned, and speaking of poisons…

"Mr Aguillon, it's time for your medicine."

"Thank you, Marie. What day it is today?" I asked after putting in my teeth."

"Thursday."

"What's the date?"

"November 1st."

"Toussaint!"

"Your memory is excellent, Mr Aguillon."

"Toussaint Rouge."

How could I forget? Whoever would have thought that the man who attempted to use the *Black Hand* to initiate Sicilian Vespers in Sarajevo would live long enough to witness *Red All Saints' Day* in 1954 and witness the *Red Hand* cause a disaster?

The National Liberation Front, or FLN, a group of fewer than five hundred Algerians, attacked military and civilian targets throughout Algeria. Seven people were killed that day. The Algerian people didn't support them at first. Ironically, the damage would be done by the Red Hand itself. They killed many people, which led the Algerian population to join the FLN.

I'd lived through the *Pig War*, we were currently experiencing the *Cold War* and in 1954, the *War without a Name* began. It was named as such because Algiers was not a colony. It was France on the opposite side of the sea. There was simply no name to describe it and I'm sure Bismarck would have agreed with me.

On January 6th 1955, I locked up my shop and my home and left for France with just one suitcase. I was ninety-two years old and should already have been dead. All I wanted to do was what Mr Elazar had done - go to my promised land and be buried there. I had no one to leave my property to and what's more, I didn't care. It was over.

"You left Algiers straight after the Red All Saints' Day, Mr Edward?" asked Marie while making the bed.

"A few months later," I answered slowly.

"What about your family?"

Marie received no answer but carried on making the bed. She turned to me when she had finished.

I was dead.

The war without a name or the *Algerian War of Independence* lasted until 1962. Once the war was over,

900.000 French people left Algeria in just three months, fearing the revenge of the FLN. Their propaganda was cruel and deadly for all the members of the *Pied-Noir* community. *The Suitcase or the Coffin* was their motto. La valise ou le cercueil.

I'd already had both, and some years in advance. Quite proactive for an old *Pied-Noir*, don't you think?

In the damned year of 1962, 928 other shots were taken.

More specifically, on Sunday, October 14th 1962, 928 pictures were taken by pilot Richard S. Heyser, capturing images of what turned out to be USSR missiles. If a war had broken out then, it would have been a nuclear war and not only the end of the *Belle Epoch* but the end of all epochs.

On the morning of Tuesday, October 16th, the forty-three-year-old president of the United States John Kennedy - less than a year in office - was shown photographs of Russian missiles located in Cuba.

At 6:30 that evening, John Fitzgerald Kennedy convened a meeting of the nine members of the National Security Council and five other key advisers in a group he formally named the Executive Committee of the National Security Council, known as EXCOMM. President Kennedy recorded the proceedings without their prior consent.

The EXCOMM discussed several possible courses of action, from no action at all to diplomacy, invasion, air strike or blockade.

The Joint Chiefs of Staff, i.e. the generals, unanimously agreed that a full-scale attack and invasion was the only solution. They believed the Soviets would not attempt to stop the US from conquering Cuba.

'If Cuba should possess a capacity to carry out offensive actions against the United States... the United States would act', Kennedy had promised the American people less than a month before.

Historians claimed the Great War was inevitable. It was obvious. Anyone could have seen it coming. A cold war would undeniably lead to a nuclear catastrophe in less than twenty years. But this time, there would be no one left to talk about the inevitability of war.

Enter Edward Aguillon to stop the madness and save the world! But how? How could a *Pied-Noir* who had died alone in a French hospital in Nice years earlier have saved the world during the October missile crisis?

Be patient and allow me to tell you what had gone before.

John Fitzgerald Kennedy, a.k.a. JFK, decided not to bungle into war but move on with a naval blockade of Cuba and use diplomatic pressure instead. And he succeeded. It wasn't easy; it was too complicated for that, but he succeeded.

Only some damned foolish thing could ruin his tremendous and extraordinary effort. And there were quite a few of those towards the end of the crisis, on the *Black Saturday* of October 27th.

Direct orders from the Soviet President Nikita Khrushchev were violated and at midday approximately, a US aircraft was shot down by a Soviet missile and the pilot, thirty-seven-year-old-year-old Rudolf Anderson, was killed.

Later, at about 3:41 p.m., Cuban antiaircraft fired against other US reconnaissance aircraft and against Khrushchev's direct orders to Castro. However, Kennedy acted against advice not to stage a military response to the attack. Please note he took this decision without knowing that the shooting had gone against Khrushchev's orders and whilst under pressure from everyone, not just his 'Conrads'.

Furthermore, the Soviet President received a letter that day from Fidel Castro. He wrote:

'I believe the imperialists' aggressiveness is extremely dangerous and if they carry out the brutal act of invading Cuba in violation of international law and morality, that would be the moment to eliminate such danger forever through an act of clear legitimate defence, however harsh and terrible the solution would be.'

Read the last part once again. 'However, harsh and terrible the solution would be'. Kennedy and Khrushchev knew that a nuclear war would likely kill a third of humanity with most or all of those deaths in the US, the USSR, Europe and China. Castro knew that every human in Cuba would likely die as a result. However 'harsh and terrible the solution would be'. However!

Even the eighteen-year-old Gavrilo Prinzip wouldn't have dared say such a thing at such a crucial moment. But Castro, double his age at thirty-six, said it, no, wrote it. Luckily, it wasn't Stalin who received the *Armageddon Letter.*

Later on Black Saturday, the US Navy dispatched signalling depth charges, explosives intended to force a Soviet submarine to come to the surface for identification.

But the submarine was armed with a nuclear-tipped torpedo with orders that allowed it to be used if necessary. It was too deep to monitor any radio traffic and the captain, Valentin Grigorievitch Savitsky, decided that a war might already have started and prepared to launch a nuclear torpedo.

Fortunately, wise Russian generals had previously issued strict instructions indicating that the launch of a nuclear torpedo required agreement from all three officers on board - the captain, the political officer and the commodore. The commodore, thirty-six-year-old Vasily Arkhipov, strongly objected. An argument broke out with only Arkhipov against the launch. Eventually, he persuaded Savitsky to surface and await orders from Moscow. The nuclear launch was averted.

Arthur M. Schlesinger Jr., historian and advisor to the Kennedy administration, stated that 'this was not only the most dangerous moment of the Cold War. It was the most dangerous moment in human history.'

This is where Edward Aguillon enters the scene.

Do you remember young Barbara Wertheim, Ambassador Morgenthau's granddaughter?

She grew up to become a journalist. She kept her promise, however, and wrote the book I told her to. How could she not? I'd given her the Mona Lisa, after all.

An academic historian, obviously jealous, described Barbara's book as 'hopelessly unscholarly' but students loved it.

The book was titled *Guns of August*. I'm sure you know why. She'd been inspired by that painting of August hanging in Mr Elazar's shop since 1914. Fortunately, it was published earlier in 1962. Barbara became known as Barbara Tuchman after marrying Mr Lester Tuchman, a nice enough fellow.

Fortunately once again, the newly elected president read it and loved it, as the students had. He was so impressed by the book that he gave copies to his cabinet and principal military advisers, ordering them to read it. He demanded that every army officer read it, too.

Subsequently, the armed forces secretary sent copies to every U.S. military base in the world. While dealing with the crisis in Cuba, Kennedy had seriously understood the profound and unpredictable implications a rapid escalation of the situation could have had.

Robert McNamara, United States Secretary of Defense at the time, clarified what happened. Kennedy said *The Guns of August* graphically portrayed how Europe's leaders had bungled into the debacle of World War I. 'We are not going to bungle into war', he said.

Graham Allison, a political scientist who covered the Cuban Missile Crisis in *Essence of Decision*, noted the effect Barbara's book had on Kennedy but also its implications for proper analysis of decision-making and warfare. Allison created an entire model of decision-making, which he called the Organizational Process Model, based on issues such as those covered by Tuchman, a model that directly countered game theory and other rationalistic means of explaining events.

So now you can appreciate Kennedy's initial decision to blockade and negotiate, as well as his consistency - even on that Black Saturday - against all advice, with the generals who claimed that a simple two-minute delay could mean defeat.

It was relatively late in the Great War that the generals discovered that three men with machine guns could eliminate a battalion of heroes. In 1963, any idiot could have done the same, simply by pressing a button.

Thank you, Barbara. Thank you, Mona Lisa. Thank you, Leonardo.

But it wasn't just the book. There was another important issue that gave Kennedy the strength to say no to his 'Conrads'.

A year before, President Kennedy, less than three months in office at the time, ordered an invasion of Cuba. Barbara was yet to publish her book and the idea of overthrowing Castro's dictatorship first emerged within the CIA in early 1960. They even tried to kill Castro and never ceased with their efforts.

There were extensive economic reasons for such a move. In June 1960, Castro had nationalised the Esso refineries, as well as those of Shell and Texaco because they refused to refine Soviet oil. In September, all U.S. banks were expropriated. Last but not least, in October, casinos and hotel chains were confiscated.

On April 15th 1961, at about 6 a.m. Cuban time, eight bombers in three groups simultaneously attacked three Cuban airfields at San Antonio de los Baños, and on April 17th, the invasion took place. It was held on the southwestern coast known as Bay of Pigs. It failed.

Remember the War of Pigs?

As you can probably imagine, JFK was very suspicious when his overconfident generals asked for war after the Cuban failure.

Imagine if Franz Joseph Karl, FJK, if you like, had accepted one of Conrad's proposals for war against Italy, for example. Conrad had indeed asked for a war against Italy when the Italians attacked the Ottomans in Libya. If Conrad had failed in an earlier confrontation when the answer to the ultimatum arrived on July 28th, having accepted all but the sixth demand, the conversation would probably have gone something like this:

"Ok, they don't accept the sixth demand but it's a great diplomatic victory. We don't have to go to war and…"

"Your Highness, you told me that..."
"Shut up, Conrad!"
"But the monarchy is at stake and..."
"You will marry your Gina!"
"Ok!"

Thanks to the failure of the invasion at the Bay of Pigs, President JFK was able to keep the peace by continuing with a naval blockade of Cuba and using diplomatic pressure.

The question is, why was President Kennedy in so much of a hurry to invade Cuba? He was sworn in as the 35th president on January 20th and approved the final invasion plan on April 4th.

Indeed, Eisenhower had worked on the plan, but still, it was too early for Kennedy, no matter how serious the economic reasons were. However, one of the reasons couldn't wait. Which reason was that?

The casinos!

The Italian-American Mafia controlled the drug, gambling, and prostitution businesses in Havana, before the Cuban revolution. Cosa Nostra supported Kennedy's election and the president, once elected, would be under pressure to return these businesses to Havana as soon as possible and before Castro came to power. The new presidential candidate made an agreement with the Mafia, which stated that if he were elected, he would get rid of Castro so they could reclaim the casino in Havana.

Kennedy wanted to make a start on this obligation, which was conducive to American interests. The CIA had even used the Mafia to try and kill Castro. The mobster that took the job, Sam Giancana, said that the CIA and Cosa Nostra were 'different sides of the same coin'.

As you remember it was I, Edward Aguillon, who initiated the expansion of the Sicilian Mafia's business in America in 1892. Thus, if Conte Cucinotta and Barbara Wertheim had not done as they were told, a nuclear war in 1962 would have been inevitable. So all those minor accidents had a sacred cause after all, did they not?

"Von Reininghaus, this young girl is extremely beautiful. A classic Italian beauty. Aristocratic, unique. Probably the most beautiful girl in Trieste. I came across her by accident a week ago on the Piazza Grande, in the Caffè Specchi. She was with a Frenchman I know from the past.

"I know all about her. She's quite something. Her father is a poor painter. He would be glad to give his daughter's hand in marriage to your son instead of a French salesman."

"Thank you for your interest, von Kalchberg. It seems the Österreichische Lloyd bank is much more than a bank, to us."

"You are my best client and I always take care of my clients."

Damned Prussians!

A knife

I always carry tightly fastened to my belt
a small African steel knife
-like those the Africans play with-
that I bought from an old merchant in Algiers.

I remember, as if it were now, the old antique dealer,
who looked like an old oil-painting by Goya,
standing next to long swords and torn uniforms,
saying in a hoarse voice the following words.

"This knife you want to buy
is surrounded by strange stories,
and everybody knows that those who ever held it,
murdered one of their own.

Don Basilio murdered with it Donna Julia,
his beautiful wife because she was unfaithful.
Conte Antonio one night, his unfortunate brother
with this here knife secretly murdered.

An African his little lover because of jealousy
and some Italian sailor a Greek boatswain.
From hand to hand it came to mine.
Many things my eyes have seen, but this one terrifies me.

Look closely at it, it has an anchor and a crest
it's light, take it, it's not even a quarter,
but I would advise you to buy something else…"
-How much is it? - Only seven francs. Since you want it, take it.

A small knife sits tightly on my belt,
I made it my own on a whim,
and since I hate no one in the world to kill
I fear one day I will turn it on myself…

Nikos Kavvadias, 'Marabou' collection of poems, 1933

The Antique Dealer of Algiers was mainly inspired by the historical and political book 'The War that Ended Peace', by Margaret MacMillan and by the poem 'A Knife' by Nikos Kavvadias.

Made in the USA
Columbia, SC
09 June 2021

39527130R00290